POKÉMON™

SUN & MOON

POCKET COMICS

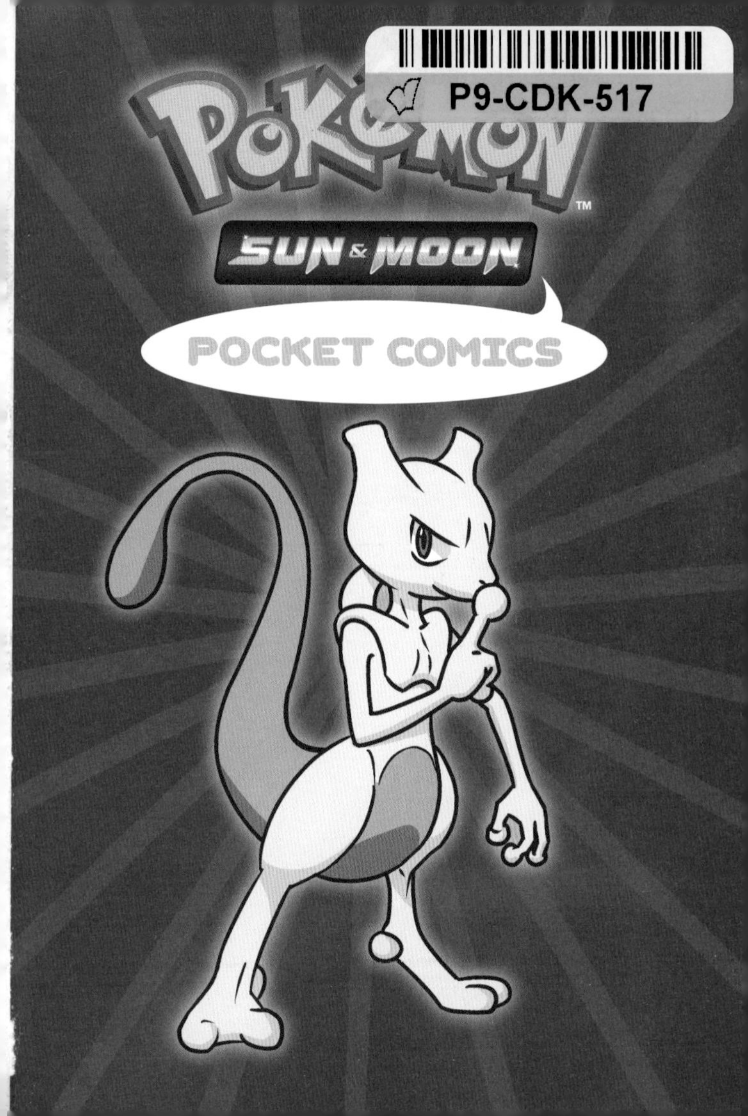

POPPLIO

Let's Have Pun!

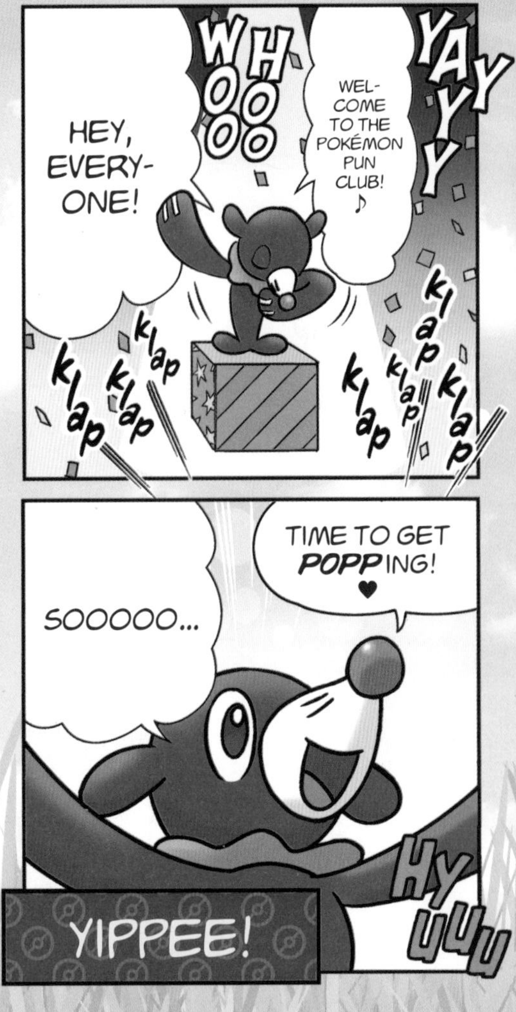
HEY, EVERY-ONE!
WHOOOOO
WEL-COME TO THE POKÉMON PUN CLUB! ♪
YAYYY
klap klap klap
klap klap klap klap
TIME TO GET POPPING! ♥
SOOOOO...
HYUUU
YIPPEE!

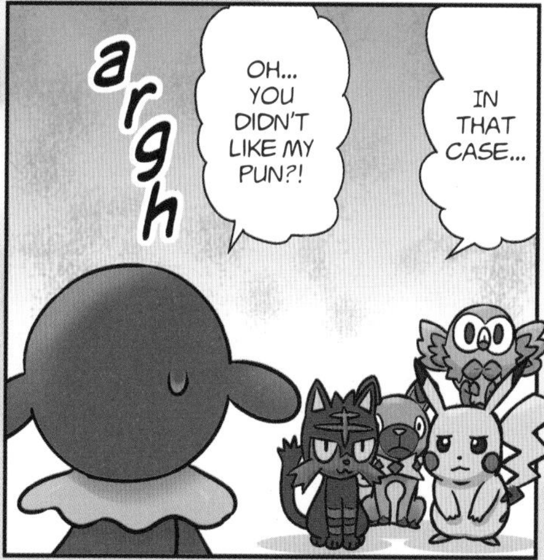
argh
OH... YOU DIDN'T LIKE MY PUN?!
IN THAT CASE...

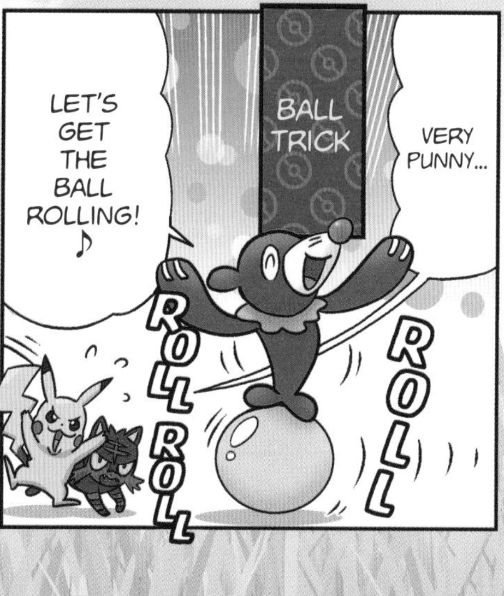
LET'S GET THE BALL ROLLING! ♪
BALL TRICK
VERY PUNNY...
ROLL ROLL
ROLL

POKÉMON MINIDEX

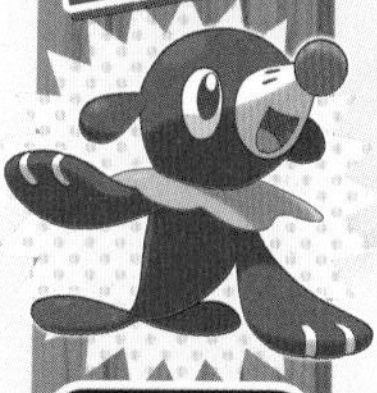

POPPLIO

CATEGORY

Sea Lion

TYPE

Water

It is good at creating water bubbles. It practices diligently to learn to make big ones. It's such a hard worker it'll blow you away...like a bubble!

ALOLA REGION

Neither Here nor There

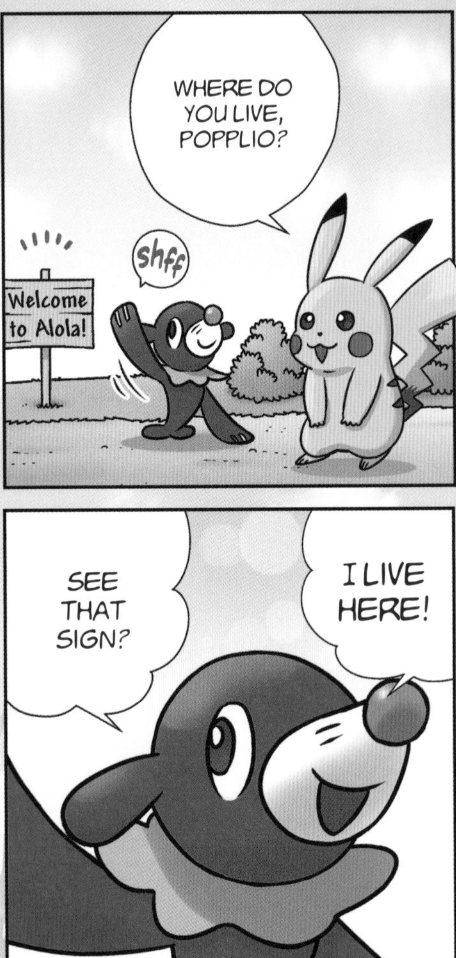
WHERE DO YOU LIVE, POPPLIO?
Welcome to Alola!
shff
SEE THAT SIGN?
I LIVE HERE!

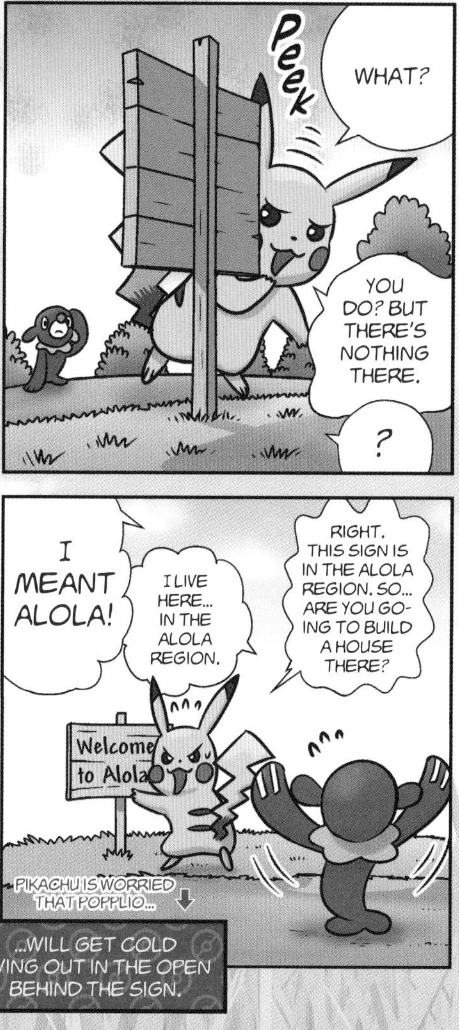

PEEK
WHAT?
YOU DO? BUT THERE'S NOTHING THERE.
?
I MEANT ALOLA!
I LIVE HERE... IN THE ALOLA REGION.
RIGHT. THIS SIGN IS IN THE ALOLA REGION. SO... ARE YOU GO-ING TO BUILD A HOUSE THERE?
Welcome to Alola
PIKACHU IS WORRIED THAT POPPLIO...
...WILL GET COLD LIVING OUT IN THE OPEN BEHIND THE SIGN.

POKÉMON MINIDEX

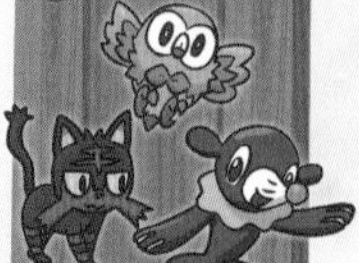

Which of the following is a specialty of Alola that everybody, both young and old, loves to eat?

1. Masalada
2. Salamada
3. Malasada
4. Dasamala

Quiz Answer: ③

LITTEN

Any Which Way

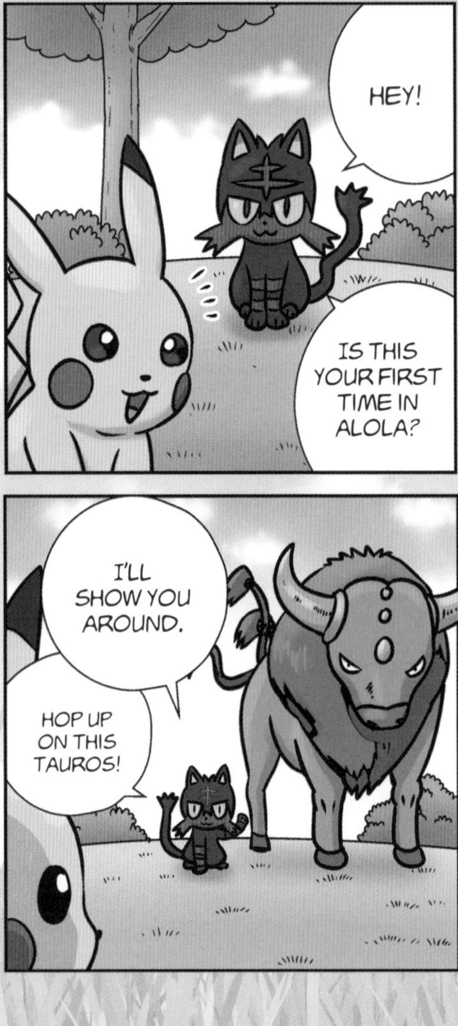

HEY!
IS THIS YOUR FIRST TIME IN ALOLA?
I'LL SHOW YOU AROUND.
HOP UP ON THIS TAUROS!

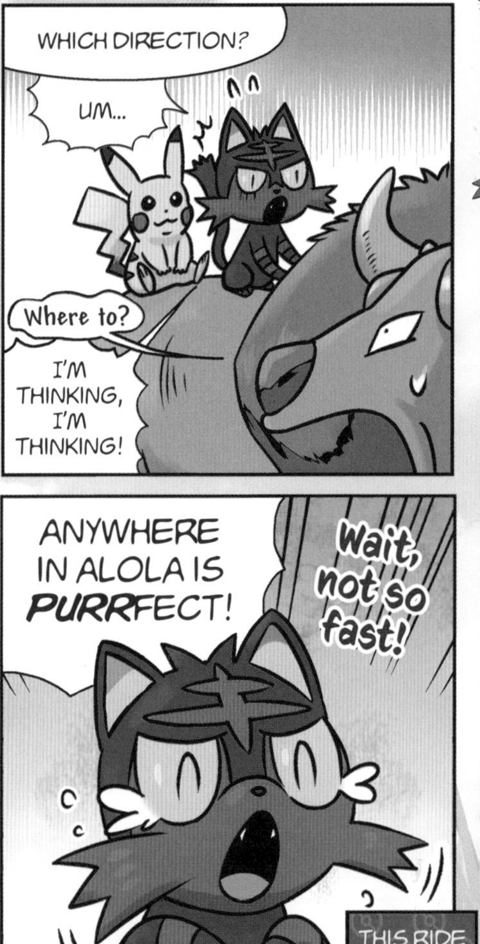
WHICH DIRECTION?
UM...
Where to?
I'M THINKING, I'M THINKING!
ANYWHERE IN ALOLA IS ***PURR***FECT!
Wait, not so fast!
THIS RIDE IS ***LIT***!

POKÉMON MINIDEX

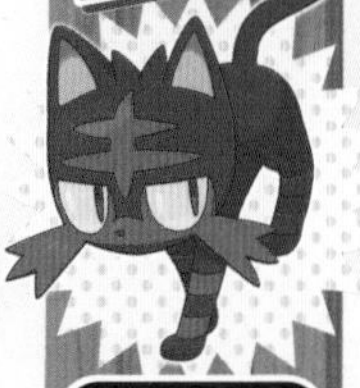

LITTEN

CATEGORY

Fire Cat

TYPE

Fire

It likes to be alone. This skittish Pokémon shows very ***litten*** emotion.

ROCKRUFF

Keep Your Day Job

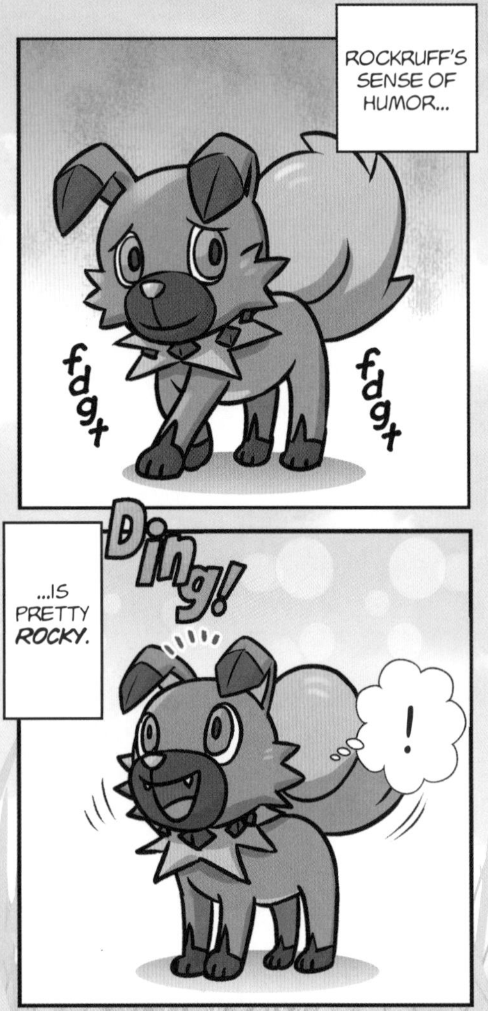
ROCKRUFF'S SENSE OF HUMOR...
fdgt
fdgt
Ding!
...IS PRETTY *ROCKY*.
!

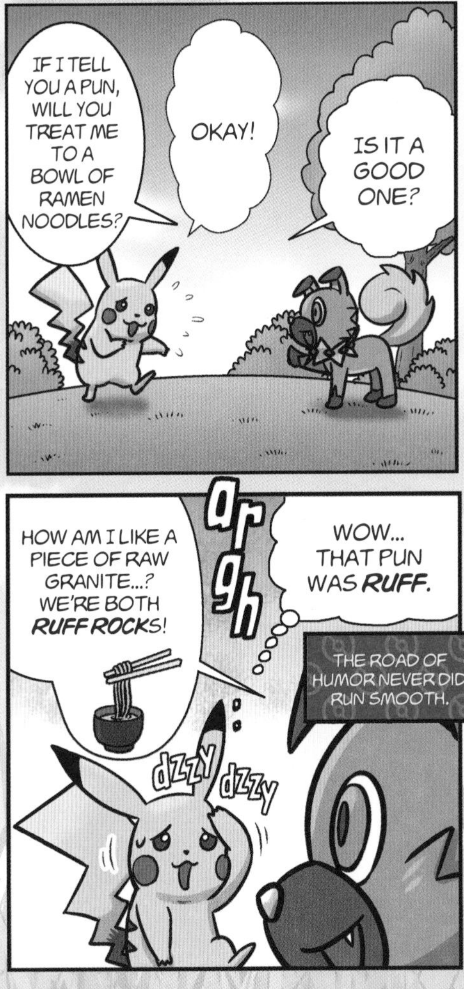
IF I TELL YOU A PUN, WILL YOU TREAT ME TO A BOWL OF RAMEN NOODLES?
OKAY!
IS IT A GOOD ONE?
HOW AM I LIKE A PIECE OF RAW GRANITE...? WE'RE BOTH ***RUFF ROCK***S!
argh
WOW... THAT PUN WAS ***RUFF***.
THE ROAD OF HUMOR NEVER DID RUN SMOOTH.
dzzy dzzy

POKÉMON MINIDEX

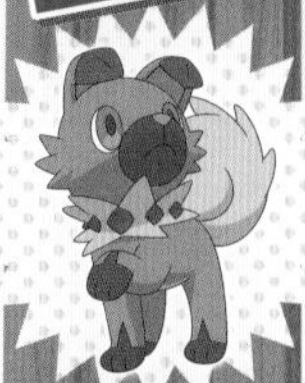

ROCKRUFF

CATEGORY

Puppy

TYPE

Rock

It can sense when its Trainer is feeling down and will stick close by their side. So it's a partner who really ***rock***s!

WISHIWASHI: SCHOOL FORM

Danger in Numbers

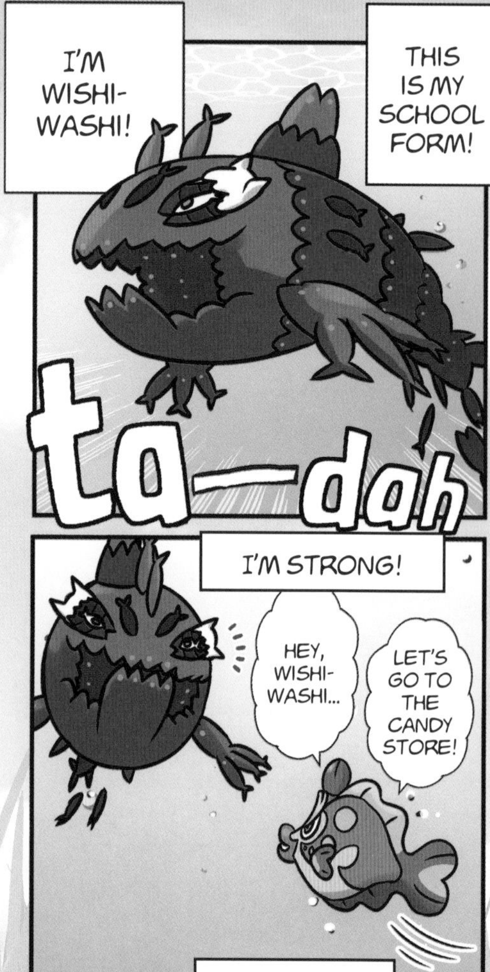

I'M WISHI-WASHI!
THIS IS MY SCHOOL FORM!
ta-dah
I'M STRONG!
HEY, WISHI-WASHI...
LET'S GO TO THE CANDY STORE!
AND I'M BIG!

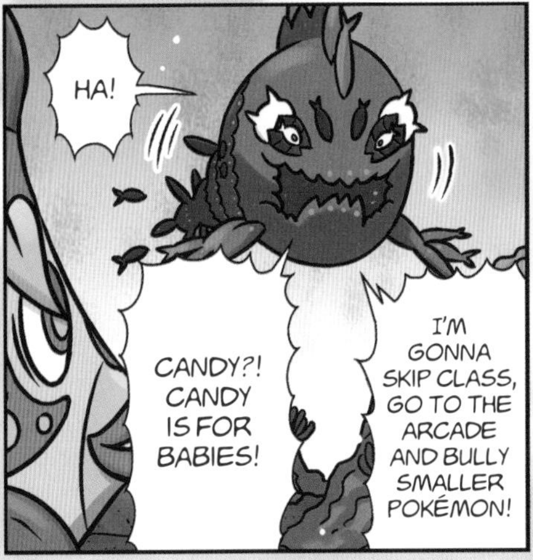
HA!
CANDY?! CANDY IS FOR BABIES!
I'M GONNA SKIP CLASS, GO TO THE ARCADE AND BULLY SMALLER POKÉMON!

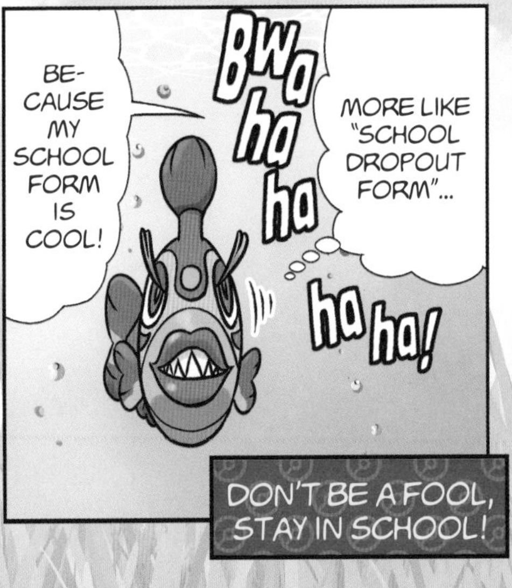
BE-CAUSE MY SCHOOL FORM IS COOL!
Bwa ha ha ha
MORE LIKE "SCHOOL DROPOUT FORM"...
ha ha ha!
DON'T BE A FOOL, STAY IN SCHOOL!

POKÉMON MINIDEX

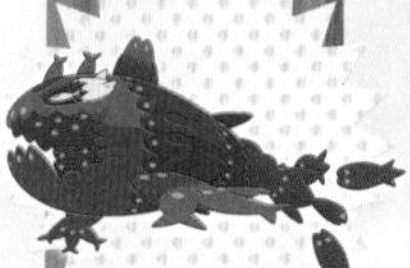

WISHIWASHI: S. F.

CATEGORY

Small Fry

TYPE

Water

Even Gyarados is afraid of the power of Water Gun, wielded by Wishiwashi in its School Form. Despite its name, Wishiwashi isn't wishy-washy but decisive—even when it makes bad choices!

PIKIPEK

Pokémon Word Chain ①

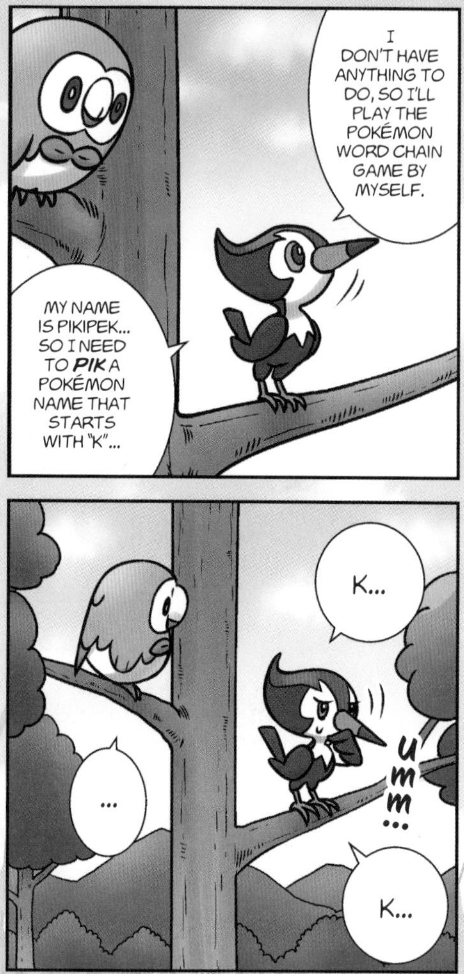
I DON'T HAVE ANYTHING TO DO, SO I'LL PLAY THE POKÉMON WORD CHAIN GAME BY MYSELF.
MY NAME IS PIKIPEK... SO I NEED TO ***PIK*** A POKÉMON NAME THAT STARTS WITH "K"...
K...
...
UMMM...
K...

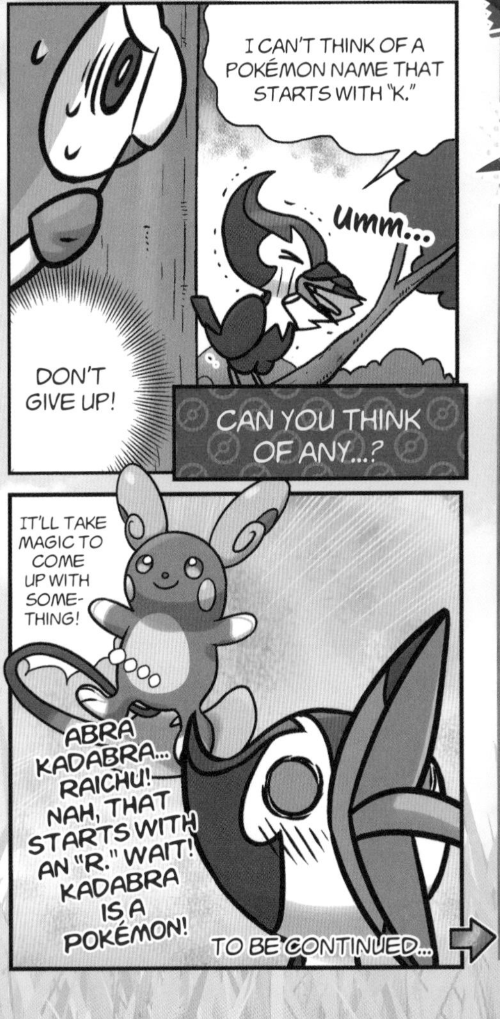

DON'T GIVE UP!
I CAN'T THINK OF A POKÉMON NAME THAT STARTS WITH "K."
UMM...
CAN YOU THINK OF ANY...?
IT'LL TAKE MAGIC TO COME UP WITH SOME-THING!
ABRA KADABRA... RAICHU! NAH, THAT STARTS WITH AN "R." WAIT! KADABRA IS A POKÉMON!
TO BE CONTINUED...

POKÉMON MINIDEX

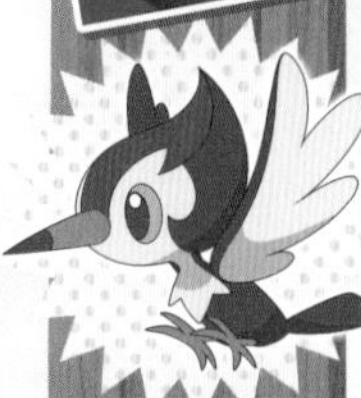

PIKIPEK

CATEGORY

Woodpecker

TYPE

Normal, Flying

This Pokémon shoots leftover seeds of berries it has eaten from its mouth. It can ***pik*** off opposing Pokémon with ease.

Pokémon Word Chain ②

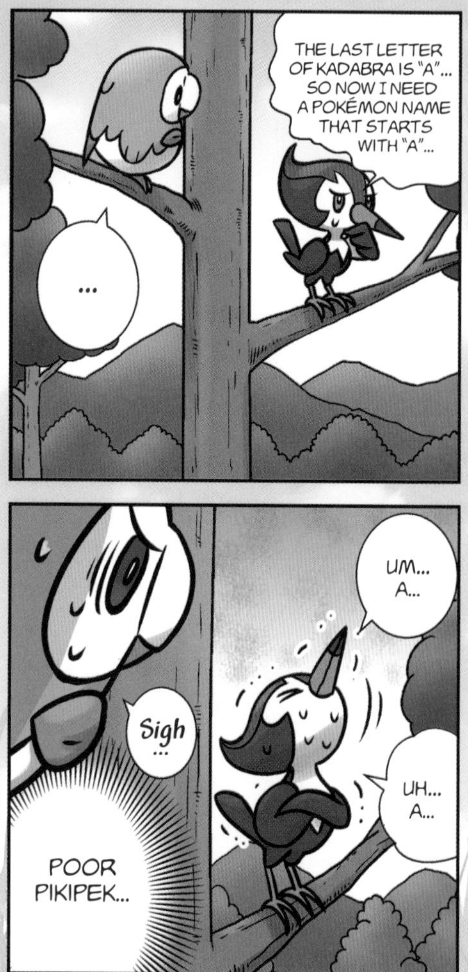
...
THE LAST LETTER OF KADABRA IS "A"... SO NOW I NEED A POKÉMON NAME THAT STARTS WITH "A"...
Sigh...
POOR PIKIPEK...
UM... A...
UH... A...

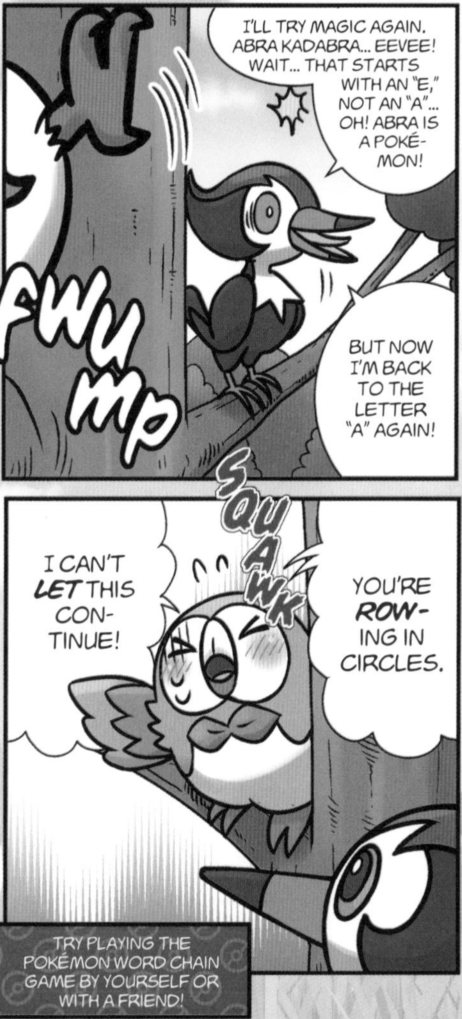
FWUMP
I'LL TRY MAGIC AGAIN. ABRA KADABRA... EEVEE! WAIT... THAT STARTS WITH AN "E," NOT AN "A"... OH! ABRA IS A POKÉMON!
BUT NOW I'M BACK TO THE LETTER "A" AGAIN!
SQUAWK
I CAN'T *LET* THIS CONTINUE!
YOU'RE *ROW*-ING IN CIRCLES.
TRY PLAYING THE POKÉMON WORD CHAIN GAME BY YOURSELF OR WITH A FRIEND!

POKÉMON MINIDEX

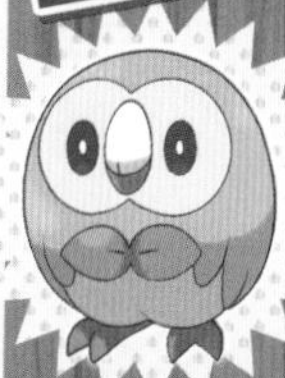

ROWLET

CATEGORY

Grass Quill

TYPE

Grass, Flying

Rowlet is a nocturnal Pokémon. It quietly photosynthesizes during the day. The energy Rowlet store up during the day lets them move actively at night...when they often ***row*** with one another.

MAGNEMITE

Do You Like This Pokémon?

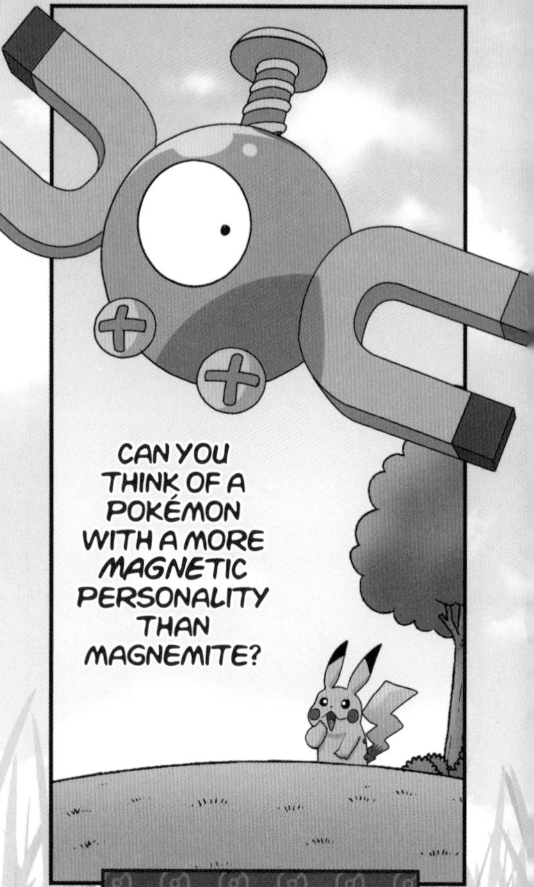
CAN YOU THINK OF A POKÉMON WITH A MORE *MAGNETIC* PERSONALITY THAN MAGNEMITE?

OR MAYBE WE SHOULD SAY A MORE ***ATTRACTIVE*** PERSONALITY?

POKÉMON FUN CLUB

POKÉMON CLOSE-UP QUIZ

The following pictures are close-ups of parts of Pokémon. Can you tell which Pokémon they belong to? Quiz your friends!

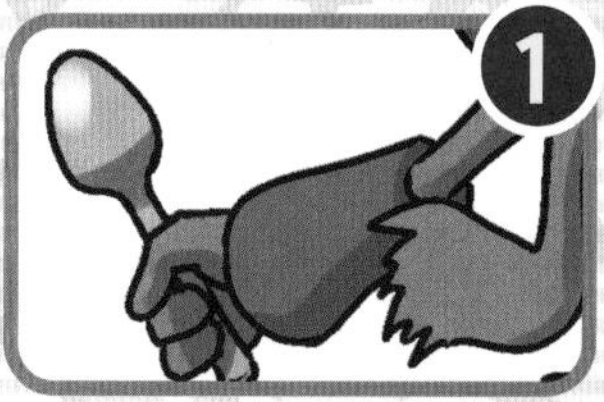

1

Answer (   )

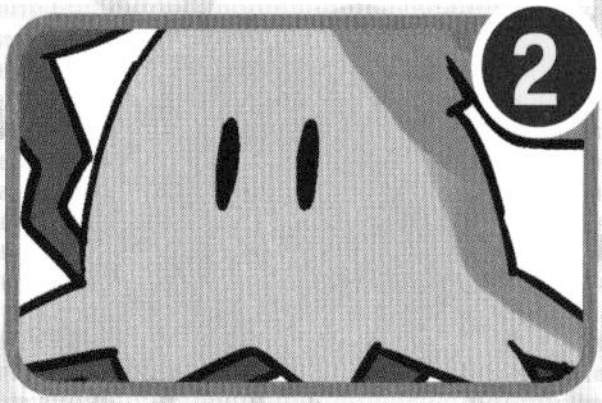

2

Answer (   )

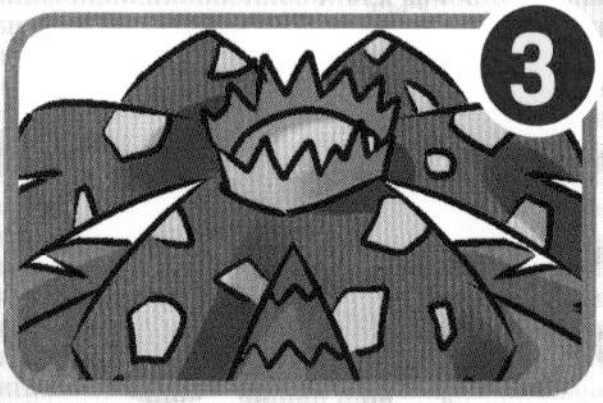

3

Answer (   )

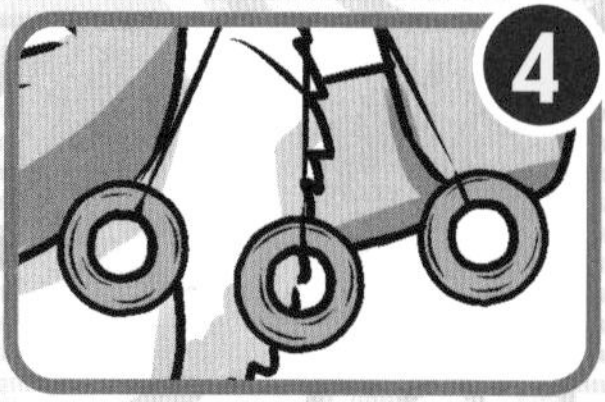

4

Answer (   )

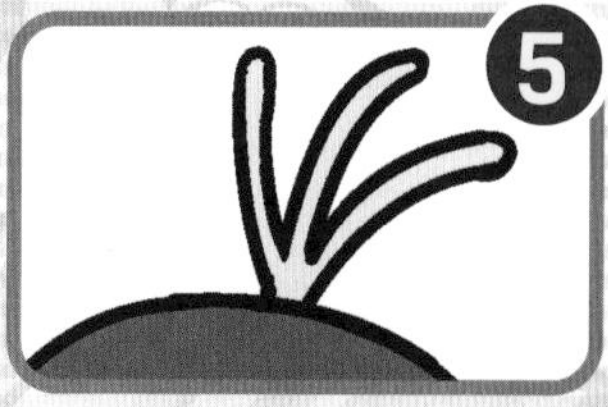

5

Answer (   )

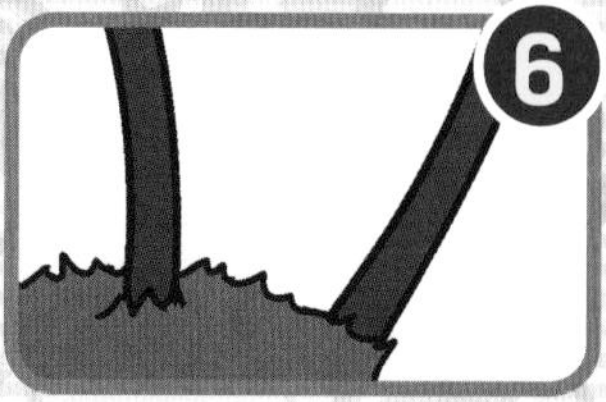

6

Answer (   )

Answers on page 186!

MORELULL

One Word, Two Meanings

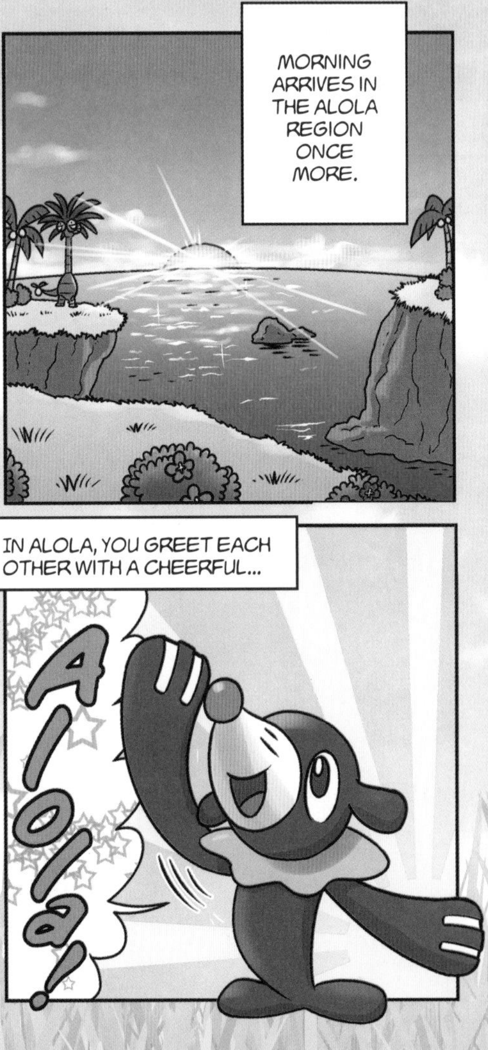

MORNING ARRIVES IN THE ALOLA REGION ONCE MORE.
IN ALOLA, YOU GREET EACH OTHER WITH A CHEERFUL...
A-OLA!

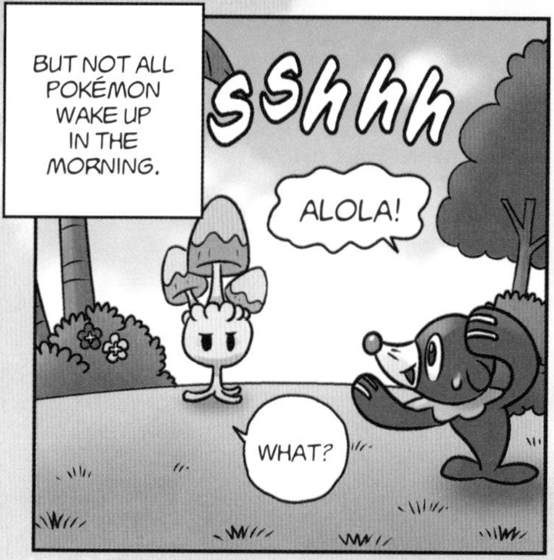
BUT NOT ALL POKÉMON WAKE UP IN THE MORNING.
SSHHHH
ALOLA!
WHAT?

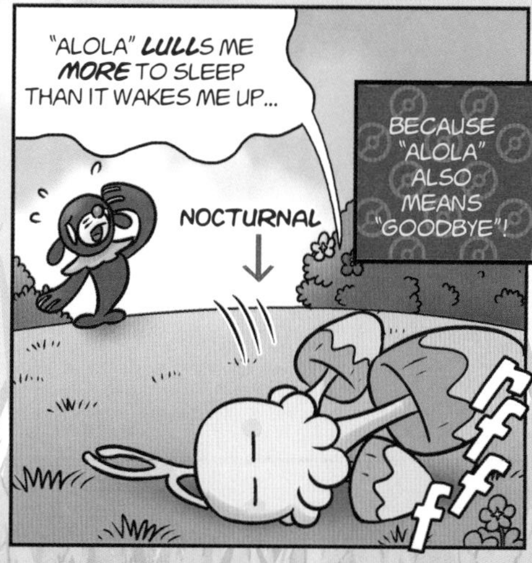
"ALOLA" LULLS ME MORE TO SLEEP THAN IT WAKES ME UP...
BECAUSE "ALOLA" ALSO MEANS "GOODBYE"!
NOCTURNAL
FFFFF

POKÉMON MINIDEX

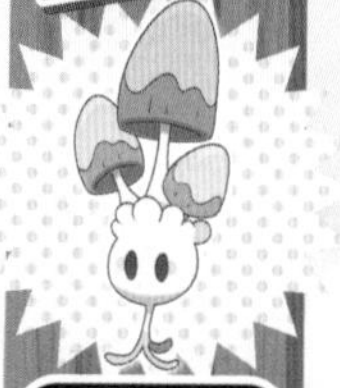

MORELULL

CATEGORY

Illuminating

TYPE

Grass, Fairy

Morelull scatters spores that put others to sleep. The spores glow. That is why Morelull is called the Illuminating Pokémon.

MIMIKYU

By Any Other Name

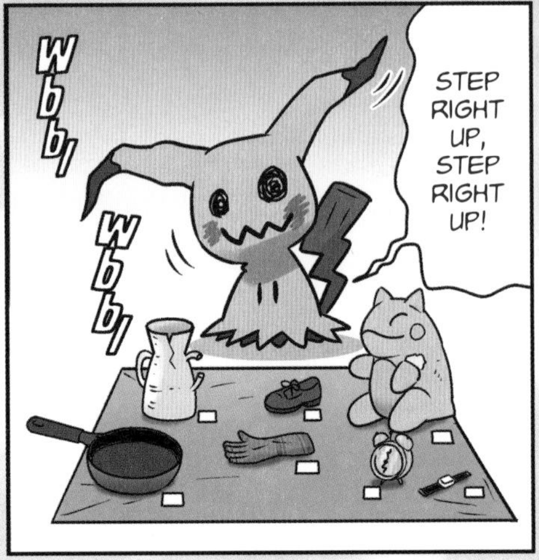

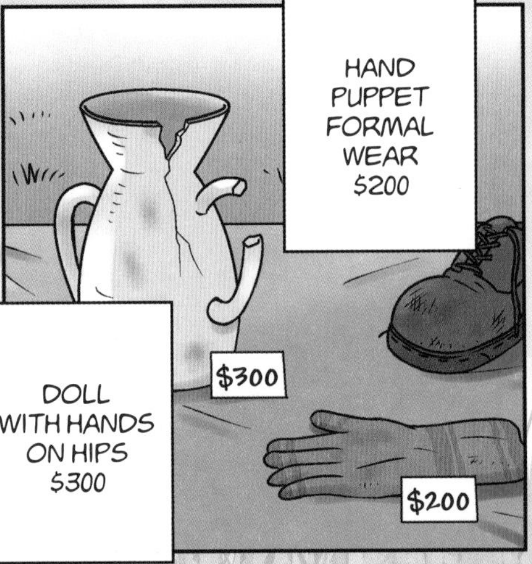

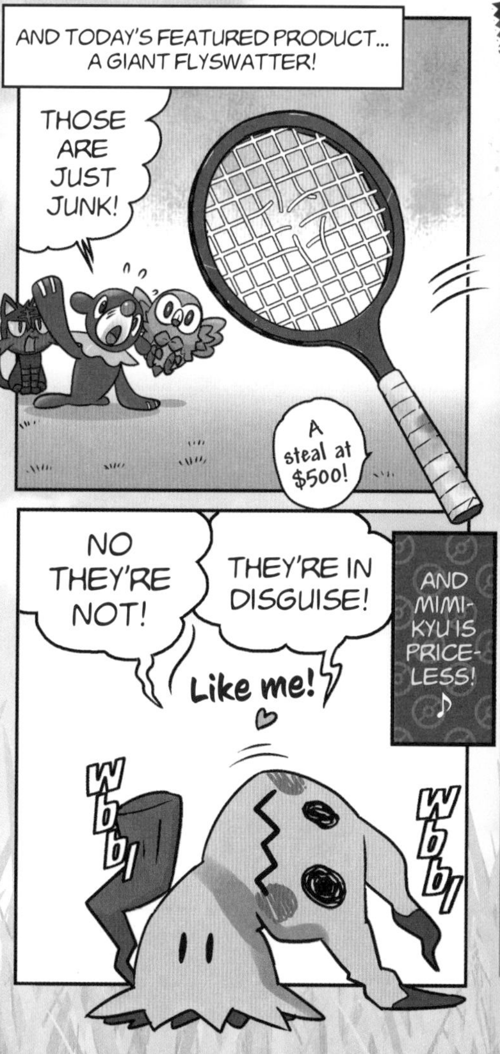
AND TODAY'S FEATURED PRODUCT... A GIANT FLYSWATTER!
THOSE ARE JUST JUNK!
A steal at $500!
NO THEY'RE NOT!
THEY'RE IN DISGUISE!
AND MIMI-KYU IS PRICE-LESS! ♪
Like me!
wbbl
wbbl

POKÉMON MINIDEX

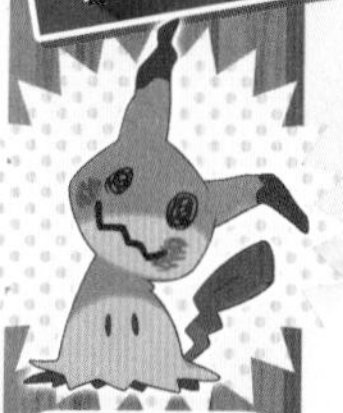

MIMIKYU

CATEGORY

Disguise

TYPE

Ghost, Fairy

Rumor has is that if you see what Mimikyu really looks like under its sheet, you'll die of shock! Would you want to look...?

Give Me a Break

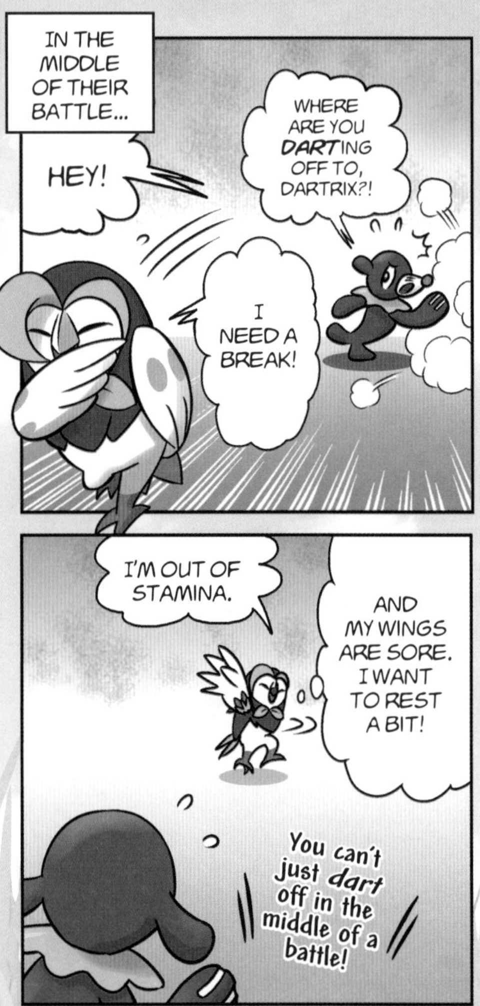
IN THE MIDDLE OF THEIR BATTLE...
HEY!
WHERE ARE YOU DARTING OFF TO, DARTRIX?!
I NEED A BREAK!
I'M OUT OF STAMINA.
AND MY WINGS ARE SORE. I WANT TO REST A BIT!
You can't just dart off in the middle of a battle!

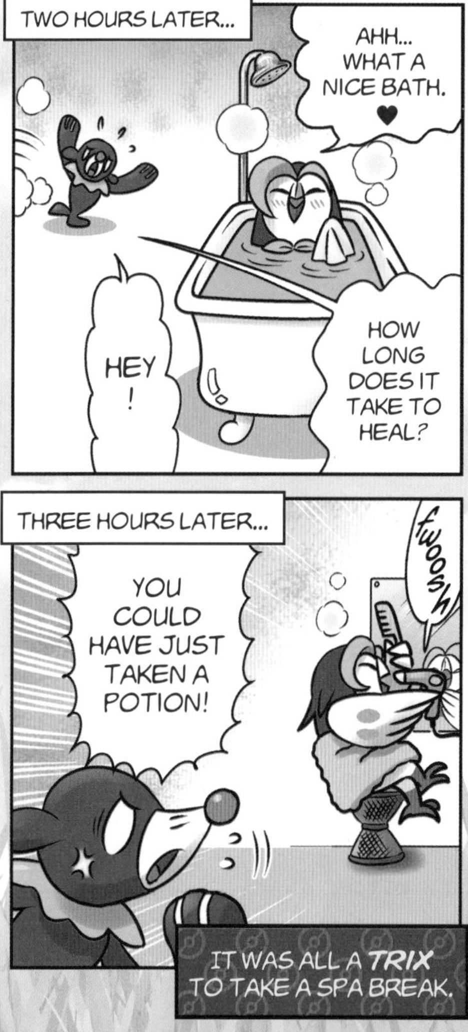
TWO HOURS LATER...
AHH... WHAT A NICE BATH. ♥
HEY !
HOW LONG DOES IT TAKE TO HEAL?
THREE HOURS LATER...
fwoosh
YOU COULD HAVE JUST TAKEN A POTION!
IT WAS ALL A ***TRIX*** TO TAKE A SPA BREAK.

POKÉMON MINIDEX

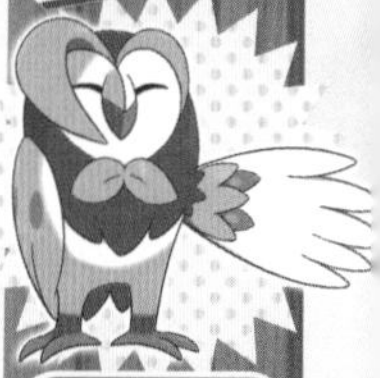

DARTRIX

CATEGORY

Blade Quill

TYPE

Grass, Flying

It throws sharp feathers called blade quills at enemies or prey. The feather darts never miss a ***trix***.

TORRACAT

I Need My Beauty Rest

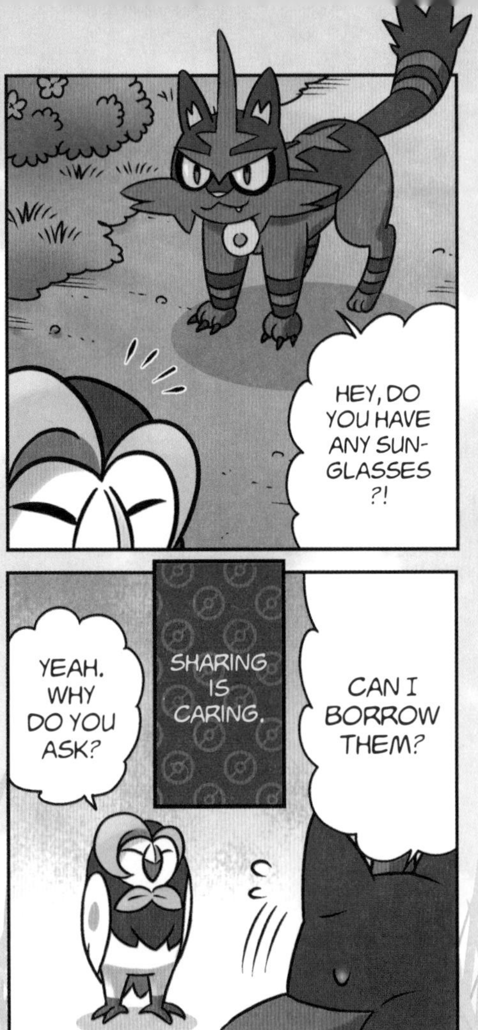
HEY, DO YOU HAVE ANY SUN-GLASSES?!
YEAH. WHY DO YOU ASK?
SHARING IS CARING.
CAN I BORROW THEM?

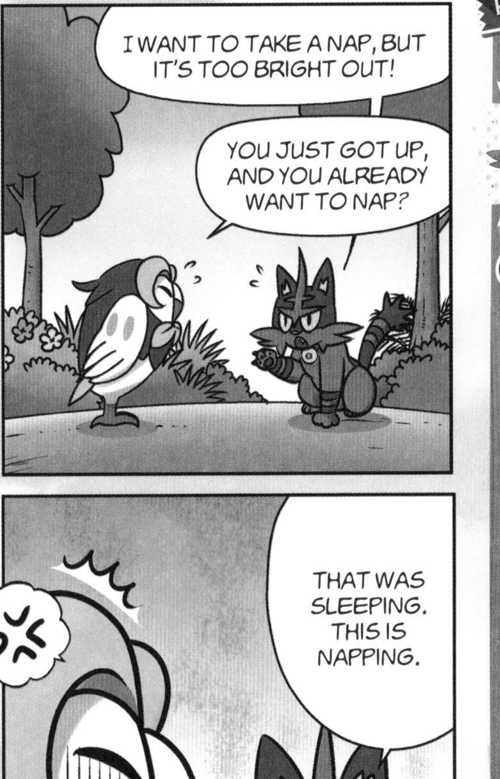
I WANT TO TAKE A NAP, BUT IT'S TOO BRIGHT OUT!
YOU JUST GOT UP, AND YOU ALREADY WANT TO NAP?
THAT WAS SLEEPING. THIS IS NAPPING.
Sheesh
TO BE CONTINUED...

POKÉMON MINIDEX

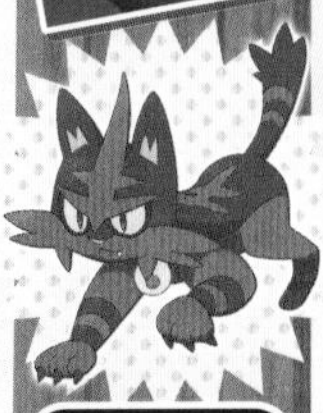

TORRACAT

CATEGORY

Fire Cat

TYPE

Fire

A punch from Torracat's front leg is strong enough to bend an iron bar. Even Pokémon who brag about their strength are no match for it! Match... Fire Cat... Get it?

BRIONNE

Dance Away the Pain

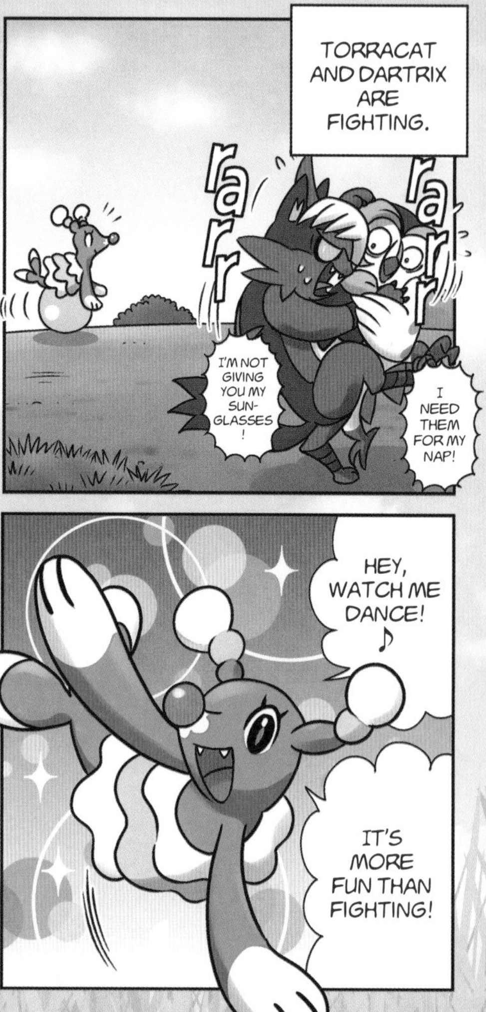
TORRACAT AND DARTRIX ARE FIGHTING.
rarr
rarr
I'M NOT GIVING YOU MY SUN-GLASSES!
I NEED THEM FOR MY NAP!
HEY, WATCH ME DANCE! ♪
IT'S MORE FUN THAN FIGHTING!

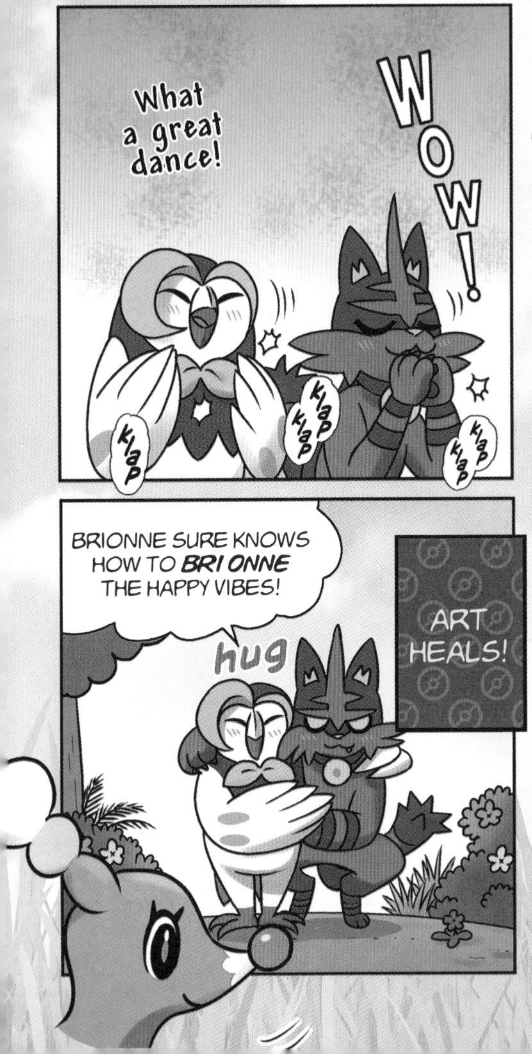
What a great dance!
WOW!
klap klap
klap klap
klap klap
BRIONNE SURE KNOWS HOW TO BRI ONNE THE HAPPY VIBES!
hug
ART HEALS!

POKÉMON MINIDEX

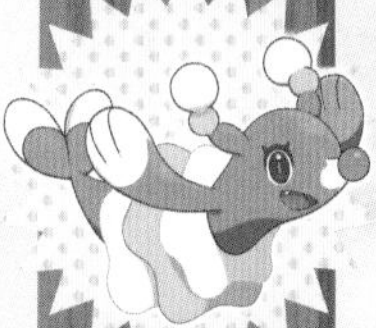

BRIONNE

CATEGORY

Pop Star

TYPE

Water

When its Trainer feels down, it performs a dance to cheer them up. Taking care of its friends is Brionne's strength!

Walk on By ①

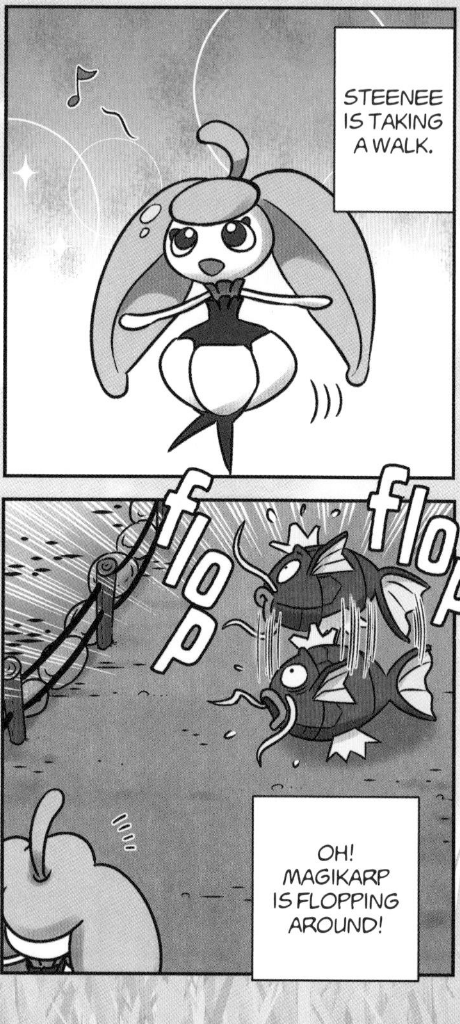
STEENEE IS TAKING A WALK.
flop flop
flop flop
OH! MAGIKARP IS FLOPPING AROUND!

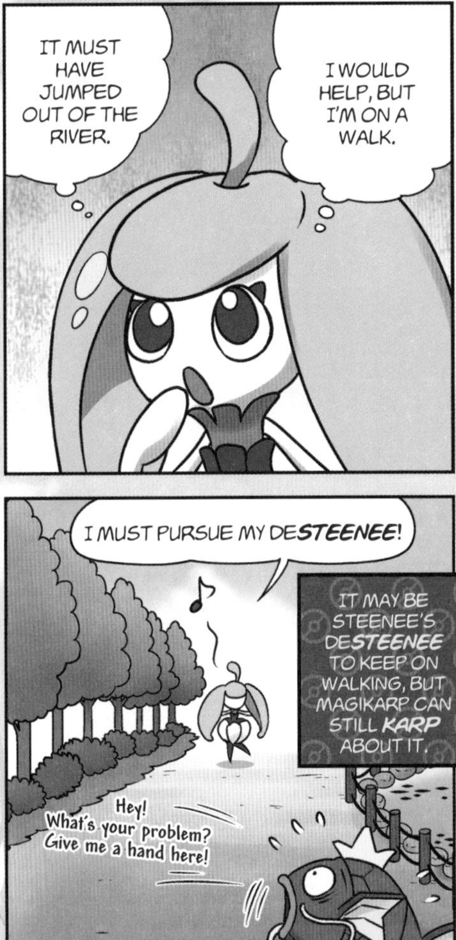
IT MUST HAVE JUMPED OUT OF THE RIVER.
I WOULD HELP, BUT I'M ON A WALK.
I MUST PURSUE MY DE*STEENEE*!
IT MAY BE STEENEE'S DE*STEENEE* TO KEEP ON WALKING, BUT MAGIKARP CAN STILL *KARP* ABOUT IT.
Hey! What's your problem? Give me a hand here!

POKÉMON MINIDEX

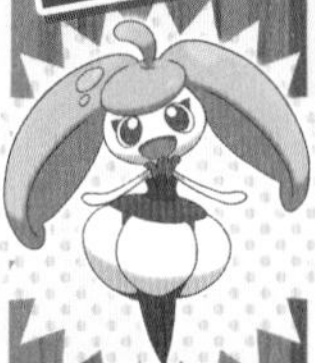

STEENEE

CATEGORY

Fruit

TYPE

Grass

This Pokémon is always bouncing around energetically. Other Pokémon are attracted to its liveliness and pleasant aroma.

Walk on By ②

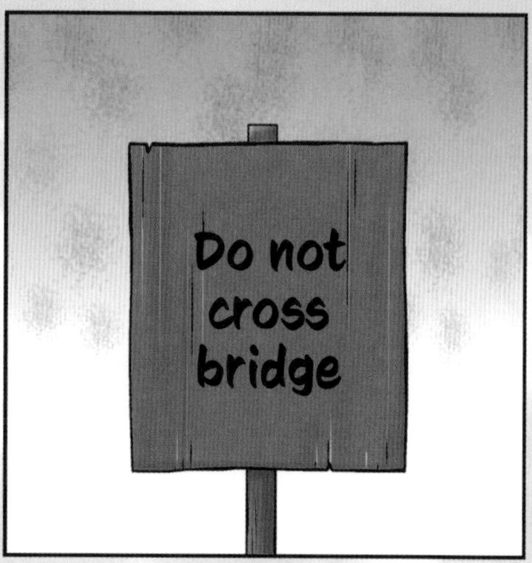
Do not cross bridge

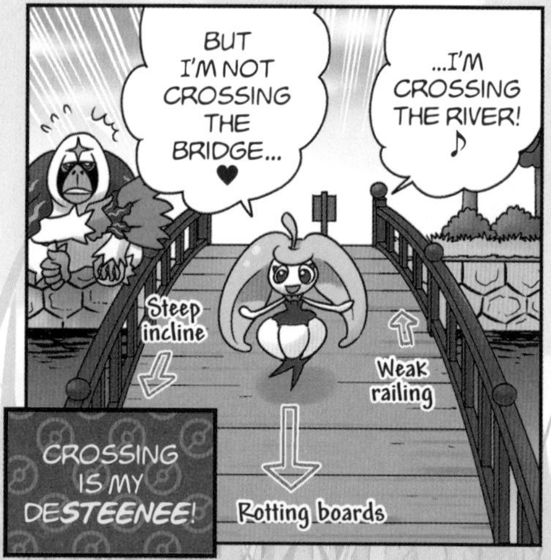
BUT I'M NOT CROSSING THE BRIDGE... ♥
...I'M CROSSING THE RIVER! ♪
Steep incline
Weak railing
Rotting boards
CROSSING IS MY DESTEENEE!

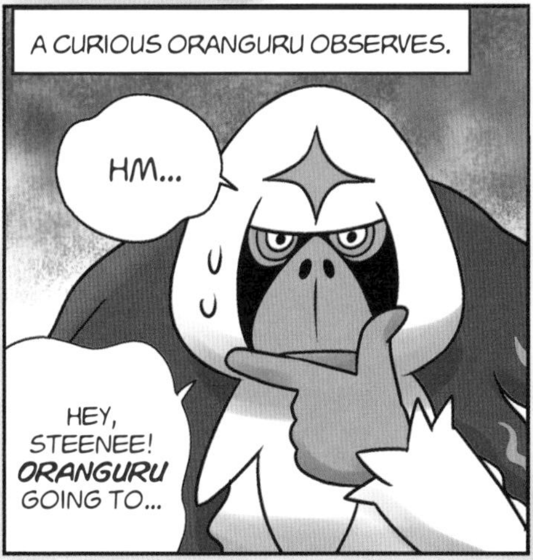
A CURIOUS ORANGURU OBSERVES.
HM...
HEY, STEENEE! **ORANGURU** GOING TO...

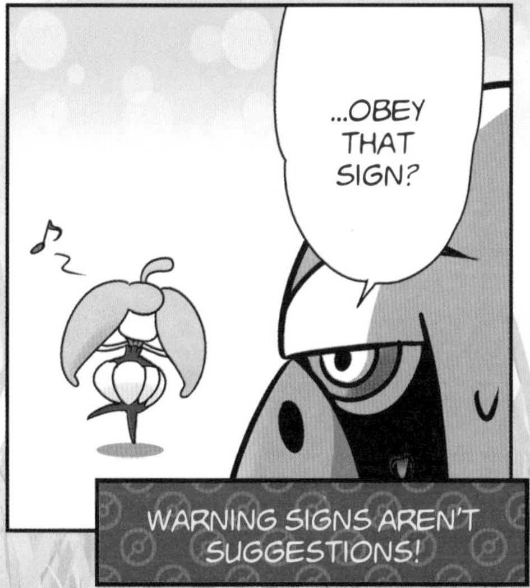
...OBEY THAT SIGN?
WARNING SIGNS AREN'T SUGGESTIONS!

POKÉMON MINIDEX

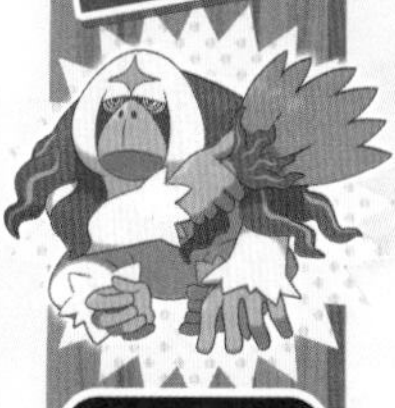

ORANGURU

CATEGORY

Sage

TYPE

Normal, Psychic

A very smart Pokémon who lives deep in the jungle and ponders the meaning of things. Knock, knock. Who's there? Oranguru. Oranguru who? Orangaru going to let me in?

PRIMARINA

Sports Festival ①

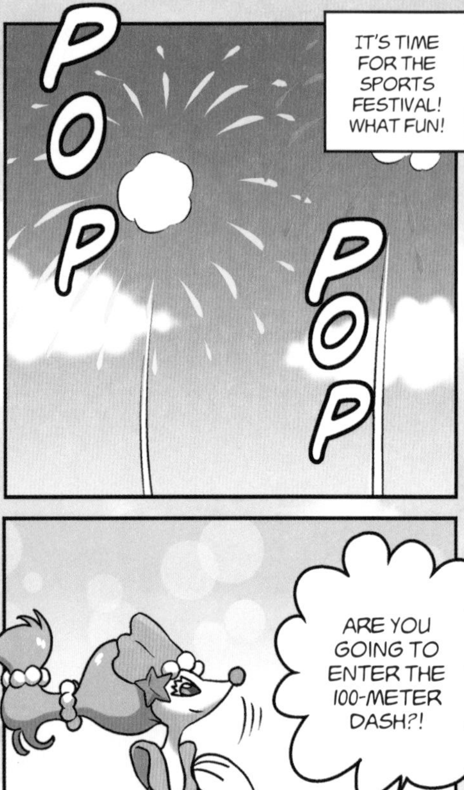

POP
POP
IT'S TIME FOR THE SPORTS FESTIVAL! WHAT FUN!
POP
POP
ARE YOU GOING TO ENTER THE 100-METER DASH?!
nod
nod

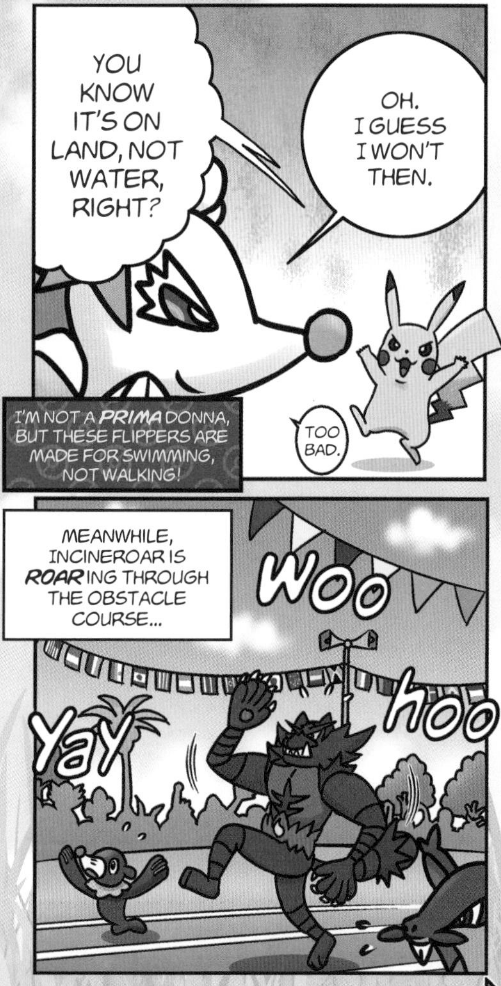
YOU KNOW IT'S ON LAND, NOT WATER, RIGHT?
OH. I GUESS I WON'T THEN.
I'M NOT A PRIMA DONNA, BUT THESE FLIPPERS ARE MADE FOR SWIMMING, NOT WALKING!
TOO BAD.
MEANWHILE, INCINEROAR IS ROARING THROUGH THE OBSTACLE COURSE...
WOO
YAY
HOO

TO BE CONTINUED...

POKÉMON MINIDEX

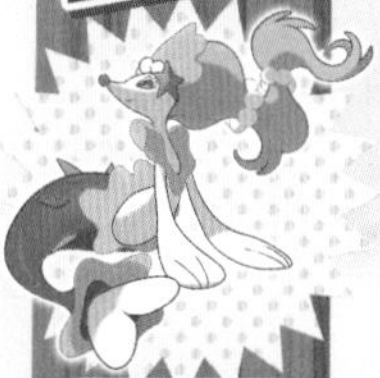

PRIMARINA

CATEGORY

Soloist

TYPE

Water, Fairy

Primarina's beautiful singing is passed down through the generations. It can control water balloons with its singing voice.

Sports Festival ②

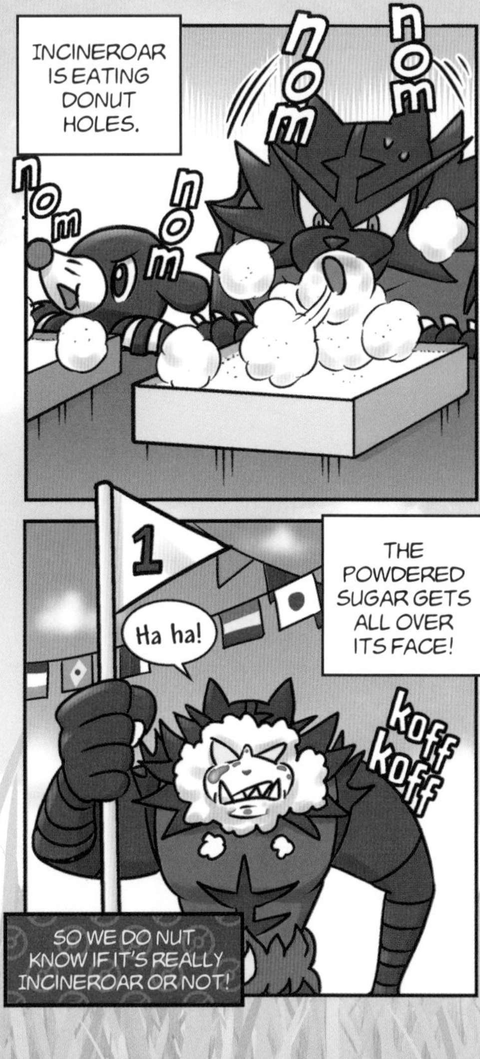
INCINEROAR IS EATING DONUT HOLES.
nom
nom
nom
nom
Ha ha!
THE POWDERED SUGAR GETS ALL OVER ITS FACE!
koff koff
SO WE DO NUT KNOW IF IT'S REALLY INCINEROAR OR NOT!

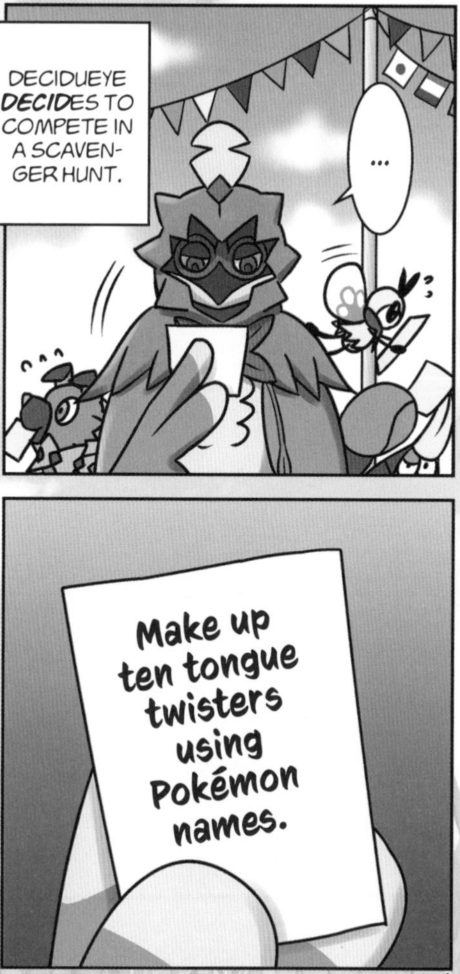
DECIDUEYE *DECID*ES TO COMPETE IN A SCAVENGER HUNT.
...
Make up ten tongue twisters using Pokémon names.

TO BE CONTINUED...

POKÉMON MINIDEX

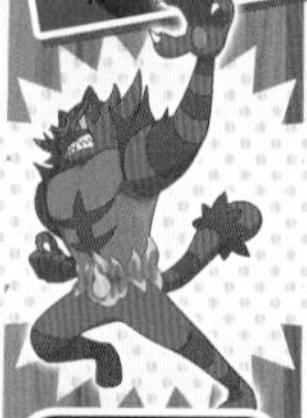

INCINEROAR

CATEGORY

Heel

TYPE

Fire, Dark

After hurling ferocious punches and flinging furious kicks, it finishes opponents off by spewing fire from around its navel. So it incinerates everything with the touch of a button...a belly button!

Sports Festival ③

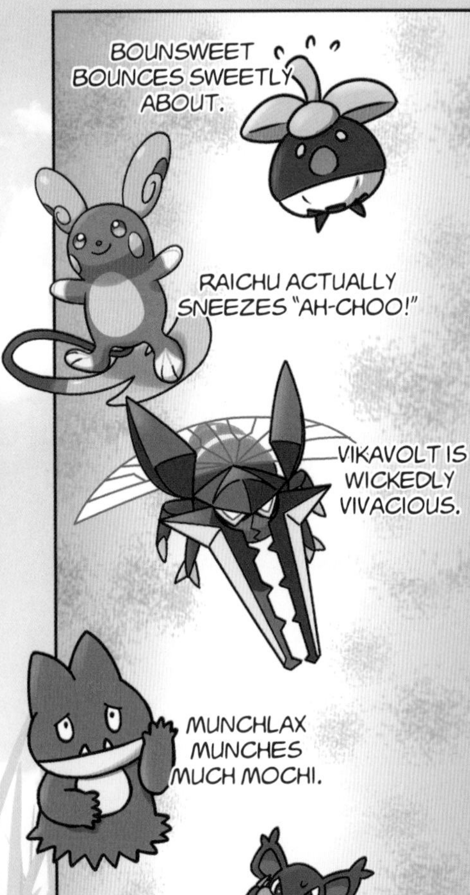
BOUNSWEET BOUNCES SWEETLY ABOUT.
RAICHU ACTUALLY SNEEZES "AH-CHOO!"
VIKAVOLT IS WICKEDLY VIVACIOUS.
MUNCHLAX MUNCHES MUCH MOCHI.
RATTATA RANTS RIDICULOUSLY AT RATICATE.

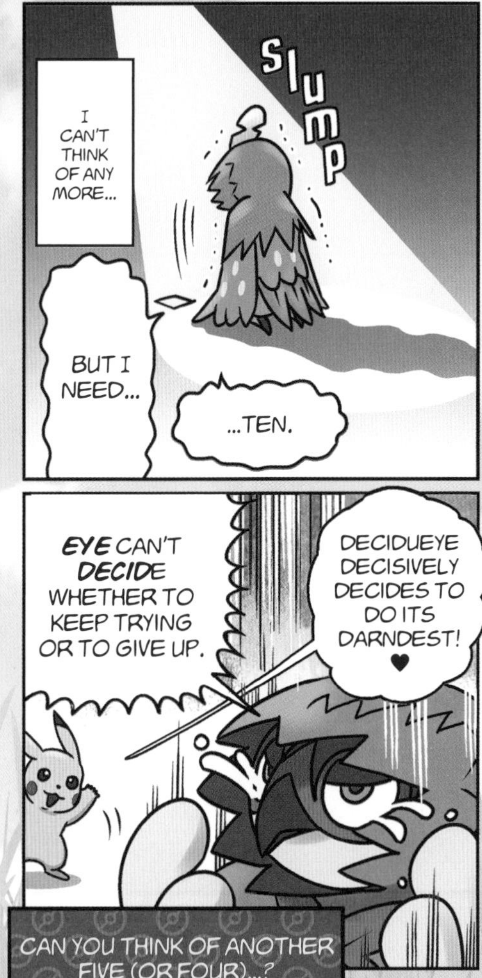
I CAN'T THINK OF ANY MORE...
SLUMP
BUT I NEED...
...TEN.
EYE CAN'T DECIDE WHETHER TO KEEP TRYING OR TO GIVE UP.
DECIDUEYE DECISIVELY DECIDES TO DO ITS DARNDEST! ♥
CAN YOU THINK OF ANOTHER FIVE (OR FOUR)...?

POKÉMON MINIDEX

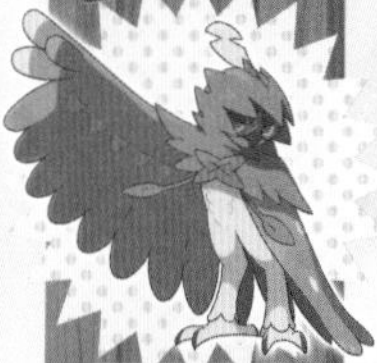

DECIDUEYE

CATEGORY

Arrow Quill

TYPE

Grass, Ghost

Although basically cool and cautious, when it's under pressure, it panics.

Hair Today, Gone Tomorrow

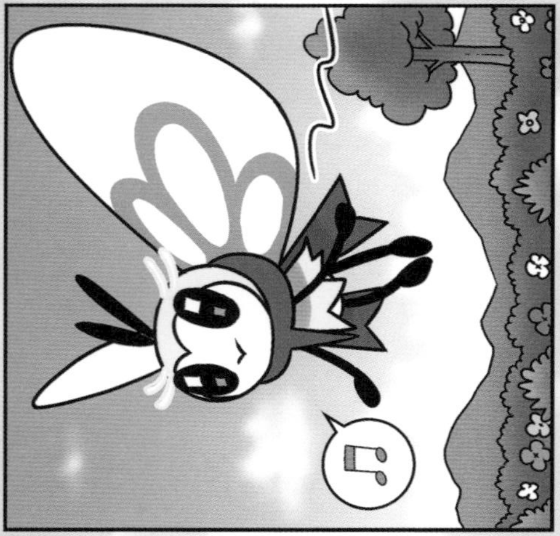

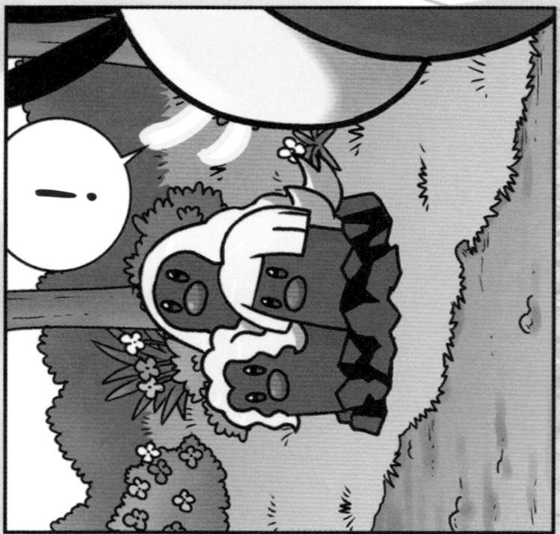
!

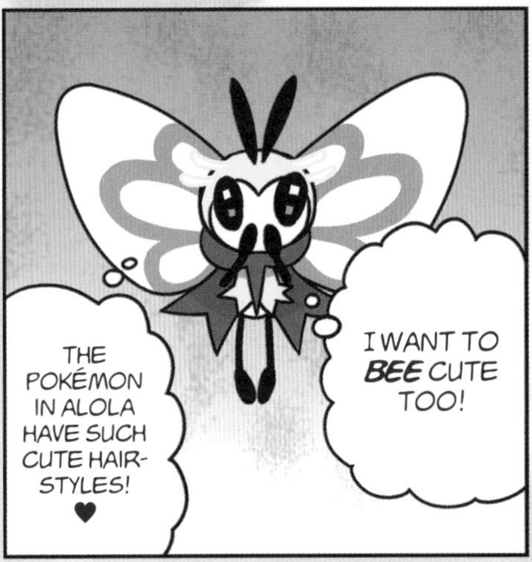
THE POKÉMON IN ALOLA HAVE SUCH CUTE HAIR-STYLES! ♥
I WANT TO **BEE** CUTE TOO!

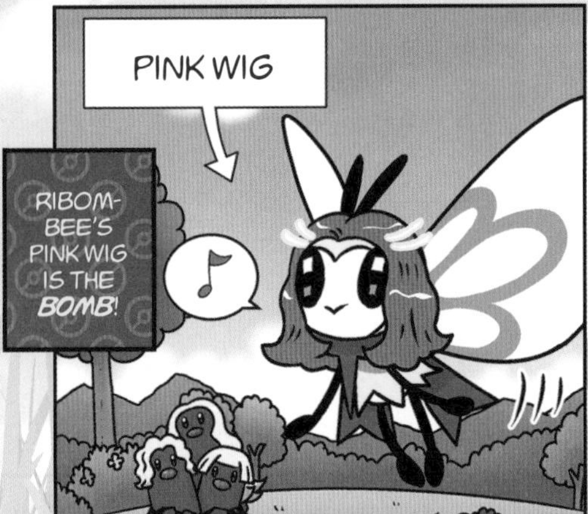
PINK WIG
RIBOM-BEE'S PINK WIG IS THE ***BOMB***!
♪

POKÉMON MINIDEX

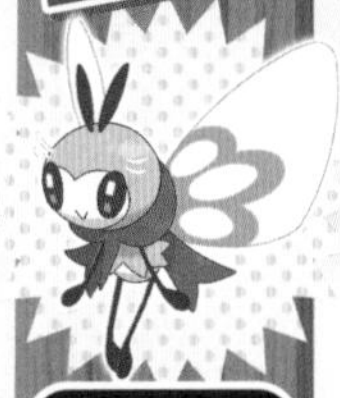

RIBOMBEE

CATEGORY

Bee Fly

TYPE

Bug, Fairy

It rolls pollen into puffs and eats them or uses them as weapons in battle. It is an un***bee***lievably cute Pokémon!

To the Bitter End

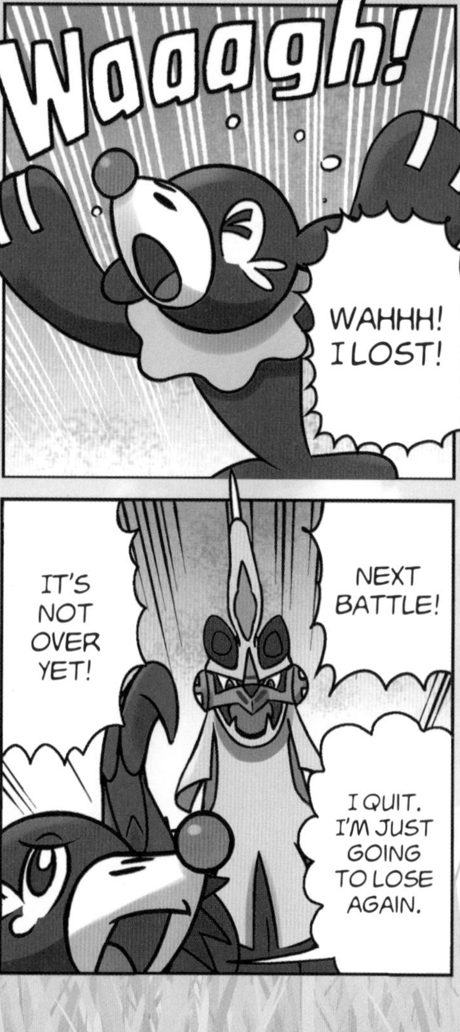
Waaagh!
WAHHH! I LOST!
IT'S NOT OVER YET!
NEXT BATTLE!
I QUIT. I'M JUST GOING TO LOSE AGAIN.

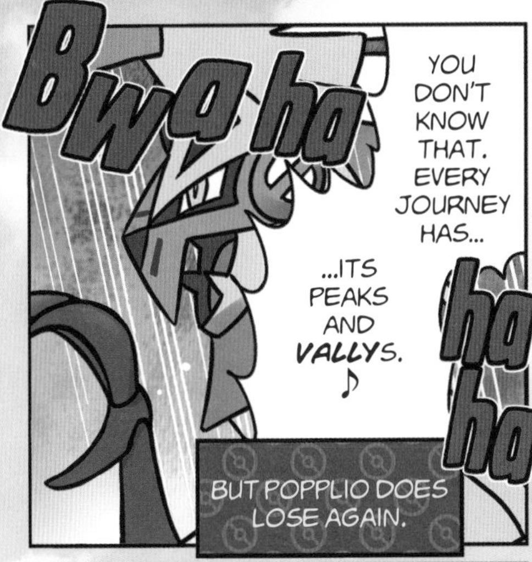

Bwa ha
YOU DON'T KNOW THAT. EVERY JOURNEY HAS...
...ITS PEAKS AND VALLYS. ♪
ha ha
BUT POPPLIO DOES LOSE AGAIN.

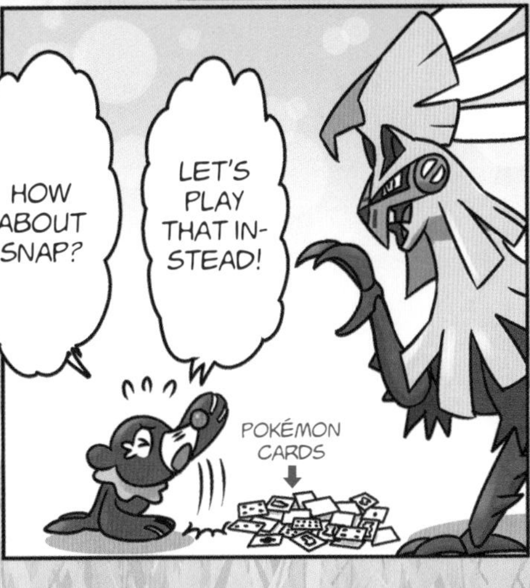

HOW ABOUT SNAP?
LET'S PLAY THAT IN-STEAD!
POKÉMON CARDS

POKÉMON MINIDEX

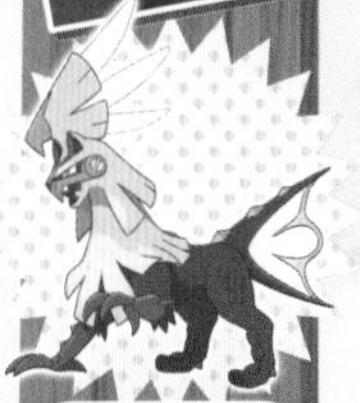

SILVALLY

CATEGORY

Synthetic

TYPE

Normal

Type: Null ***type***cally evolves into Silvally after deepening its friendship with its Trainer. It can change its Pokémon type freely depending on the memory it holds on to.

Respect Your Elders

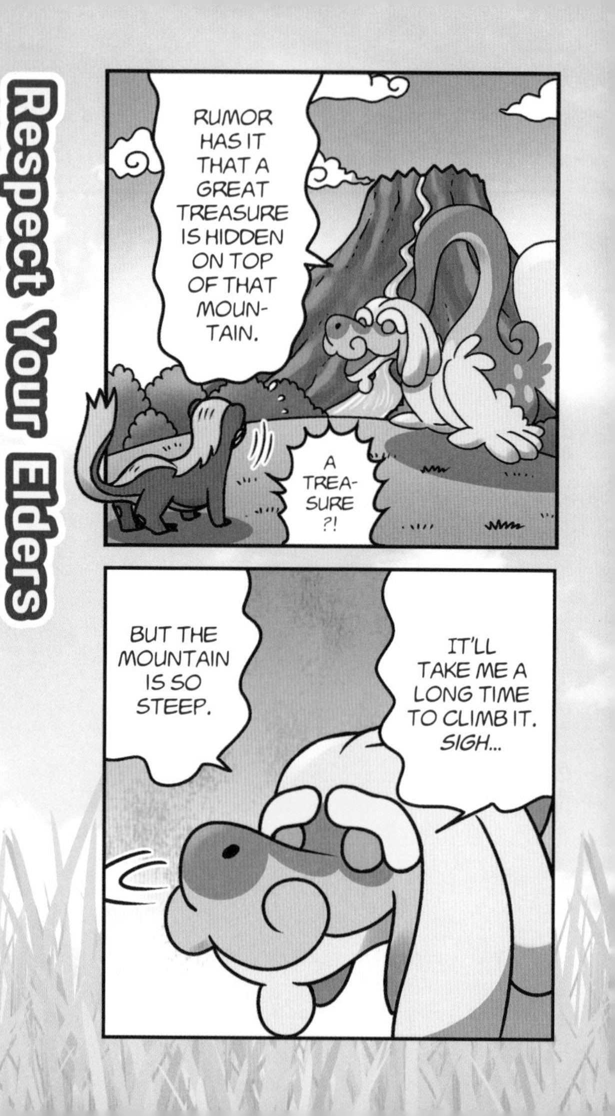
RUMOR HAS IT THAT A GREAT TREASURE IS HIDDEN ON TOP OF THAT MOUN-TAIN.
A TREA-SURE ?!
BUT THE MOUNTAIN IS SO STEEP.
IT'LL TAKE ME A LONG TIME TO CLIMB IT. SIGH...

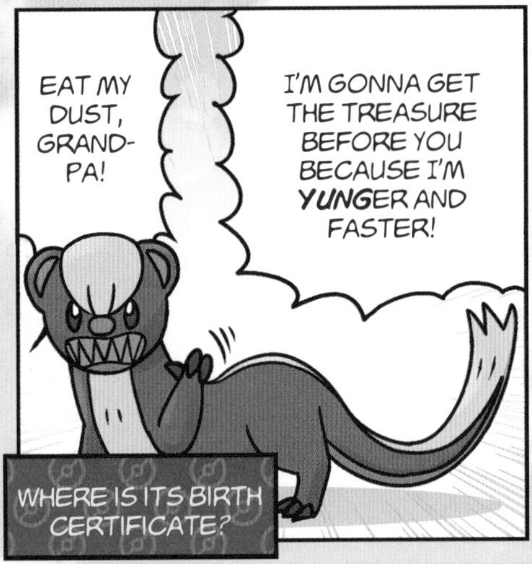
EAT MY DUST, GRAND-PA!
I'M GONNA GET THE TREASURE BEFORE YOU BECAUSE I'M **YUNG**ER AND FASTER!
WHERE IS ITS BIRTH CERTIFICATE?

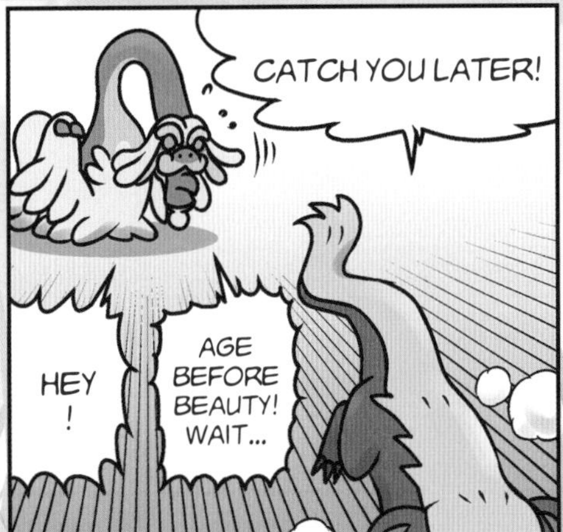
CATCH YOU LATER!
HEY !
AGE BEFORE BEAUTY! WAIT...

POKÉMON MINIDEX

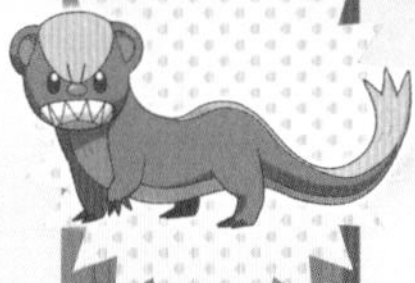

YUNGOOS

CATEGORY

Loitering

TYPE

Normal

It wanders around in a never-ending search for food. At dusk it collapses from exhaustion and falls asleep on the spot.

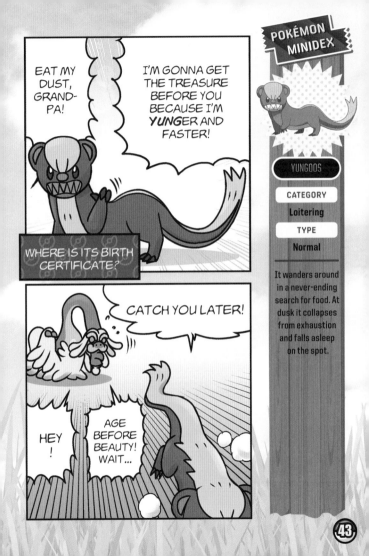

Butter Up!

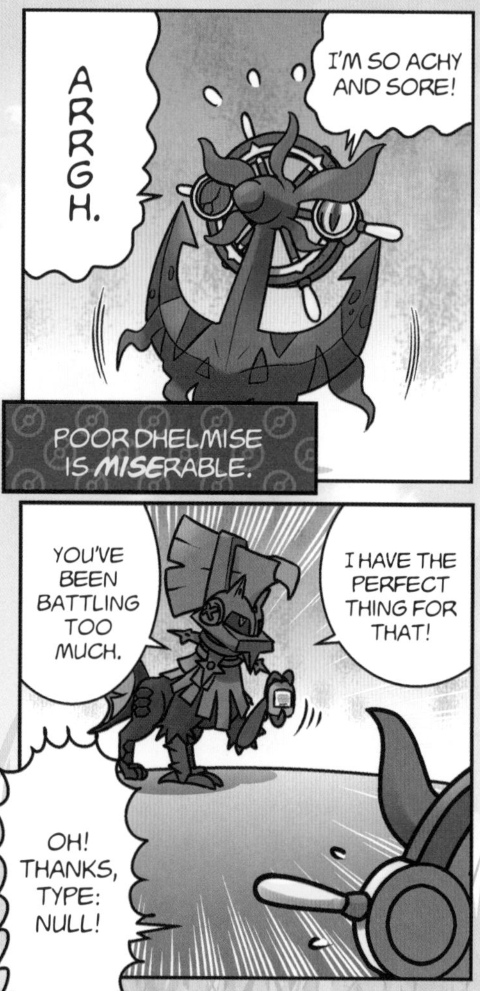
ARRGH.
I'M SO ACHY AND SORE!
POOR DHELMISE IS *MISE*RABLE.
YOU'VE BEEN BATTLING TOO MUCH.
I HAVE THE PERFECT THING FOR THAT!
OH! THANKS, TYPE: NULL!

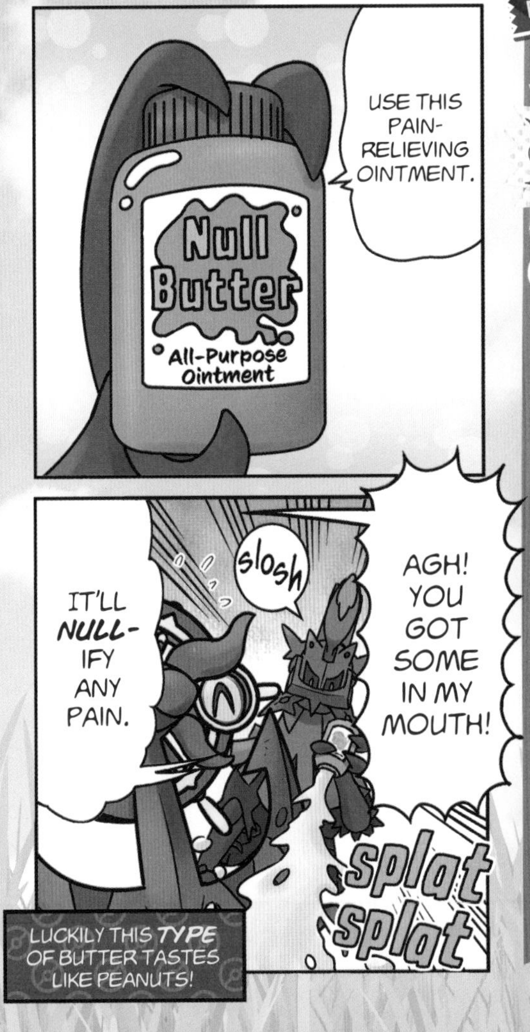
Null Butter
All-Purpose Ointment
USE THIS PAIN-RELIEVING OINTMENT.
IT'LL *NULL*-IFY ANY PAIN.
slosh
AGH! YOU GOT SOME IN MY MOUTH!
splat splat
LUCKILY THIS *TYPE* OF BUTTER TASTES LIKE PEANUTS!

POKÉMON MINIDEX

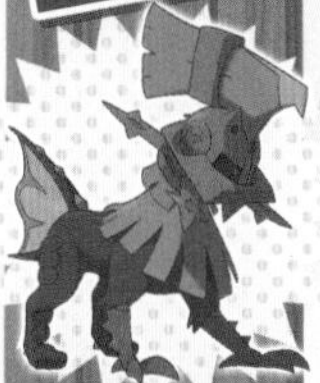

TYPE: NULL

CATEGORY

Synthetic

TYPE

Normal

It wears a mask to control its true power due to the potential of it going on a rampage. Its true power is incredible! You don't want to miss its battles!

Missed Me!

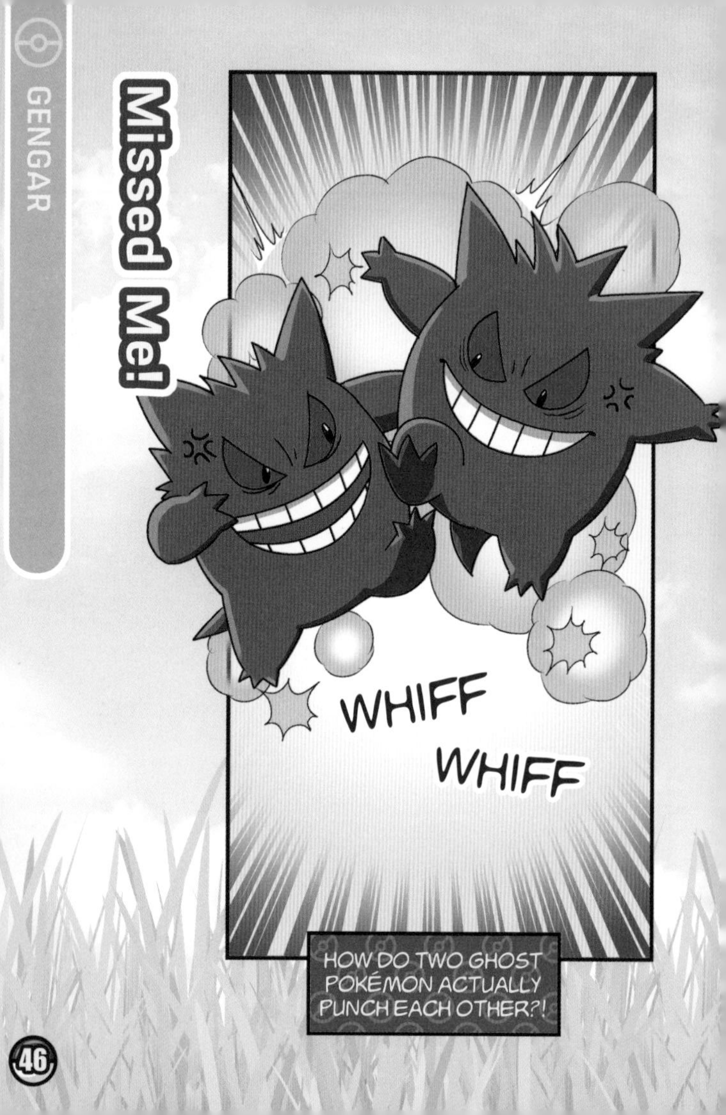
WHIFF
WHIFF
HOW DO TWO GHOST POKÉMON ACTUALLY PUNCH EACH OTHER?!

POKÉMON FUN CLUB

SILHOUETTE QUIZ

Which of the following silhouettes has the greatest number of Pokémon in it?

1

Pokémon (   )

2

Pokémon (   )

3

Pokémon (   )

Answers on page 187!

Three Out of Seven

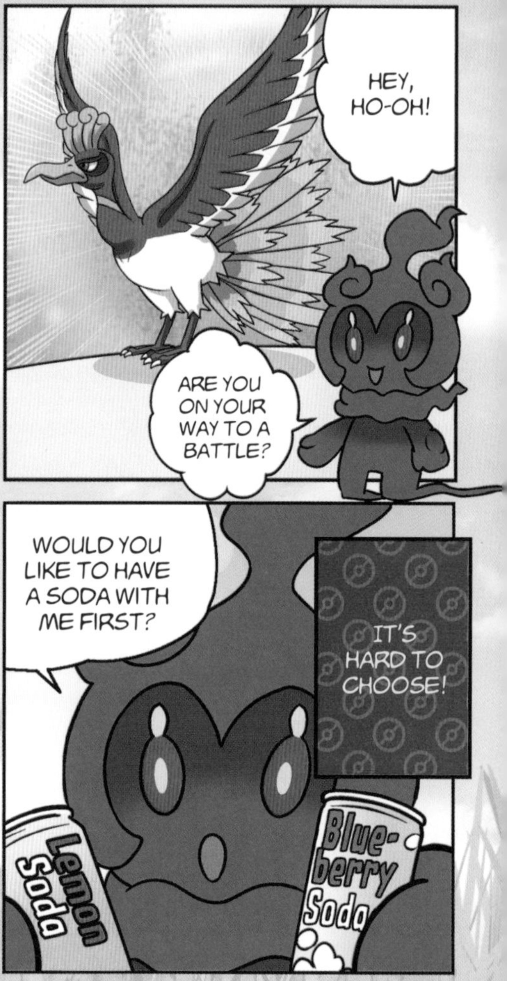
HEY, HO-OH!
ARE YOU ON YOUR WAY TO A BATTLE?
WOULD YOU LIKE TO HAVE A SODA WITH ME FIRST?
IT'S HARD TO CHOOSE!
Lemon Soda
Blue-berry Soda

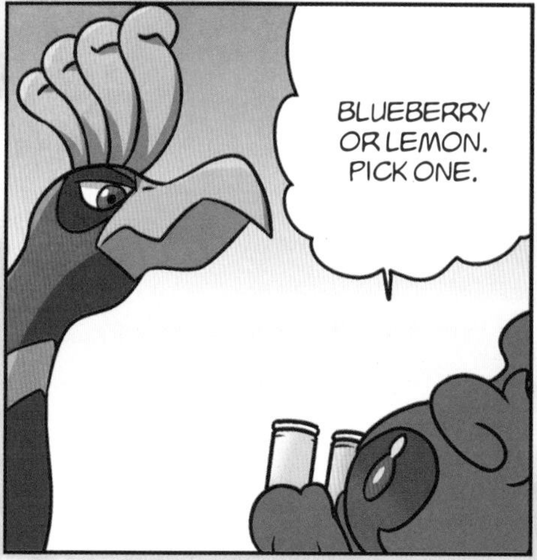
BLUEBERRY OR LEMON. PICK ONE.

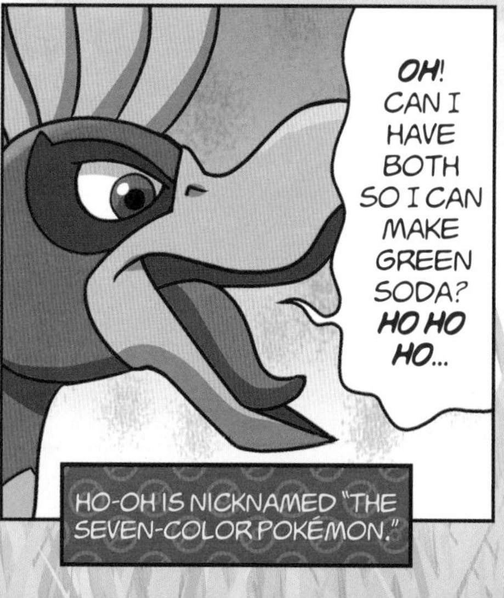
OH! CAN I HAVE BOTH SO I CAN MAKE GREEN SODA? HO HO HO...
HO-OH IS NICKNAMED "THE SEVEN-COLOR POKÉMON."

POKÉMON MINIDEX

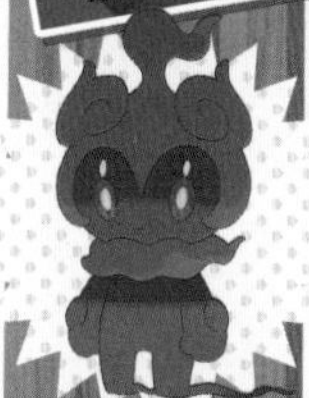

MARSHADOW

CATEGORY

Gloomdweller

TYPE

Fighting, Ghost

It lurks in the shadows of others, copying their movements and powers. It prefers to remain hidden, so it is hardly ever seen by anyone.

Escape Plan

POPPLIO'S STRATEGY

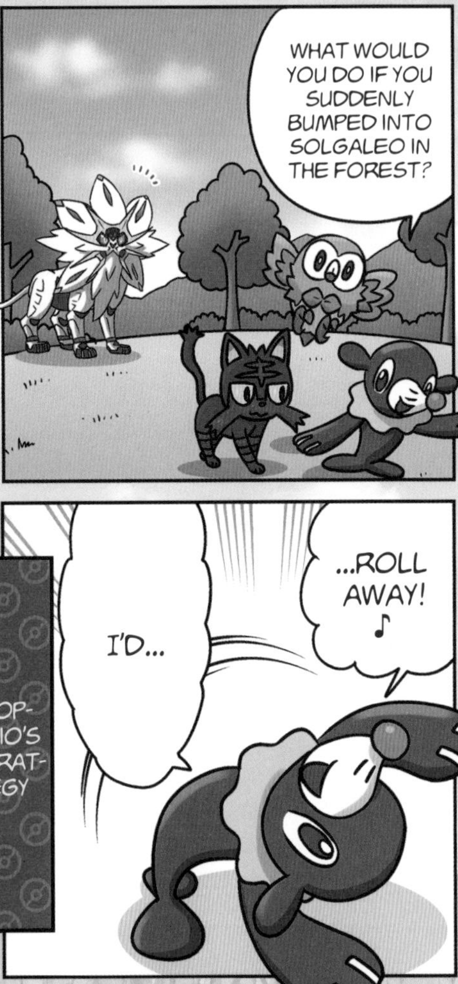
WHAT WOULD YOU DO IF YOU SUDDENLY BUMPED INTO SOLGALEO IN THE FOREST?
I'D...
...ROLL AWAY! ♪

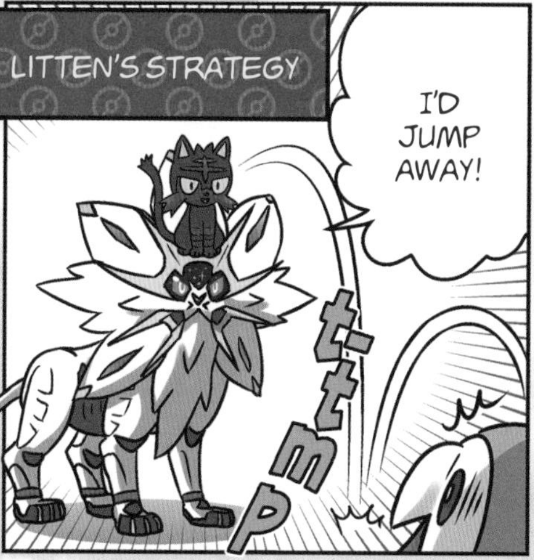
LITTEN'S STRATEGY
I'D JUMP AWAY!
t-tmp

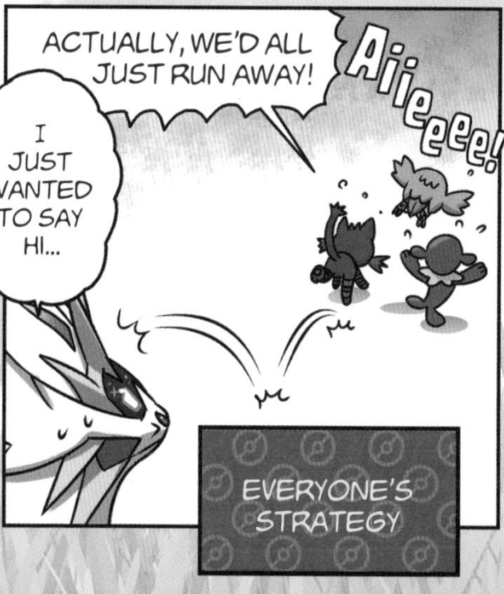
ACTUALLY, WE'D ALL JUST RUN AWAY!
Aiieeeee!
I JUST WANTED TO SAY HI...
EVERYONE'S STRATEGY

POKÉMON MINIDEX

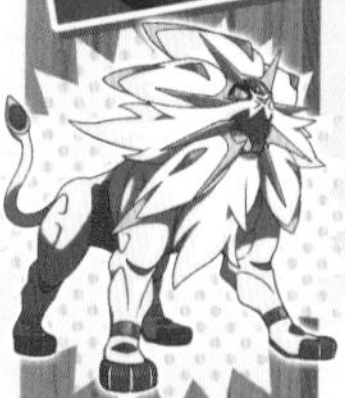

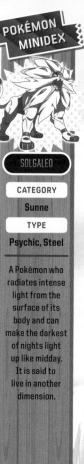

SOLGALEO

CATEGORY

Sunne

TYPE

Psychic, Steel

A Pokémon who radiates intense light from the surface of its body and can make the darkest of nights light up like midday. It is said to live in another dimension.

Time for a Picnic

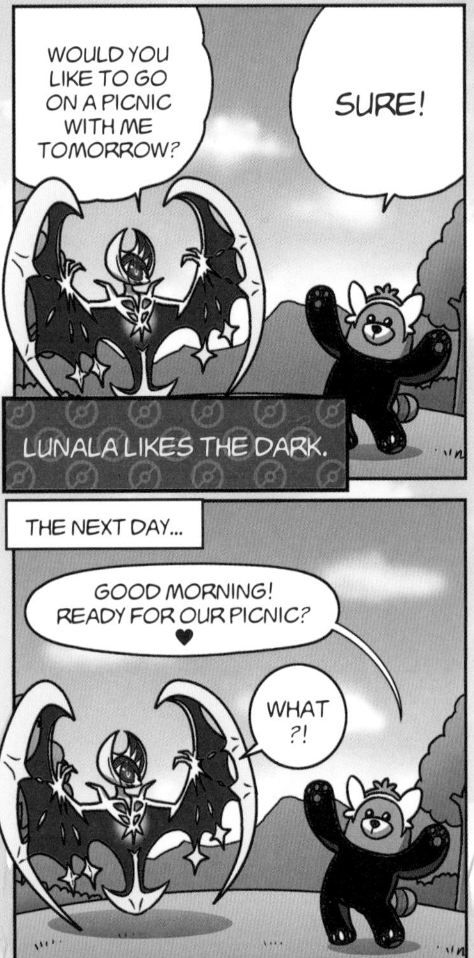
WOULD YOU LIKE TO GO ON A PICNIC WITH ME TOMORROW?
SURE!
LUNALA LIKES THE DARK.
THE NEXT DAY...
GOOD MORNING! READY FOR OUR PICNIC? ♥
WHAT ?!

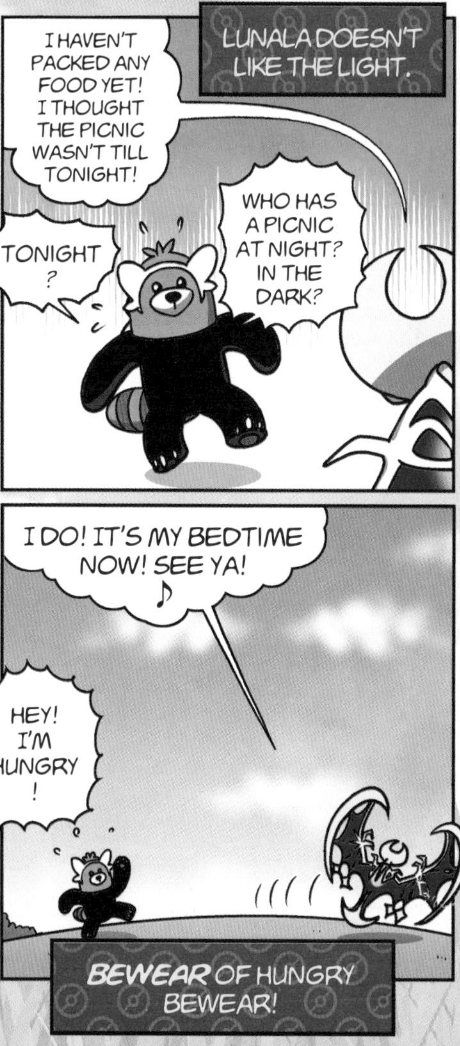
LUNALA DOESN'T LIKE THE LIGHT.
I HAVEN'T PACKED ANY FOOD YET! I THOUGHT THE PICNIC WASN'T TILL TONIGHT!
TONIGHT?
WHO HAS A PICNIC AT NIGHT? IN THE DARK?
I DO! IT'S MY BEDTIME NOW! SEE YA! ♪
HEY! I'M HUNGRY!
BEWEAR OF HUNGRY BEWEAR!

POKÉMON MINIDEX

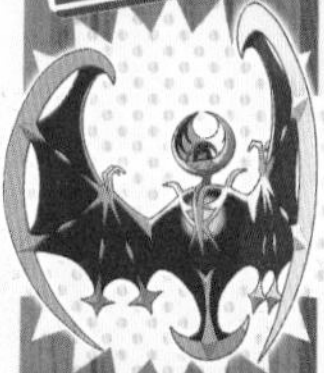

LUNALA

CATEGORY

Moone

TYPE

Psychic, Ghost

A Pokémon who absorbs light, drawing the moonless dark veil of night over the brightness of day.

Mop Dreams

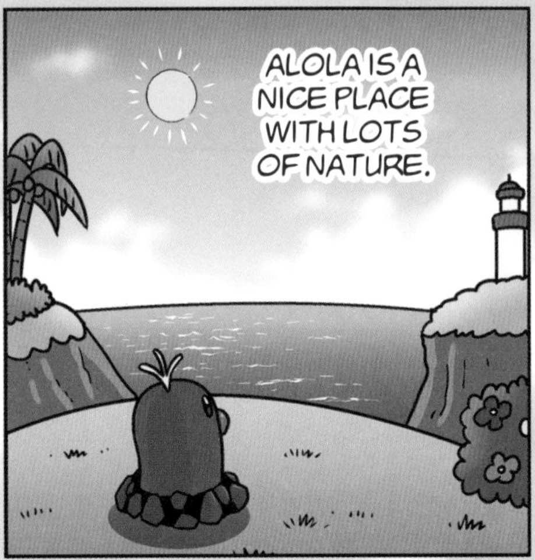
ALOLA IS A NICE PLACE WITH LOTS OF NATURE.

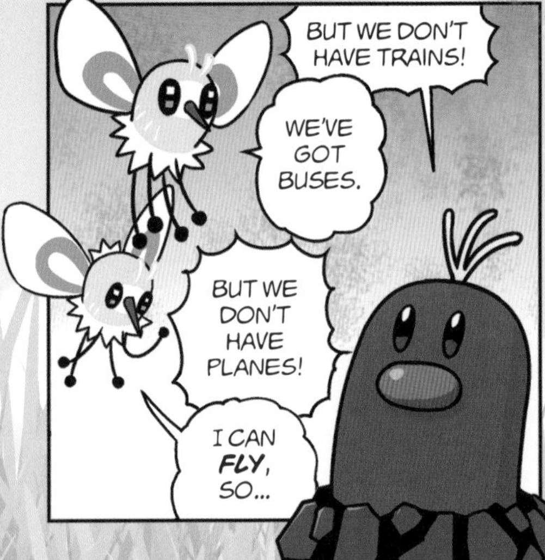
BUT WE DON'T HAVE TRAINS!
WE'VE GOT BUSES.
BUT WE DON'T HAVE PLANES!
I CAN **FLY**, SO...

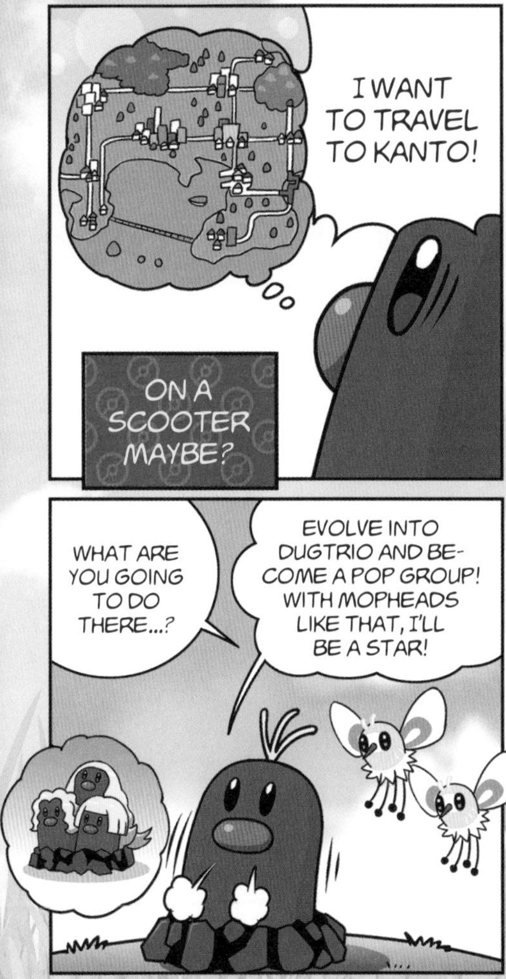
I WANT TO TRAVEL TO KANTO!
ON A SCOOTER MAYBE?
WHAT ARE YOU GOING TO DO THERE...?
EVOLVE INTO DUGTRIO AND BE-COME A POP GROUP! WITH MOPHEADS LIKE THAT, I'LL BE A STAR!
...

POKÉMON MINIDEX

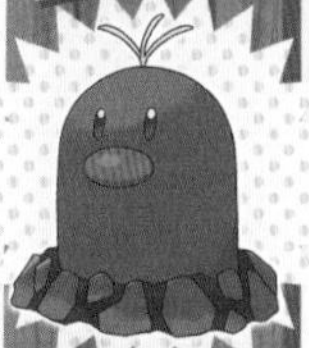

A. DIGLETT

CATEGORY

Mole

TYPE

Ground, Steel

The hair growing out of its head is actually its whiskers. It pokes them out of a hole to sense its surroundings! That way it can predict if it's about to have a hair-raising experience.

Don't Forget To...

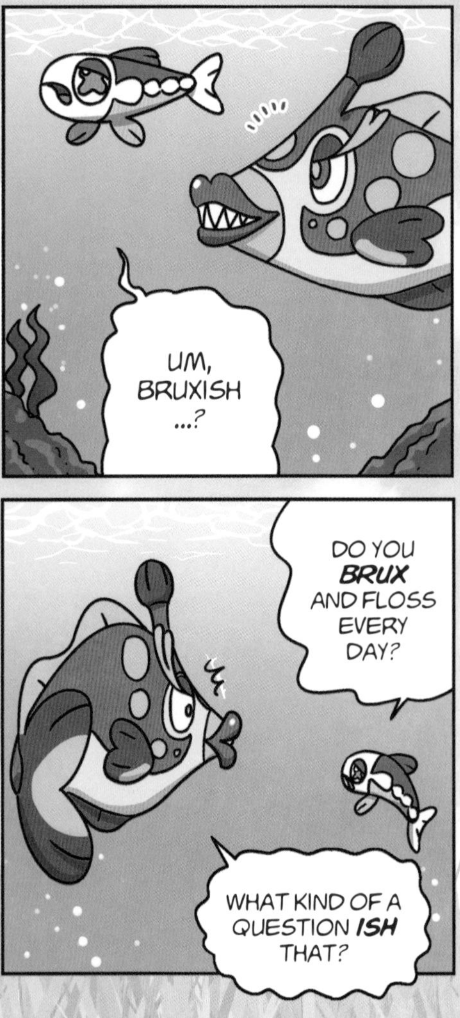
UM, BRUXISH ...?
DO YOU BRUX AND FLOSS EVERY DAY?
WHAT KIND OF A QUESTION ISH THAT?

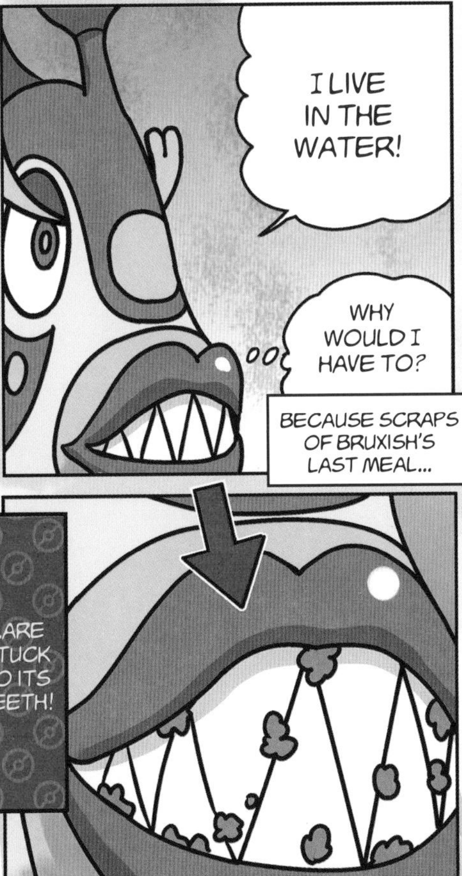
I LIVE IN THE WATER!
WHY WOULD I HAVE TO?
BECAUSE SCRAPS OF BRUXISH'S LAST MEAL...
...ARE STUCK TO ITS TEETH!

POKÉMON MINIDEX

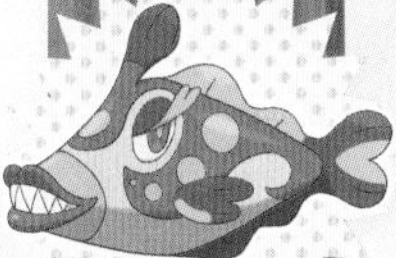

BRUXISH

CATEGORY

Gnash Teeth

TYPE

Water, Psychic

Beware the sound of Bruxish's gnashing teeth. It stuns its prey with Psychokinesis, then grinds them to mush with its powerful chompers!

Crack Up

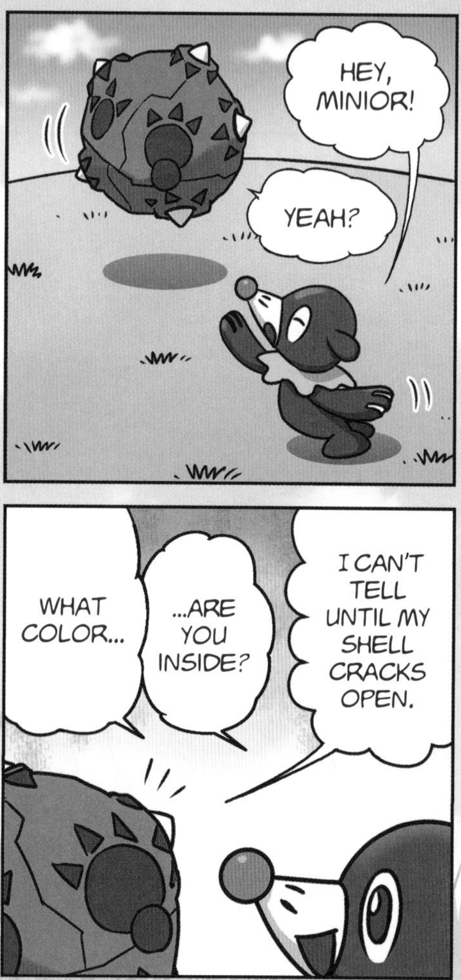
HEY, MINIOR!
YEAH?
WHAT COLOR...
...ARE YOU INSIDE?
I CAN'T TELL UNTIL MY SHELL CRACKS OPEN.

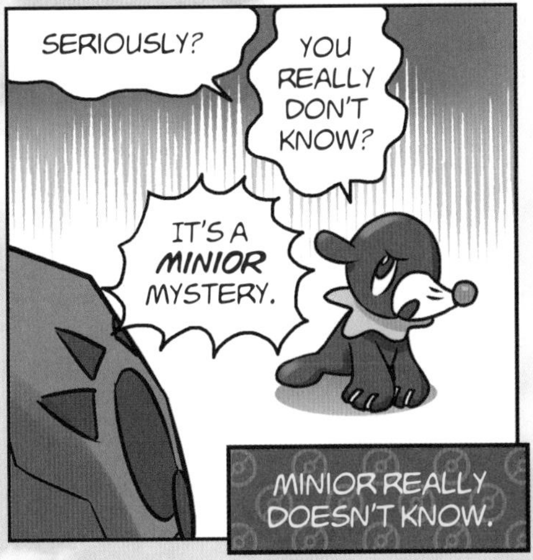
SERIOUSLY?
YOU REALLY DON'T KNOW?
IT'S A MINIOR MYSTERY.
MINIOR REALLY DOESN'T KNOW.

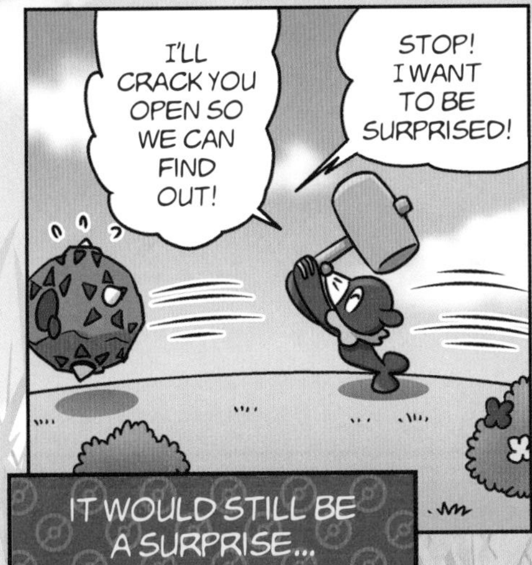
I'LL CRACK YOU OPEN SO WE CAN FIND OUT!
STOP! I WANT TO BE SURPRISED!
IT WOULD STILL BE A SURPRISE...

POKÉMON MINIDEX

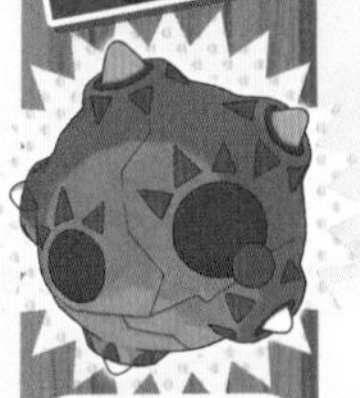

MINIOR

CATEGORY

Meteor

TYPE

Rock, Flying

The color of its core depends on the substance it absorbed in the atmosphere.

WIMPOD

Meet and Don't Greet

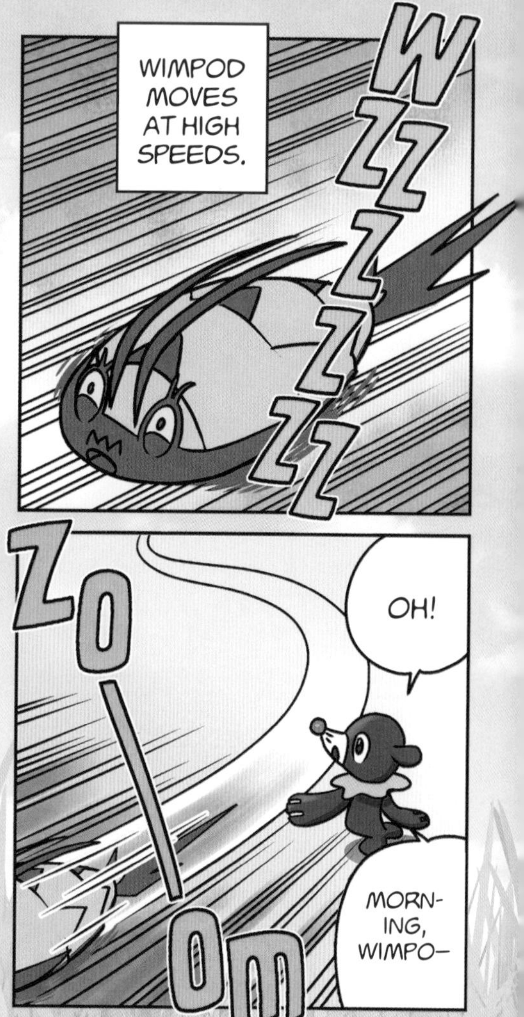
WIMPOD MOVES AT HIGH SPEEDS.
WZZZZZZ
ZO—OM
OH!
MORNING, WIMPO—

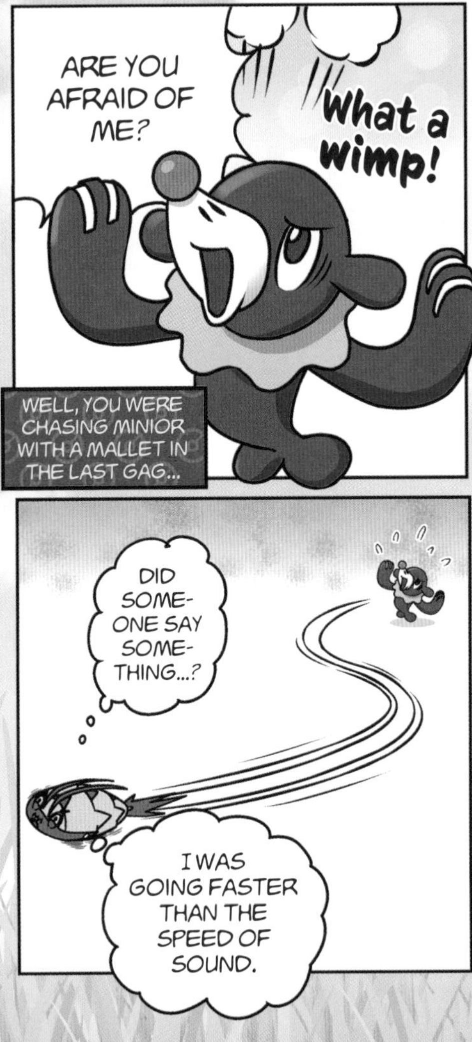
ARE YOU AFRAID OF ME?
What a wimp!
WELL, YOU WERE CHASING MINIOR WITH A MALLET IN THE LAST GAG...
DID SOME-ONE SAY SOME-THING...?
I WAS GOING FASTER THAN THE SPEED OF SOUND.

POKÉMON MINIDEX

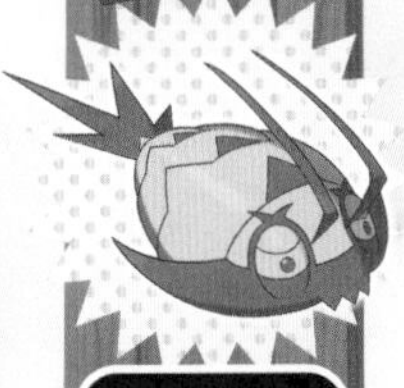

WIMPOD

CATEGORY

Turn Tail

TYPE

Bug, Water

A very cowardly Pokémon. If you try to catch it, it will flail its many legs at high speed and run away!

In the Dark

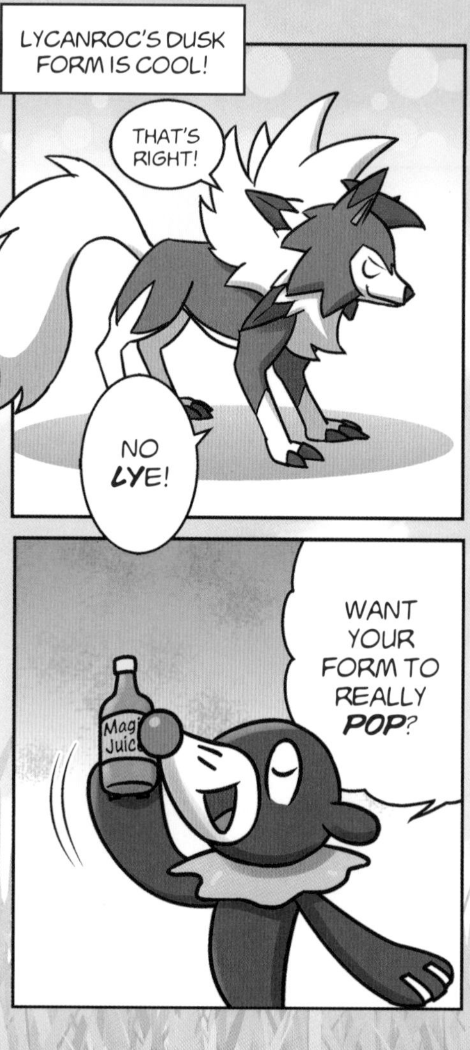
LYCANROC'S DUSK FORM IS COOL!
THAT'S RIGHT!
NO LYE!
WANT YOUR FORM TO REALLY POP?
Magi Juic

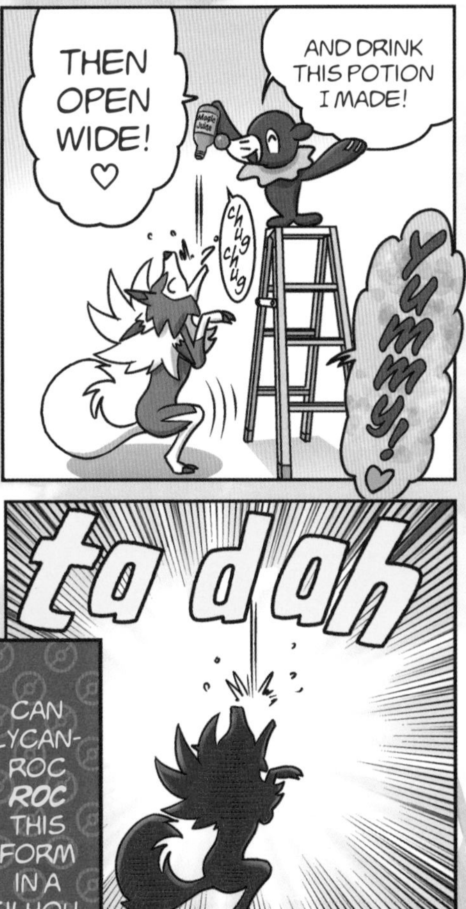
THEN OPEN WIDE! ♡
AND DRINK THIS POTION I MADE!
Magic Juice
chug chug
Yummy! ♡
ta dah

CAN LYCANROC ROC THIS FORM IN A SILHOUETTE?

POKÉMON MINIDEX

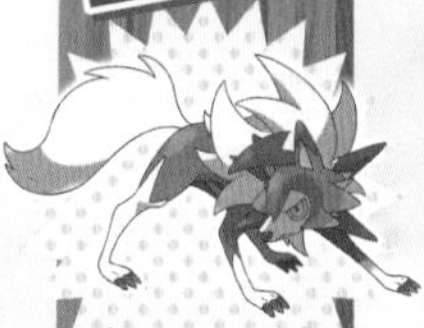

LYCANROC: D. F.

CATEGORY

Wolf

TYPE

Rock

Bathed in the setting sun, Lycanroc undergoes a special kind of evolution. An intense fighting spirit underlies its calm exterior.

COSMOG

Peace and Not So Quiet

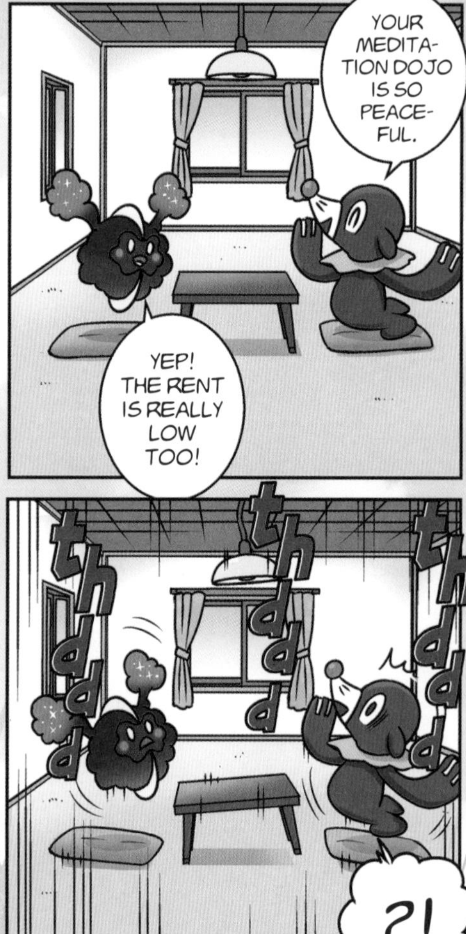
YOUR MEDITA-TION DOJO IS SO PEACE-FUL.
YEP! THE RENT IS REALLY LOW TOO!
?!

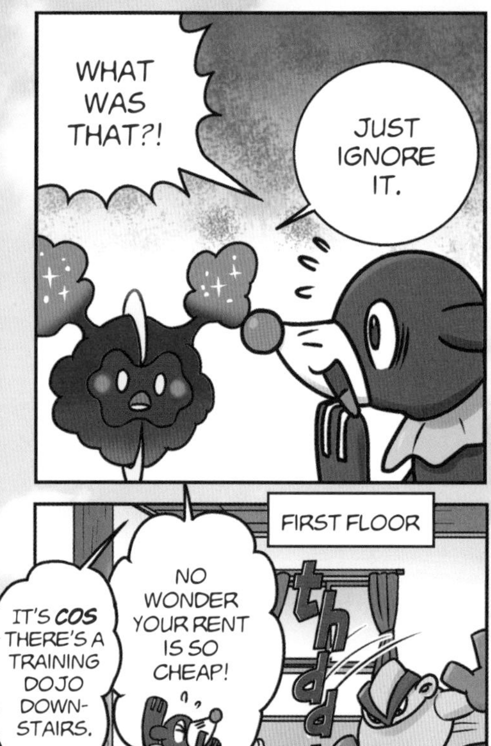
WHAT WAS THAT?!
JUST IGNORE IT.
FIRST FLOOR
IT'S **COS** THERE'S A TRAINING DOJO DOWN-STAIRS.
NO WONDER YOUR RENT IS SO CHEAP!
thdd
YOU GET WHAT YOU PAY FOR.

POKÉMON MINIDEX

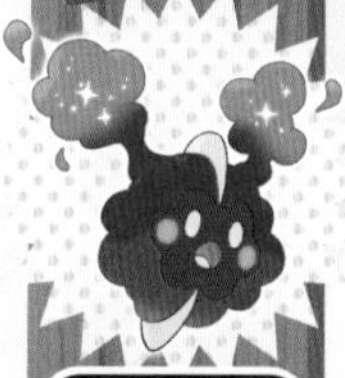

COSMOG

CATEGORY

Nebula

TYPE

Psychic

A rare Pokémon that only a handful of Alola residents know about. Its body is like a cloud of smog that can be blown hither and thither by the wind.

JANGMO-O

In the Wrong Field

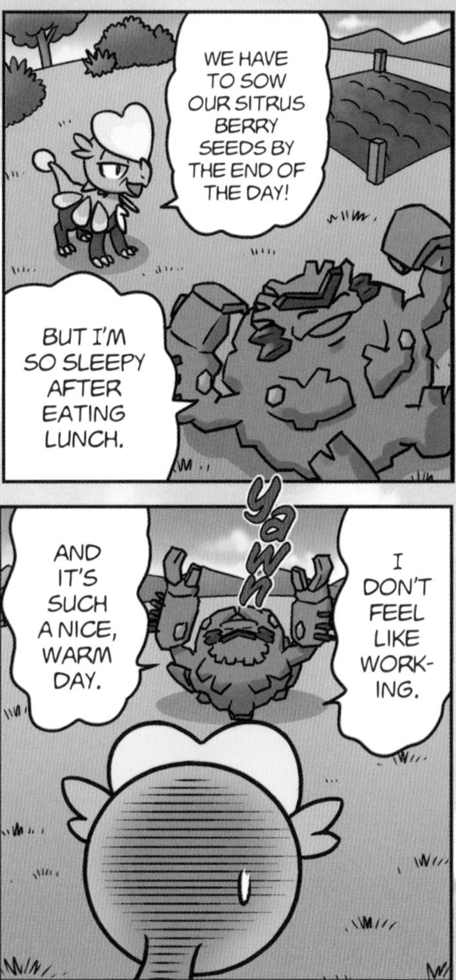
WE HAVE TO SOW OUR SITRUS BERRY SEEDS BY THE END OF THE DAY!
BUT I'M SO SLEEPY AFTER EATING LUNCH.
AND IT'S SUCH A NICE, WARM DAY.
yawn
I DON'T FEEL LIKE WORK-ING.

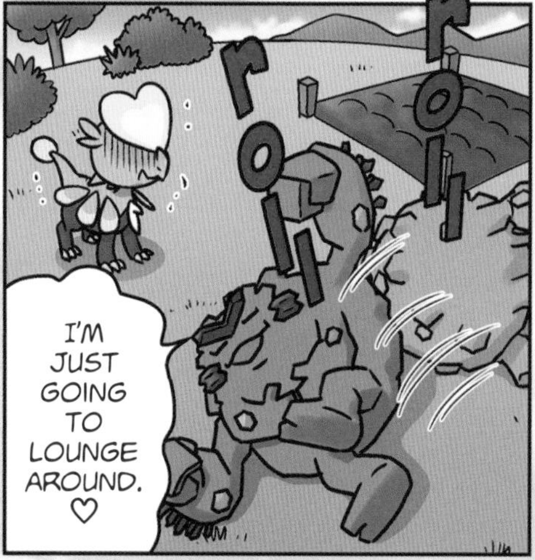
roll
roll
I'M JUST GOING TO LOUNGE AROUND. ♡

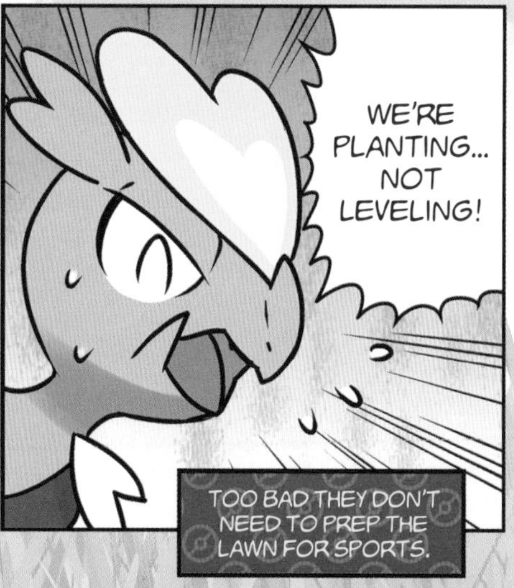
WE'RE PLANTING... NOT LEVELING!
TOO BAD THEY DON'T NEED TO PREP THE LAWN FOR SPORTS.

POKÉMON MINIDEX

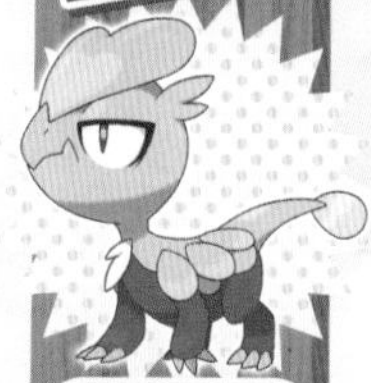

JANGMO-O

CATEGORY

Scaly

TYPE

Dragon

Metallic sounds echo through the high mountains—the sound of Jangmo-o's ***jang***led nerves.

DRAMPA

Let Sleeping Pokémon Lie

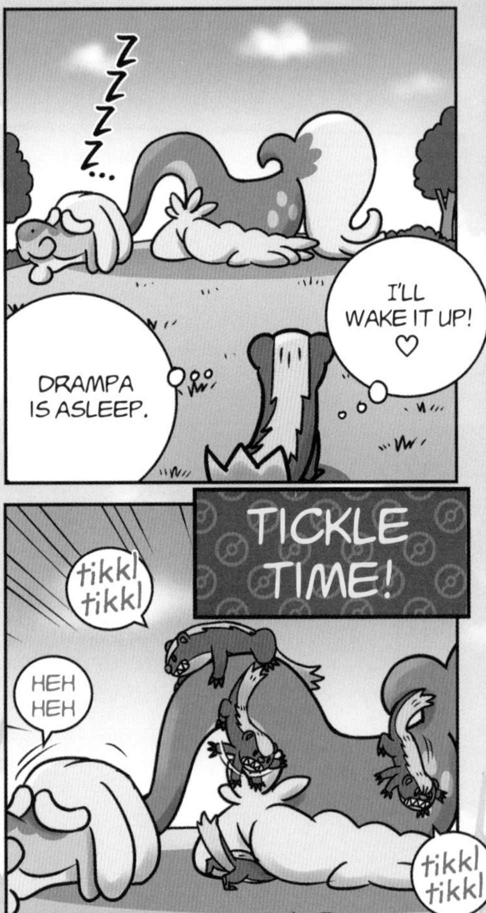
ZZZZ...
DRAMPA IS ASLEEP.
I'LL WAKE IT UP! ♡
TICKLE TIME!
tikkl tikkl
HEH HEH
tikkl tikkl
tikkl tikkl

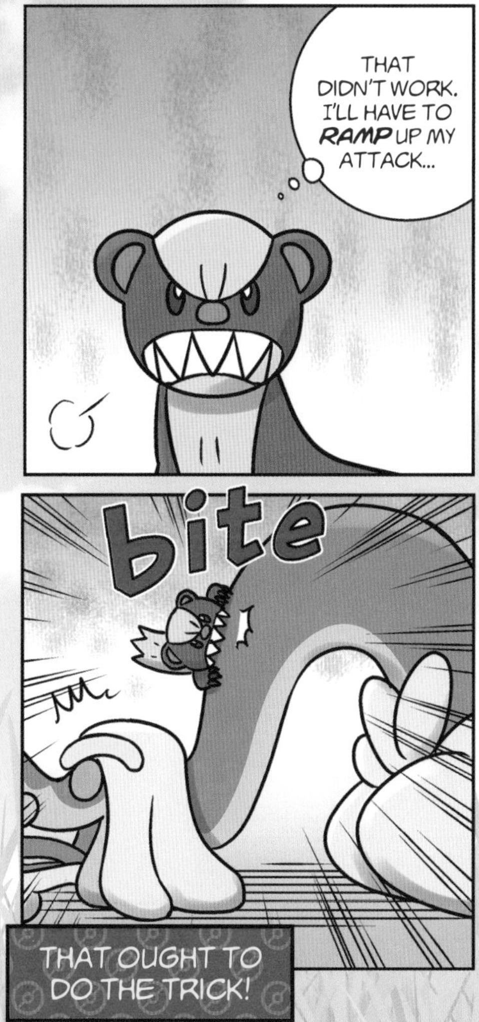
THAT DIDN'T WORK. I'LL HAVE TO *RAMP* UP MY ATTACK...
bite
THAT OUGHT TO DO THE TRICK!

POKÉMON MINIDEX

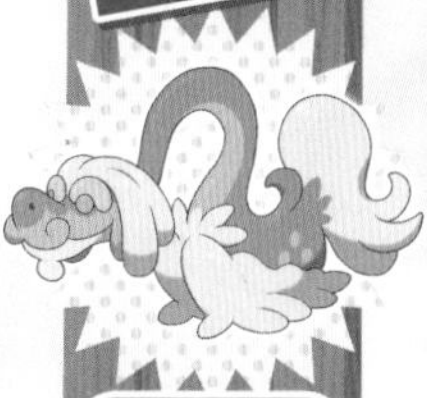

DRAMPA

CATEGORY

Placid

TYPE

Normal, Dragon

A kind Pokémon who explodes in anger when children are in danger. The power of its move Dragon Breath can be devastating at such times. Protecting others can really ***amp*** up your motivation!

A Matter of Table Manners

SALANDIT

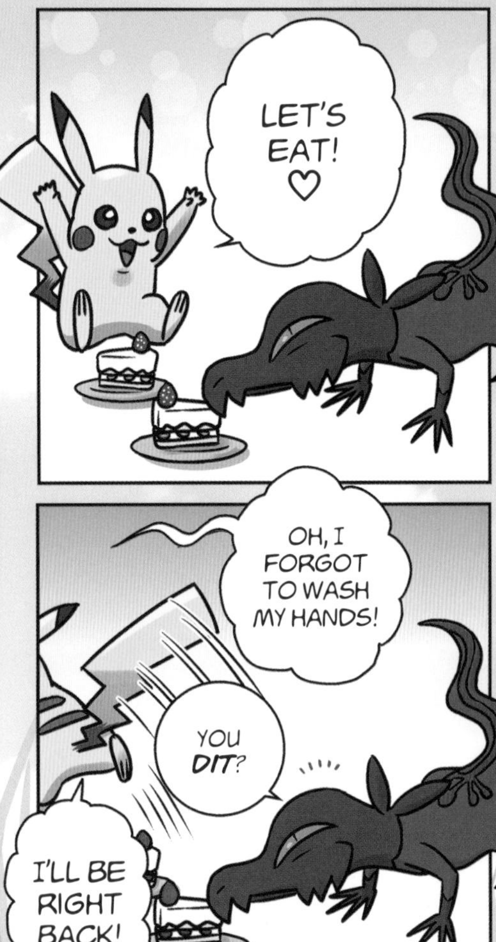
LET'S EAT! ♡
OH, I FORGOT TO WASH MY HANDS!
YOU **DIT**?
I'LL BE RIGHT BACK!

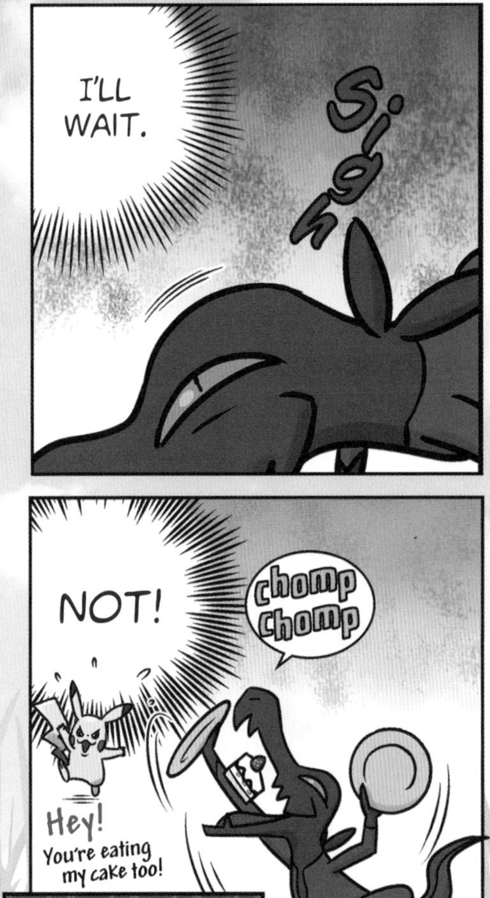
I'LL WAIT.
Sigh
NOT!
chomp chomp
Hey! You're eating my cake too!
AND THAT'S WHY YOU SHOULD ALWAYS REMEMBER TO WASH YOUR HANDS BEFORE MEALS.

POKÉMON MINIDEX

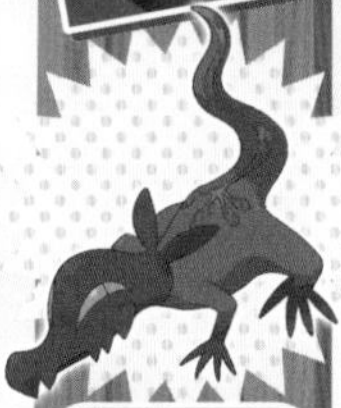

SALANDIT

CATEGORY

Toxic Lizard

TYPE

Poison, Fire

It burns its bodily fluids to create a sweet-smelling poisonous gas that immobilizes Bug Pokémon, then eats them. Gas that smells good? That's a first!

Don't Do the Crime If...

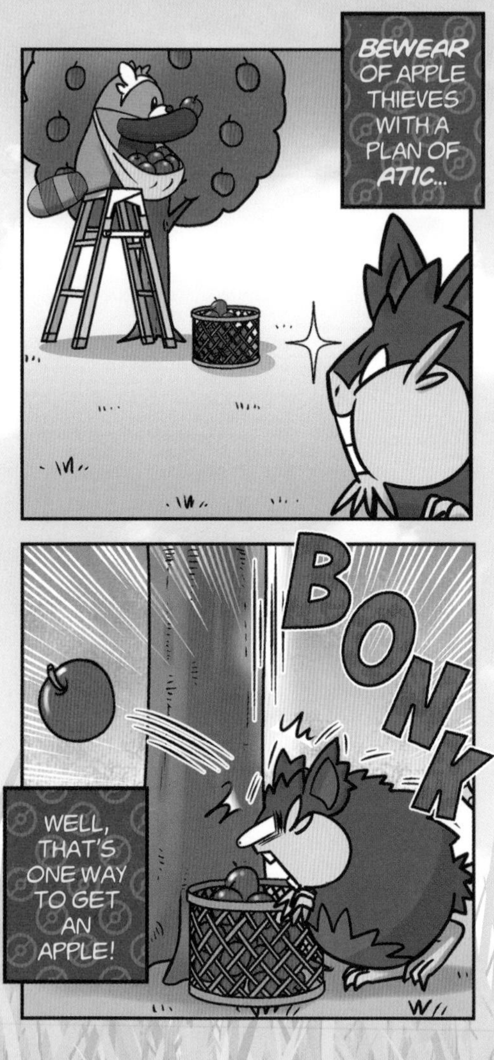
BEWEAR OF APPLE THIEVES WITH A PLAN OF ATIC...
BONK
WELL, THAT'S ONE WAY TO GET AN APPLE!

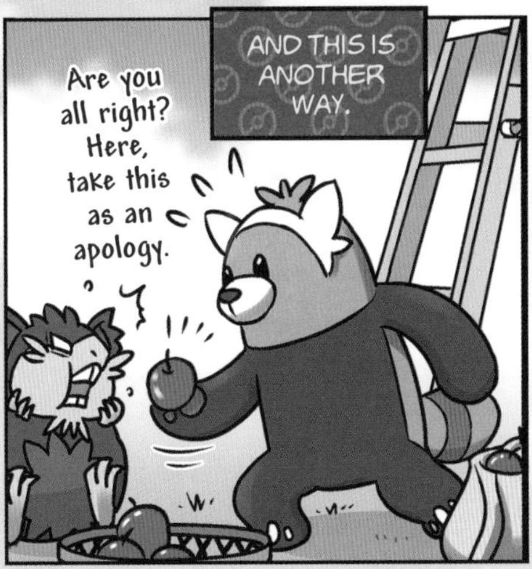
AND THIS IS ANOTHER WAY.
Are you all right? Here, take this as an apology.

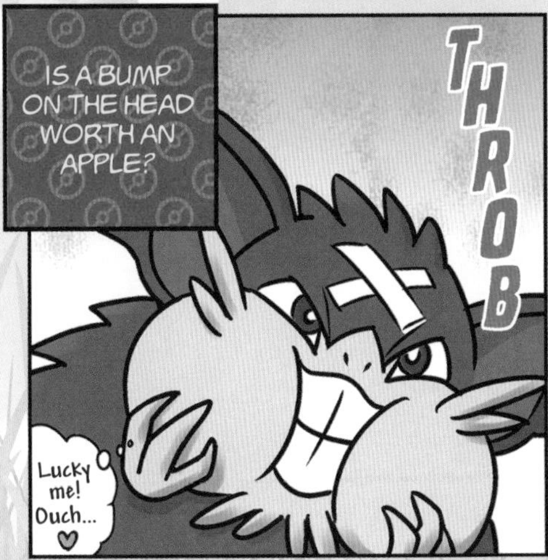
IS A BUMP ON THE HEAD WORTH AN APPLE?
THROB
Lucky me! Ouch... ♡

POKÉMON MINIDEX

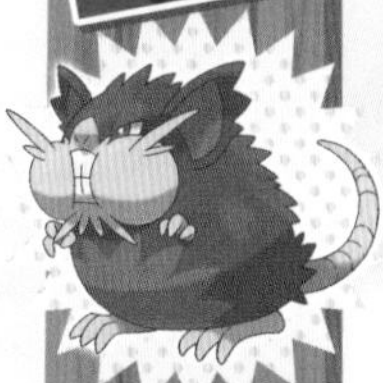

A. RATICATE

CATEGORY

Mouse

TYPE

Dark, Normal

A fat Pokémon who usually lives in cities. It commands Rattata to gather food and then eats it all up! What a ***ratt***en boss!

Bridging the Gap

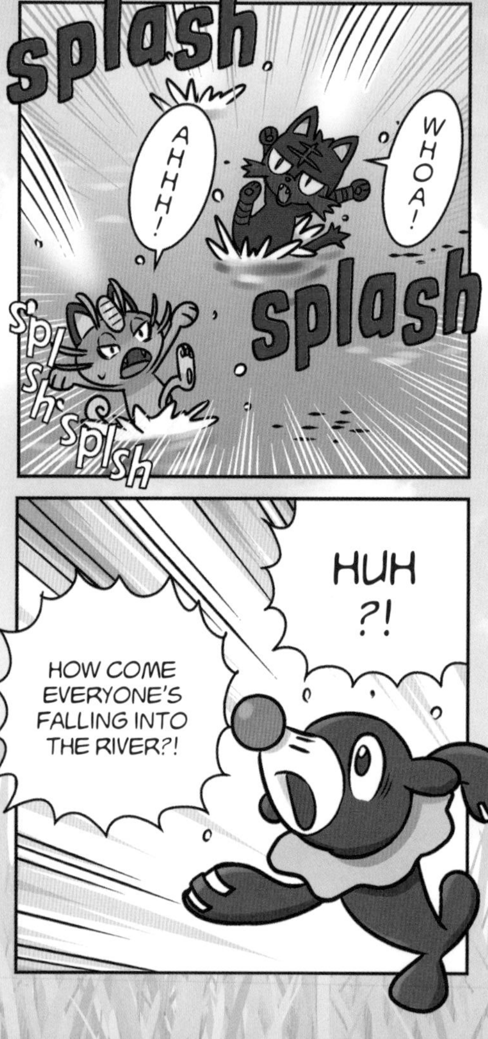
splash
AHHHH!
WHOA!
splash
splsh
splsh
HUH ?!
HOW COME EVERYONE'S FALLING INTO THE RIVER?!

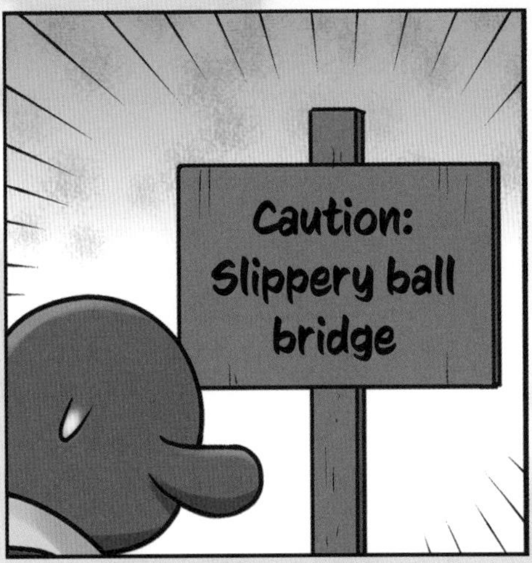
Caution:
Slippery ball
bridge

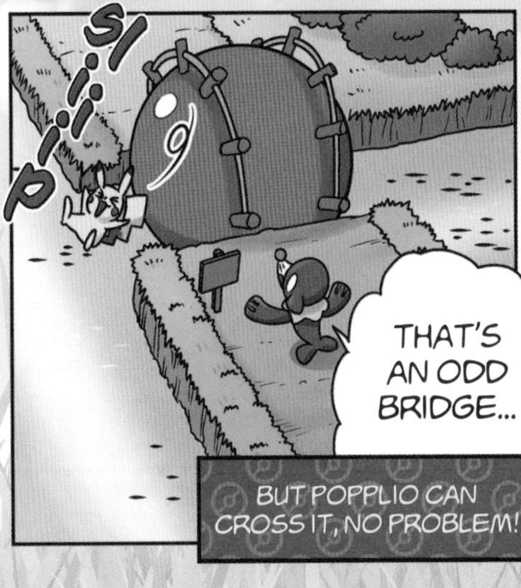
Sliiiip
THAT'S AN ODD BRIDGE...
BUT POPPLIO CAN CROSS IT, NO PROBLEM!

POKÉMON MINIDEX

Which of the three below is a Sea Lion Pokémon like Popplio?

1
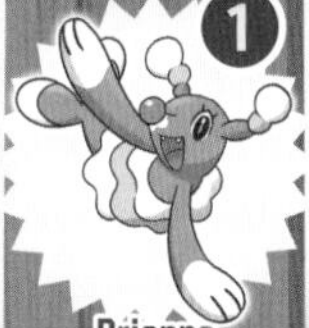
Brionne

2
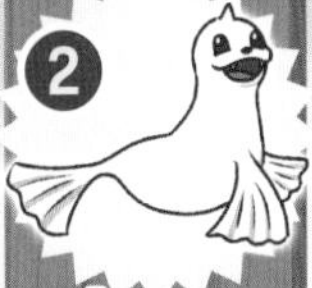
Dewgong

3
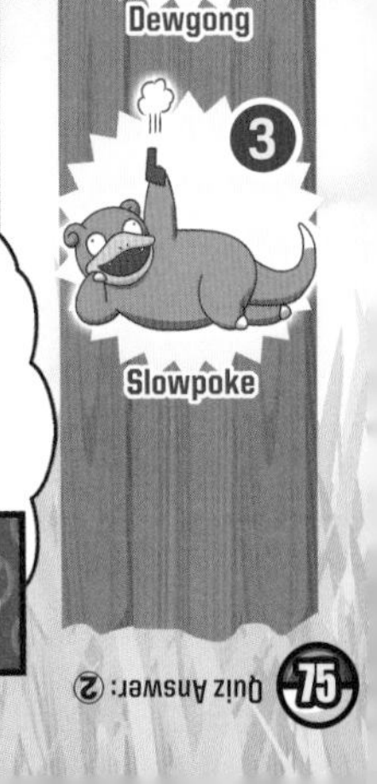
Slowpoke

Quiz Answer: 2

How Many Are There?

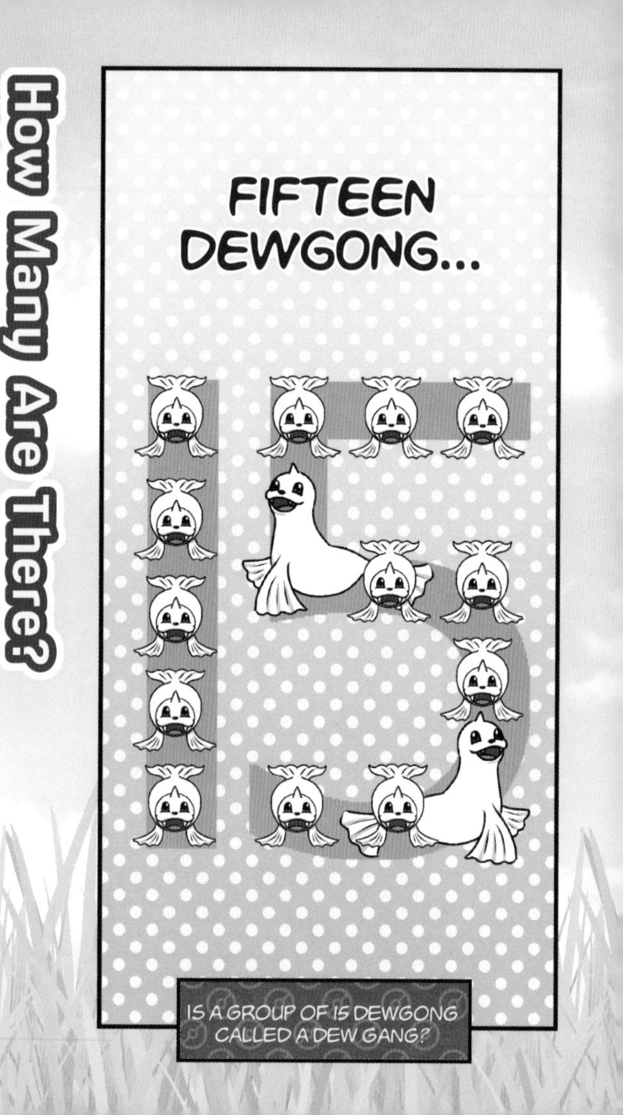
FIFTEEN DEWGONG...
IS A GROUP OF 15 DEWGONG CALLED A DEW GANG?

POKÉMON FUN CLUB

MAKE UP YOUR OWN JOKES!

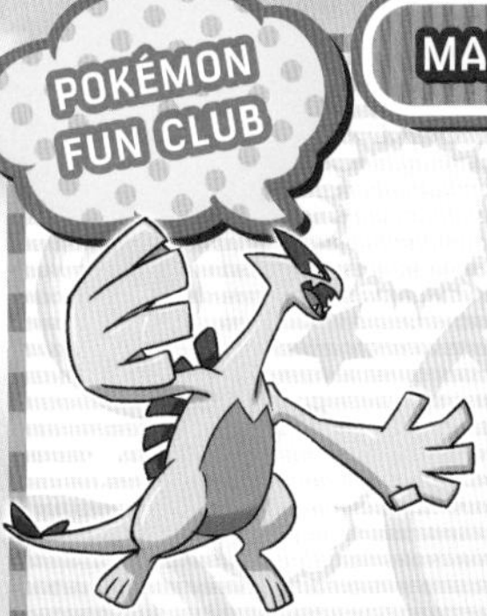

Use the Pokémon illustrations below to play along.

Come up with clever puns or tongue twisters based on the names of these Pokémon.

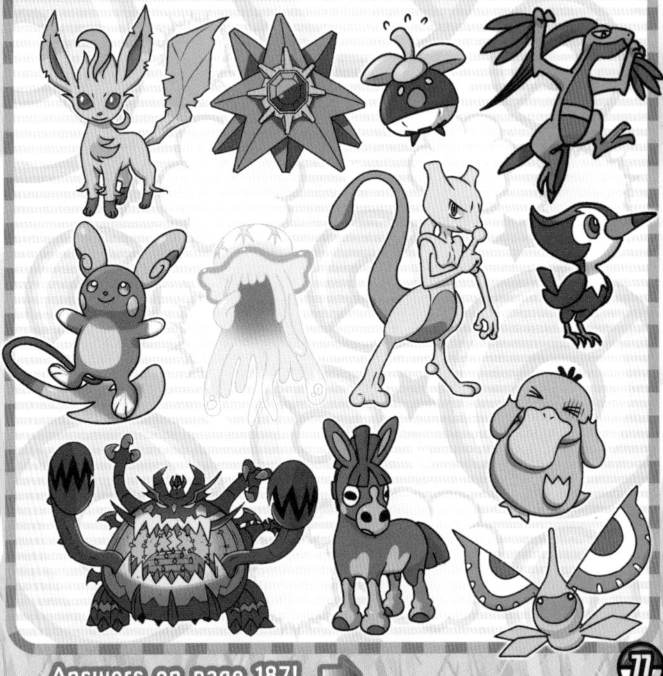

Answers on page 187!

Bragging Rights

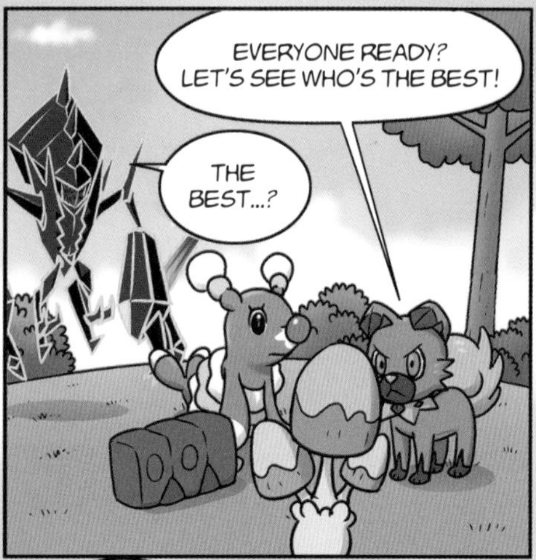
THE BEST...?
EVERYONE READY? LET'S SEE WHO'S THE BEST!

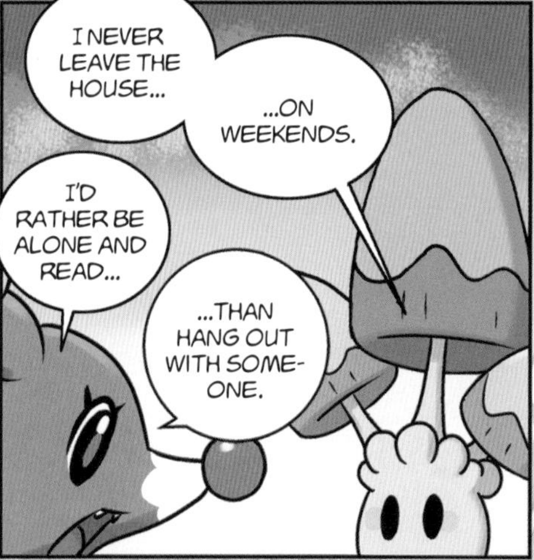
I NEVER LEAVE THE HOUSE...
...ON WEEKENDS.
I'D RATHER BE ALONE AND READ...
...THAN HANG OUT WITH SOME-ONE.

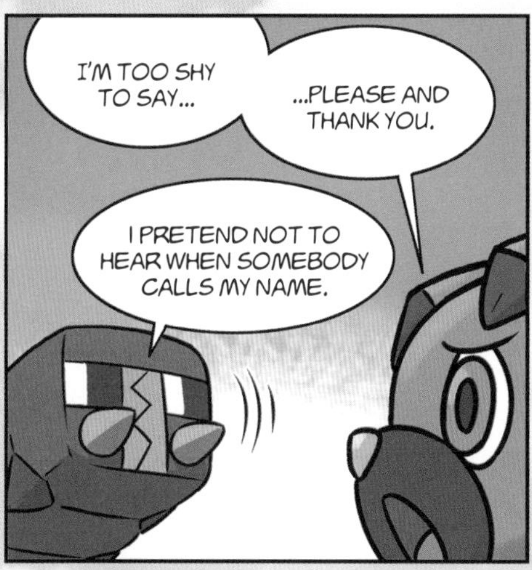
I'M TOO SHY TO SAY...
...PLEASE AND THANK YOU.
I PRETEND NOT TO HEAR WHEN SOMEBODY CALLS MY NAME.

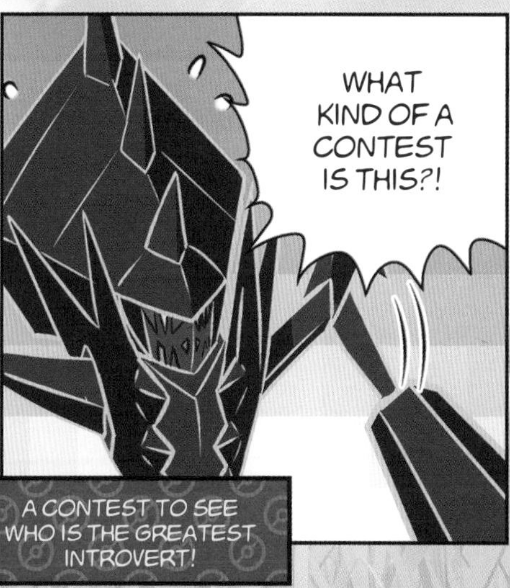
WHAT KIND OF A CONTEST IS THIS?!
A CONTEST TO SEE WHO IS THE GREATEST INTROVERT!

POKÉMON MINIDEX

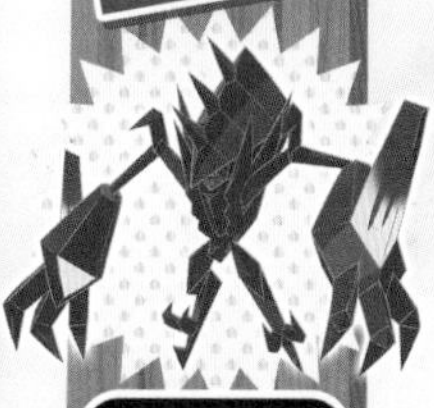

NECROZMA

CATEGORY

Prism

TYPE

Psychic

This Ultra Beast is said to have traveled to this world in ancient times. It usually sleeps underground, and its body is pitch-black.

DUSK MANE NECROZMA

Like Night and Day

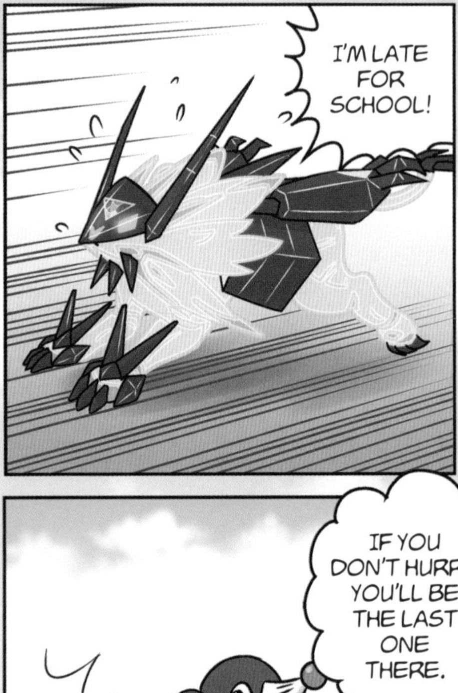

I'M LATE FOR SCHOOL!
IF YOU DON'T HURRY, YOU'LL BE THE LAST ONE THERE.
Good morning!

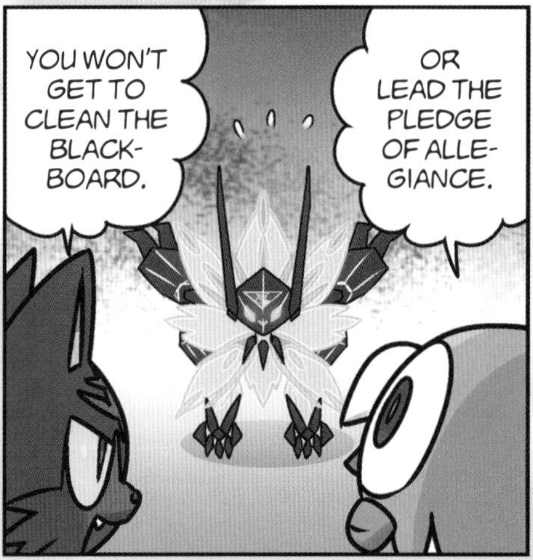
YOU WON'T GET TO CLEAN THE BLACK-BOARD.
OR LEAD THE PLEDGE OF ALLE-GIANCE.

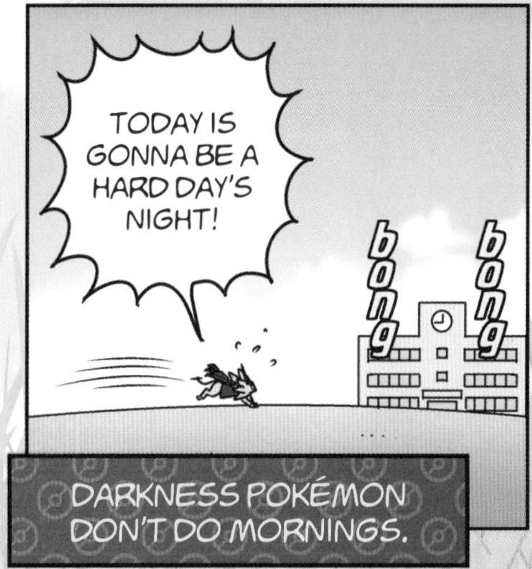
TODAY IS GONNA BE A HARD DAY'S NIGHT!
bong
bong
DARKNESS POKÉMON DON'T DO MORNINGS.

POKÉMON MINIDEX

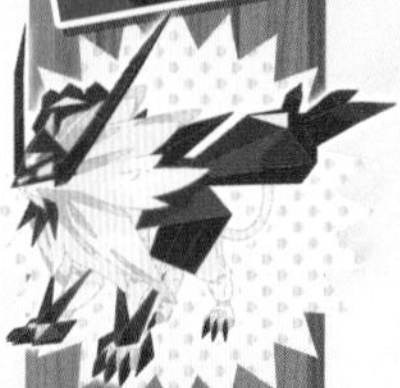

D. M. NECROZMA

CATEGORY

Prism

TYPE

Psychic, Steel

Necrozma takes on its Dusk Mane form when it devours the light of Solgaleo. Its incredible power to ward off opponents is the ***mane*** reason Trainers admire it.

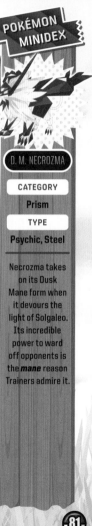

It's All in the Name

DAWN WINGS NECROZMA

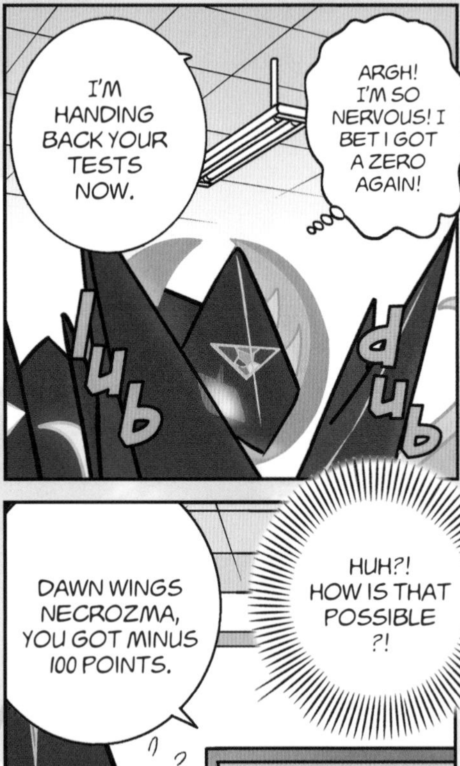
I'M HANDING BACK YOUR TESTS NOW.
ARGH! I'M SO NERVOUS! I BET I GOT A ZERO AGAIN!
DAWN WINGS NECROZMA, YOU GOT MINUS 100 POINTS.
HUH?! HOW IS THAT POSSIBLE ?!
-100

POKÉMON
MINIDEX

D. W. NECROZMA

CATEGORY
Prism

TYPE
Psychic, Ghost

This is Necrozma's form when it has taken control of Lunala. It radiates dark shining energy out of its large wings.

YOU EVEN FORGOT TO WRITE YOUR NAME!

X-100

Name

Soda   Sitrus Berry   Five

I COULDN'T REMEMBER WHAT FORM I WAS IN.

URK.

POKÉMON PROBLEMS, THE STRUGGLE IS REAL.

Like Day and Night

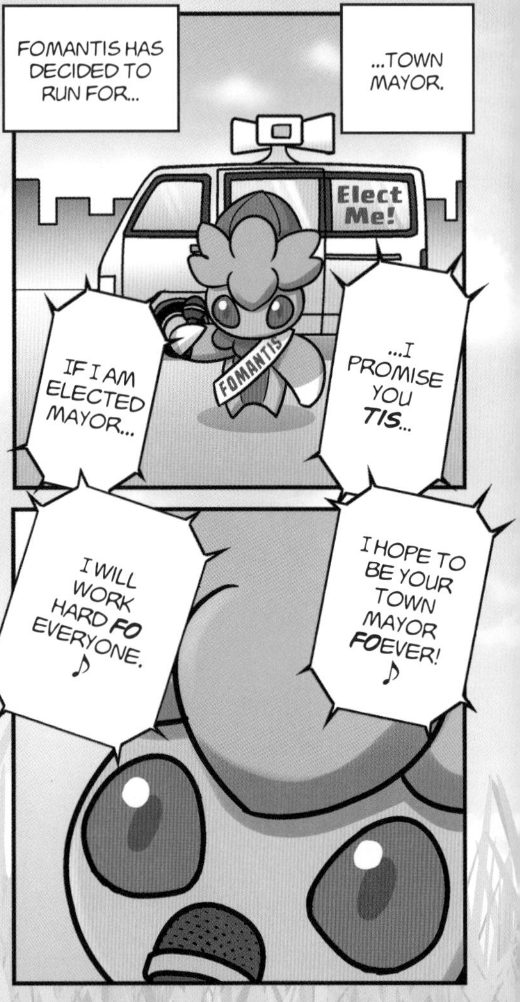
FOMANTIS HAS DECIDED TO RUN FOR...
...TOWN MAYOR.
Elect Me!
FOMANTIS
IF I AM ELECTED MAYOR...
...I PROMISE YOU ***TIS***...
I WILL WORK HARD ***FO*** EVERYONE. ♪
I HOPE TO BE YOUR TOWN MAYOR ***FO***EVER! ♪

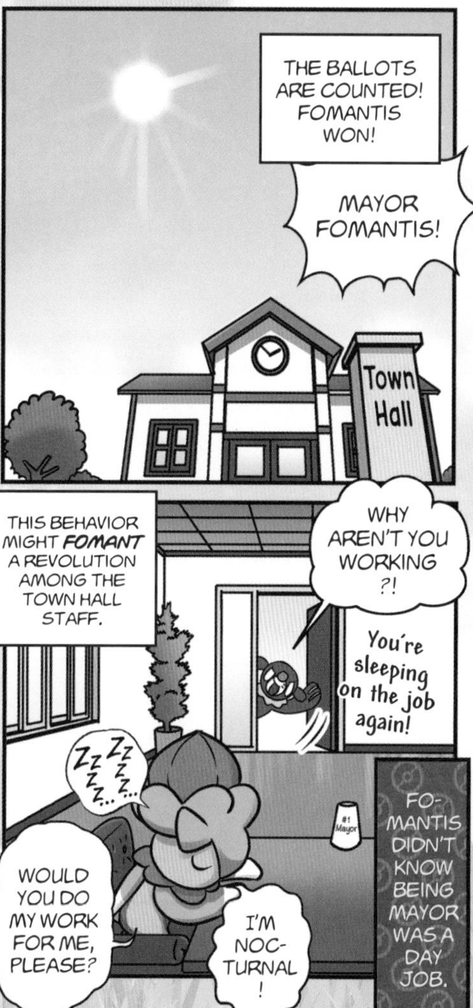
THE BALLOTS ARE COUNTED! FOMANTIS WON!
MAYOR FOMANTIS!
Town Hall
THIS BEHAVIOR MIGHT ***FOMANT*** A REVOLUTION AMONG THE TOWN HALL STAFF.
WHY AREN'T YOU WORKING ?!
You're sleeping on the job again!
ZZZ ZZZ...
#1 Mayor
WOULD YOU DO MY WORK FOR ME, PLEASE?
I'M NOC-TURNAL!
FO-MANTIS DIDN'T KNOW BEING MAYOR WAS A DAY JOB.

POKÉMON MINIDEX

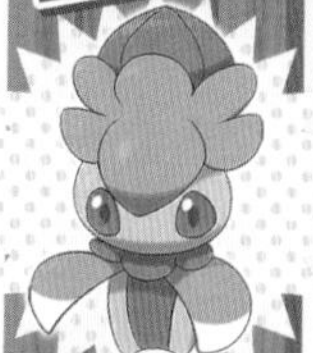

FOMANTIS

CATEGORY

Sickle Grass

TYPE

Grass

Fomantis attacks anyone who stands in its way. It is nocturnal, which means it is active at night. During the day, it is busy sleeping and basking in the sun to gain its vivid colors and grow strong. Wait...can you really be busy sleeping?

Mud Bath

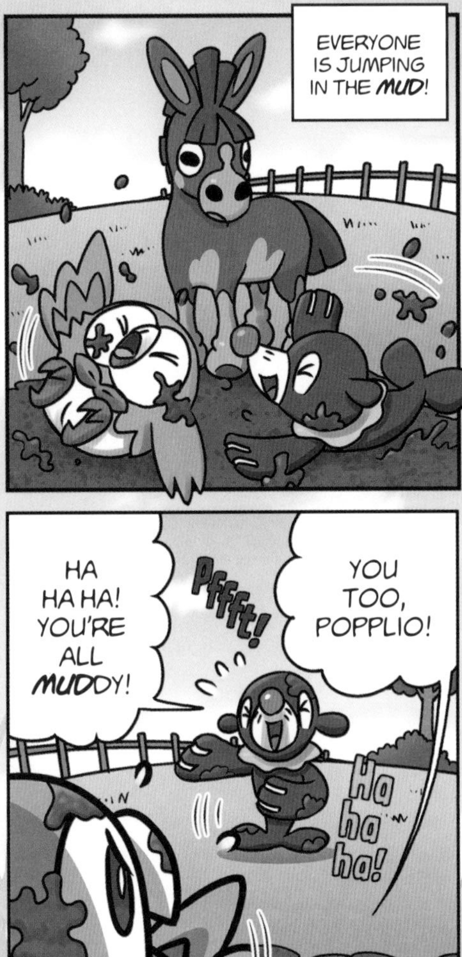
EVERYONE IS JUMPING IN THE MUD!
HA HA HA! YOU'RE ALL MUDDY!
Pfffft!
YOU TOO, POPPLIO!
Ha ha ha!

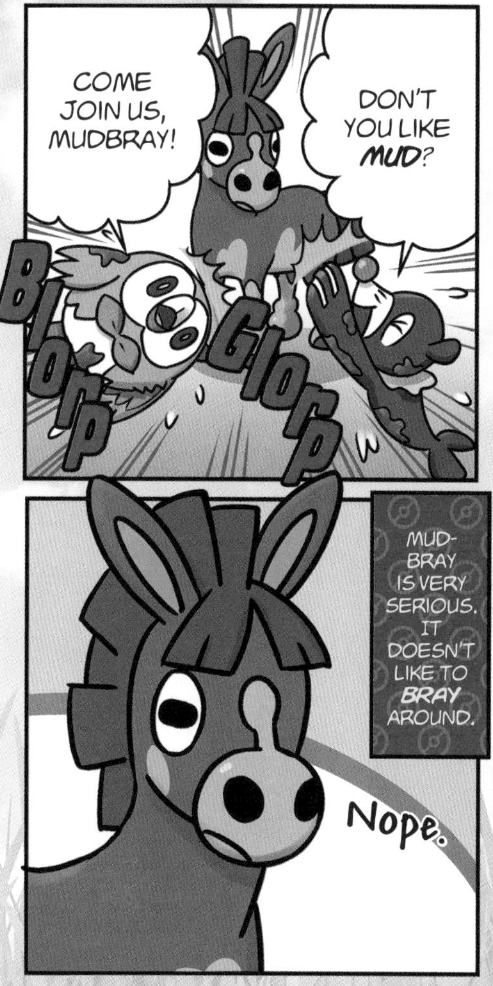
COME JOIN US, MUDBRAY!
DON'T YOU LIKE MUD?
Blorp
Glorp
MUD-BRAY IS VERY SERIOUS. IT DOESN'T LIKE TO BRAY AROUND.
Nope.

POKÉMON MINIDEX

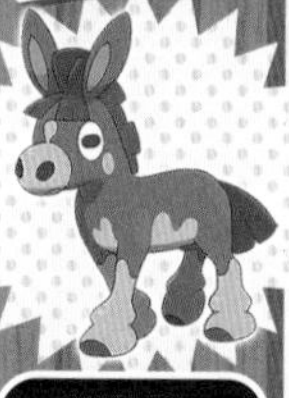

MUDBRAY

CATEGORY

Donkey

TYPE

Ground

Mudbray may be small, but it can carry up to 50 times its own body weight. Looks can be deceiving.

Command Performance

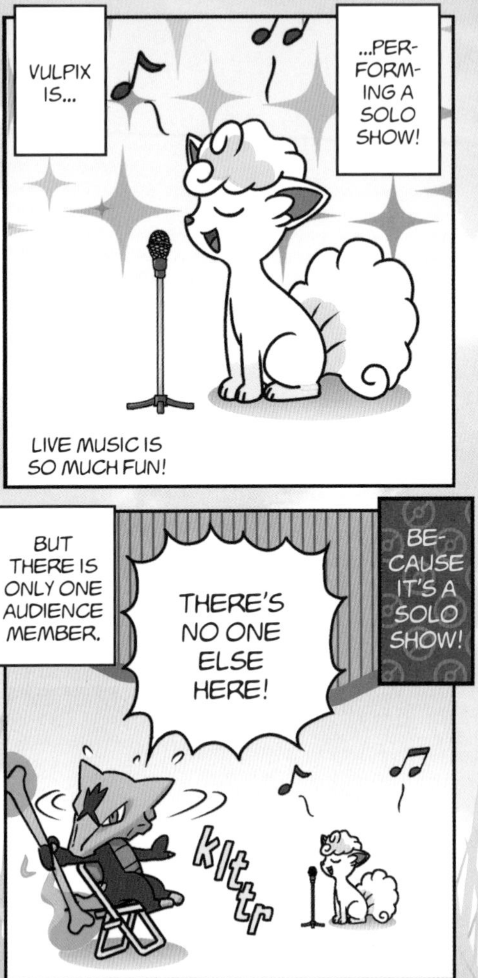
VULPIX IS...
...PER-FORM-ING A SOLO SHOW!
LIVE MUSIC IS SO MUCH FUN!
BUT THERE IS ONLY ONE AUDIENCE MEMBER.
THERE'S NO ONE ELSE HERE!
BE-CAUSE IT'S A SOLO SHOW!
klttr

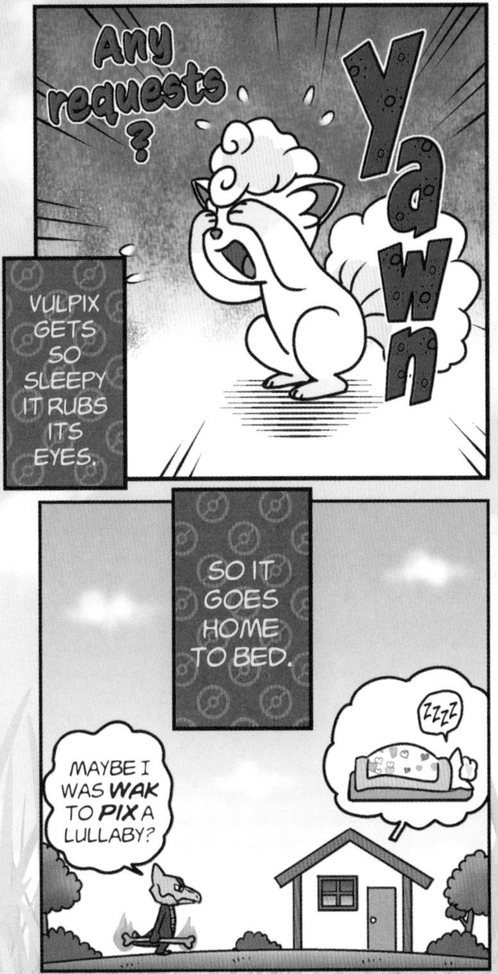
Any requests?
Yawn
VULPIX GETS SO SLEEPY IT RUBS ITS EYES.
SO IT GOES HOME TO BED.
ZZZZ
MAYBE I WAS WAK TO PIX A LULLABY?

POKÉMON MINIDEX

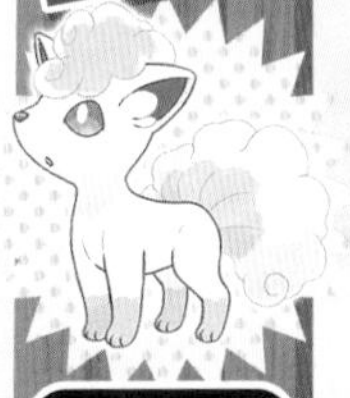

A. VULPIX

CATEGORY

Fox

TYPE

Ice

This Vulpix lives up in the snowy mountains. It freezes its prey solid with its -58°F breath!

Roll on By

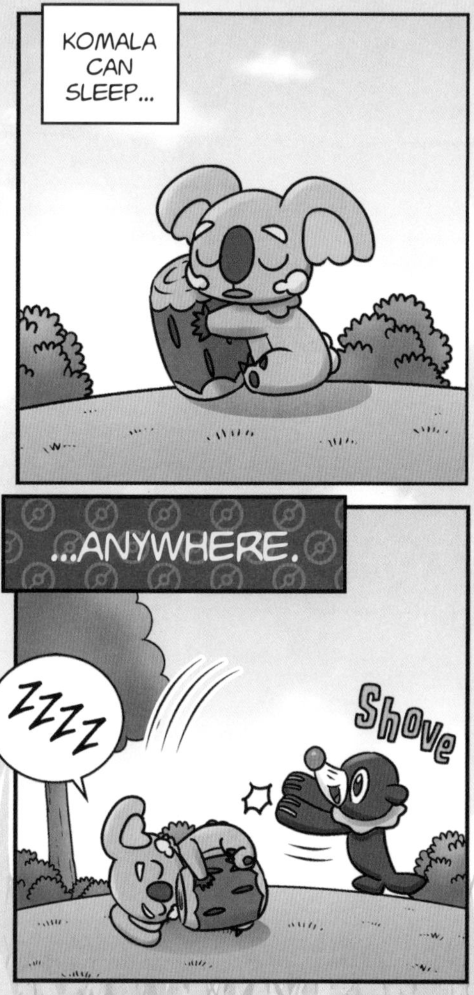
KOMALA CAN SLEEP...
...ANYWHERE.
ZZZZ
Shove

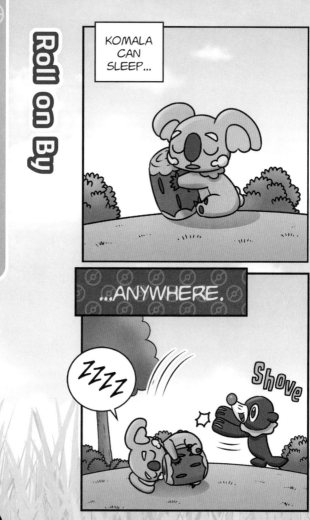

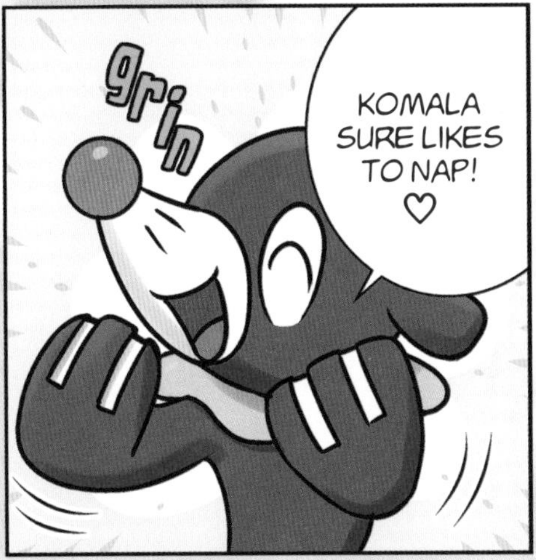
grin
KOMALA SURE LIKES TO NAP! ♡

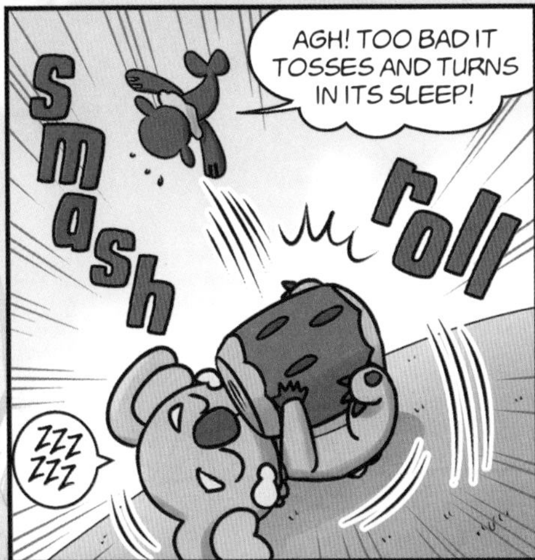
AGH! TOO BAD IT TOSSES AND TURNS IN ITS SLEEP!
smash
roll
ZZZ ZZZ

POKÉMON MINIDEX

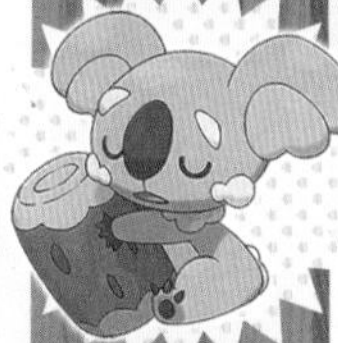

KOMALA

CATEGORY

Drowsing

TYPE

Normal

An interesting Pokémon who remains asleep its whole life. All its movements are the result of what it is dreaming about.

GUZZLORD

Try Baking Banana Bread

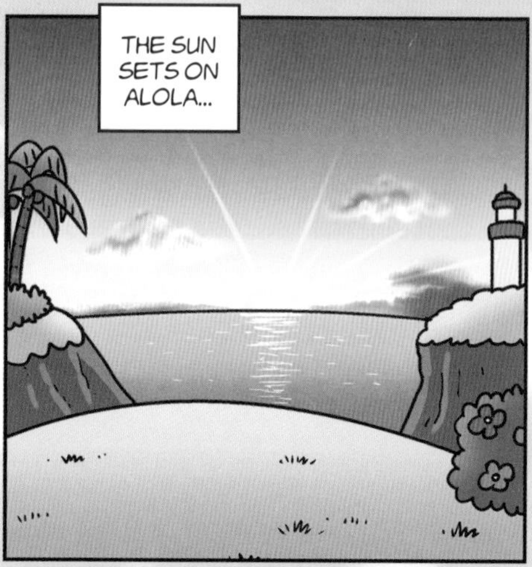
THE SUN SETS ON ALOLA...

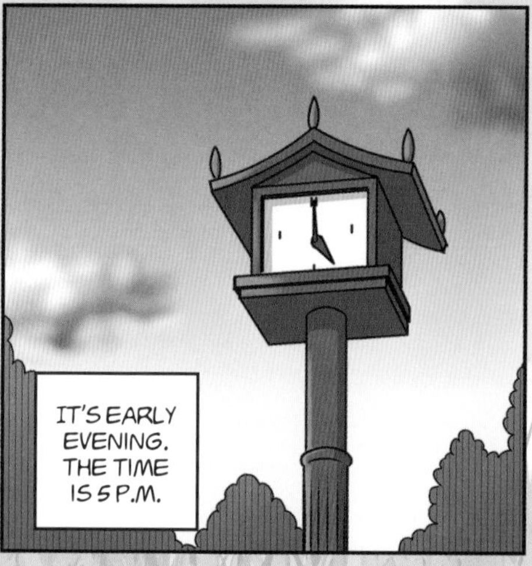
IT'S EARLY EVENING. THE TIME IS 5 P.M.

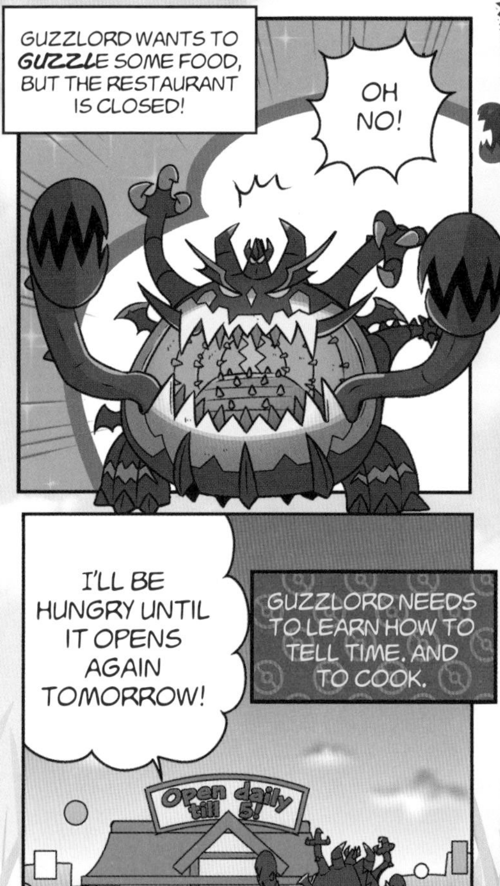
GUZZLORD WANTS TO *GUZZLE* SOME FOOD, BUT THE RESTAURANT IS CLOSED!
OH NO!
I'LL BE HUNGRY UNTIL IT OPENS AGAIN TOMORROW!
GUZZLORD NEEDS TO LEARN HOW TO TELL TIME. AND TO COOK.
Open daily till 5!

POKÉMON MINIDEX

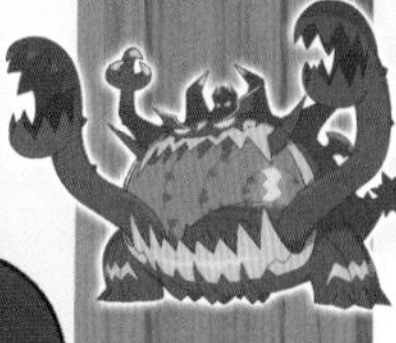

GUZZLORD

CATEGORY

Junkivore

TYPE

Dark, Dragon

Is it the most dangerous Ultra Beast of all? It is said to ***guzzl***e mountains and swallow buildings whole. Wow!

On Blast

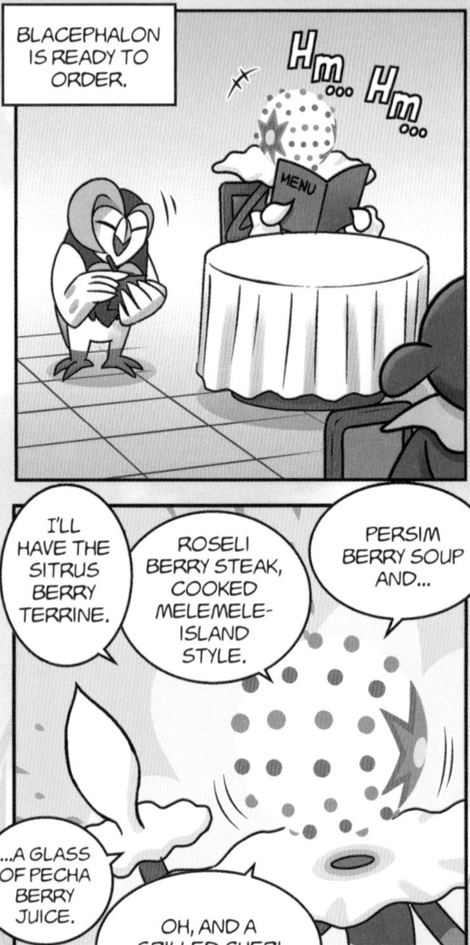
BLACEPHALON IS READY TO ORDER.
Hm... Hm...
MENU
I'LL HAVE THE SITRUS BERRY TERRINE.
ROSELI BERRY STEAK, COOKED MELEMELE-ISLAND STYLE.
PERSIM BERRY SOUP AND...
...A GLASS OF PECHA BERRY JUICE.
OH, AND A GRILLED CHERI BERRY TOO!

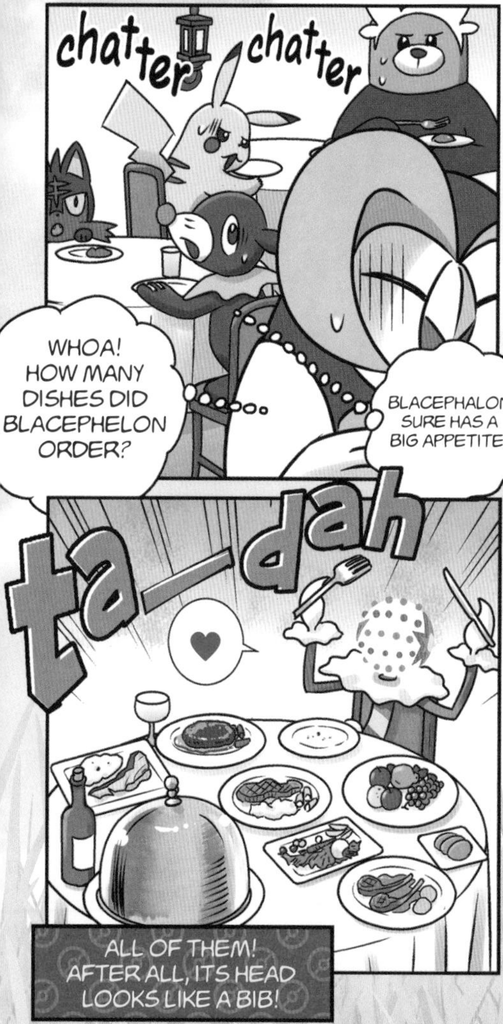
chatter chatter
WHOA! HOW MANY DISHES DID BLACEPHELON ORDER?
BLACEPHALON SURE HAS A BIG APPETITE!
ta-dah
ALL OF THEM! AFTER ALL, ITS HEAD LOOKS LIKE A BIB!

POKÉMON MINIDEX

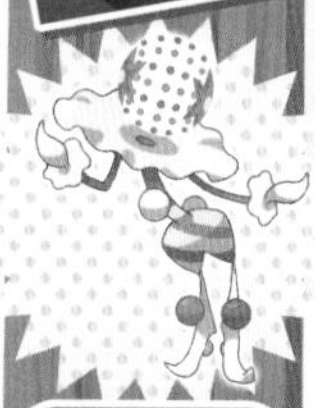

BLACEPHALON

CATEGORY

Fireworks

TYPE

Fire, Ghost

One of the Ultra Beasts who appeared out of the Ultra Wormhole. It explodes with a ***blac***t and robs its opponent of its vitality.

If You Can't Take the Heat...

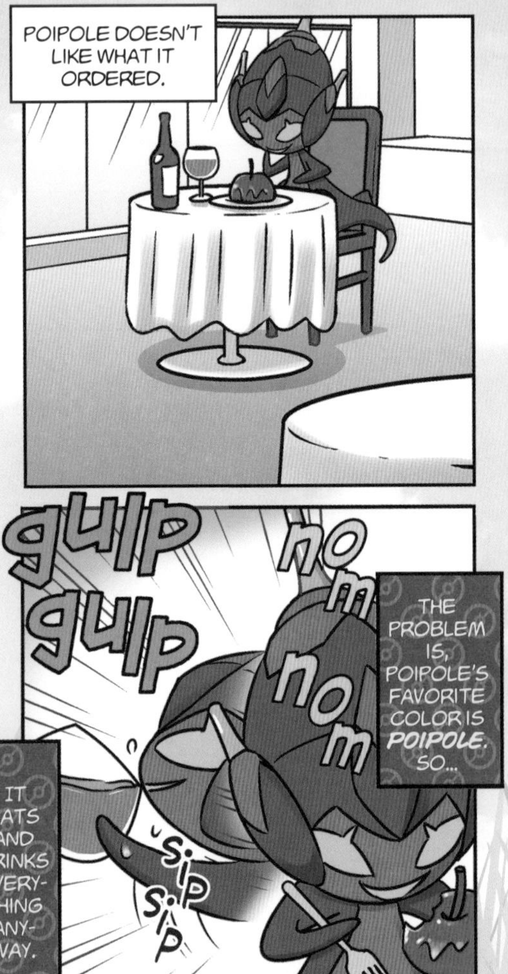
POIPOLE DOESN'T LIKE WHAT IT ORDERED.
gulp gulp
nom nom
THE PROBLEM IS, POIPOLE'S FAVORITE COLOR IS ***POIPOLE***. SO...
IT EATS AND DRINKS EVERY-THING ANY-WAY.
sip sip

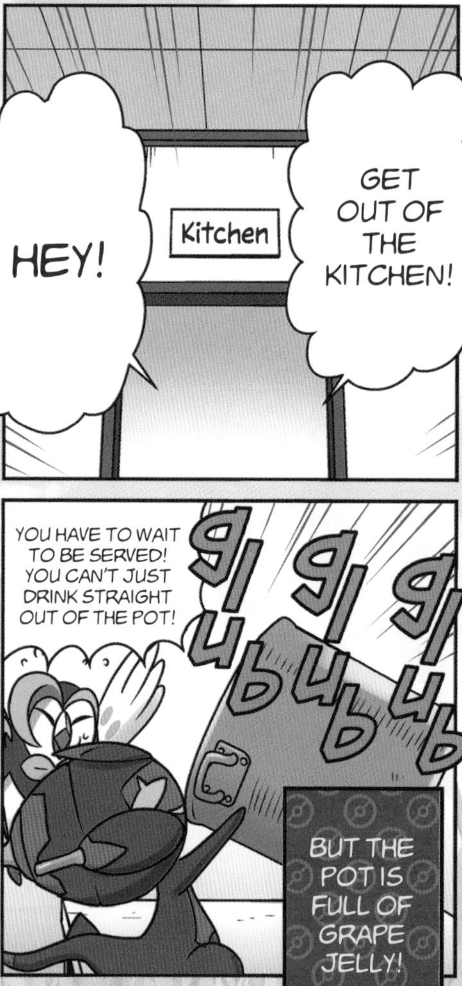
Kitchen
HEY!
GET OUT OF THE KITCHEN!
YOU HAVE TO WAIT TO BE SERVED! YOU CAN'T JUST DRINK STRAIGHT OUT OF THE POT!
glub glub glub
BUT THE POT IS FULL OF GRAPE JELLY!

POKÉMON MINIDEX

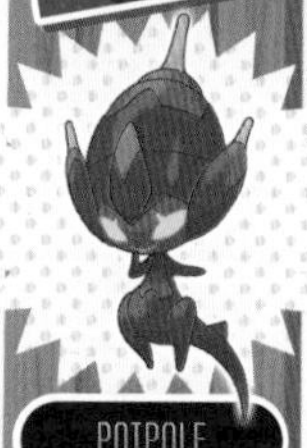

POIPOLE

CATEGORY

Poison Pin

TYPE

Poison

An Ultra Beast who lives in a different world. It sprays its opponents with poison from the poles on its head on ***poipo***se. When that happens, watch out!

Begging for Trouble

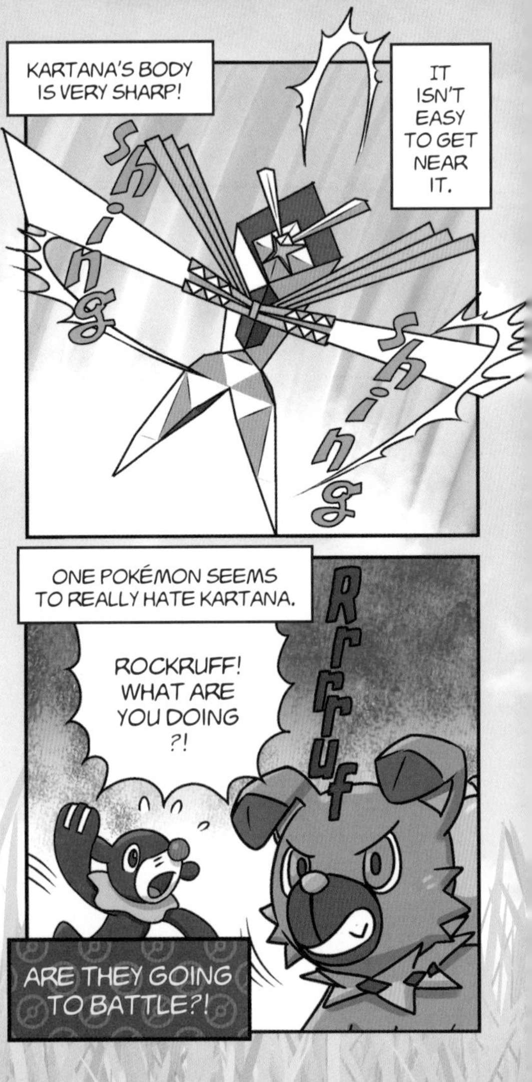
KARTANA'S BODY IS VERY SHARP!
IT ISN'T EASY TO GET NEAR IT.
shing
shing
ONE POKÉMON SEEMS TO REALLY HATE KARTANA.
ROCKRUFF! WHAT ARE YOU DOING ?!
Rrrruff
ARE THEY GOING TO BATTLE?!

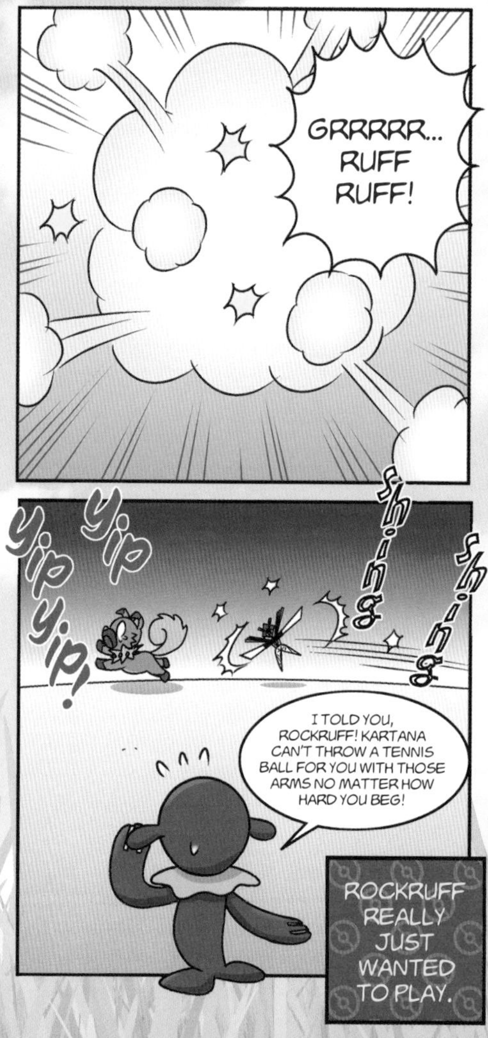
GRRRRR... RUFF RUFF!
yip yip yip yip!
shing shing
I TOLD YOU, ROCKRUFF! KARTANA CAN'T THROW A TENNIS BALL FOR YOU WITH THOSE ARMS NO MATTER HOW HARD YOU BEG!
ROCKRUFF REALLY JUST WANTED TO PLAY.

POKÉMON MINIDEX

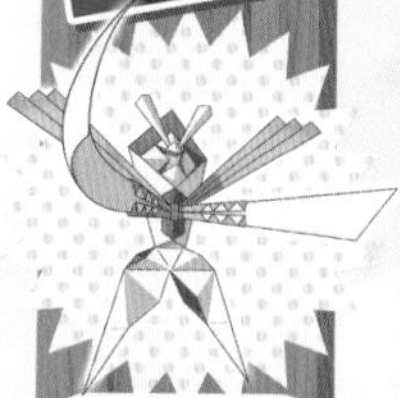

KARTANA

CATEGORY

Drawn Sword

TYPE

Grass, Steel

This Drawn Sword Pokémon can even cut down a gigantic steel tower. Don't annoy it, or it might chase you!

CELESTEELA

I Don't Wanna Hold Your Hand

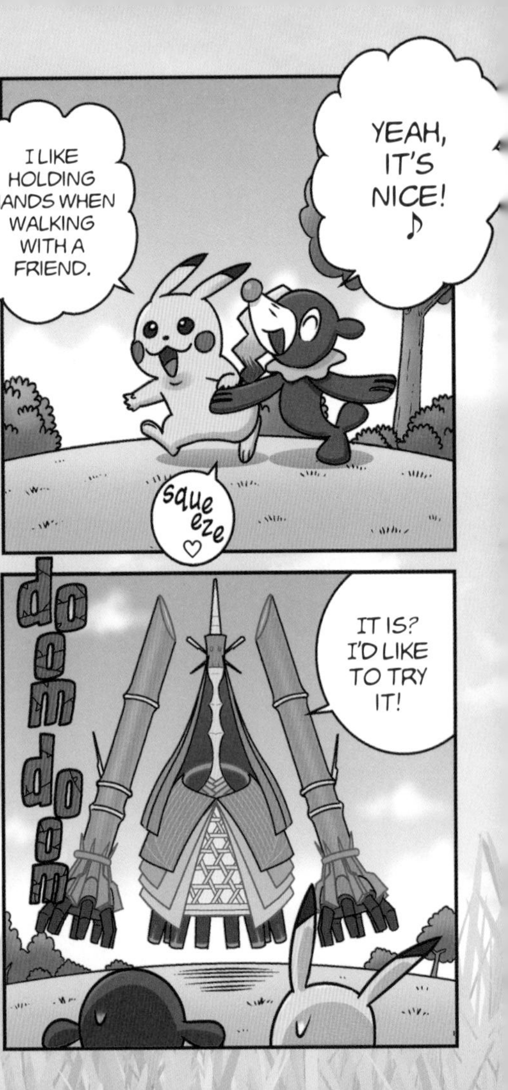
I LIKE HOLDING HANDS WHEN WALKING WITH A FRIEND.
YEAH, IT'S NICE! ♪
squeeze ♡
doon doon
IT IS? I'D LIKE TO TRY IT!

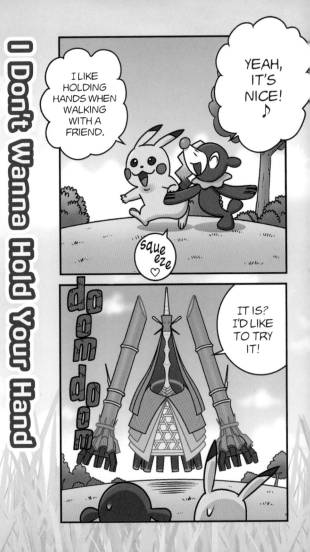

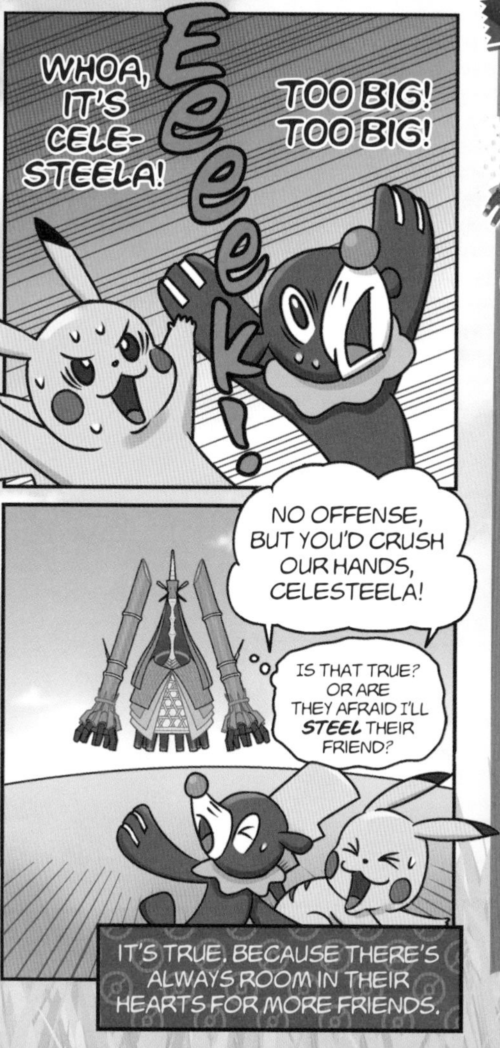
WHOA, IT'S CELE-STEELA!
Eeeeek!
TOO BIG! TOO BIG!
NO OFFENSE, BUT YOU'D CRUSH OUR HANDS, CELESTEELA!
IS THAT TRUE? OR ARE THEY AFRAID I'LL STEEL THEIR FRIEND?
IT'S TRUE. BECAUSE THERE'S ALWAYS ROOM IN THEIR HEARTS FOR MORE FRIENDS.

POKÉMON MINIDEX

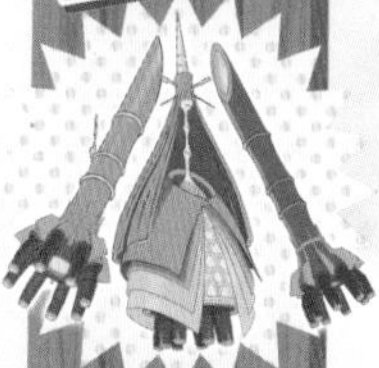

CELESTEELA

CATEGORY

Launch

TYPE

Steel, Flying

One of the Ultra Beasts. Witnesses have seen it burn down a forest by expelling gas from its two arms. It is unbelievably huge!

PHEROMOSA

What's in a Name?

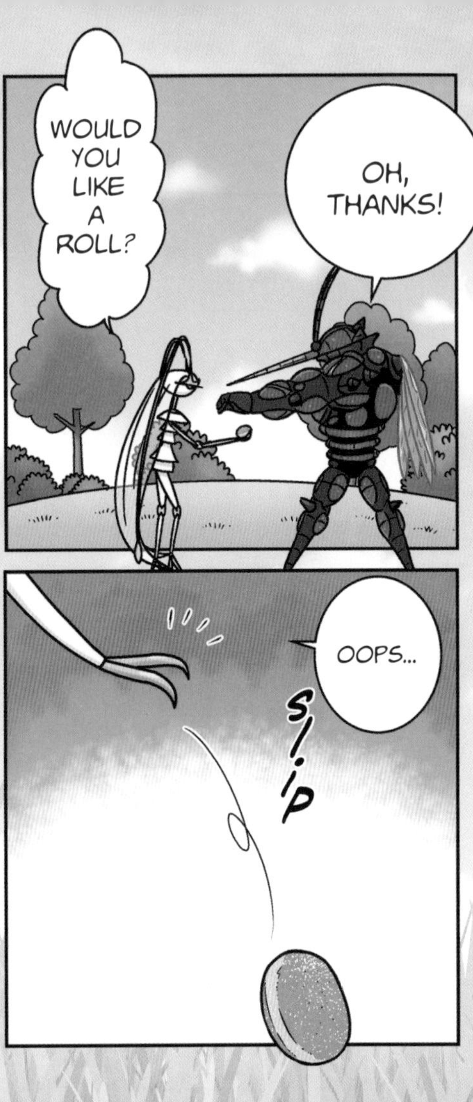

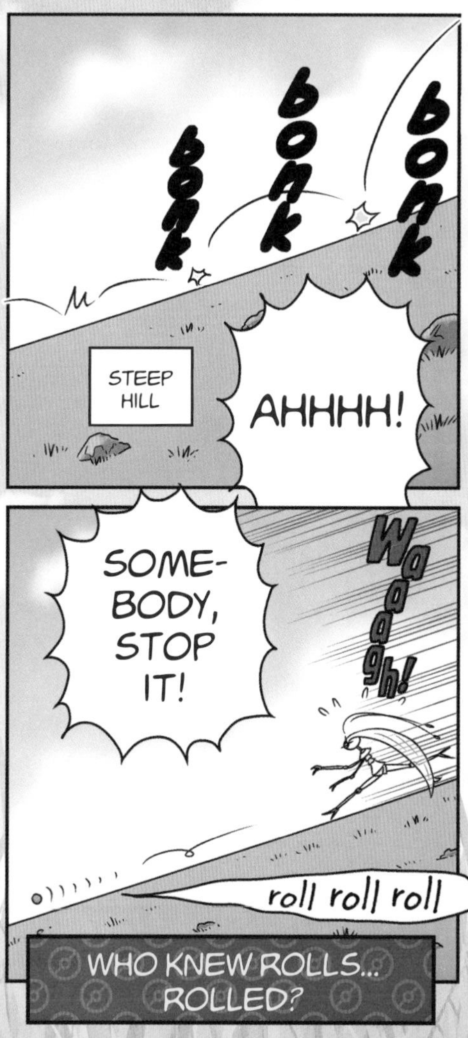
bonk
bonk
bonk
STEEP HILL
AHHHH!
SOME-BODY, STOP IT!
Waaaagh!
roll roll roll
WHO KNEW ROLLS... ROLLED?

POKÉMON MINIDEX

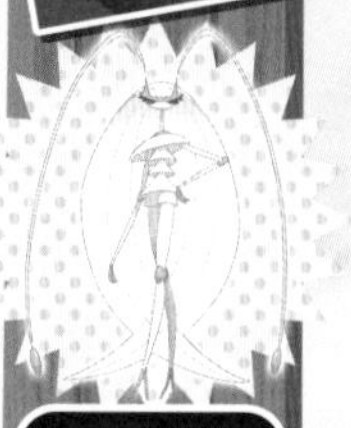

PHEROMOSA

CATEGORY

Lissome

TYPE

Bug, Fighting

An Ultra Beast who runs at terrific speeds. In a race, it leaves all the other Pokémon in the dust.

NIHILEGO

Neither Here nor There

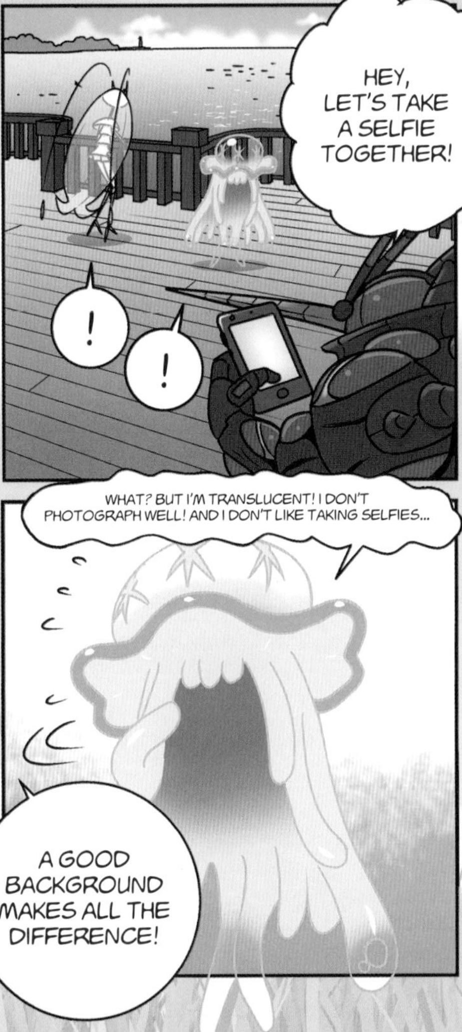
HEY, LET'S TAKE A SELFIE TOGETHER!
!
!
WHAT? BUT I'M TRANSLUCENT! I DON'T PHOTOGRAPH WELL! AND I DON'T LIKE TAKING SELFIES...
A GOOD BACKGROUND MAKES ALL THE DIFFERENCE!

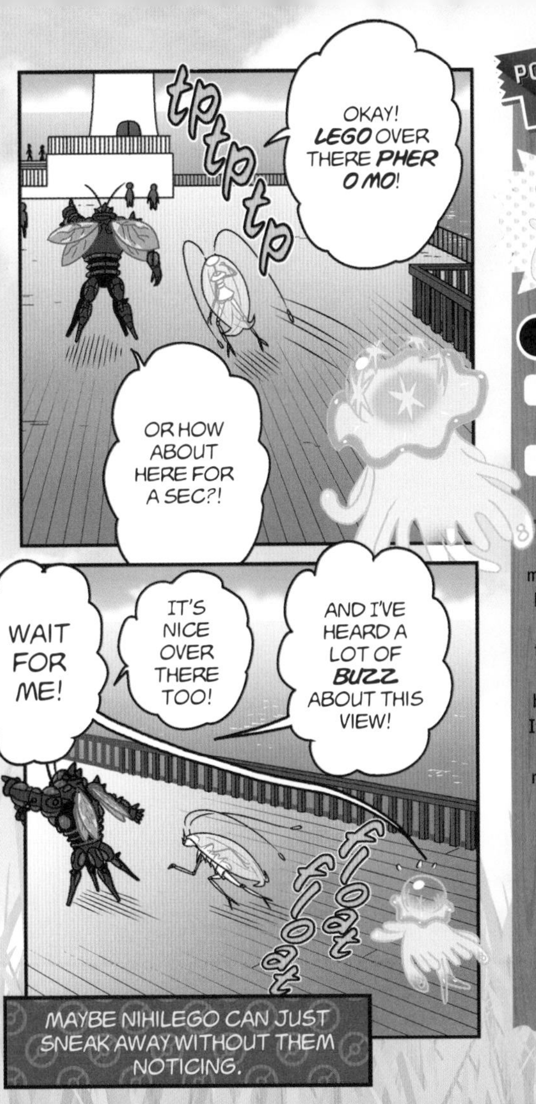
tp tp tp tp
OKAY! LEGO OVER THERE PHER O MO!
OR HOW ABOUT HERE FOR A SEC?!
WAIT FOR ME!
IT'S NICE OVER THERE TOO!
AND I'VE HEARD A LOT OF BUZZ ABOUT THIS VIEW!
float float
MAYBE NIHILEGO CAN JUST SNEAK AWAY WITHOUT THEM NOTICING.

POKÉMON MINIDEX

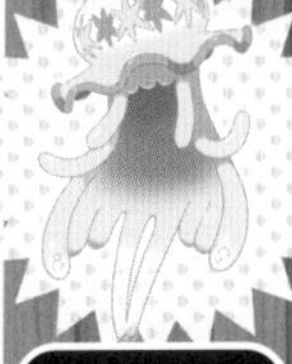

NIHILEGO

CATEGORY

Parasite

TYPE

Rock, Poison

One of several mysterious Ultra Beasts. People report that those infected by it suddenly become violent. If someone gets infected, they really want it to ***lego*** of them!

Fan Club

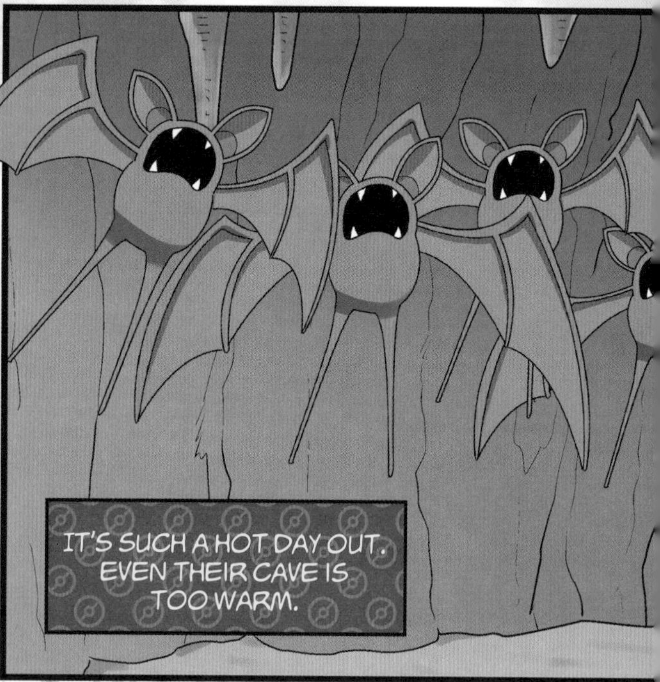
IT'S SUCH A HOT DAY OUT. EVEN THEIR CAVE IS TOO WARM.

POKÉMON MINIDEX

ZUBAT

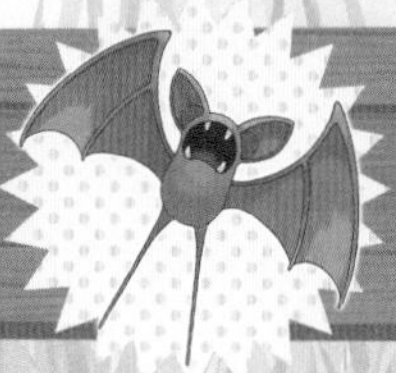

CATEGORY

Bat Pokémon

TYPE

Poison, Flying

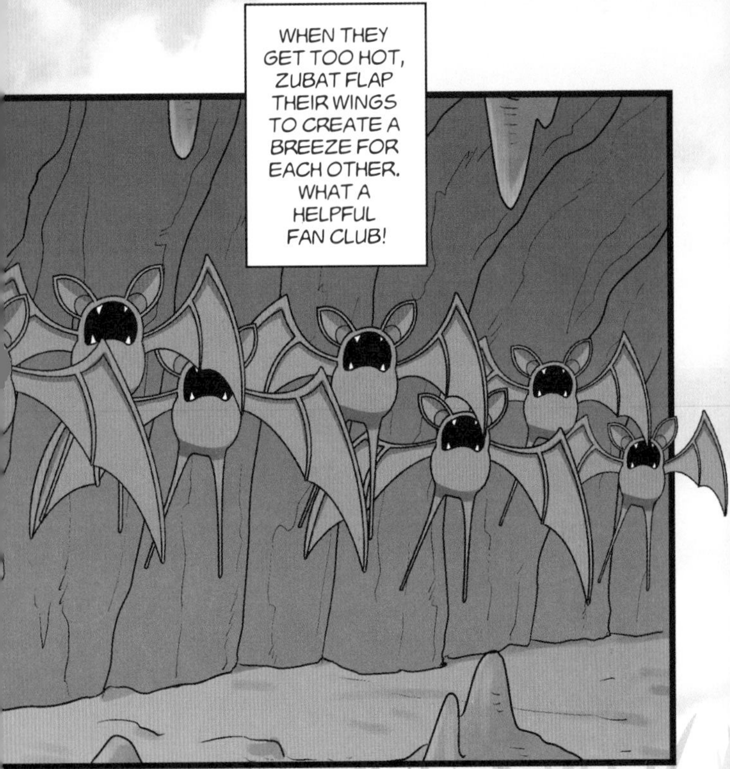
WHEN THEY GET TOO HOT, ZUBAT FLAP THEIR WINGS TO CREATE A BREEZE FOR EACH OTHER. WHAT A HELPFUL FAN CLUB!

Did ***zu*** know that Zubat's skin is so thin they get burned if sunlight hits them? They also gather to warm each other when they get too cold.

PALKIA

Ace the Interview ①

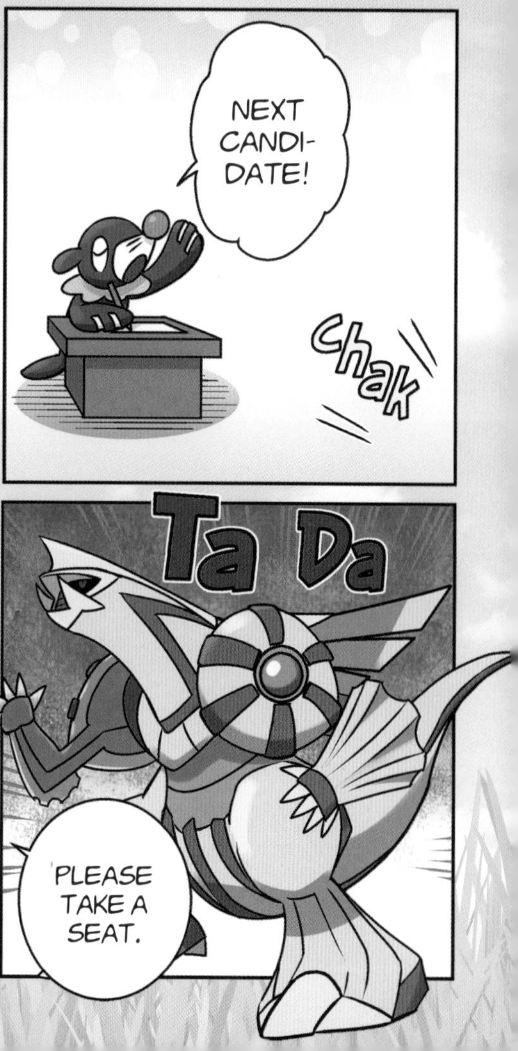
NEXT CANDI-DATE!
Chak
Ta Da
PLEASE TAKE A SEAT.

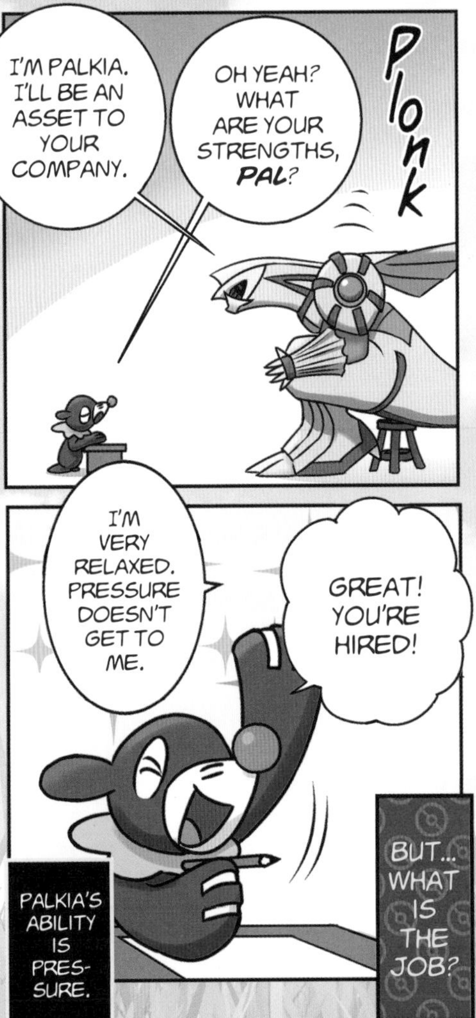
I'M PALKIA. I'LL BE AN ASSET TO YOUR COMPANY.
OH YEAH? WHAT ARE YOUR STRENGTHS, PAL?
Plonk
I'M VERY RELAXED. PRESSURE DOESN'T GET TO ME.
GREAT! YOU'RE HIRED!
PALKIA'S ABILITY IS PRES-SURE.
BUT... WHAT IS THE JOB?

POKÉMON MINIDEX

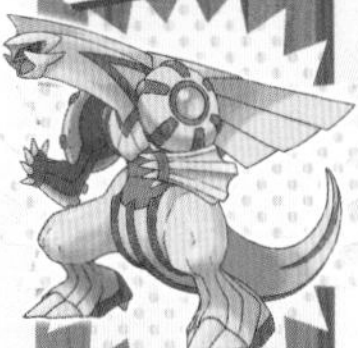

PALKIA

CATEGORY

Spatial

TYPE

Water, Dragon

A Legendary Pokémon revered as a deity in the Sinnoh region. No ordinary Pokémon ***kia*** beat it!

Ace the Interview ②

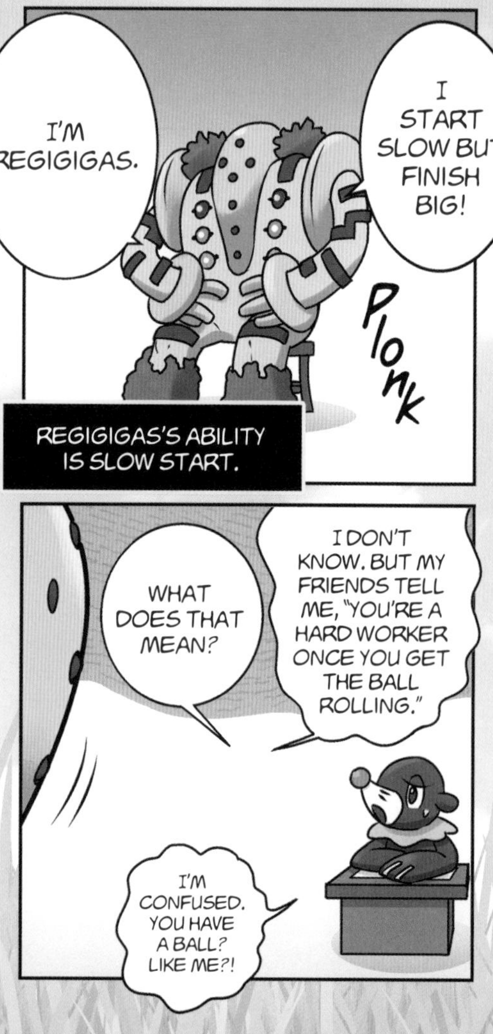
I'M REGIGIGAS.
I START SLOW BUT FINISH BIG!
Plonk
REGIGIGAS'S ABILITY IS SLOW START.
WHAT DOES THAT MEAN?
I DON'T KNOW. BUT MY FRIENDS TELL ME, "YOU'RE A HARD WORKER ONCE YOU GET THE BALL ROLLING."
I'M CONFUSED. YOU HAVE A BALL? LIKE ME?!

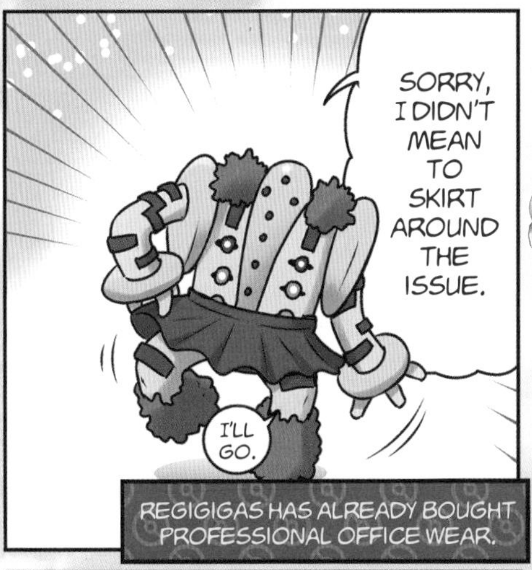
SORRY, I DIDN'T MEAN TO SKIRT AROUND THE ISSUE.
I'LL GO.
REGIGIGAS HAS ALREADY BOUGHT PROFESSIONAL OFFICE WEAR.

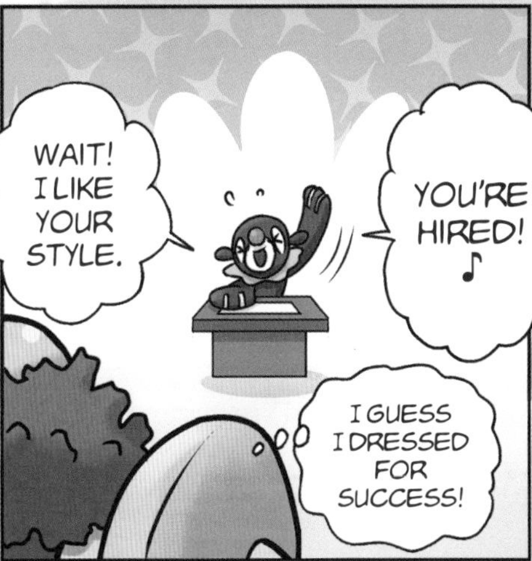
WAIT! I LIKE YOUR STYLE.
YOU'RE HIRED! ♪
I GUESS I DRESSED FOR SUCCESS!

POKÉMON MINIDEX

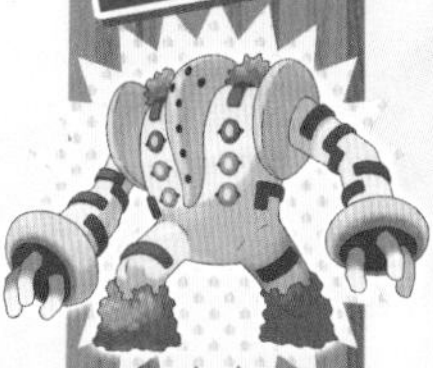

REGIGIGAS

CATEGORY

Colossal

TYPE

Normal

There is a famous ***regi***nd passed on through the generations that this massive Pokémon once towed continents around with ropes.

Have a Blast

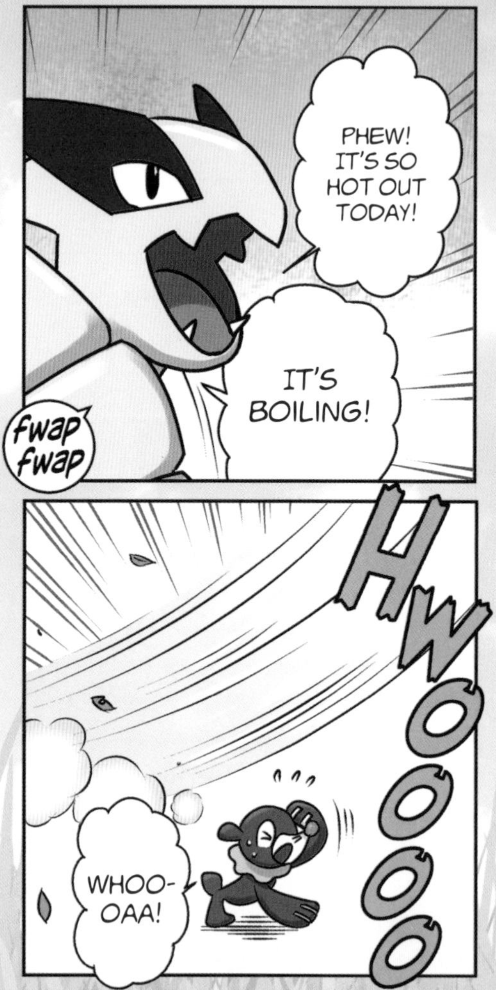
PHEW! IT'S SO HOT OUT TODAY!
IT'S BOILING!
fwap fwap
HWOOOOO
WHOO-OAA!

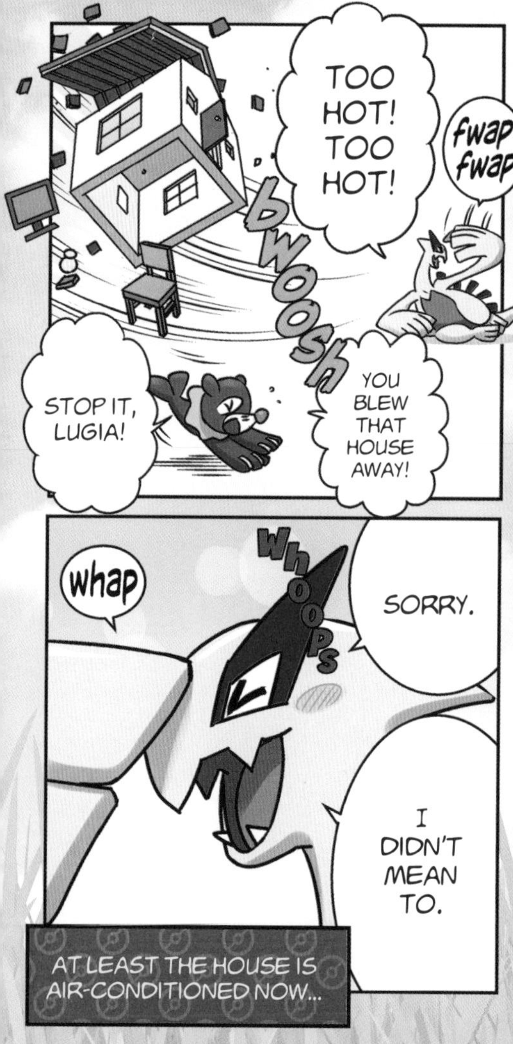
TOO HOT! TOO HOT!
fwap fwap
bwoosh
STOP IT, LUGIA!
YOU BLEW THAT HOUSE AWAY!
whap
whoops
SORRY.
I DIDN'T MEAN TO.
AT LEAST THE HOUSE IS AIR-CONDITIONED NOW...

POKÉMON MINIDEX

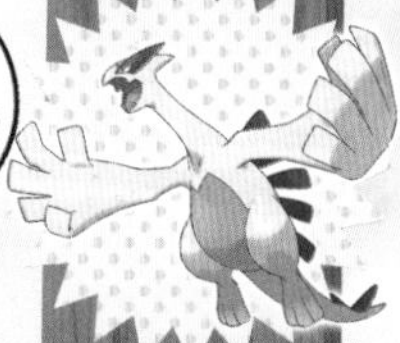

LUGIA

CATEGORY

Diving

TYPE

Psychic, Flying

A Pokémon who spends its time at the bottom of the sea because its powers are so strong.

Senior Competition

ARTICUNO, ZAPDOS, MOLTRES

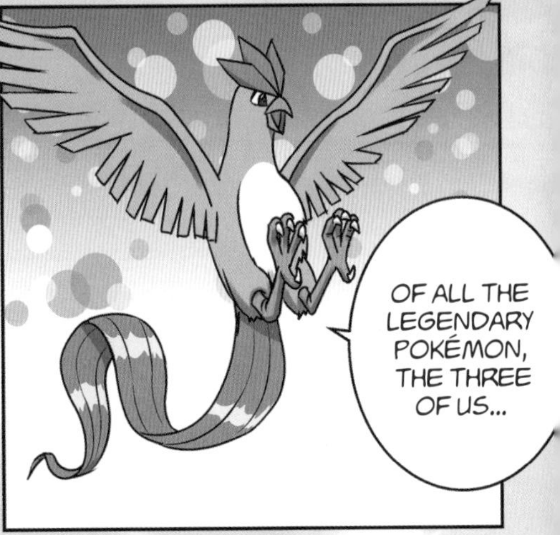
OF ALL THE LEGENDARY POKÉMON, THE THREE OF US...

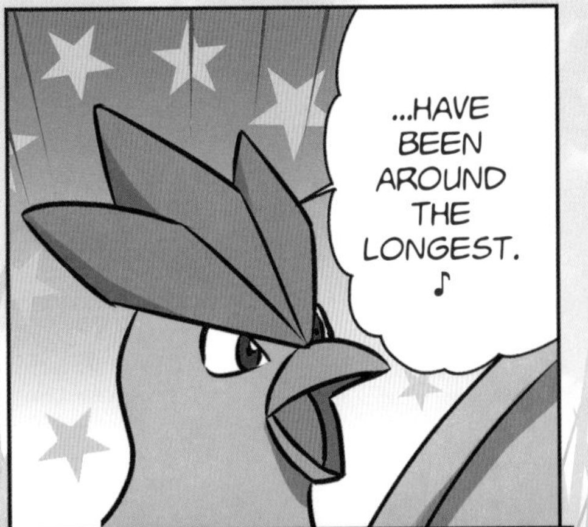
...HAVE BEEN AROUND THE LONGEST. ♪
ARTICUNO IS THE FREEZER GEEZER.

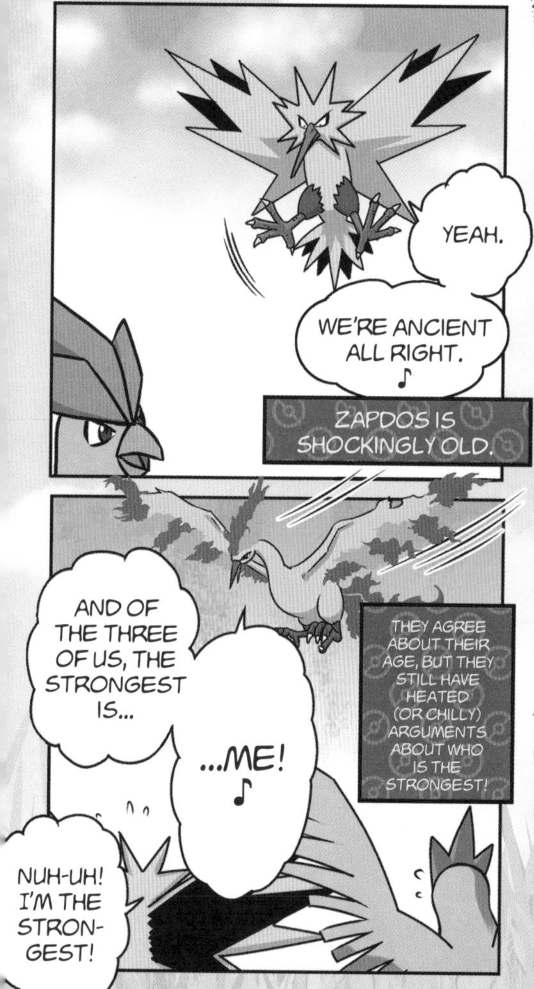
YEAH.
WE'RE ANCIENT ALL RIGHT. ♪
ZAPDOS IS SHOCKINGLY OLD.
AND OF THE THREE OF US, THE STRONGEST IS...
...ME! ♪
THEY AGREE ABOUT THEIR AGE, BUT THEY STILL HAVE HEATED (OR CHILLY) ARGUMENTS ABOUT WHO IS THE STRONGEST!
NUH-UH! I'M THE STRON-GEST!

POKÉMON MINIDEX

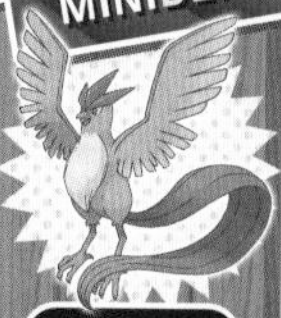

ARTICUNO

CATEGORY

Freeze

TYPE

Ice, Flying

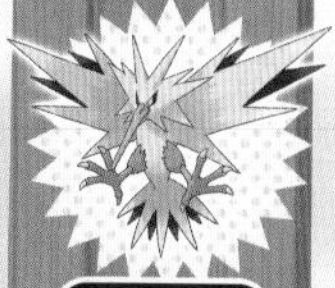

ZAPDOS

CATEGORY

Electric

TYPE

Electric, Flying

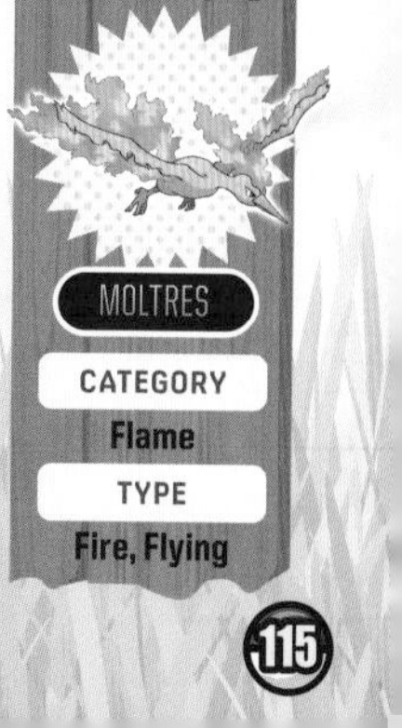

MOLTRES

CATEGORY

Flame

TYPE

Fire, Flying

The Dawn of Alola ①

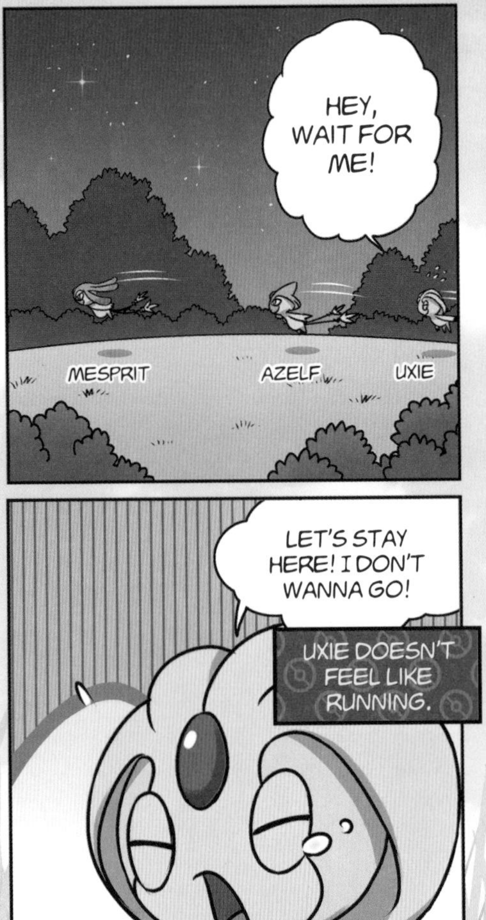
HEY, WAIT FOR ME!
MESPRIT
AZELF
UXIE
LET'S STAY HERE! I DON'T WANNA GO!
UXIE DOESN'T FEEL LIKE RUNNING.

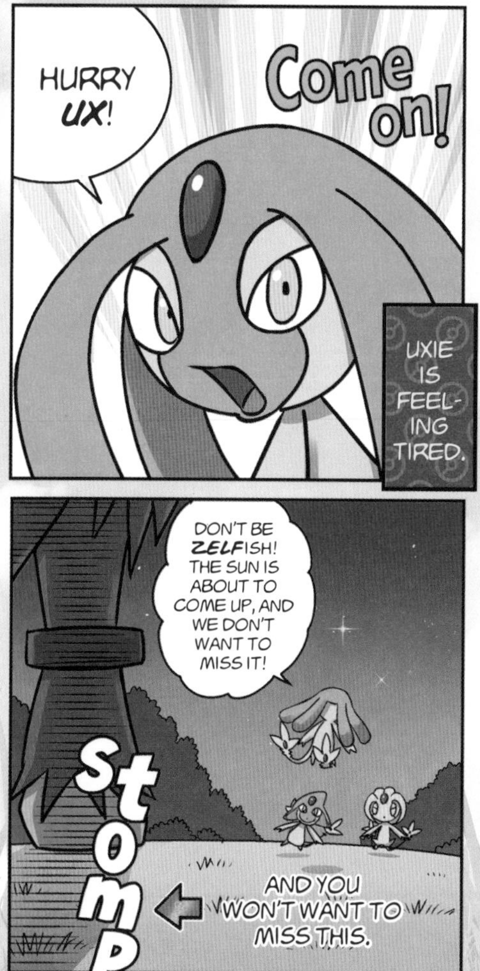
HURRY UX!
Come on!
UXIE IS FEEL-ING TIRED.
DON'T BE ZELFISH! THE SUN IS ABOUT TO COME UP, AND WE DON'T WANT TO MISS IT!
Stomp
AND YOU WON'T WANT TO MISS THIS.

POKÉMON MINIDEX

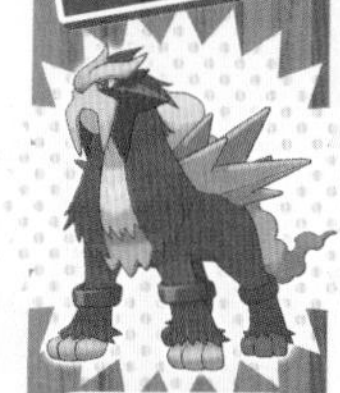

ENTEI

CATEGORY

Volcano

TYPE

Fire

A random volcano erupts when Entei roars.

The Dawn of Alola ②

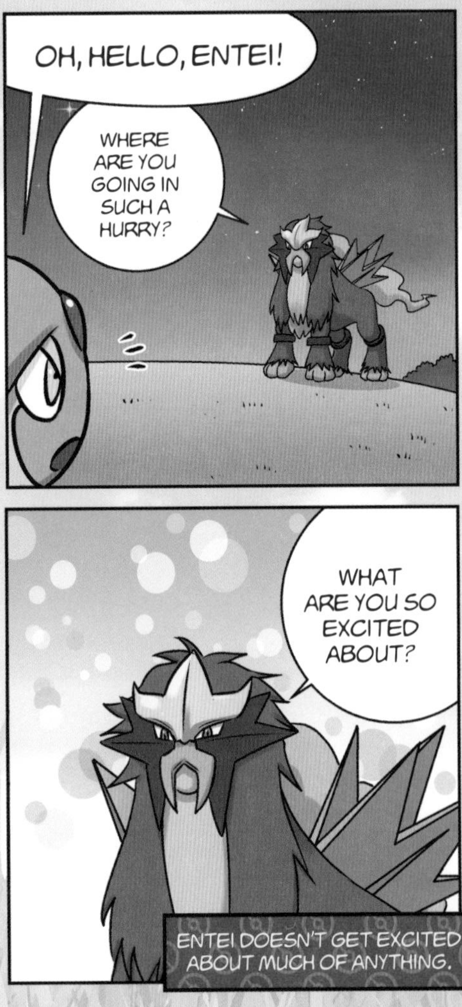
OH, HELLO, ENTEI!
WHERE ARE YOU GOING IN SUCH A HURRY?
WHAT ARE YOU SO EXCITED ABOUT?
ENTEI DOESN'T GET EXCITED ABOUT MUCH OF ANYTHING.

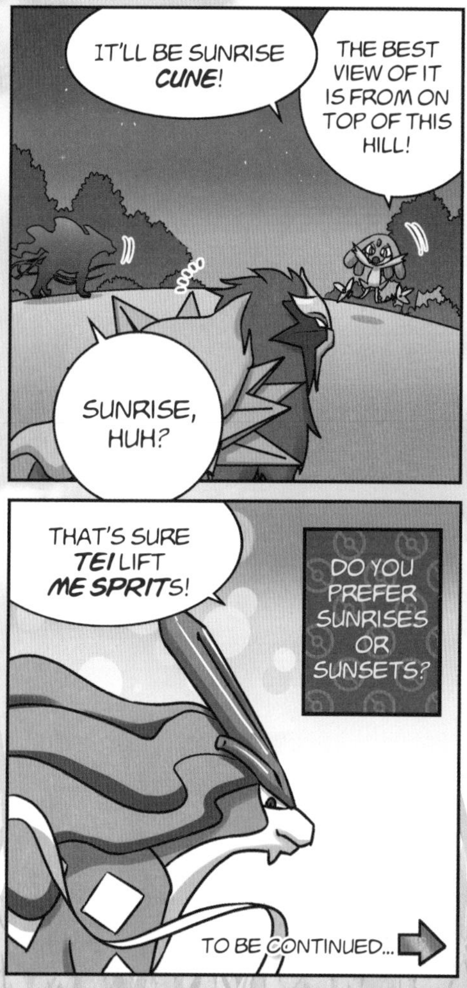
IT'LL BE SUNRISE **CUNE**!
THE BEST VIEW OF IT IS FROM ON TOP OF THIS HILL!
SUNRISE, HUH?
THAT'S SURE **TEI** LIFT **ME SPRIT**S!
DO YOU PREFER SUNRISES OR SUNSETS?
TO BE CONTINUED...

POKÉMON MINIDEX

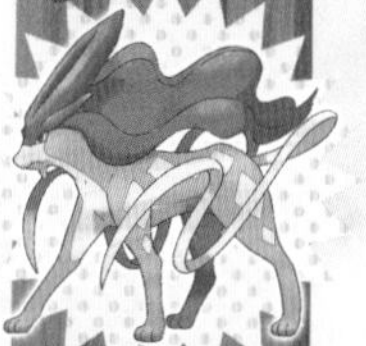

SUICUNE

CATEGORY

Aurora

TYPE

Water

It is said to be the reincarnation of the north winds. It races across the world looking for polluted, dirty water to purify. So if you are pond or detergent scum, it will ***sui cune***!

RAIKOU

The Dawn of Alola ③

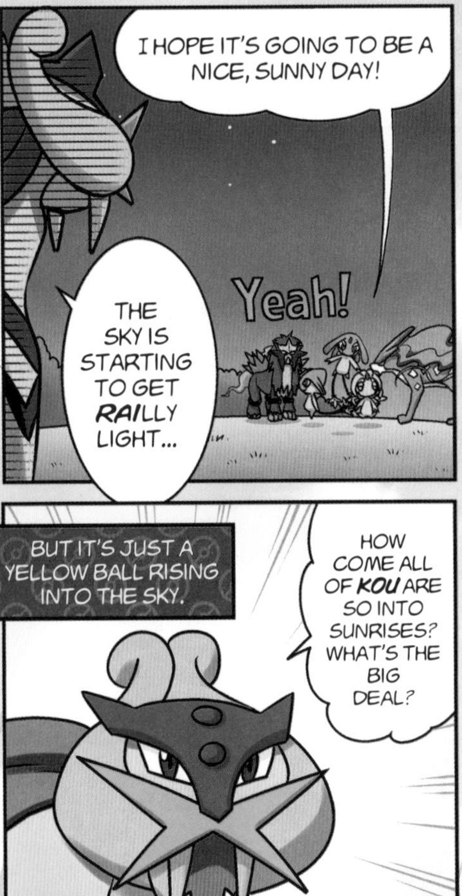
I HOPE IT'S GOING TO BE A NICE, SUNNY DAY!
Yeah!
THE SKY IS STARTING TO GET ***RAI***LLY LIGHT...
BUT IT'S JUST A YELLOW BALL RISING INTO THE SKY.
HOW COME ALL OF ***KOU*** ARE SO INTO SUNRISES? WHAT'S THE BIG DEAL?

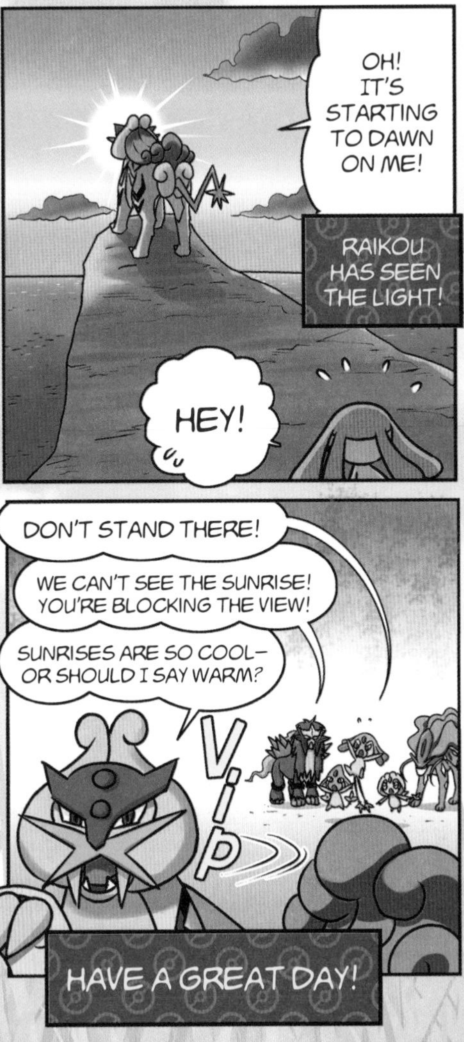
OH! IT'S STARTING TO DAWN ON ME!
RAIKOU HAS SEEN THE LIGHT!
HEY!
DON'T STAND THERE!
WE CAN'T SEE THE SUNRISE! YOU'RE BLOCKING THE VIEW!
SUNRISES ARE SO COOL— OR SHOULD I SAY WARM?
Vip
HAVE A GREAT DAY!

POKÉMON MINIDEX

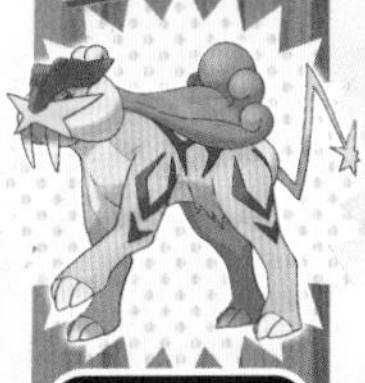

RAIKOU

CATEGORY

Thunder

TYPE

Electric

The rain cloud it carries enables it to fire thunderbolts at will. Its cry is as loud as crashing thunder.

ZERAORA

See the Light

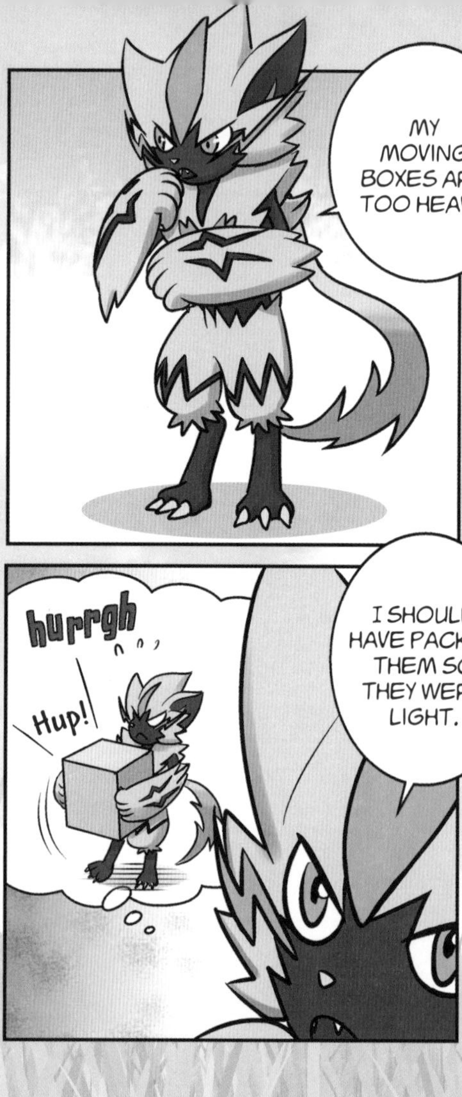
MY MOVING BOXES ARE TOO HEAVY.
hurrgh
Hup!
I SHOULD HAVE PACKED THEM SO THEY WERE LIGHT.

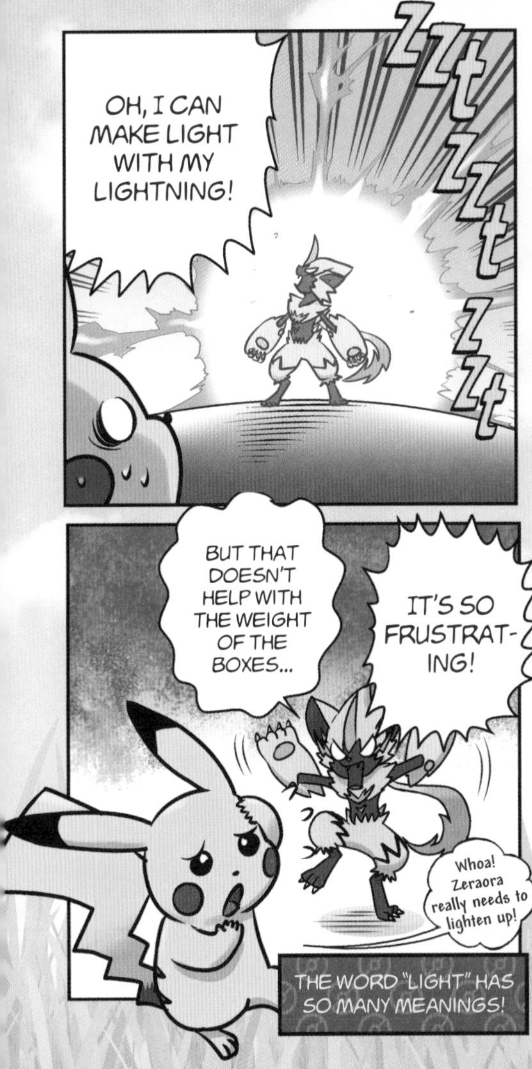
OH, I CAN MAKE LIGHT WITH MY LIGHTNING!
ZZt ZZt ZZt
BUT THAT DOESN'T HELP WITH THE WEIGHT OF THE BOXES...
IT'S SO FRUSTRAT-ING!
Whoa! Zeraora really needs to lighten up!
THE WORD "LIGHT" HAS SO MANY MEANINGS!

POKÉMON MINIDEX

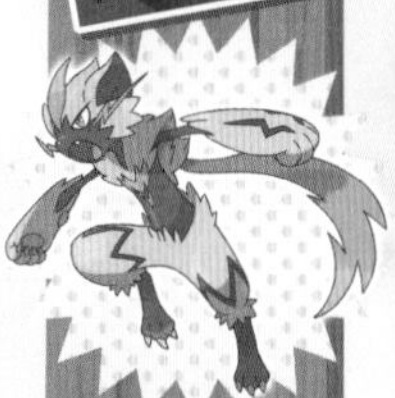

ZERAORA

CATEGORY

Thunderclap

TYPE

Electric

It electrifies its claws and tears at its opponents with them. Even if they dodge its attacks, they'll be electrocuted by ***ze aora*** of flying sparks.

A Shock to the System ①

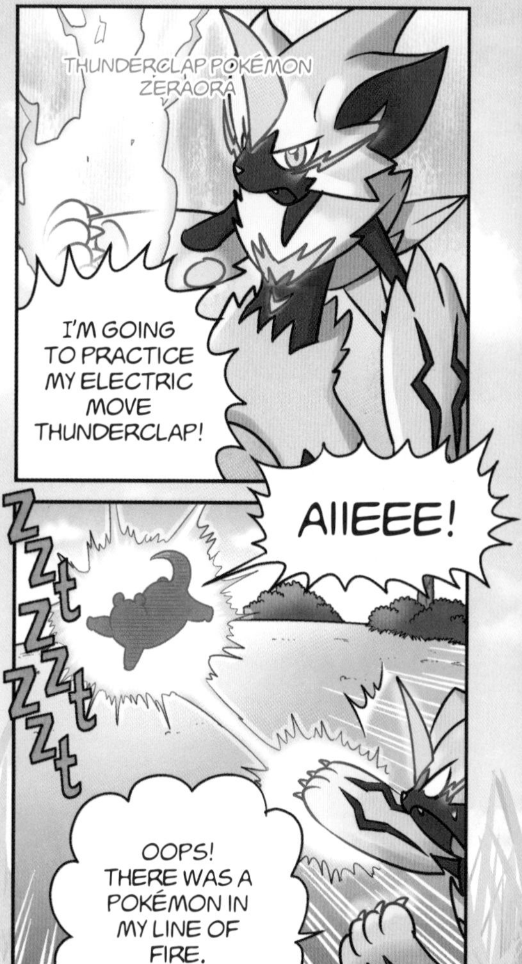
THUNDERCLAP POKÉMON ZERAORA
I'M GOING TO PRACTICE MY ELECTRIC MOVE THUNDERCLAP!
AIIEEE!
ZZt ZZt ZZt
OOPS! THERE WAS A POKÉMON IN MY LINE OF FIRE.

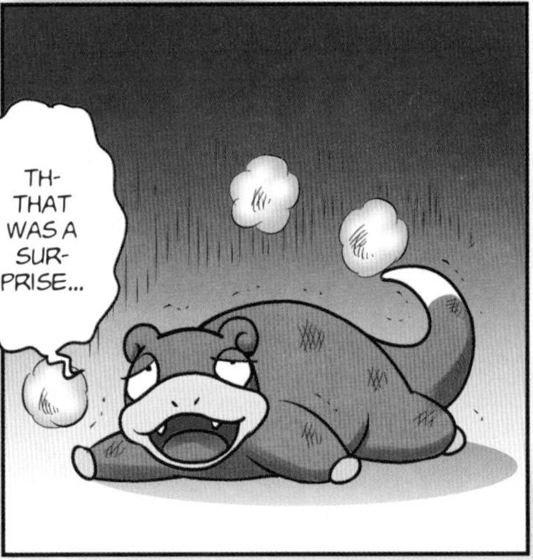
TH- THAT WAS A SUR- PRISE...

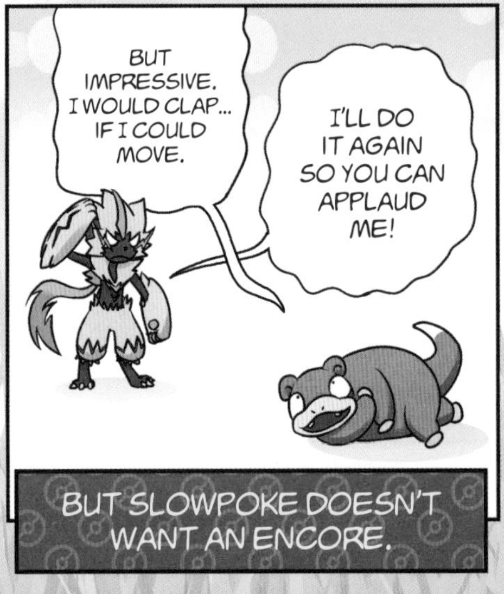
BUT IMPRESSIVE. I WOULD CLAP... IF I COULD MOVE.
I'LL DO IT AGAIN SO YOU CAN APPLAUD ME!
BUT SLOWPOKE DOESN'T WANT AN ENCORE.

POKÉMON MINIDEX

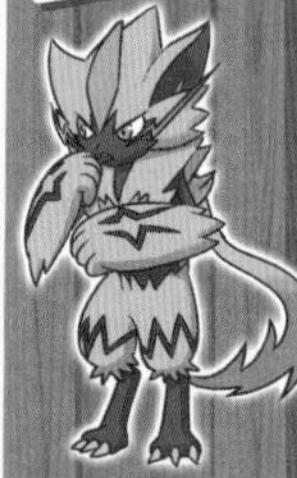

Which of the following moves can only be learned by the Mythical Pokémon Zeraora?

1. Thunderbolt
2. Plasma Fists
3. Zap Cannon

Quiz Answer: 2

EEVEE

A Shock to the System ②

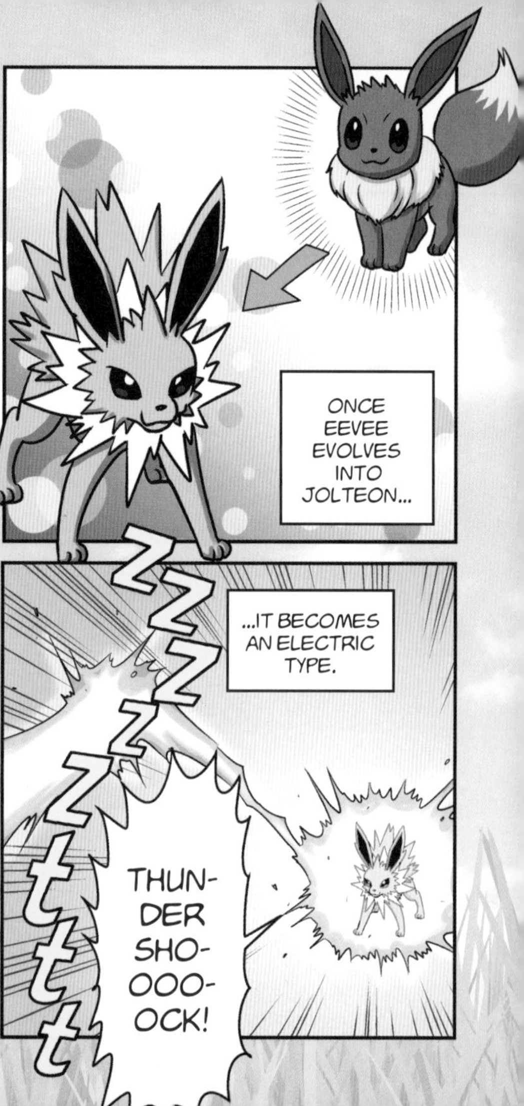
ONCE EEVEE EVOLVES INTO JOLTEON...
...IT BECOMES AN ELECTRIC TYPE.
ZZZZZtttt
THUN-DER SHO-OOO-OCK!

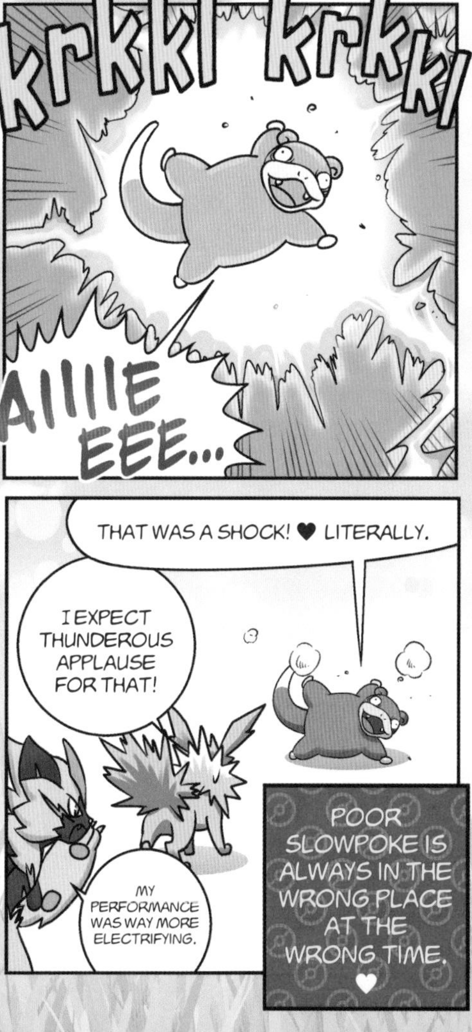
krkkl krkkl
AIIIIE EEE...
THAT WAS A SHOCK! ♥ LITERALLY.
I EXPECT THUNDEROUS APPLAUSE FOR THAT!
MY PERFORMANCE WAS WAY MORE ELECTRIFYING.
POOR SLOWPOKE IS ALWAYS IN THE WRONG PLACE AT THE WRONG TIME. ♥

POKÉMON MINIDEX

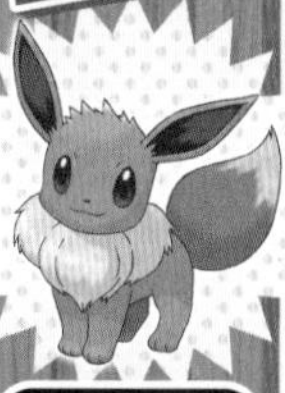

EEVEE

CATEGORY

Evolution

TYPE

Normal

This Evolution Pokémon has many possible evolutions within it. It evolves to adapt to harsh environments.

Hands Off!

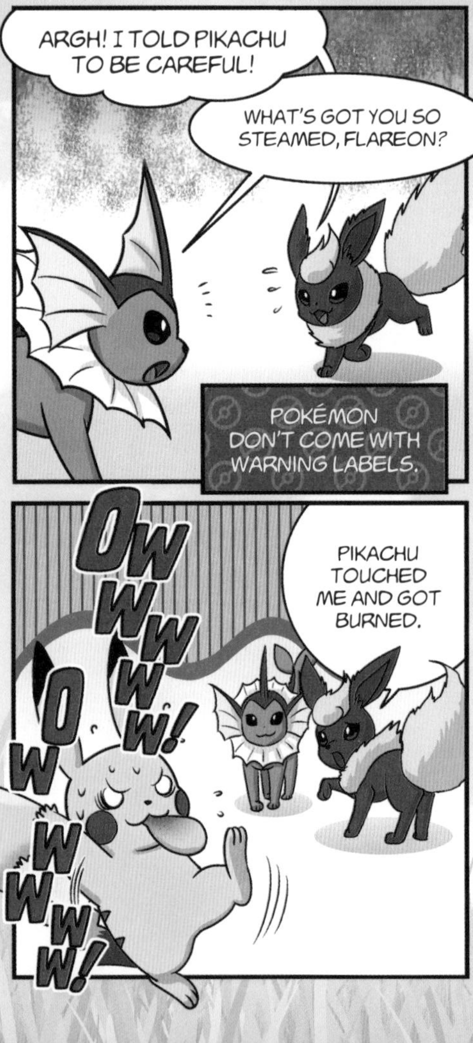
ARGH! I TOLD PIKACHU TO BE CAREFUL!
WHAT'S GOT YOU SO STEAMED, FLAREON?
POKÉMON DON'T COME WITH WARNING LABELS.
PIKACHU TOUCHED ME AND GOT BURNED.
OWWWWW!
OWWWWWW!

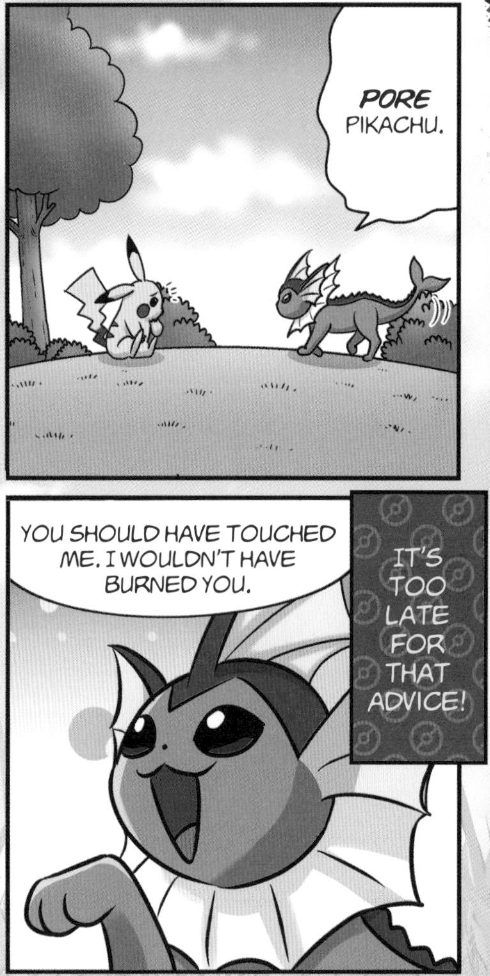
PORE PIKACHU.
YOU SHOULD HAVE TOUCHED ME. I WOULDN'T HAVE BURNED YOU.
IT'S TOO LATE FOR THAT ADVICE!

POKÉMON MINIDEX

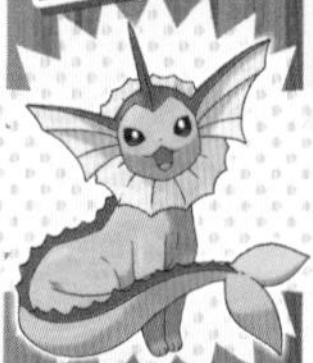

VAPOREON

CATEGORY

Bubble Jet

TYPE

Water

Its cell structure is similar to water molecules, so it melts away and becomes invisible in water.

ALOLAN NINETALES

Pokémon Hospital ①

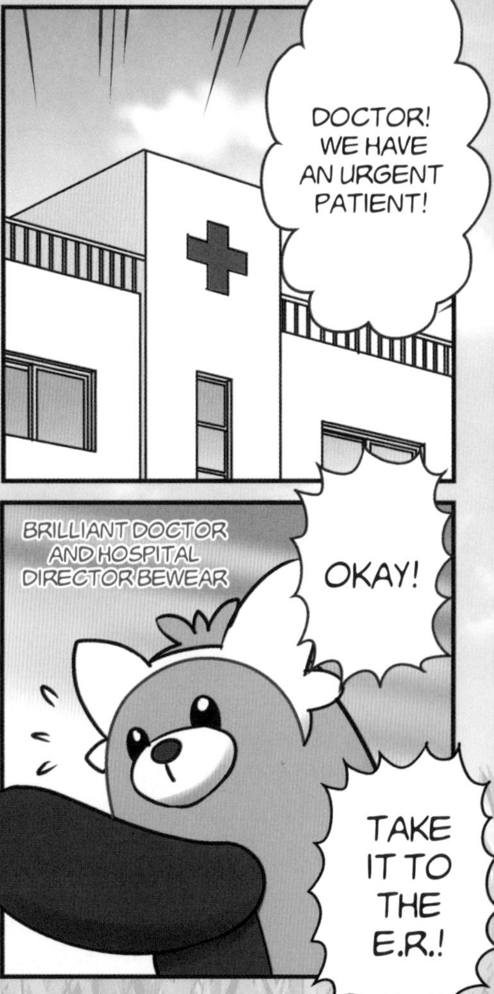
DOCTOR! WE HAVE AN URGENT PATIENT!
BRILLIANT DOCTOR AND HOSPITAL DIRECTOR BEWEAR
OKAY!
TAKE IT TO THE E.R.!

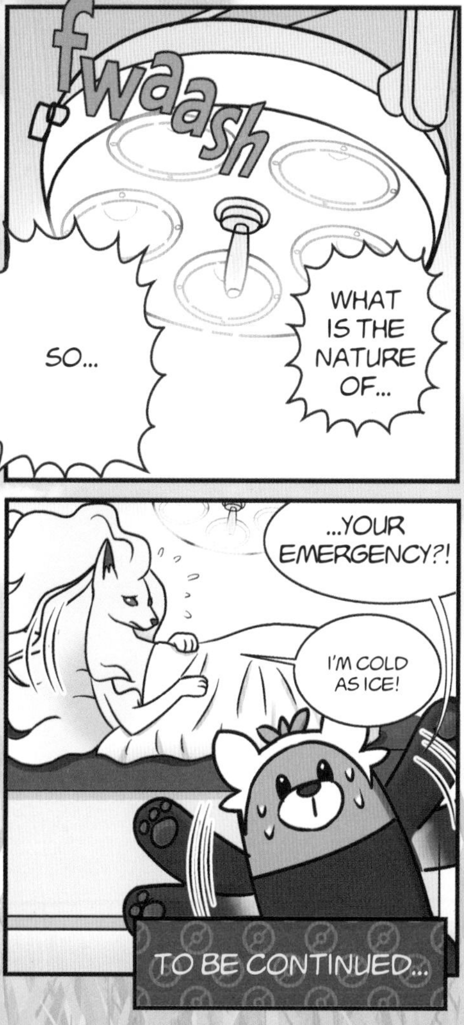
fwaash
SO...
WHAT IS THE NATURE OF...
...YOUR EMERGENCY?!
I'M COLD AS ICE!
TO BE CONTINUED...

POKÉMON MINIDEX

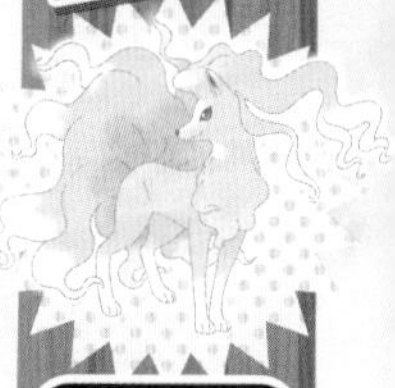

A. NINETALES

CATEGORY

Fox

TYPE

Ice, Fairy

The Alolan Ninetales creates drops of ice on its coat and showers them over its enemies.

BISHARP

Pokémon Hospital ②

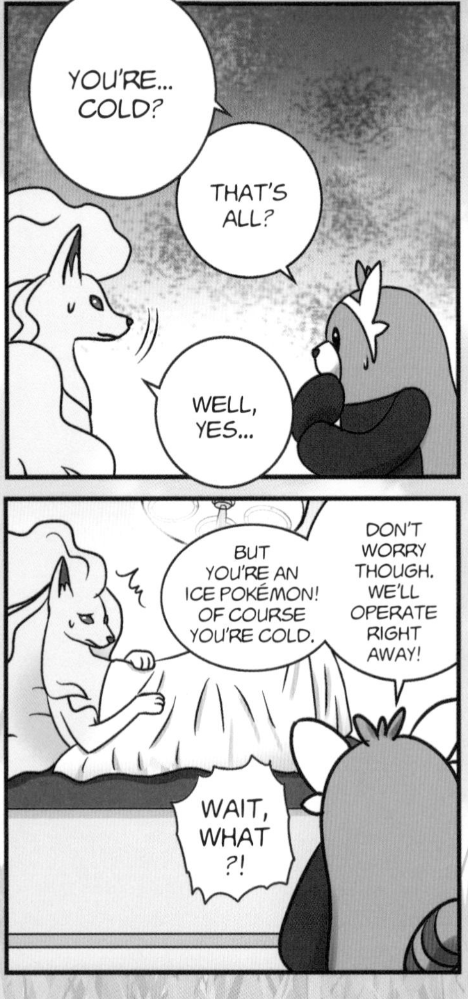
YOU'RE... COLD?
THAT'S ALL?
WELL, YES...
BUT YOU'RE AN ICE POKÉMON! OF COURSE YOU'RE COLD.
DON'T WORRY THOUGH. WE'LL OPERATE RIGHT AWAY!
WAIT, WHAT ?!

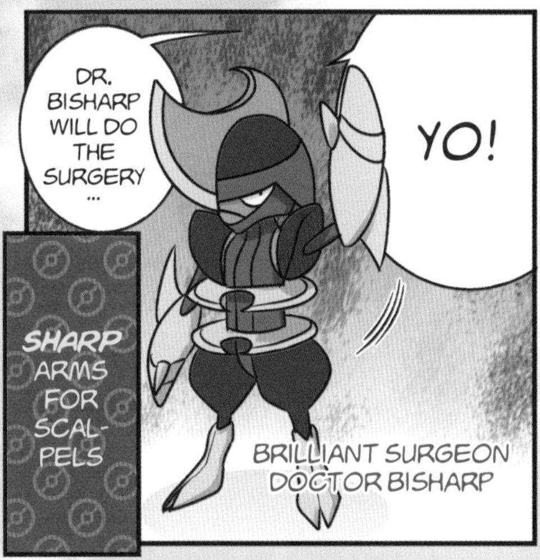
DR. BISHARP WILL DO THE SURGERY ...
YO!
SHARP ARMS FOR SCAL-PELS
BRILLIANT SURGEON DOCTOR BISHARP

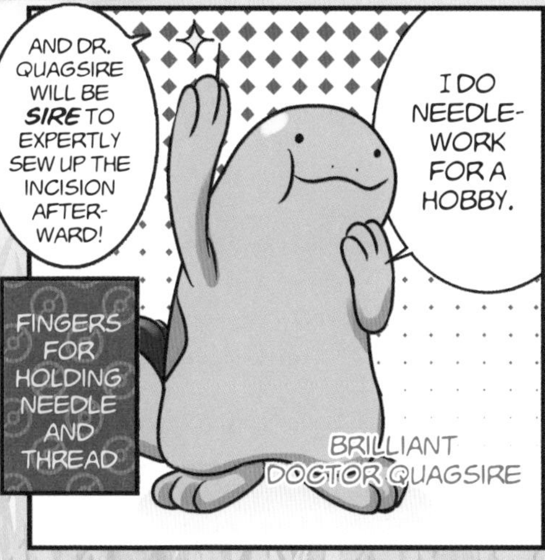
AND DR. QUAGSIRE WILL BE **SIRE** TO EXPERTLY SEW UP THE INCISION AFTER-WARD!
I DO NEEDLE-WORK FOR A HOBBY.
FINGERS FOR HOLDING NEEDLE AND THREAD
BRILLIANT DOCTOR QUAGSIRE

POKÉMON MINIDEX

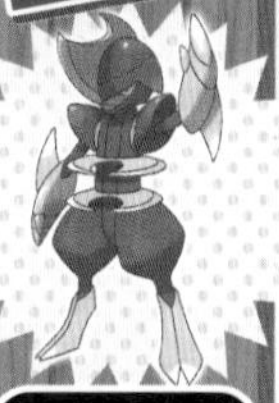

BISHARP

CATEGORY

Sword Blade

TYPE

Dark, Steel

It leads a group of Pawniard to corner its prey. The Pawniard immobilize the prey, and then Bisharp finishes it off with its sharp blade.

Pokémon Hospital ③

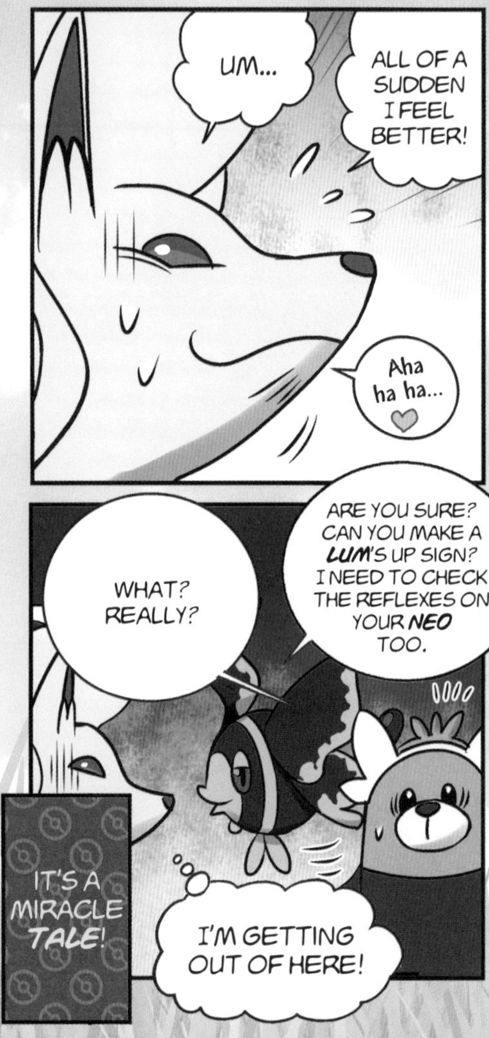
UM...
ALL OF A SUDDEN I FEEL BETTER!
Aha ha ha... ♥
WHAT? REALLY?
ARE YOU SURE? CAN YOU MAKE A ***LUM***'S UP SIGN? I NEED TO CHECK THE REFLEXES ON YOUR ***NEO*** TOO.
IT'S A MIRACLE *TALE*!
I'M GETTING OUT OF HERE!

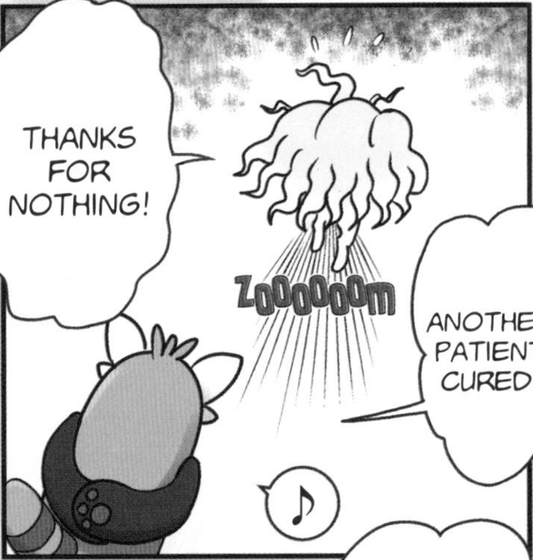
THANKS FOR NOTHING!
ZOOOOOOM
ANOTHER PATIENT CURED!
♪

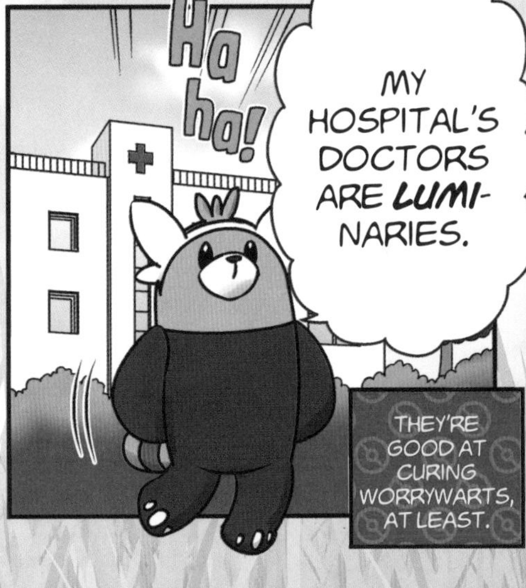
Ha ha!
MY HOSPITAL'S DOCTORS ARE *LUMI*-NARIES.
THEY'RE GOOD AT CURING WORRYWARTS, AT LEAST.

POKÉMON MINIDEX

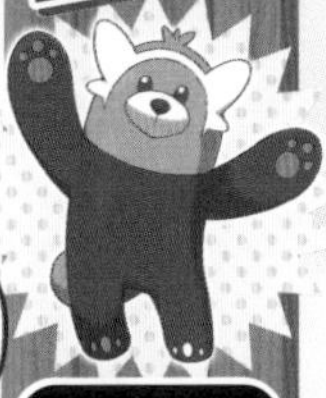

BEWEAR

CATEGORY

Strong Arm

TYPE

Normal, Fighting

It is very dangerous, so its habitat is generally off-limits. It has a habit of hugging its companions too hard. So ***bewear*** of Bewear!

TENTACOOL

When You Don't Get Enough Sleep

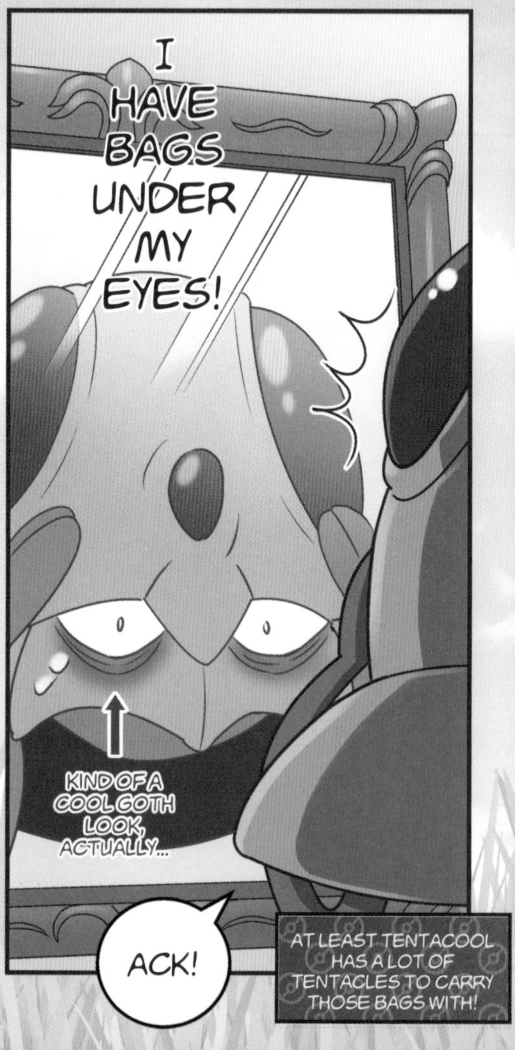

I HAVE BAGS UNDER MY EYES!
KIND OF A COOL GOTH LOOK, ACTUALLY...
ACK!
AT LEAST TENTACOOL HAS A LOT OF TENTACLES TO CARRY THOSE BAGS WITH!

MELTAN MAZE

Follow the direction of Meltan's eyes. Which route will take you to the goal—A, B or C?

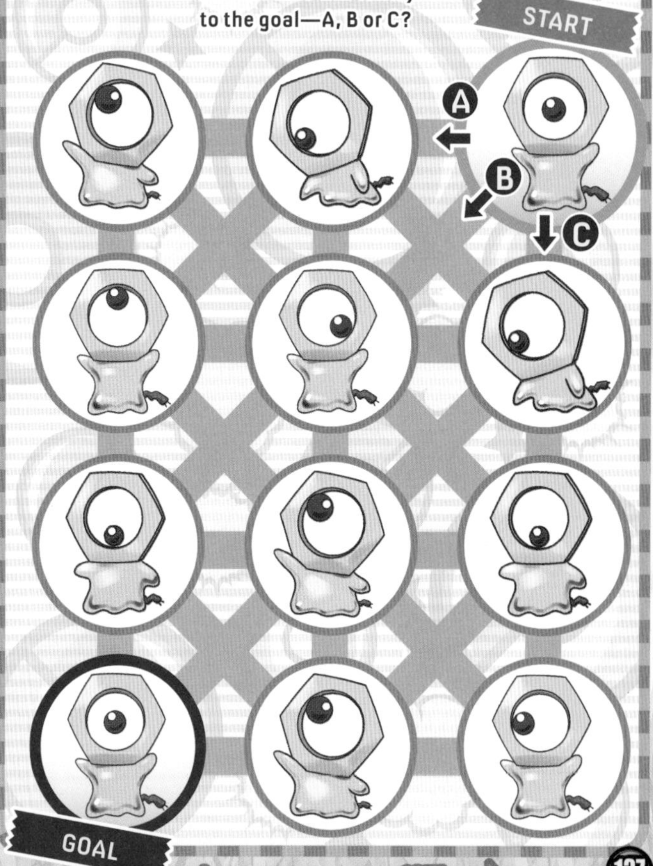
START
A
B
C
GOAL

Answers on page 187!

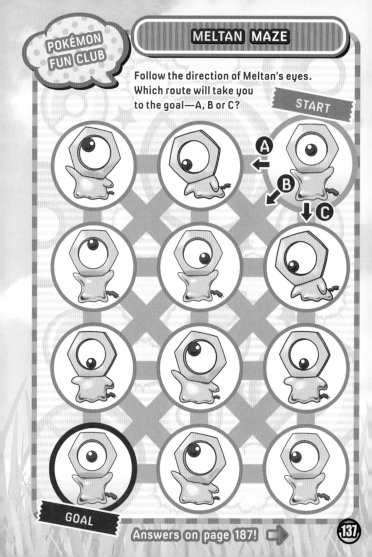

PIKACHU

On the Up and Up

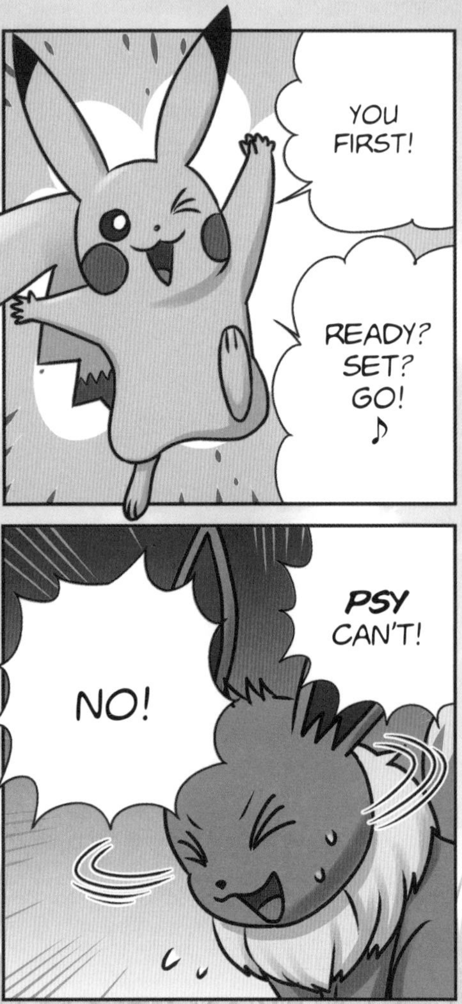
YOU FIRST!
READY? SET? GO! ♪
PSY CAN'T!
NO!

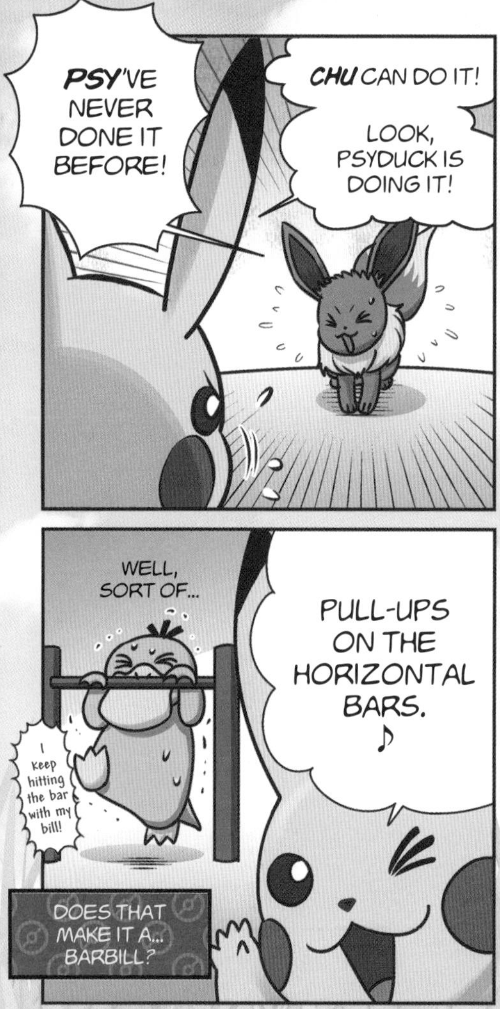
PSY'VE NEVER DONE IT BEFORE!
CHU CAN DO IT!
LOOK, PSYDUCK IS DOING IT!
WELL, SORT OF...
PULL-UPS ON THE HORIZONTAL BARS. ♪
I keep hitting the bar with my bill!
DOES THAT MAKE IT A... BARBILL?

POKÉMON MINIDEX

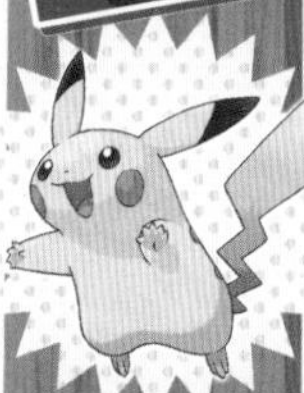

PIKACHU

CATEGORY

Mouse

TYPE

Electric

Its nature is to store up electricity. If you hear a crackle, that means Pikachu is discharging it.

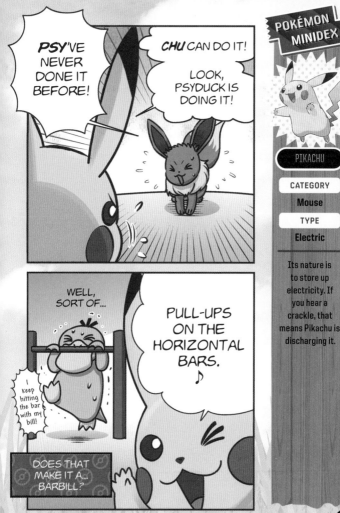

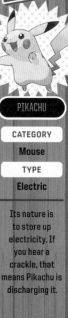

Good Job

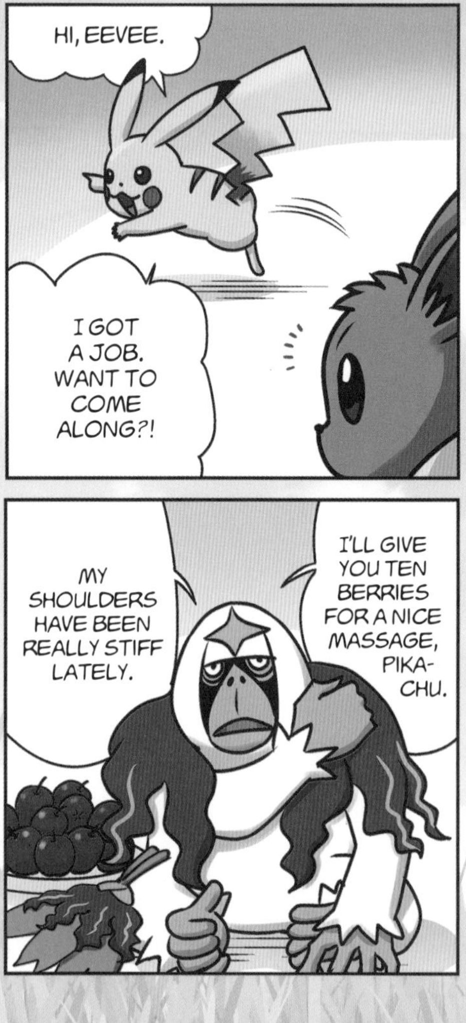
HI, EEVEE.
I GOT A JOB. WANT TO COME ALONG?!
MY SHOULDERS HAVE BEEN REALLY STIFF LATELY.
I'LL GIVE YOU TEN BERRIES FOR A NICE MASSAGE, PIKA-CHU.

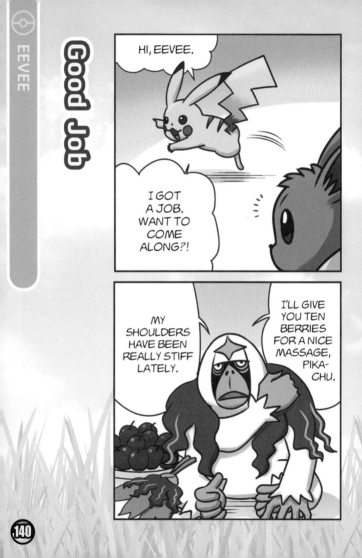

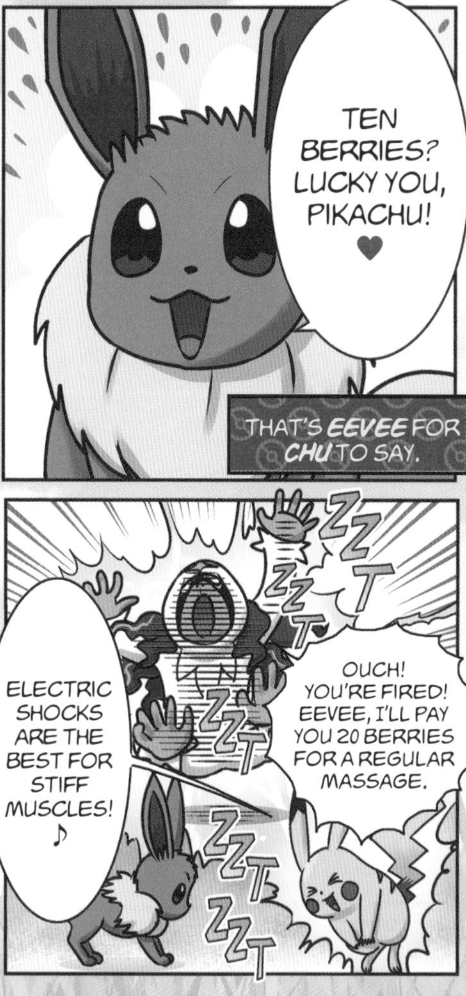
TEN BERRIES? LUCKY YOU, PIKACHU! ♥
THAT'S *EEVEE* FOR *CHU* TO SAY.
ZZZT
ZZT
ELECTRIC SHOCKS ARE THE BEST FOR STIFF MUSCLES! ♪
ZZT
OUCH! YOU'RE FIRED! EEVEE, I'LL PAY YOU 20 BERRIES FOR A REGULAR MASSAGE.
ZZT
ZZT

POKÉMON MINIDEX

Which of the following Eevee evolutions is the heaviest?

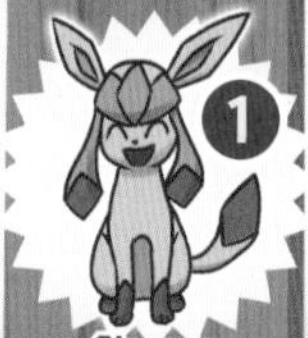
1 Glaceon

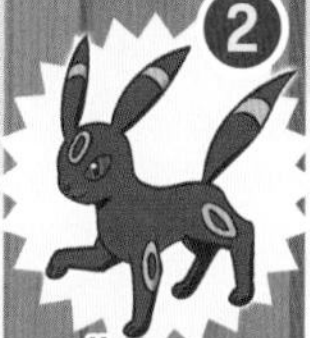
2 Umbreon

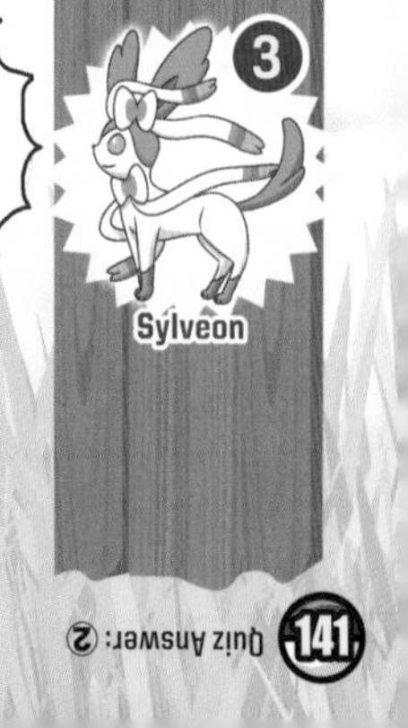
3 Sylveon

Quiz Answer: 2

GLACEON

You Are My World

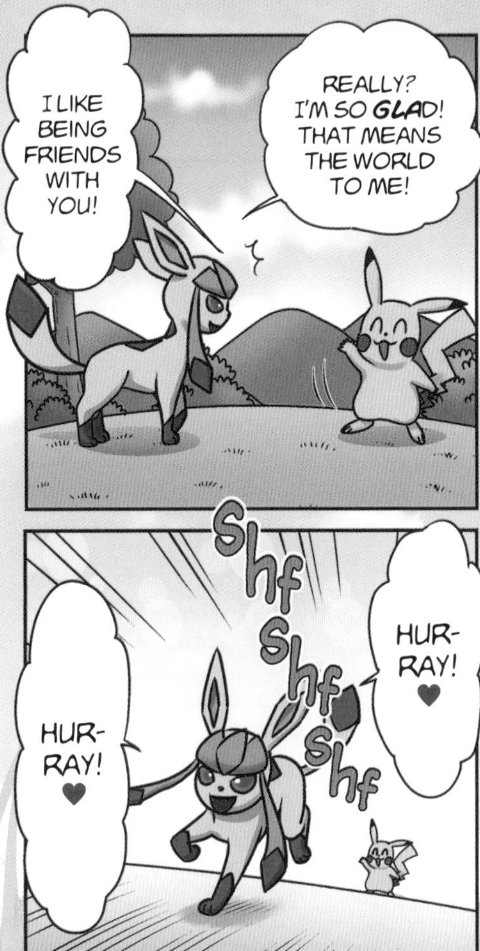
I LIKE BEING FRIENDS WITH YOU!
REALLY? I'M SO GLAD! THAT MEANS THE WORLD TO ME!
HUR-RAY! ♥
SHF SHF SHF
HUR-RAY! ♥

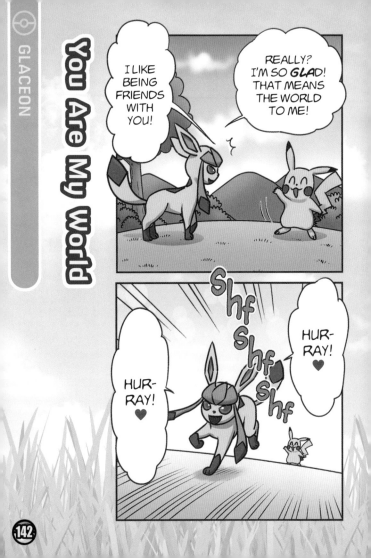

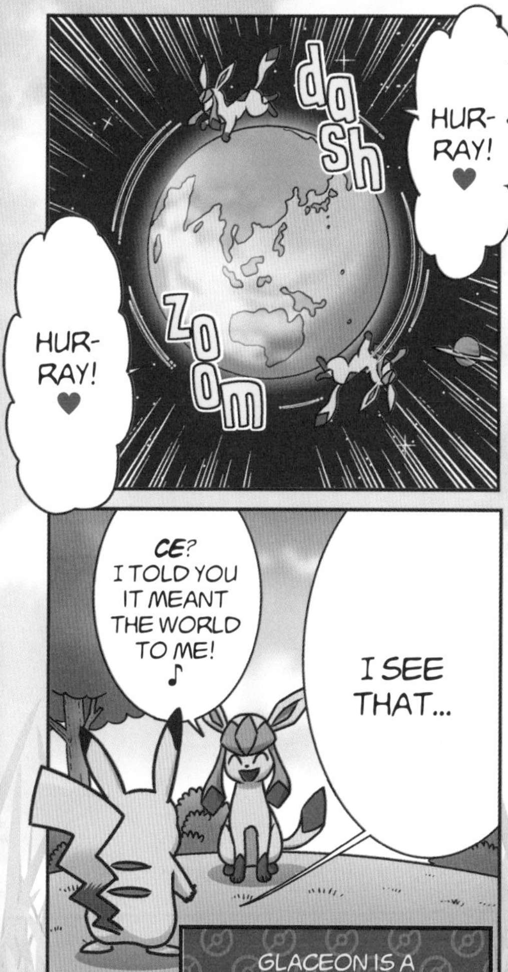
dash
HUR-RAY! ♥
ZOOM
HUR-RAY! ♥
CE? I TOLD YOU IT MEANT THE WORLD TO ME! ♪
I SEE THAT...
GLACEON IS A WORLDLY POKÉMON.

POKÉMON MINIDEX

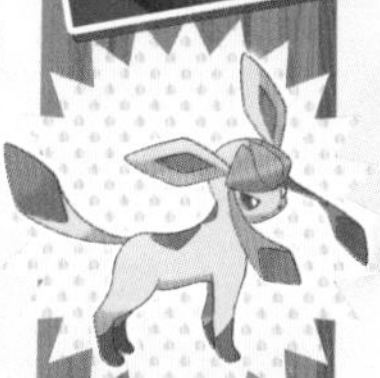

GLACEON

CATEGORY

Fresh Snow

TYPE

Ice

It can freeze the atmosphere around it to make a diamond-dust flurry. It can also drop its body temperature below -75°F.

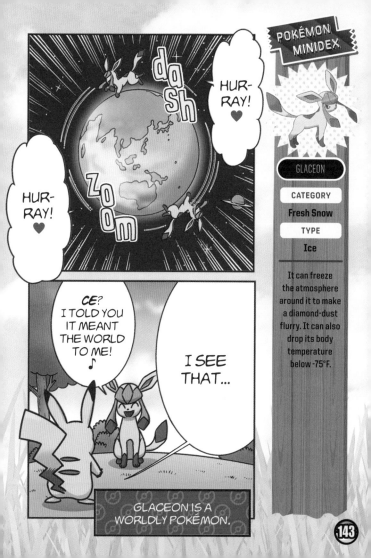

LEAFEON

Weather Report

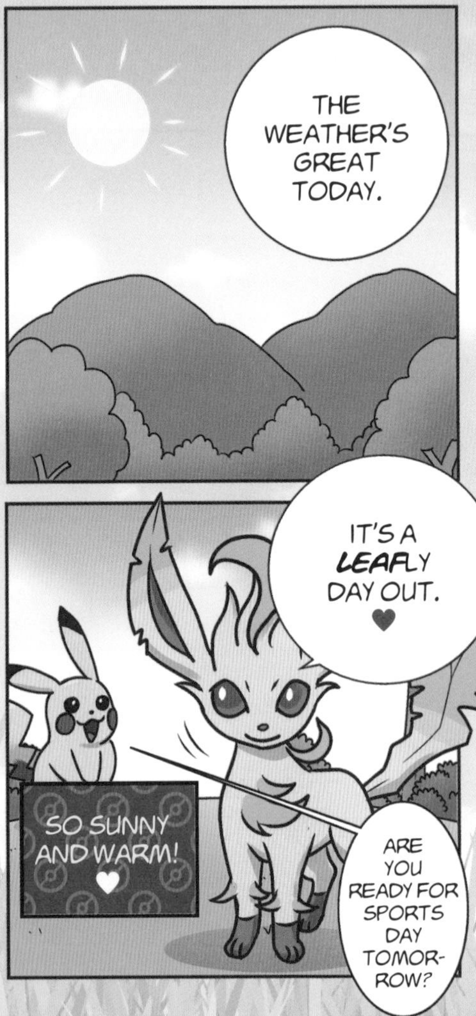
THE WEATHER'S GREAT TODAY.
IT'S A LEAFLY DAY OUT. ♥
SO SUNNY AND WARM! ♥
ARE YOU READY FOR SPORTS DAY TOMORROW?

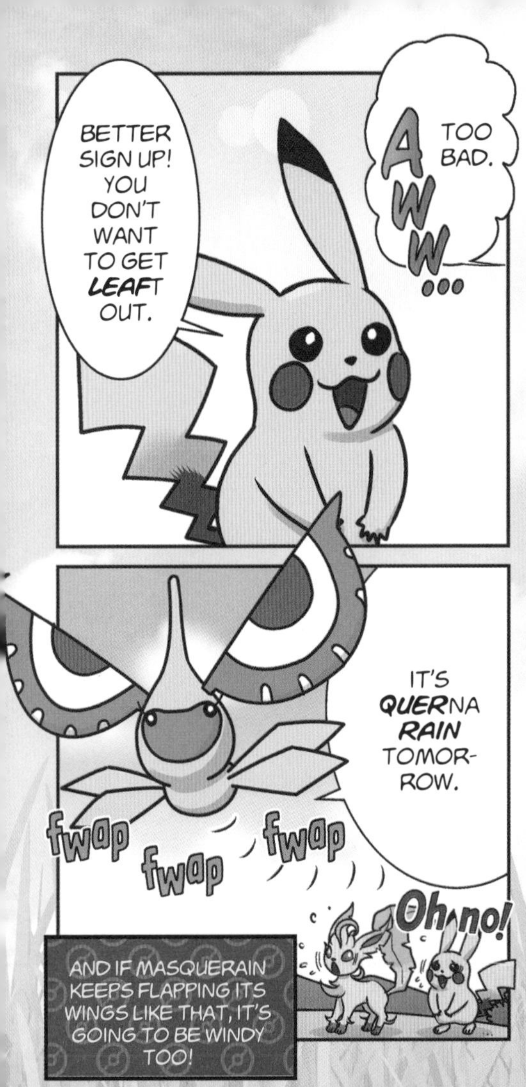
BETTER SIGN UP! YOU DON'T WANT TO GET LEAFT OUT.
AWW...
TOO BAD.
IT'S QUERNA RAIN TOMORROW.
fwap
fwap
fwap
Oh no!
AND IF MASQUERAIN KEEPS FLAPPING ITS WINGS LIKE THAT, IT'S GOING TO BE WINDY TOO!

POKÉMON MINIDEX

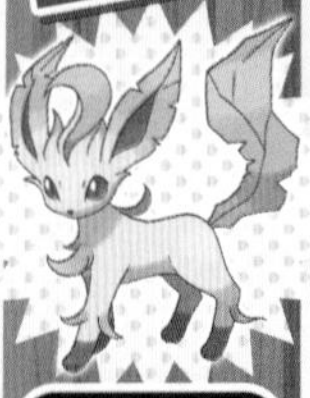

LEAFEON

CATEGORY

Verdant

TYPE

Grass

Leafeon is a Verdant Pokémon whose cells are similar to plants. It creates energy through photosynthesis.

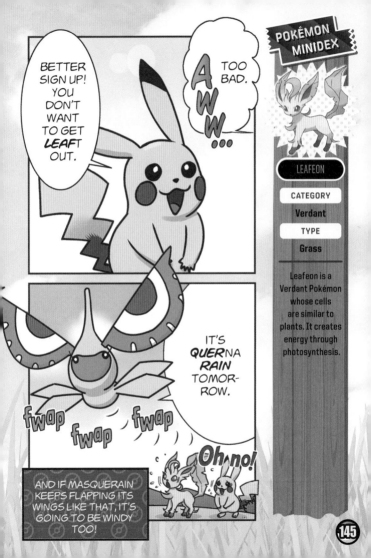

Training Dojo

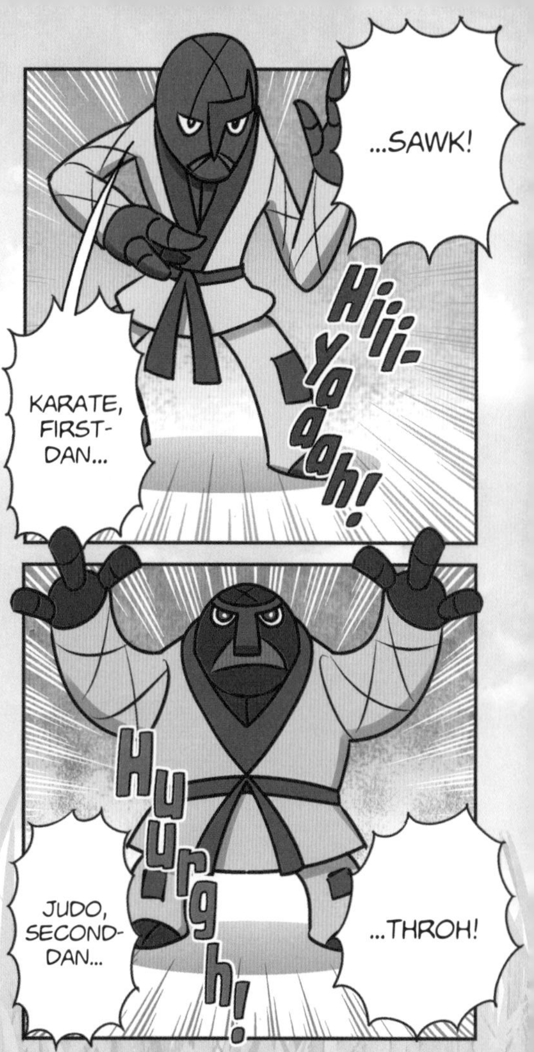
KARATE, FIRST-DAN...
...SAWK!
Hiiii-yaaah!
JUDO, SECOND-DAN...
...THROH!
Huurgh!

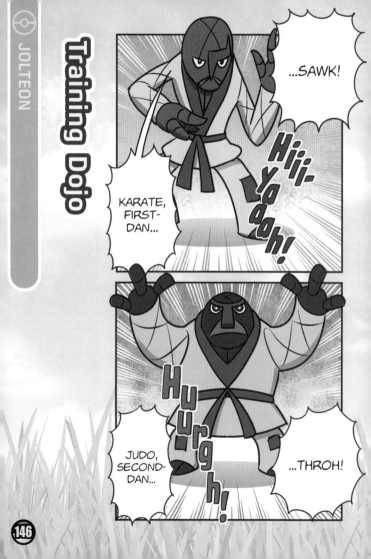

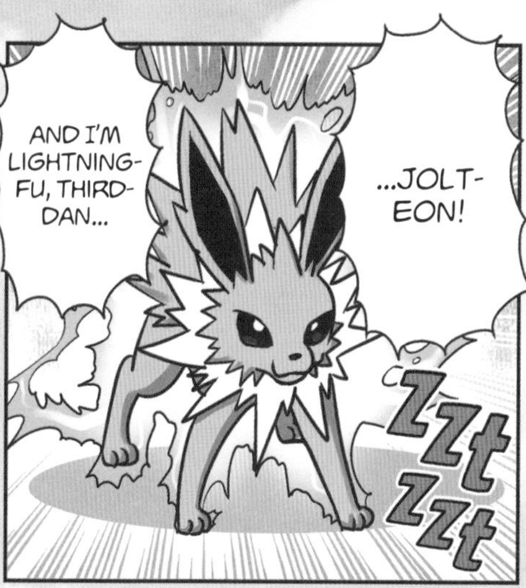
AND I'M LIGHTNING-FU, THIRD-DAN...
...JOLT-EON!
ZZt ZZt

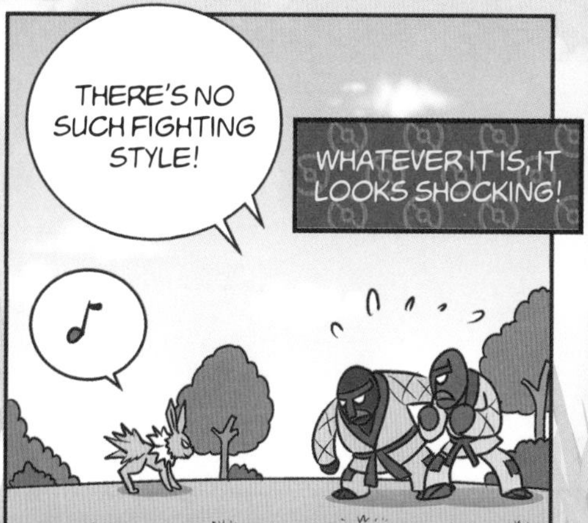
THERE'S NO SUCH FIGHTING STYLE!
WHATEVER IT IS, IT LOOKS SHOCKING!
♪

POKÉMON MINIDEX

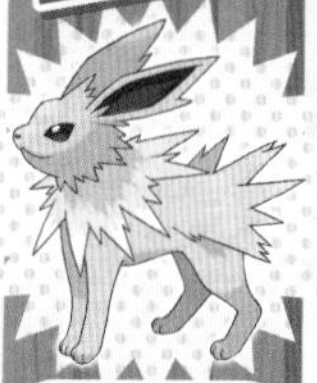

JOLTEON

CATEGORY

Lightning

TYPE

Electric

It accumulates negative ions in the atmosphere to blast out 10,000-volt lightning bolts! That would give you quite a ***jolt***!

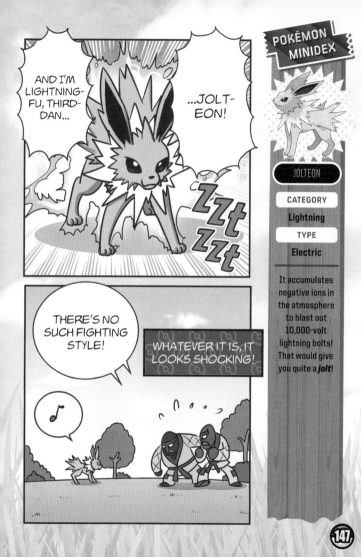

SYLVEON

Looking Good

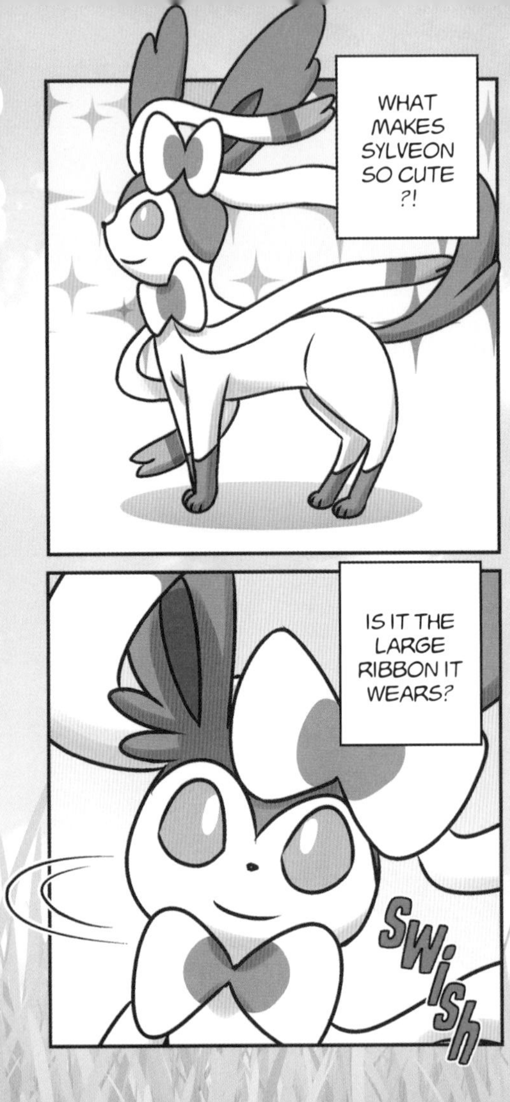

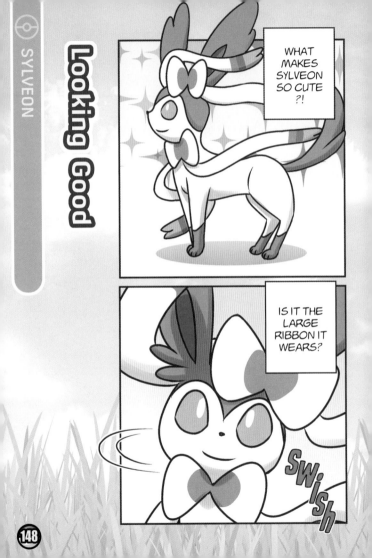

WHAT MAKES SYLVEON SO CUTE ?!
IS IT THE LARGE RIBBON IT WEARS?
SWISH

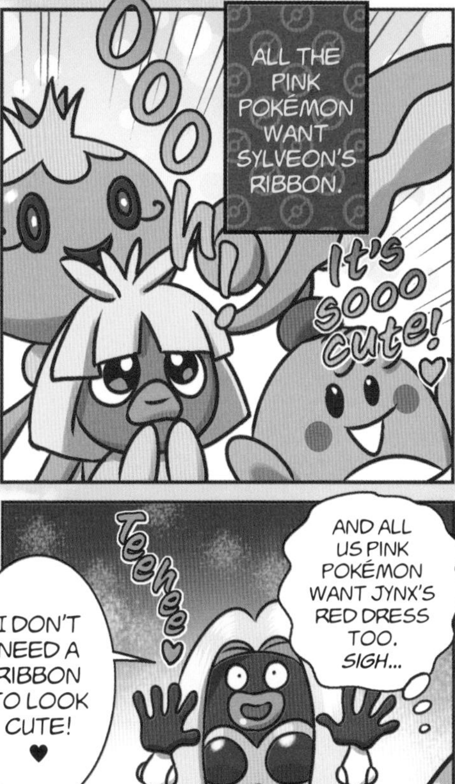
Ooooh!
ALL THE PINK POKÉMON WANT SYLVEON'S RIBBON.
It's sooo cute! ♥
Teehee ♥
I DON'T NEED A RIBBON TO LOOK CUTE! ♥
AND ALL US PINK POKÉMON WANT JYNX'S RED DRESS TOO. *SIGH*...

POKÉMON MINIDEX

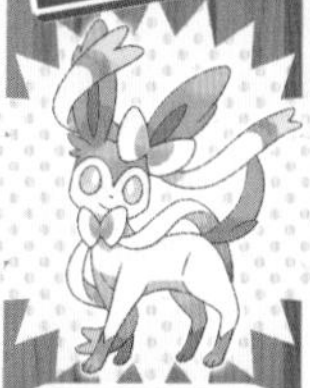

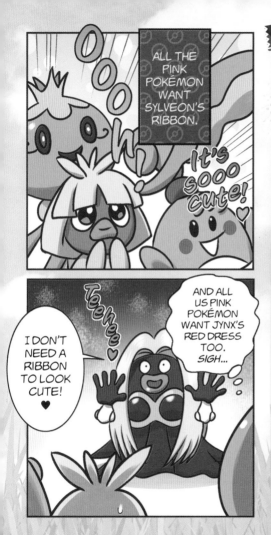

SYLVEON

CATEGORY

Intertwining

TYPE

Fairy

An Intertwining Pokémon that sends out a soothing aura from its feelers. Yet any Trainer will tell you that it is the bravest Pokémon in battle.

UMBREON

Not Guilty as Charged

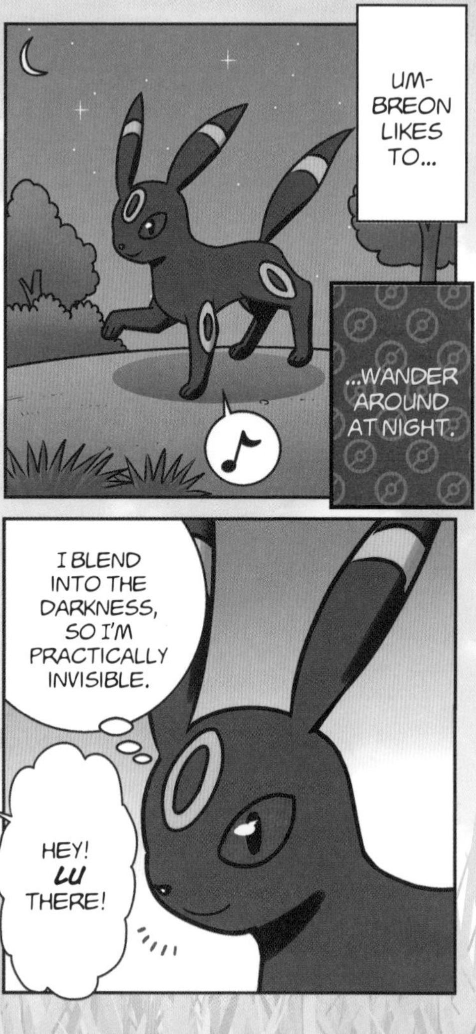
UM-BREON LIKES TO...
...WANDER AROUND AT NIGHT.
I BLEND INTO THE DARKNESS, SO I'M PRACTICALLY INVISIBLE.
HEY! LU THERE!

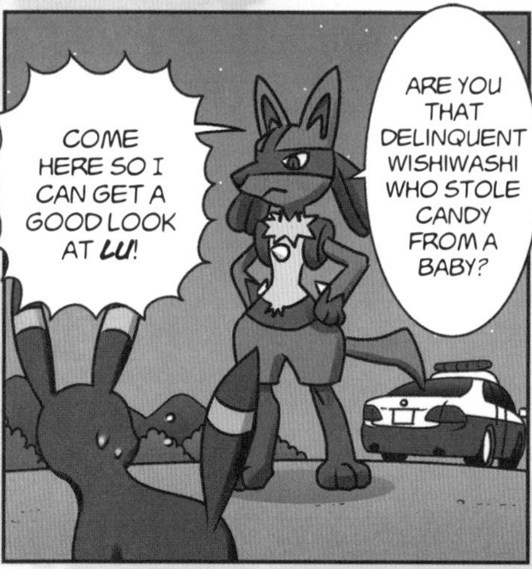
COME HERE SO I CAN GET A GOOD LOOK AT LU!
ARE YOU THAT DELINQUENT WISHIWASHI WHO STOLE CANDY FROM A BABY?

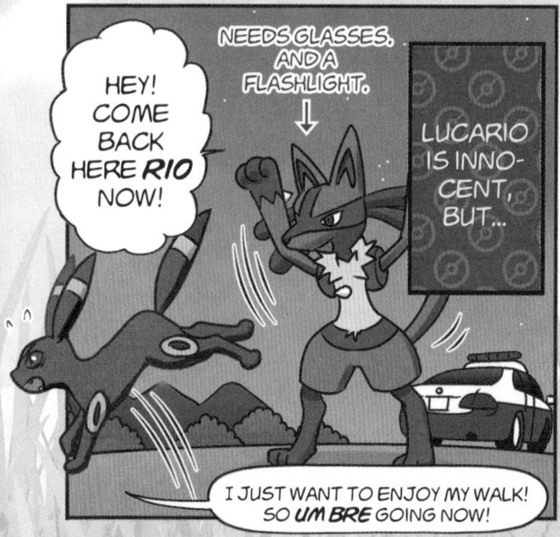
HEY! COME BACK HERE RIO NOW!
NEEDS GLASSES. AND A FLASHLIGHT.
LUCARIO IS INNO-CENT, BUT...
I JUST WANT TO ENJOY MY WALK! SO UM BRE GOING NOW!

POKÉMON MINIDEX

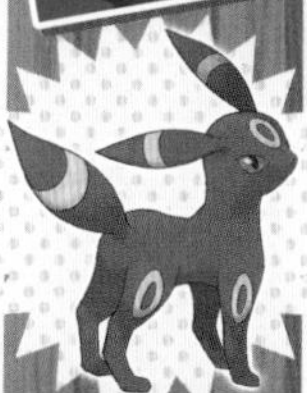

UMBREON

CATEGORY

Moonlight

TYPE

Dark

When agitated, this Pokémon protects itself by spraying poisonous sweat from its pores.

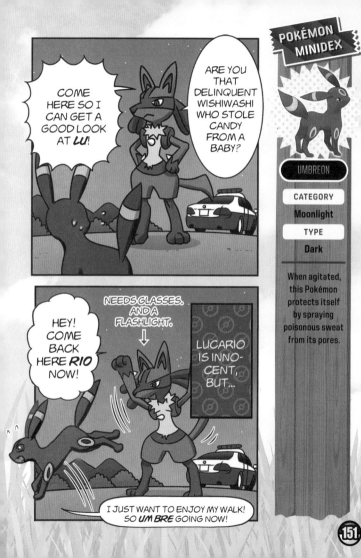

That's Nut It!

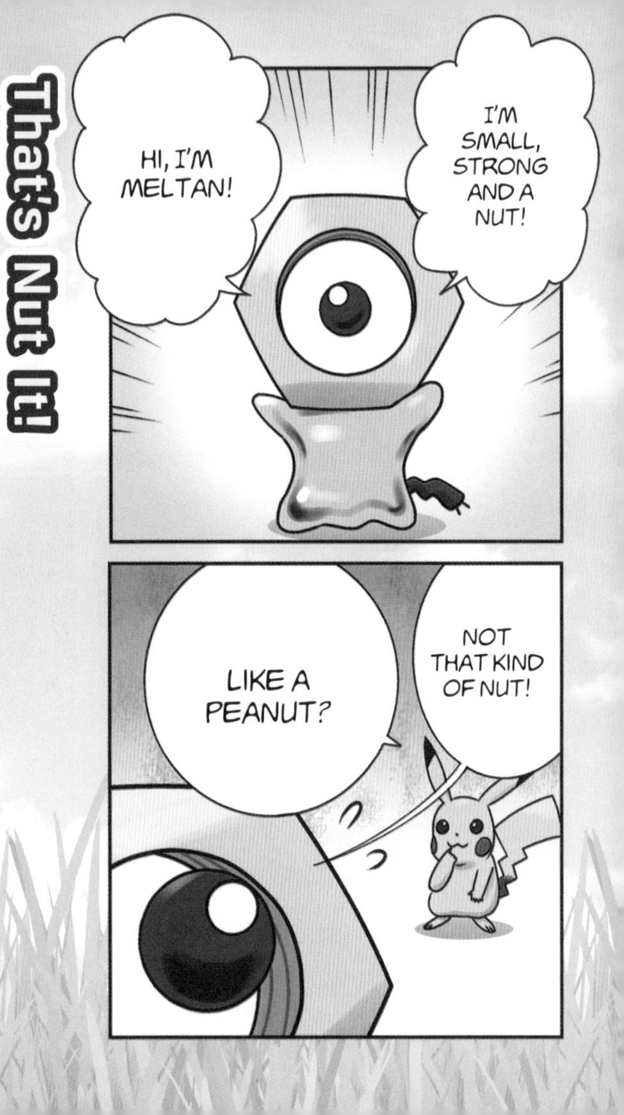
HI, I'M MELTAN!
I'M SMALL, STRONG AND A NUT!
LIKE A PEANUT?
NOT THAT KIND OF NUT!

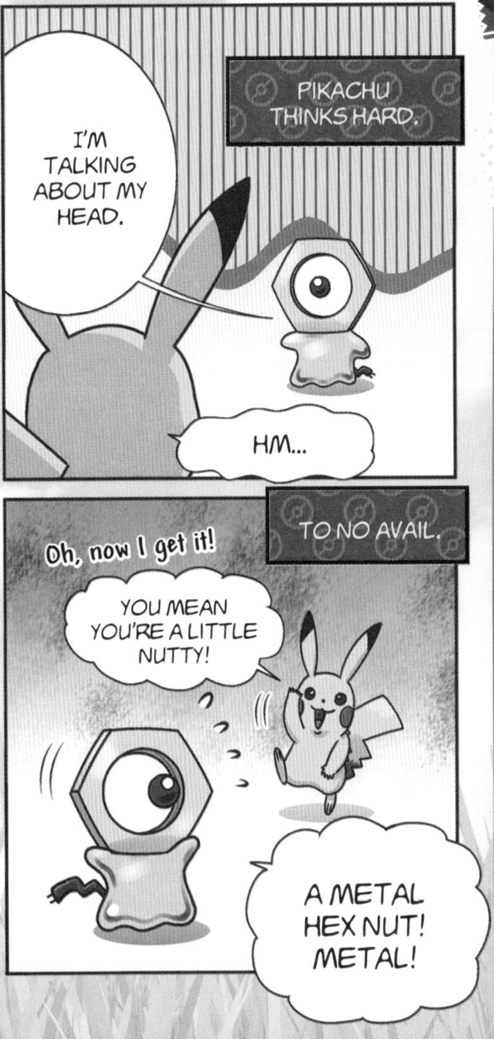
I'M TALKING ABOUT MY HEAD.
PIKACHU THINKS HARD.
HM...
TO NO AVAIL.
Oh, now I get it!
YOU MEAN YOU'RE A LITTLE NUTTY!
A METAL HEX NUT! METAL!

POKÉMON MINIDEX

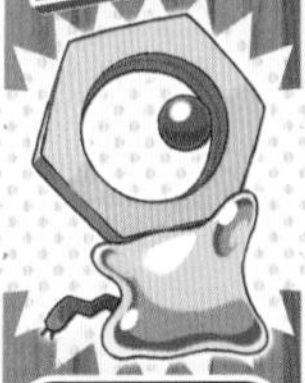

MELTAN

CATEGORY

Hex Nut

TYPE

Steel

Meltan's body is mainly made of liquid metal. It uses its liquid metal hands and legs to melt and absorb other metals!

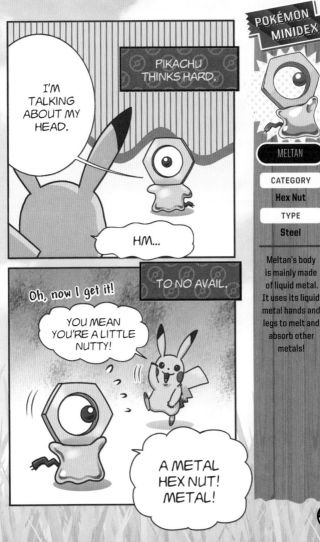

Drink Responsibly

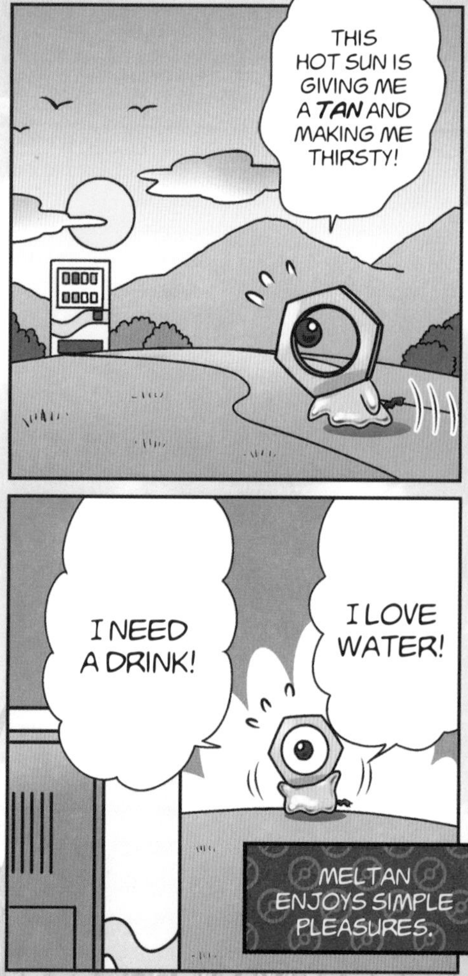
THIS HOT SUN IS GIVING ME A *TAN* AND MAKING ME THIRSTY!
I NEED A DRINK!
I LOVE WATER!
MELTAN ENJOYS SIMPLE PLEASURES.

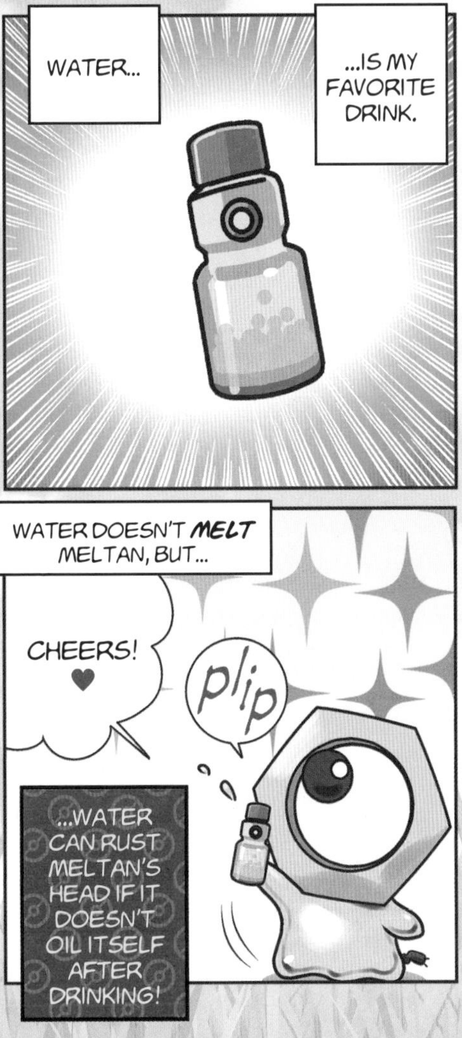
WATER...
...IS MY FAVORITE DRINK.
WATER DOESN'T ***MELT*** MELTAN, BUT...
CHEERS! ♥
plip
...WATER CAN RUST MELTAN'S HEAD IF IT DOESN'T OIL ITSELF AFTER DRINKING!

POKÉMON MINIDEX

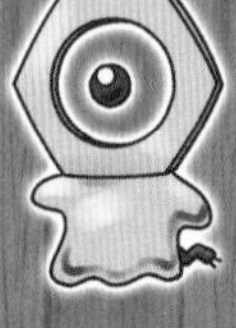

Which of the following is not true of Meltan?

① It's a Mythical Pokémon that evolves.

② Its body is made of liquid metal.

③ It came out of the Ultra Wormhole.

Quiz Answer: ③

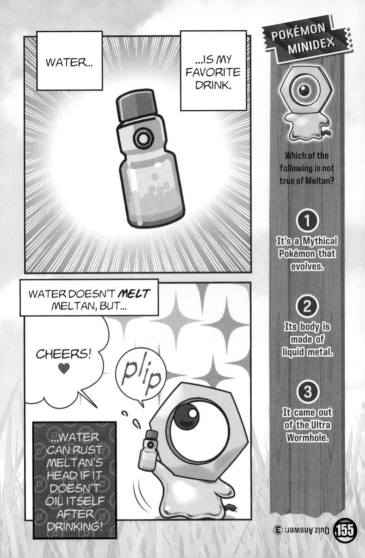

Nice to Meet Chu

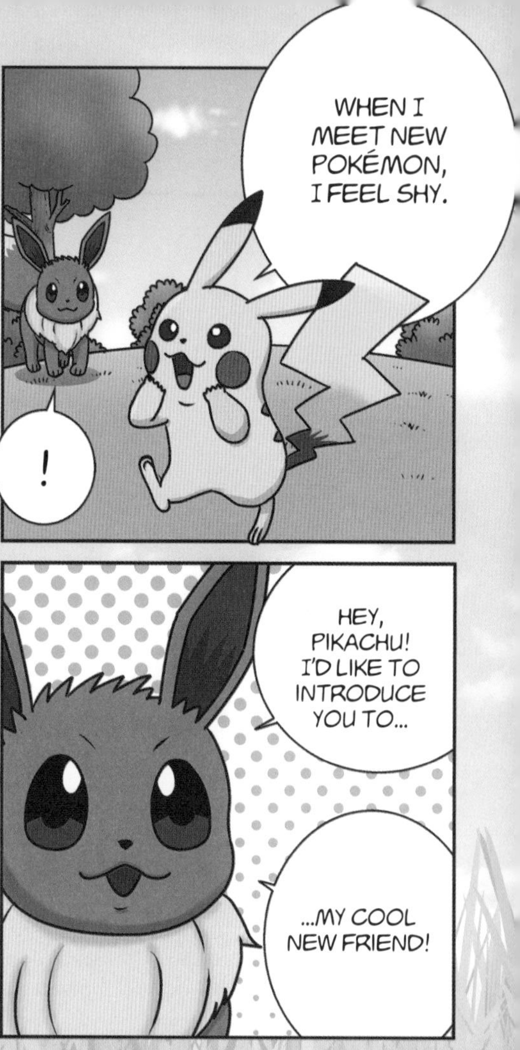
WHEN I MEET NEW POKÉMON, I FEEL SHY.
!
HEY, PIKACHU! I'D LIKE TO INTRODUCE YOU TO...
...MY COOL NEW FRIEND!

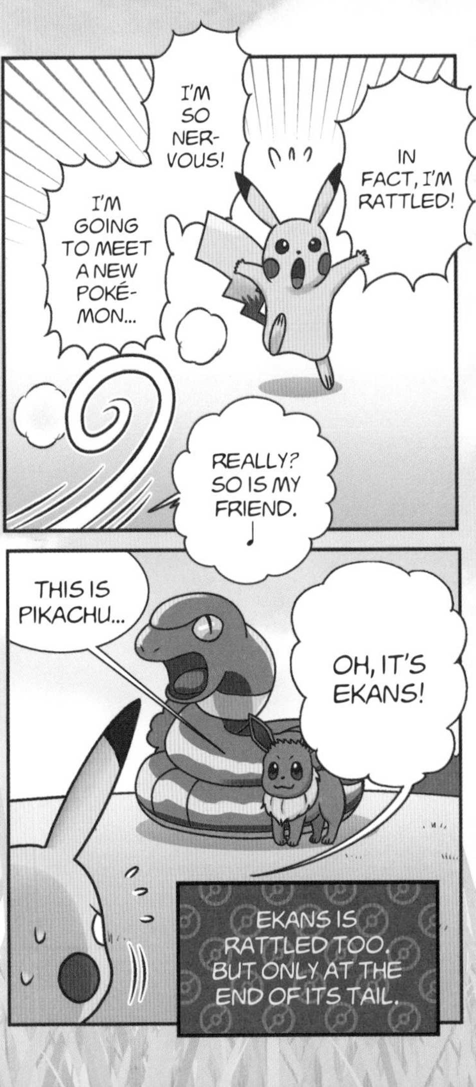
I'M GOING TO MEET A NEW POKÉMON...
I'M SO NERVOUS!
IN FACT, I'M RATTLED!
REALLY? SO IS MY FRIEND. ♩
THIS IS PIKACHU...
OH, IT'S EKANS!
EKANS IS RATTLED TOO. BUT ONLY AT THE END OF ITS TAIL.

POKÉMON MINIDEX

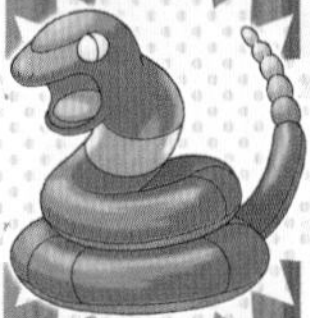

EKANS

CATEGORY

Snake

TYPE

Poison

The eggs of bird Pokémon are its favorite food. Ekans ***kan*** detach its jaw to swallow its prey whole.

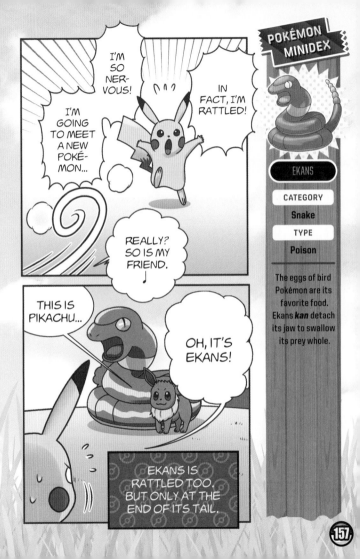

ARCANINE

A Tasty Contest

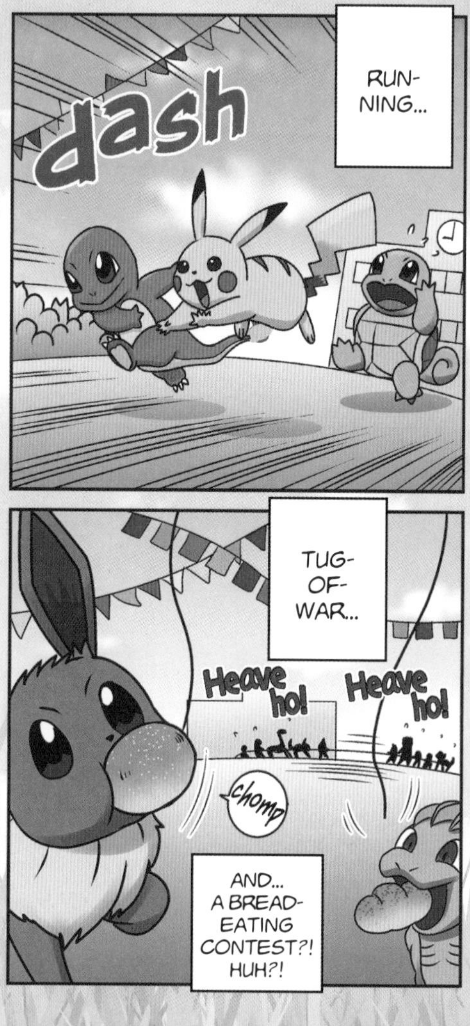
RUN-
NING...
dash
TUG-
OF-
WAR...
Heave ho!
Heave ho!
chomp
AND...
A BREAD-
EATING
CONTEST?!
HUH?!

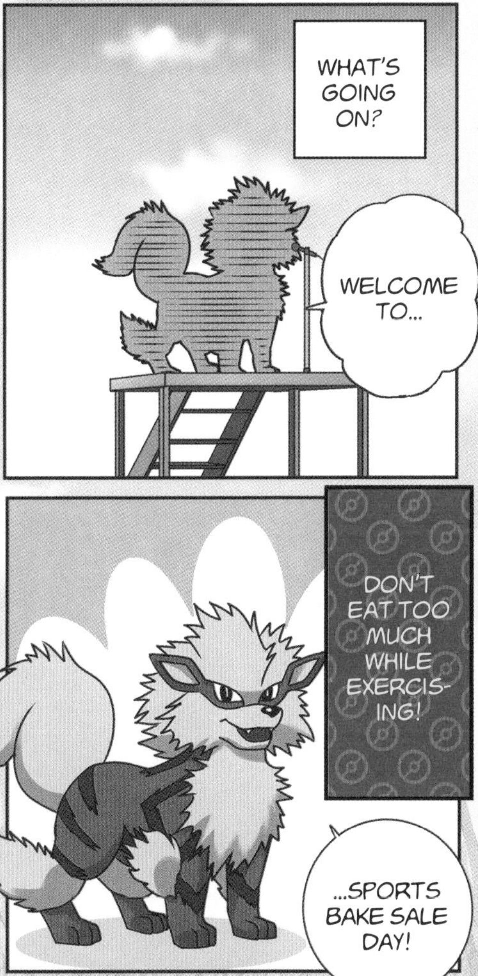
WHAT'S GOING ON?
WELCOME TO...
DON'T EAT TOO MUCH WHILE EXERCIS-ING!
...SPORTS BAKE SALE DAY!

POKÉMON MINIDEX

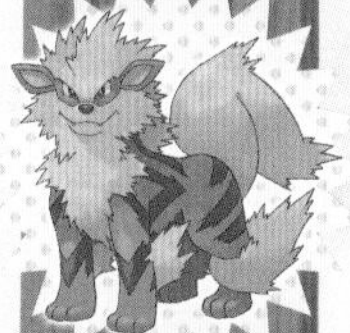

ARCANINE

CATEGORY

Legendary

TYPE

Fire

It can run over 6,200 miles in a single day and night. It appears in ancient Eastern folklore.

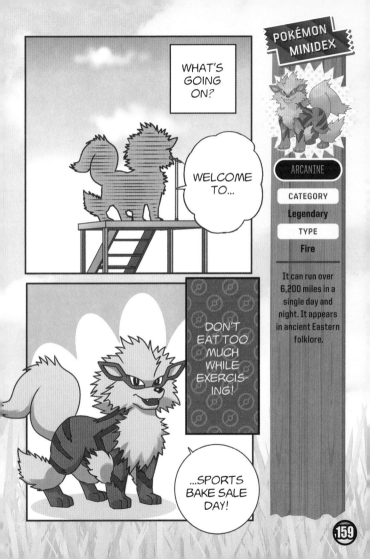

GASTLY

Stay in Your Lane

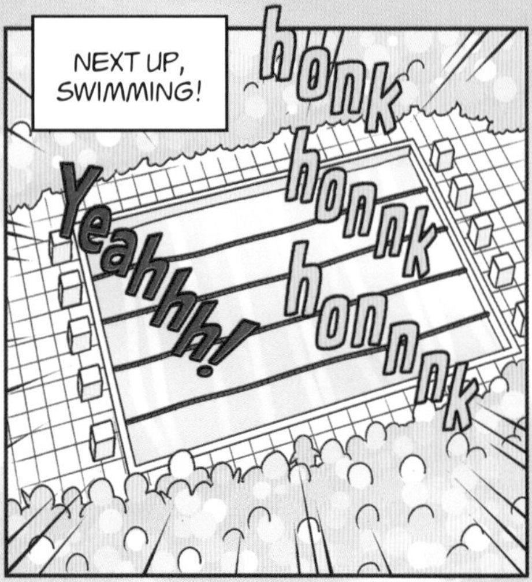

NEXT UP, SWIMMING!
honk
Yeahhhh!
honnk
honnnk

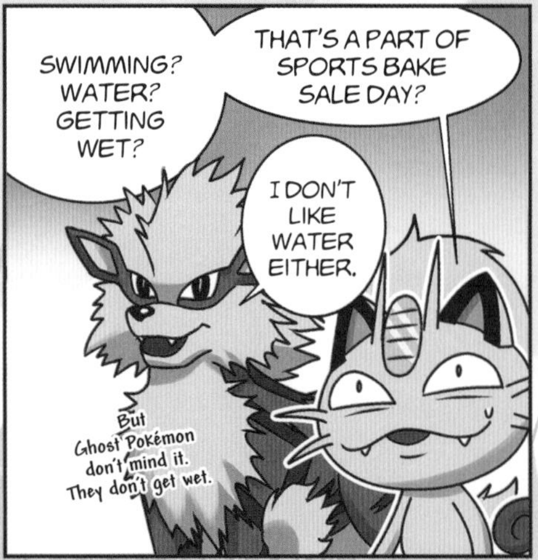

SWIMMING? WATER? GETTING WET?
THAT'S A PART OF SPORTS BAKE SALE DAY?
I DON'T LIKE WATER EITHER.
But Ghost Pokémon don't mind it. They don't get wet.

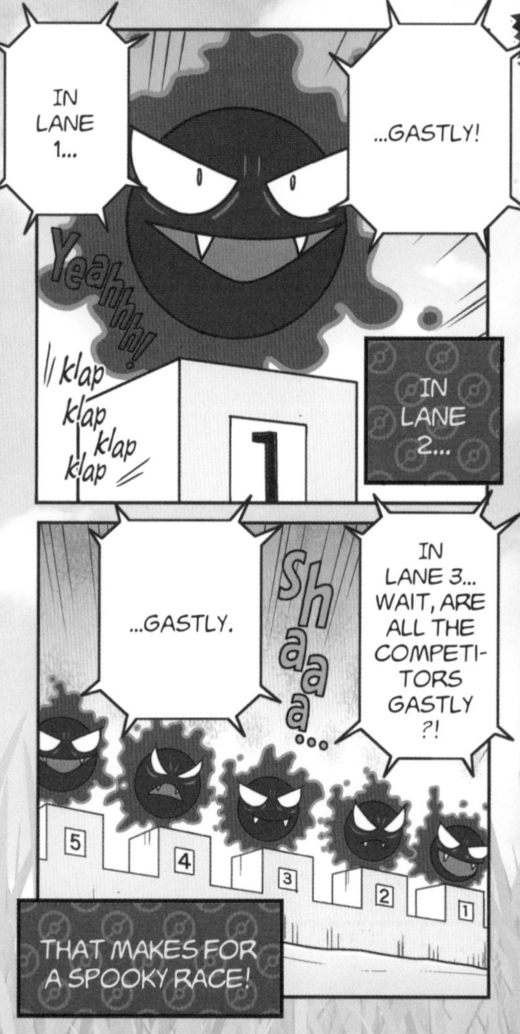
IN LANE 1...
...GASTLY!
Yeahhh!
klap klap klap klap
1
IN LANE 2...
...GASTLY.
Shaaaa...
IN LANE 3... WAIT, ARE ALL THE COMPETITORS GASTLY?!
5
4
3
2
1
THAT MAKES FOR A SPOOKY RACE!

POKÉMON MINIDEX

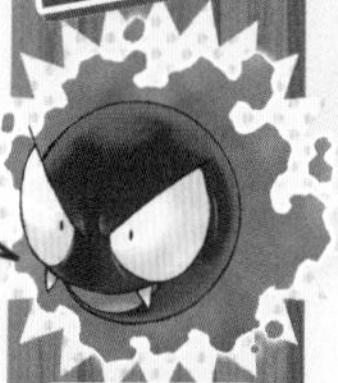

GASTLY

CATEGORY

Gas

TYPE

Ghost, Poison

This Pokémon's body is made up of 95 percent gas, which can be blown away by a strong gust of wind.

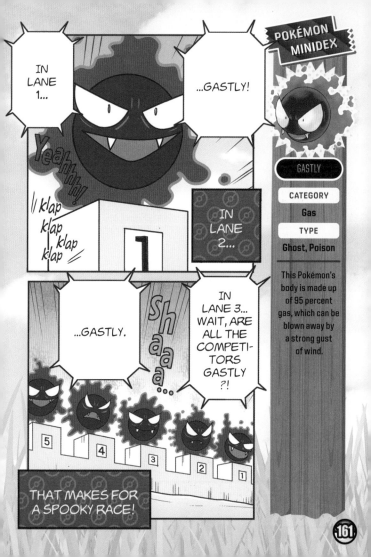

What's the Holdup?

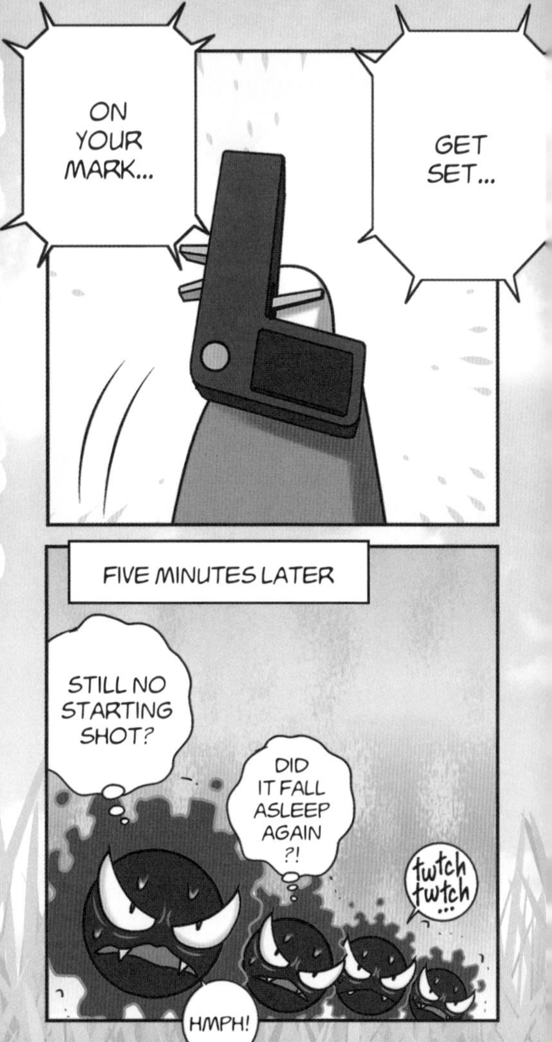
ON YOUR MARK...
GET SET...
FIVE MINUTES LATER
STILL NO STARTING SHOT?
DID IT FALL ASLEEP AGAIN?!
twtch twtch...
HMPH!

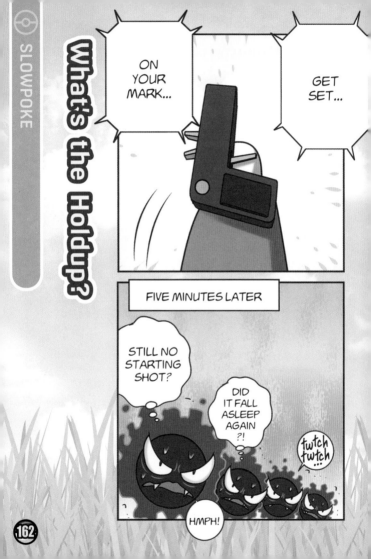

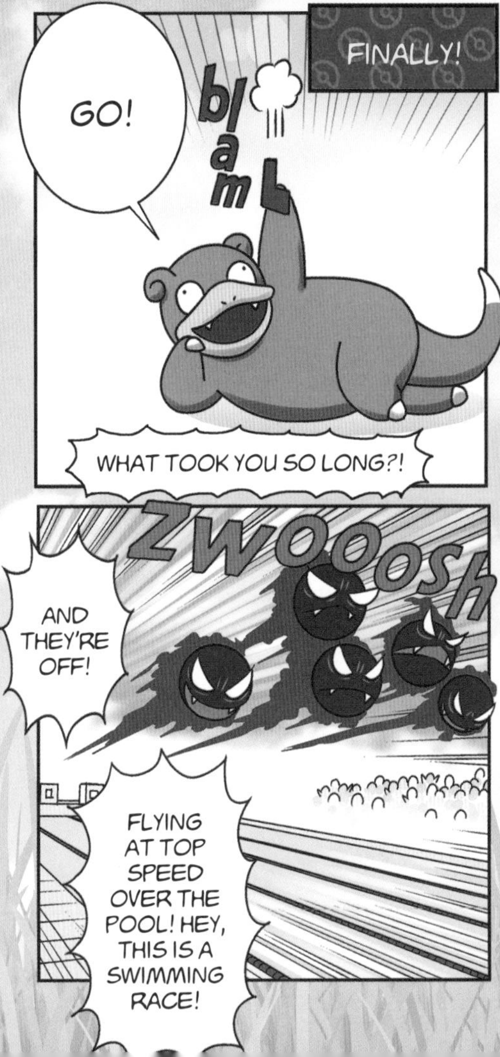
GO!
blam
FINALLY!
WHAT TOOK YOU SO LONG?!
ZWOOOSH
AND THEY'RE OFF!
FLYING AT TOP SPEED OVER THE POOL! HEY, THIS IS A SWIMMING RACE!

POKÉMON MINIDEX

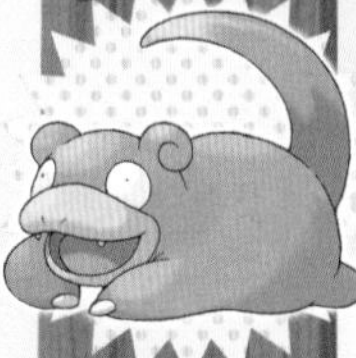

SLOWPOKE

CATEGORY

Dopey

TYPE

Water, Psychic

Even when its tail is bitten or someone hits it hard, Slowpoke is content to loll about without a care in the world.

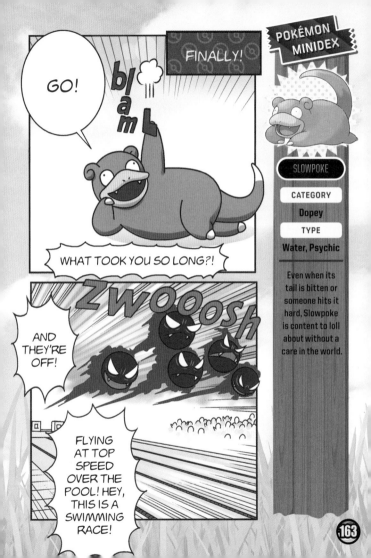

A Real Tongue Lashing

LICKI-TUNG VS. MEL-METAL!

THERE ARE BATTLES AS WELL AS RACES TODAY.

LICKITUNG USES LICK!

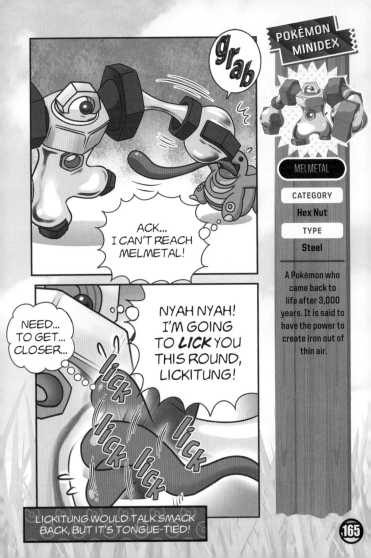

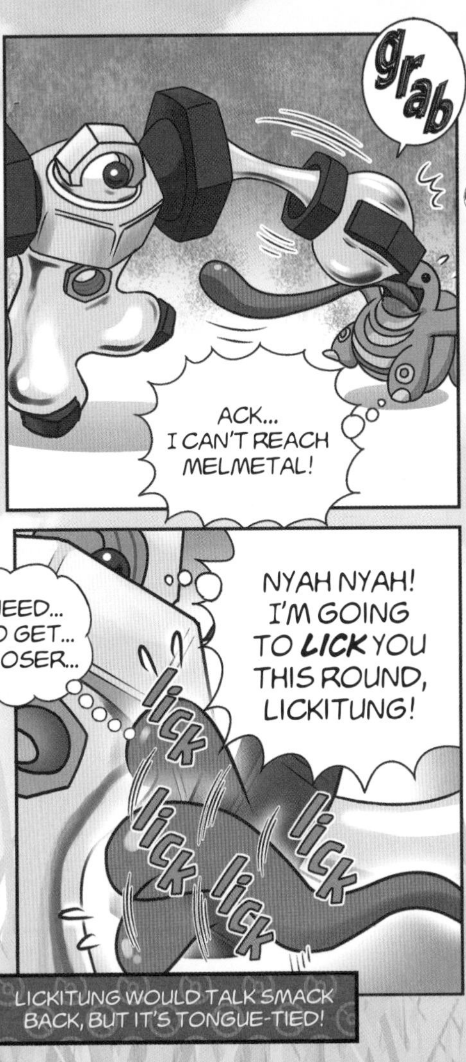
grab
ACK... I CAN'T REACH MELMETAL!
NEED... TO GET... CLOSER...
NYAH NYAH! I'M GOING TO LICK YOU THIS ROUND, LICKITUNG!
lick
lick
lick
lick
LICKITUNG WOULD TALK SMACK BACK, BUT IT'S TONGUE-TIED!

POKÉMON MINIDEX

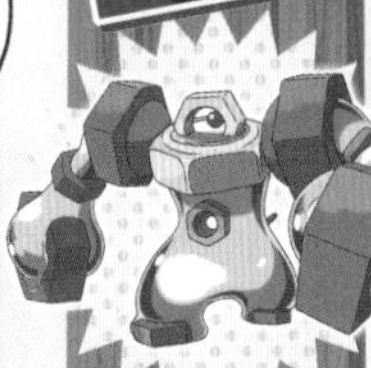

MELMETAL

CATEGORY

Hex Nut

TYPE

Steel

A Pokémon who came back to life after 3,000 years. It is said to have the power to create iron out of thin air.

DODUO

Awards Ceremony ①

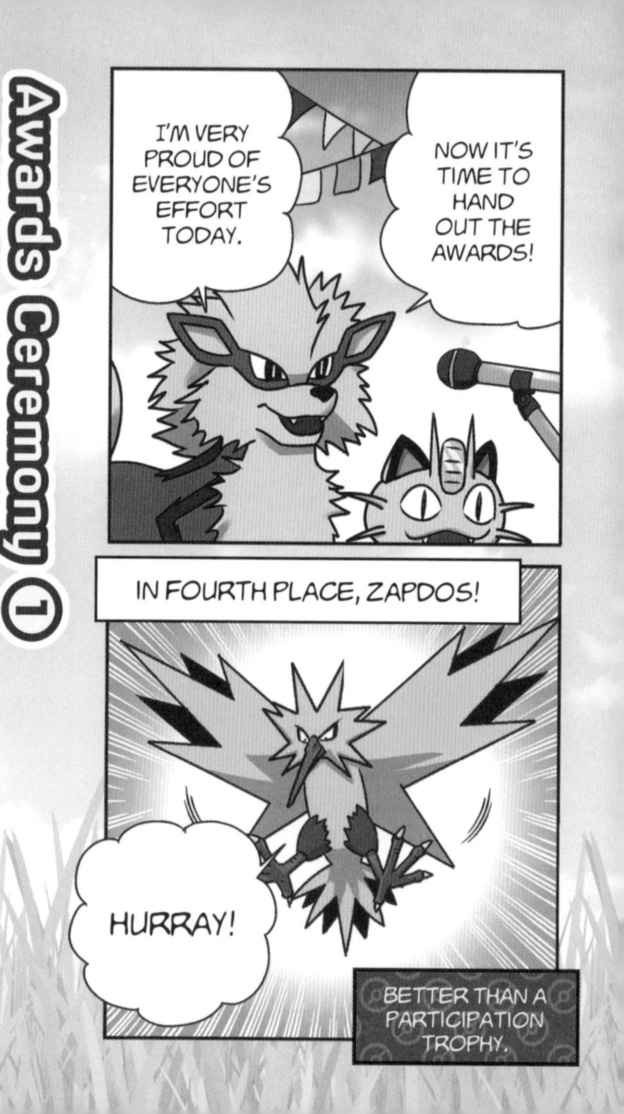
I'M VERY PROUD OF EVERYONE'S EFFORT TODAY.
NOW IT'S TIME TO HAND OUT THE AWARDS!
IN FOURTH PLACE, ZAPDOS!
HURRAY!
BETTER THAN A PARTICIPATION TROPHY.

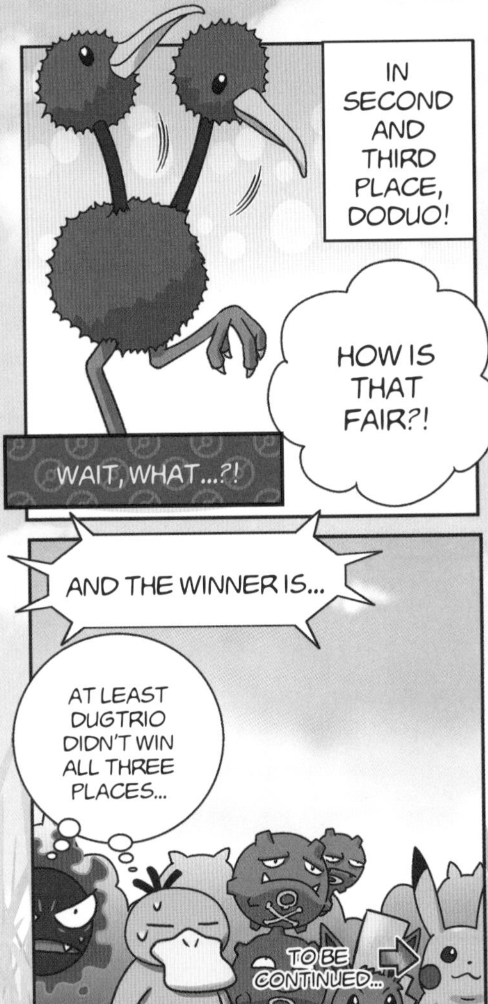
IN SECOND AND THIRD PLACE, DODUO!
HOW IS THAT FAIR?!
WAIT, WHAT...?!
AND THE WINNER IS...
AT LEAST DUGTRIO DIDN'T WIN ALL THREE PLACES...
TO BE CONTINUED...

POKÉMON MINIDEX

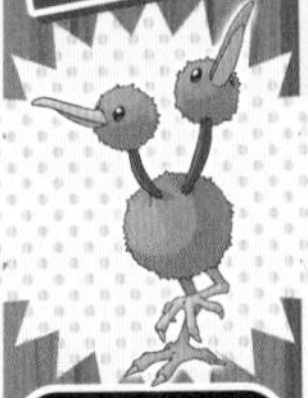

DODUO

CATEGORY

Twin Bird

TYPE

Normal, Flying

A Pokémon with two heads. Its two heads take turns sleeping, so one head can always keep watch.

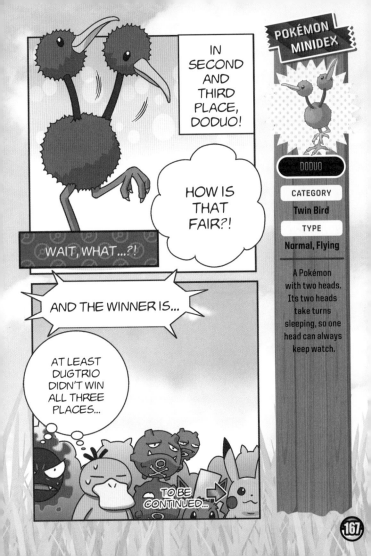

STARMIE

Awards Ceremony ②

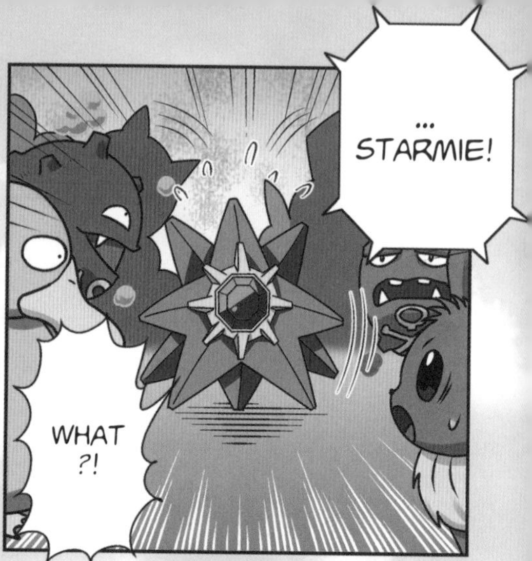
...
STARMIE!
WHAT ?!

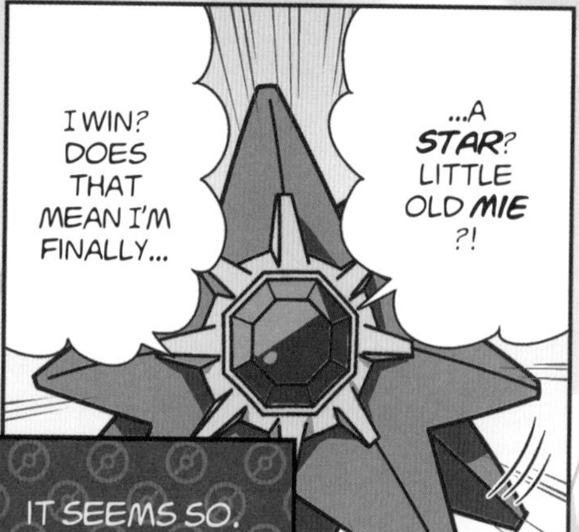
I WIN? DOES THAT MEAN I'M FINALLY...
...A STAR? LITTLE OLD MIE ?!
IT SEEMS SO.

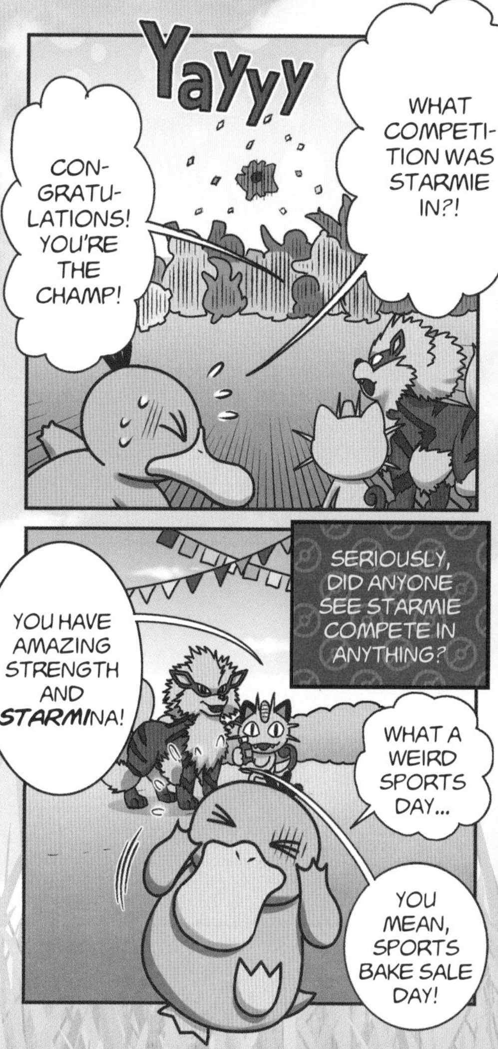
Yayyy
CONGRATULATIONS! YOU'RE THE CHAMP!
WHAT COMPETITION WAS STARMIE IN?!
YOU HAVE AMAZING STRENGTH AND STARMINA!
SERIOUSLY, DID ANYONE SEE STARMIE COMPETE IN ANYTHING?
WHAT A WEIRD SPORTS DAY...
YOU MEAN, SPORTS BAKE SALE DAY!

POKÉMON MINIDEX

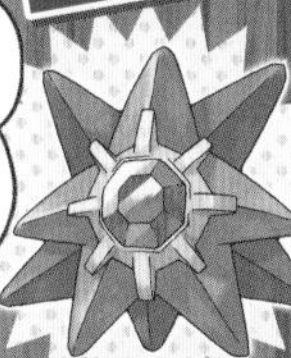

STARMIE

CATEGORY

Mysterious

TYPE

Water, Psychic

Its center section is called its core. When the core glows brightly in seven colors, it is said to be sending out mysterious radio signals.

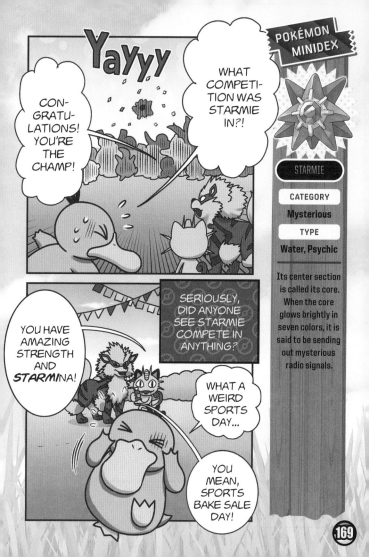

Down for the Count

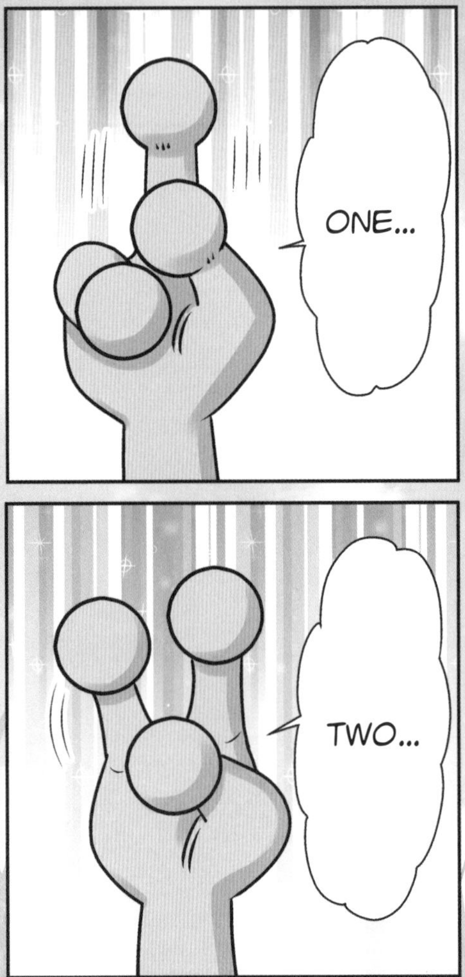
ONE...
TWO...

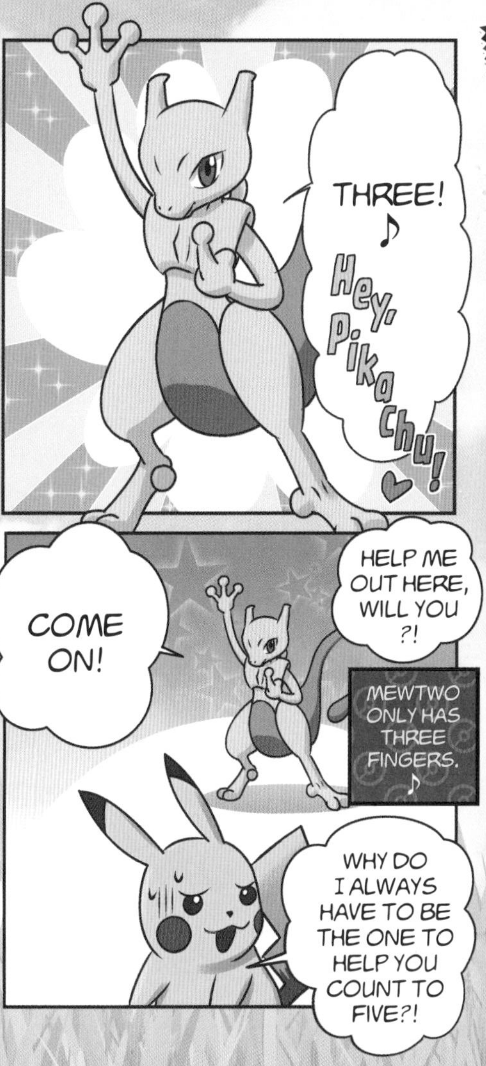
THREE! ♪
Hey, Pikachu! ♥
COME ON!
HELP ME OUT HERE, WILL YOU ?!
MEWTWO ONLY HAS THREE FINGERS. ♪
WHY DO I ALWAYS HAVE TO BE THE ONE TO HELP YOU COUNT TO FIVE?!

POKÉMON MINIDEX

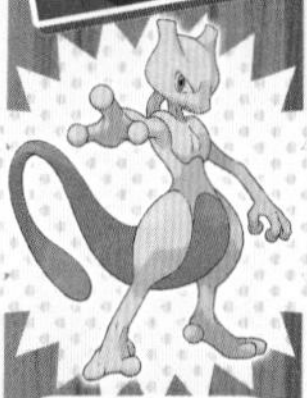

MEWTWO

CATEGORY

Genetic

TYPE

Psychic

Its battle abilities are incredible, and it is said to have the most savage heart of all the Pokémon.

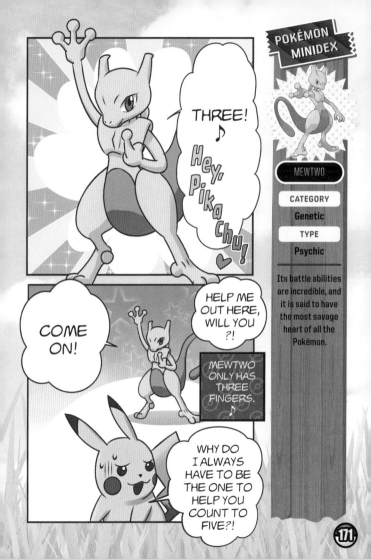

Hit Me with Your Best Shot

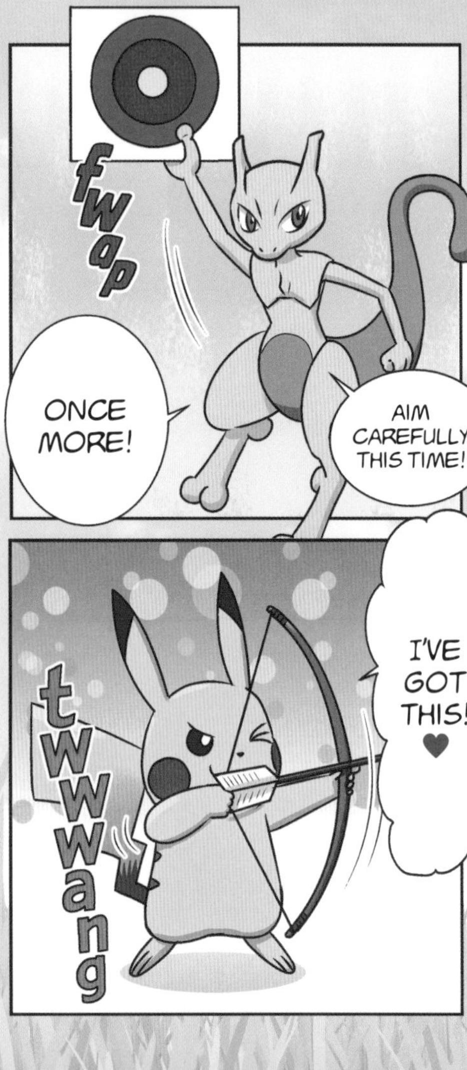

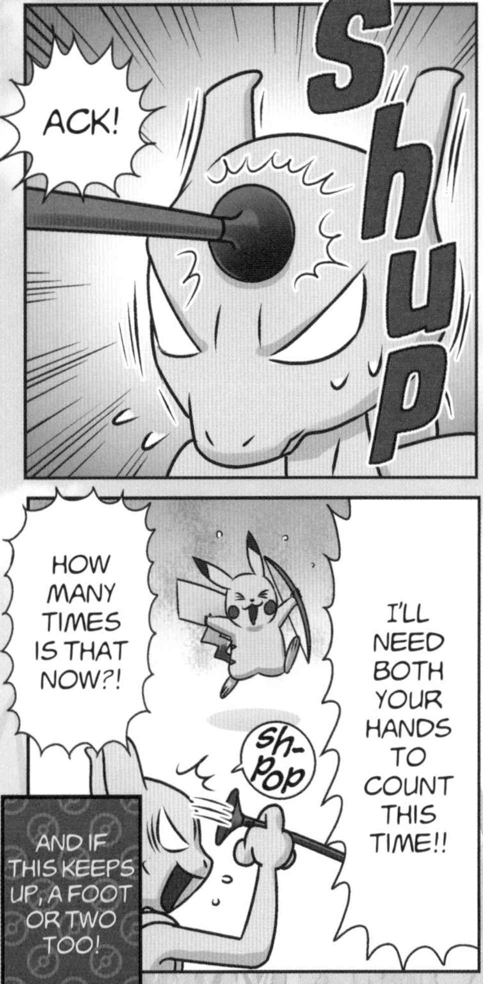
ACK!
SHUP
HOW MANY TIMES IS THAT NOW?!
I'LL NEED BOTH YOUR HANDS TO COUNT THIS TIME!!
SH-POP
AND IF THIS KEEPS UP, A FOOT OR TWO TOO!

POKÉMON MINIDEX

Which of the following Pokémon is said to be artificially made like Mewtwo?

1
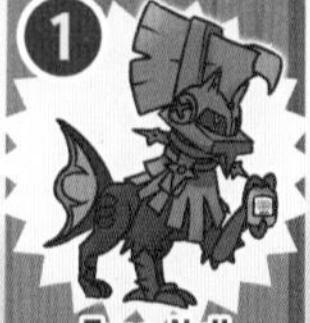
Type: Null

2
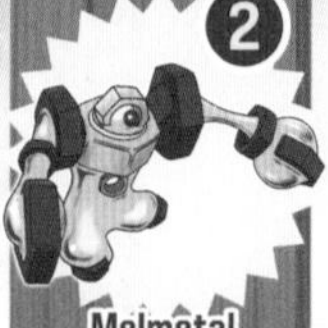
Melmetal

3
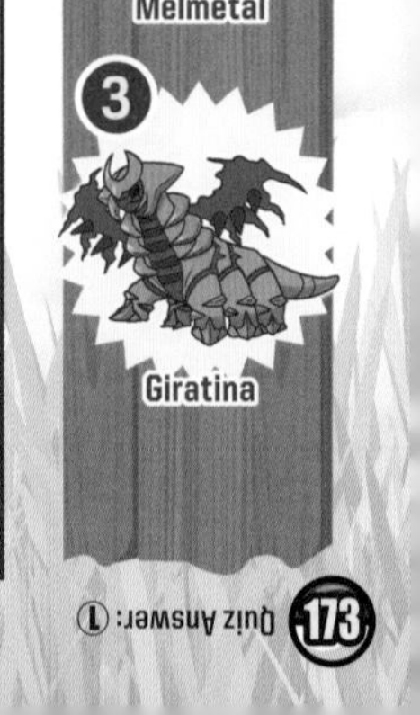
Giratina

Quiz Answer: 1

If at First You Don't Succeed...

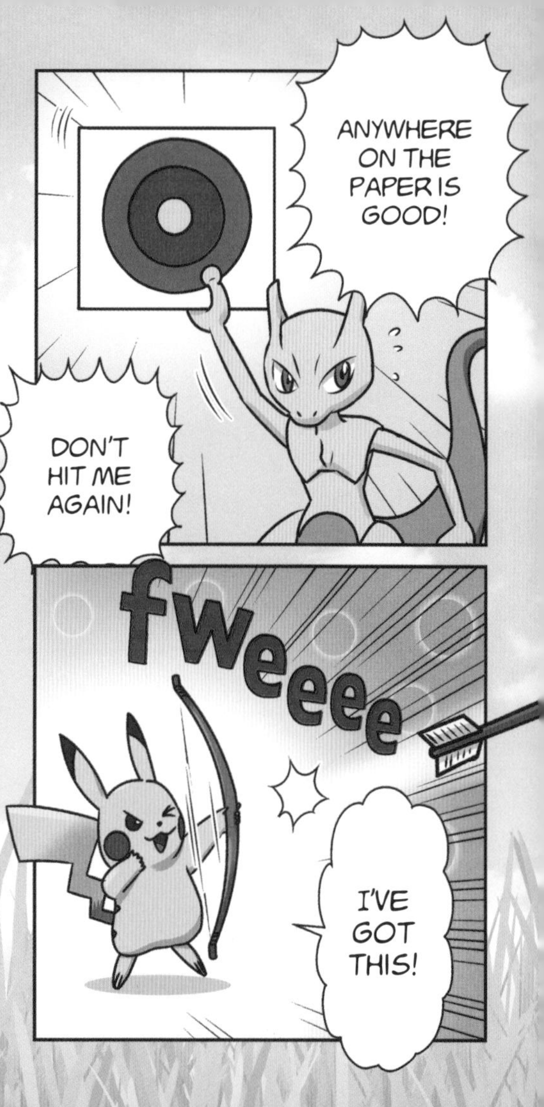
ANYWHERE ON THE PAPER IS GOOD!
DON'T HIT ME AGAIN!
fweeee
I'VE GOT THIS!

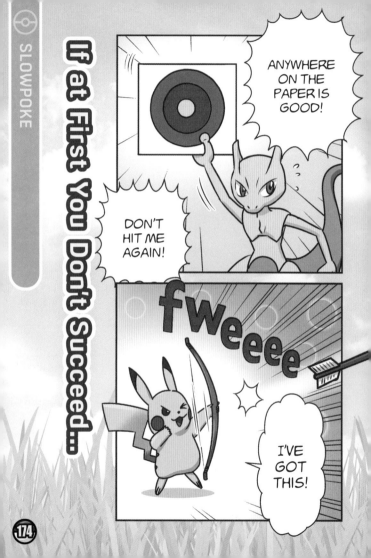

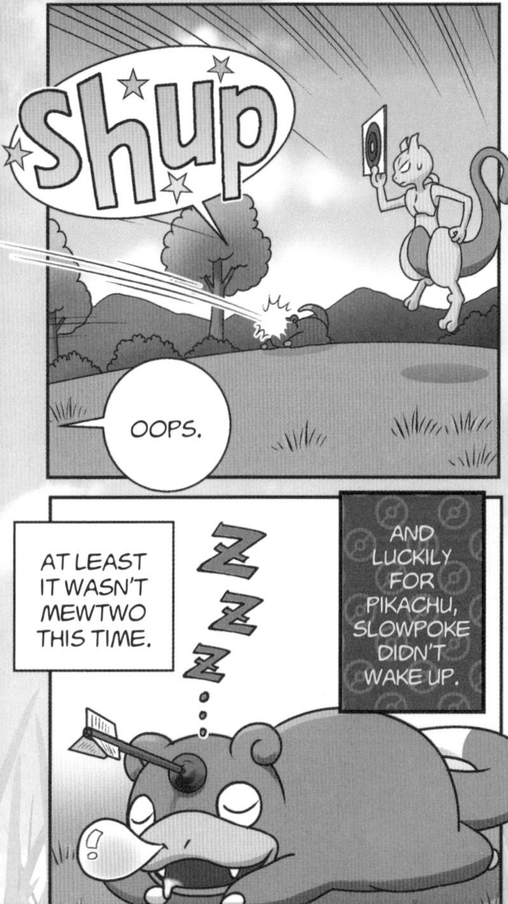

SHUP
OOPS.
AT LEAST IT WASN'T MEWTWO THIS TIME.
Z Z Z
AND LUCKILY FOR PIKACHU, SLOWPOKE DIDN'T WAKE UP.

POKÉMON MINIDEX

Which of the following is the same Water and Psychic type as Slowpoke?

1. 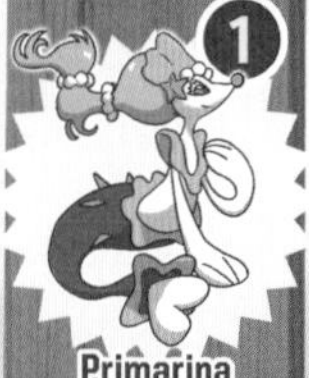
Primarina

2. 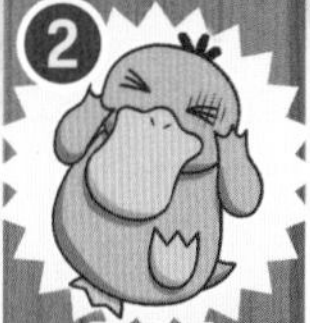
Psyduck

3. 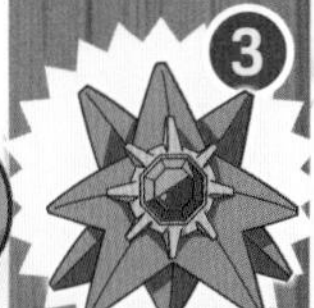
Starmie

Quiz Answer: 3

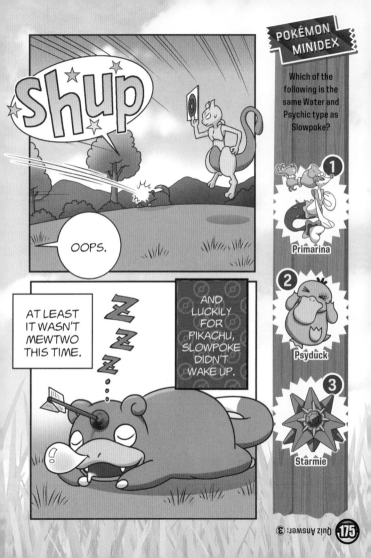

All Natural

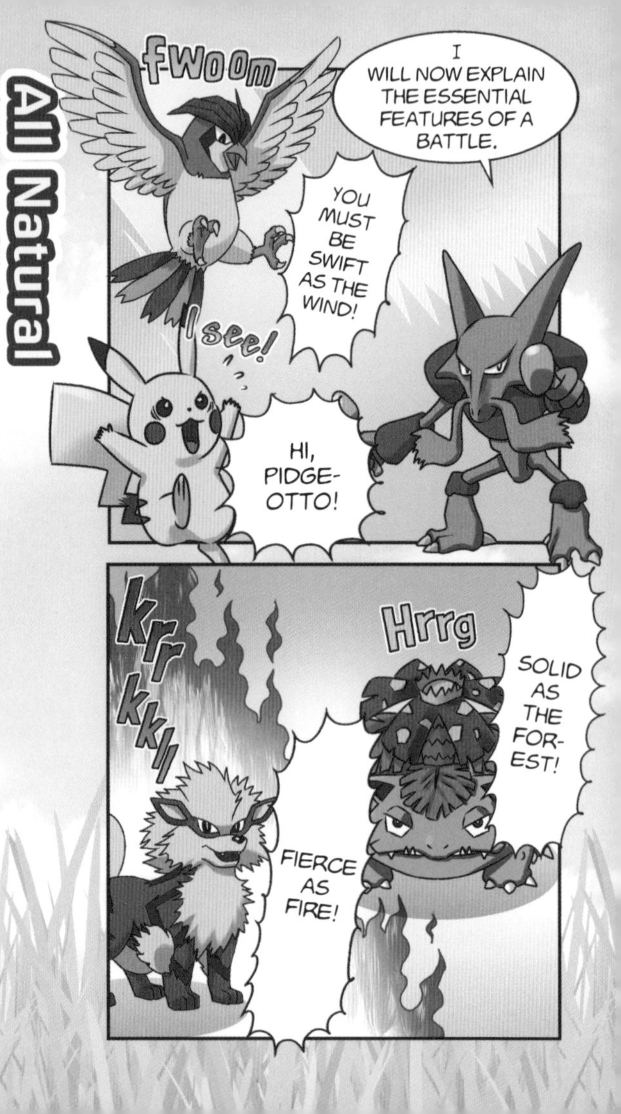
fwoom
I WILL NOW EXPLAIN THE ESSENTIAL FEATURES OF A BATTLE.
YOU MUST BE SWIFT AS THE WIND!
I see!
HI, PIDGE-OTTO!
krrkkll
Hrrg
SOLID AS THE FOR-EST!
FIERCE AS FIRE!

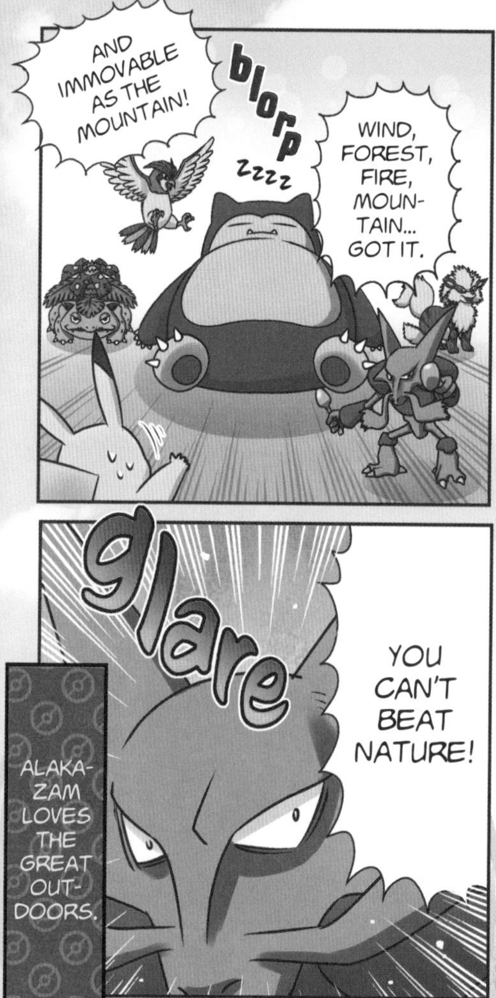
AND IMMOVABLE AS THE MOUNTAIN!
blorp
zzzz
WIND, FOREST, FIRE, MOUN-TAIN... GOT IT.
glare
ALAKA-ZAM LOVES THE GREAT OUT-DOORS.
YOU CAN'T BEAT NATURE!

POKÉMON MINIDEX

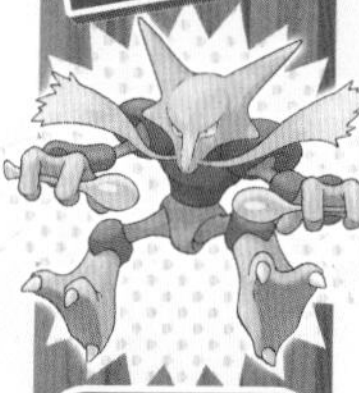

ALAKAZAM

CATEGORY

Psi

TYPE

Psychic

Its intelligence quotient is said to be 5,000. It defeats enemies with its psychic power.

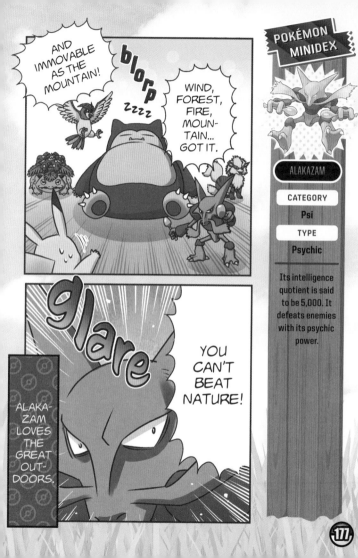

The Slipper Test

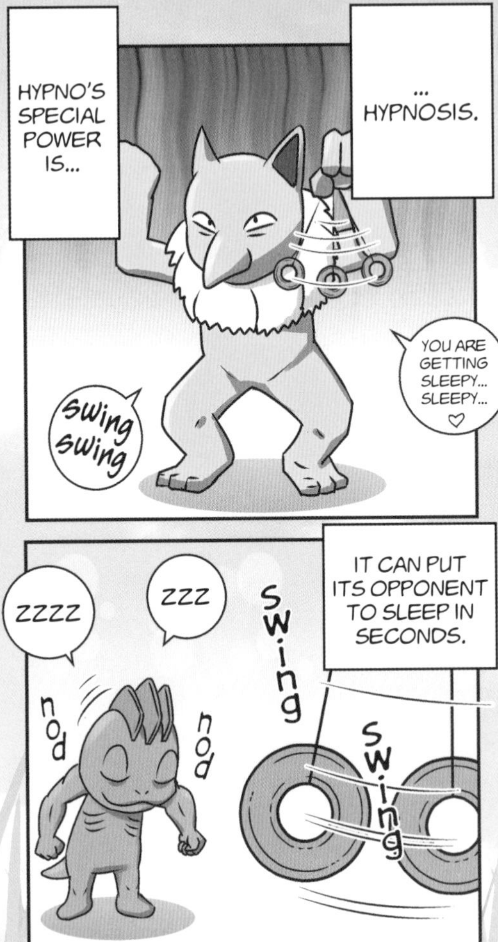
HYPNO'S SPECIAL POWER IS...
... HYPNOSIS.
swing swing
YOU ARE GETTING SLEEPY... SLEEPY... ♡
ZZZZ
ZZZ
IT CAN PUT ITS OPPONENT TO SLEEP IN SECONDS.
swing
nod
nod
swing

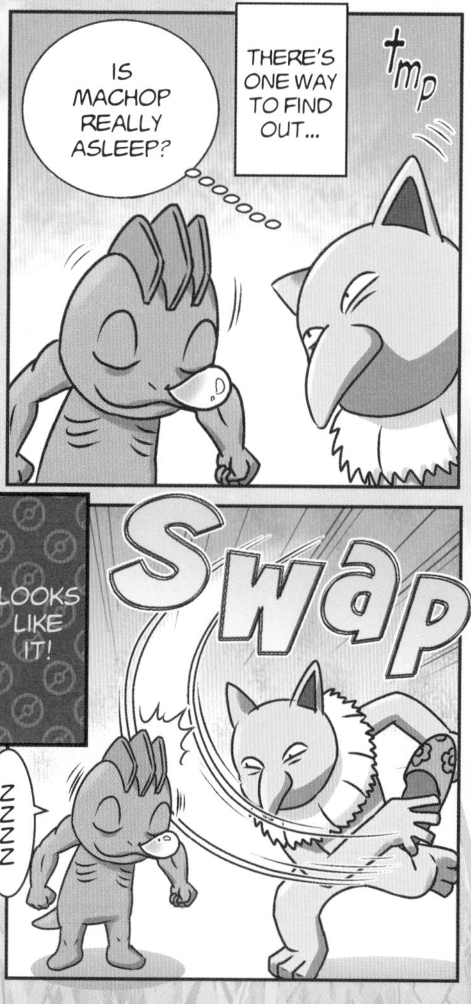

IS MACHOP REALLY ASLEEP?
THERE'S ONE WAY TO FIND OUT...
tmp
LOOKS LIKE IT!
SWAP
ZZZZ

POKÉMON MINIDEX

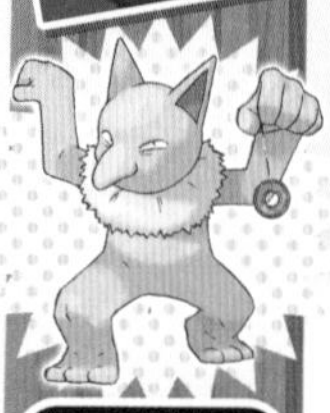

HYPNO

CATEGORY

Hypnosis

TYPE

Psychic

Be careful. Don't stare at the pendulum Hypno is always swinging with its hand, or it might hypnotize you!

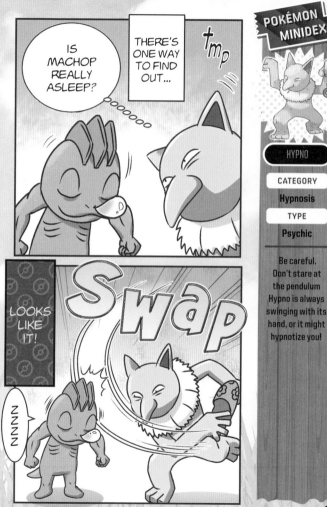

The Not-Guilty Party

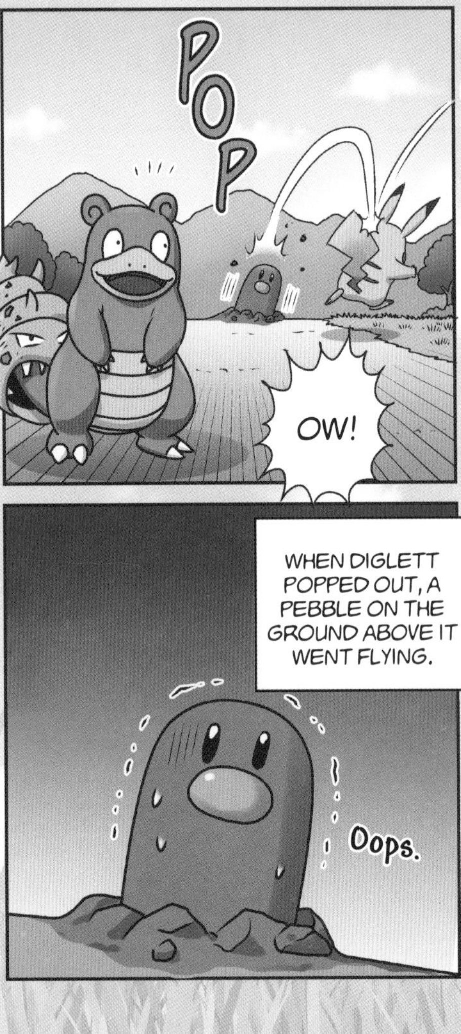
POP
OW!
WHEN DIGLETT POPPED OUT, A PEBBLE ON THE GROUND ABOVE IT WENT FLYING.
Oops.

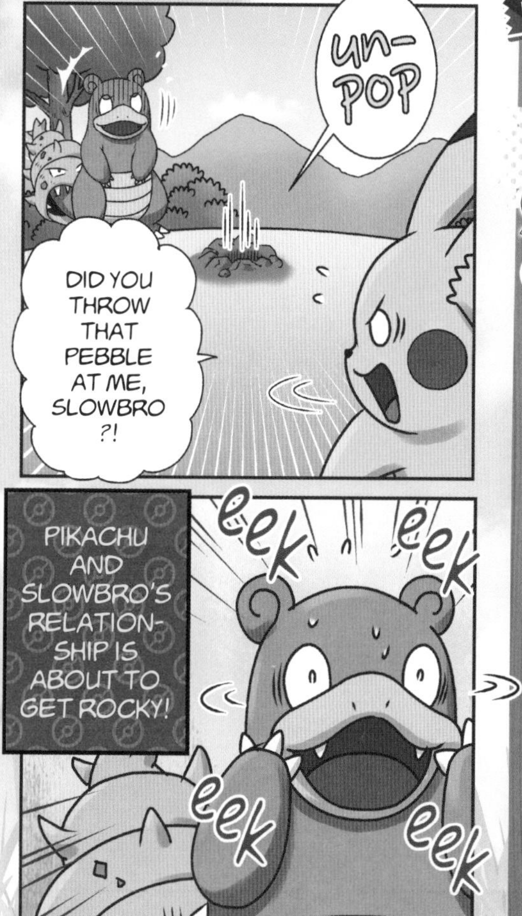
un-
POP
DID YOU THROW THAT PEBBLE AT ME, SLOWBRO?!
PIKACHU AND SLOWBRO'S RELATIONSHIP IS ABOUT TO GET ROCKY!
eek
eek
eek
eek

POKÉMON MINIDEX

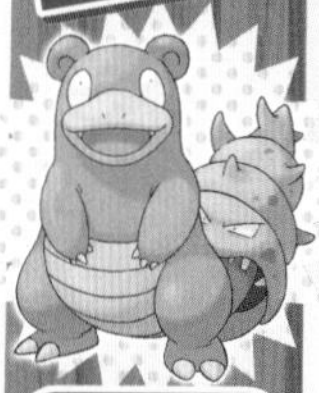

SLOWBRO

CATEGORY

Hermit Crab

TYPE

Water, Psychic

Whenever Shellder bites down hard on its tail, it gives Slowbro a flash of inspiration... which it forgets a moment later.

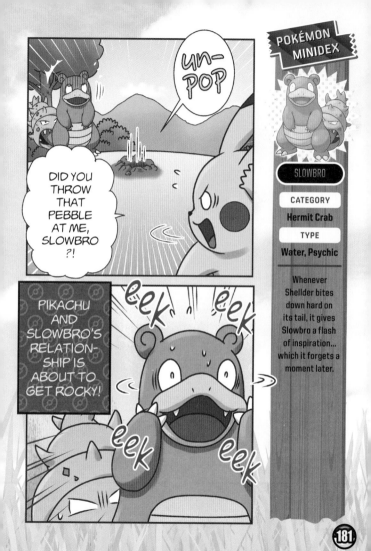

Not My Skill Set

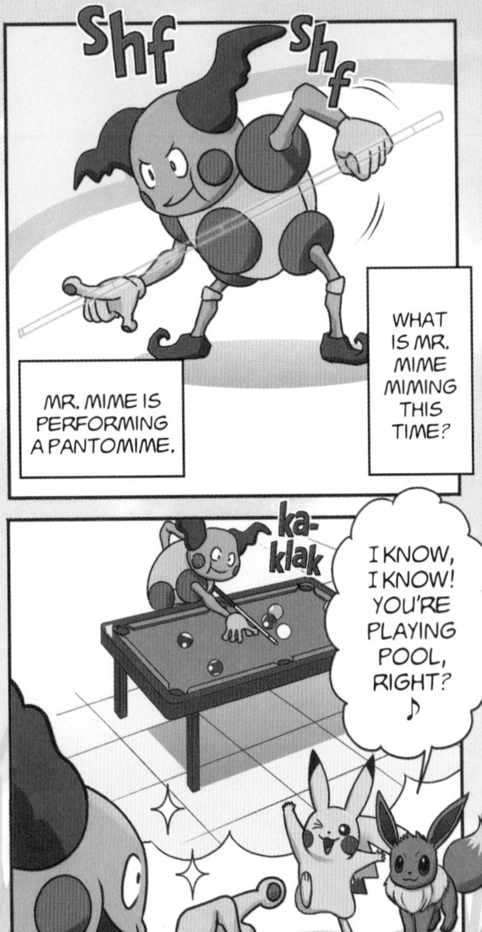
Shf Shf
WHAT IS MR. MIME MIMING THIS TIME?
MR. MIME IS PERFORMING A PANTOMIME.
ka-klak
I KNOW, I KNOW! YOU'RE PLAYING POOL, RIGHT? ♪
CORRECT!

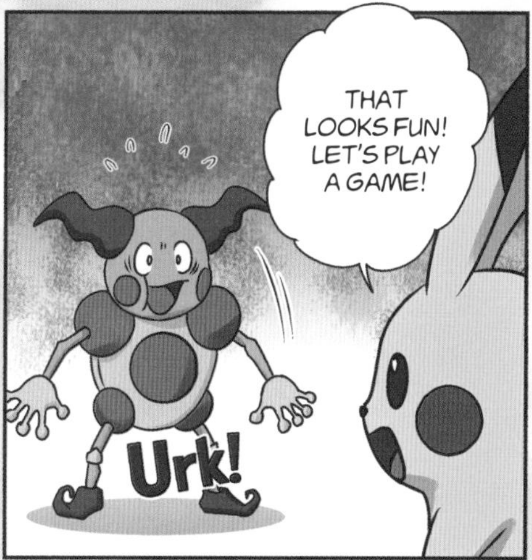
THAT LOOKS FUN! LET'S PLAY A GAME!
Urk!

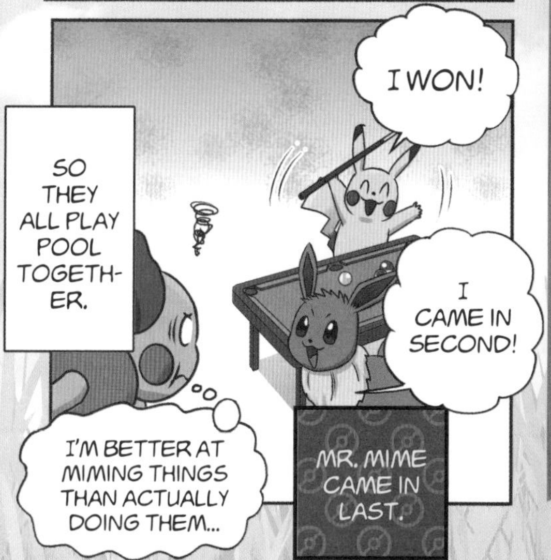
SO THEY ALL PLAY POOL TOGETH-ER.
I WON!
I CAME IN SECOND!
I'M BETTER AT MIMING THINGS THAN ACTUALLY DOING THEM...
MR. MIME CAME IN LAST.

POKÉMON MINIDEX

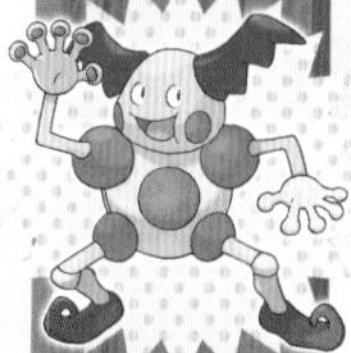

MR. MIME

CATEGORY

Barrier

TYPE

Psychic, Fairy

It can create invisible objects through pantomime.

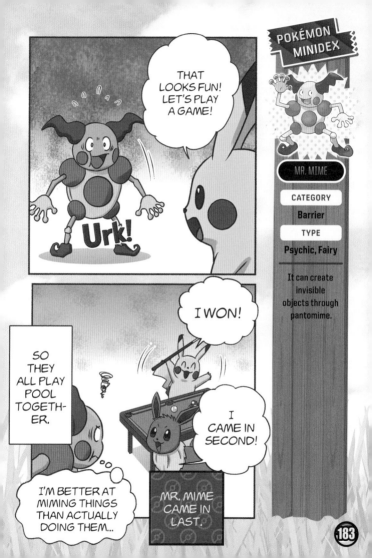

Last Pun

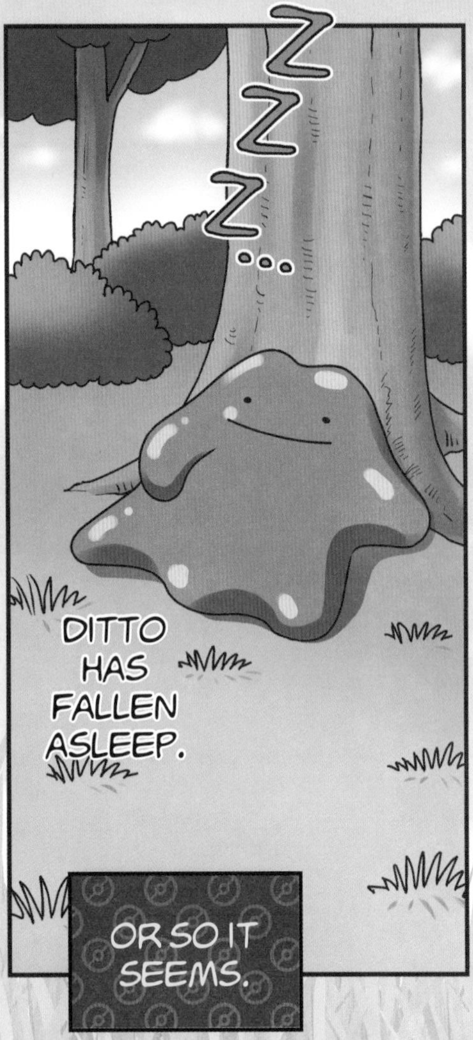
ZZZ...
DITTO HAS FALLEN ASLEEP.
OR SO IT SEEMS.

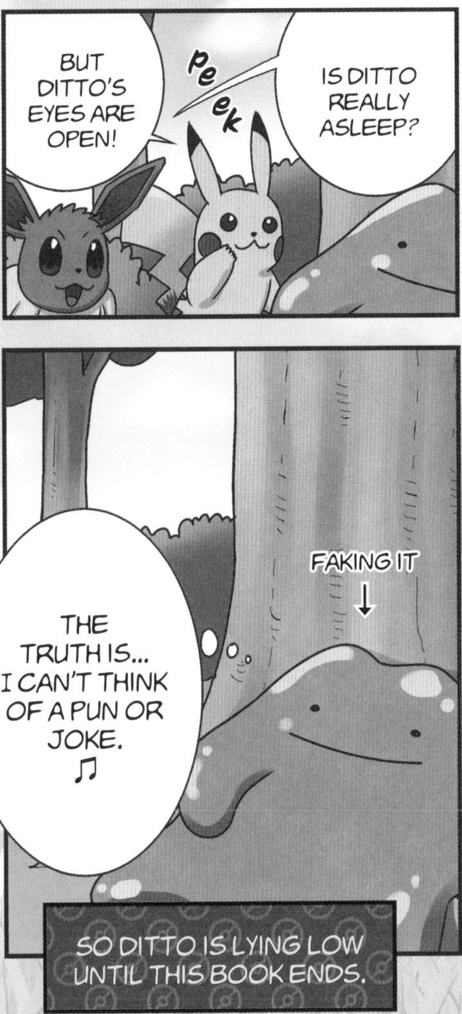
BUT DITTO'S EYES ARE OPEN!
peeek
IS DITTO REALLY ASLEEP?
THE TRUTH IS... I CAN'T THINK OF A PUN OR JOKE. ♫
FAKING IT
SO DITTO IS LYING LOW UNTIL THIS BOOK ENDS.

POKÉMON MINIDEX

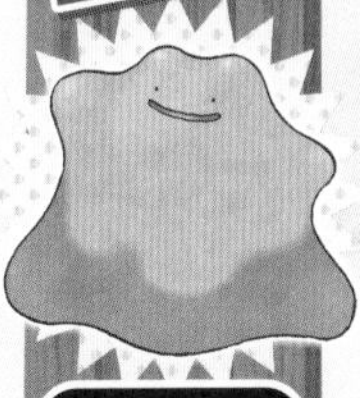

DITTO

CATEGORY

Transform

TYPE

Normal

A Pokémon who can transform into anything. Ditto has the ability to reconstitute its entire cellular structure to transform into whatever it sees.

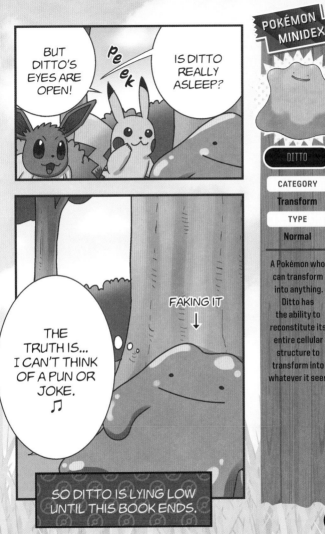

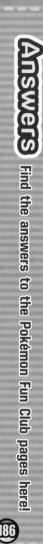

Answers for page 17

1 Alakazam

4 Hypno

2 Mimikyu

5 Alolan Diglett

3 Venusaur

6 Doduo

↑ Were you able to guess all the Pokémon based on their unique colors and physical features?

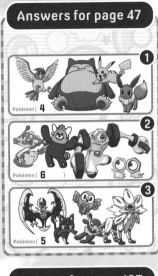

Answers for page 47

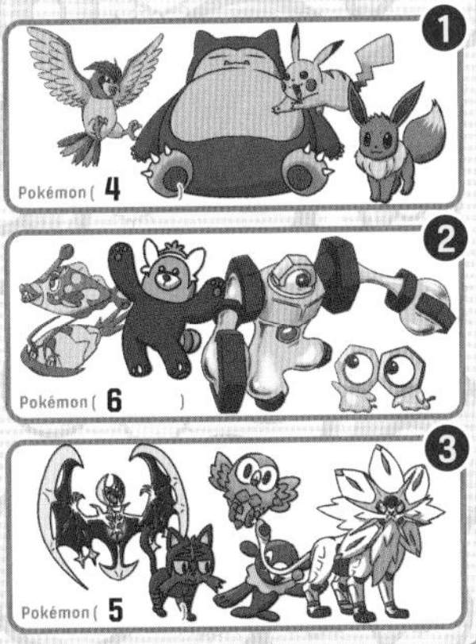
1
Pokémon (4
2
Pokémon (6)
3
Pokémon (5

← The answer is silhouette ❷. There are 4 Pokémon in silhouette ❶, 6 Pokémon in silhouette 2, and 5 Pokémon in silhouette ❸.

Answers for page 77

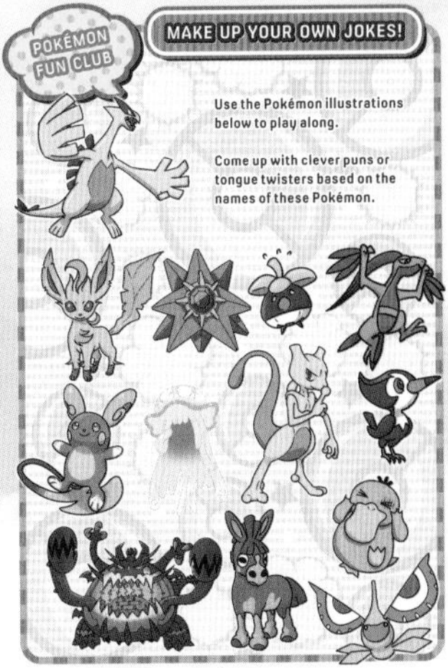
POKÉMON FUN CLUB
MAKE UP YOUR OWN JOKES!
Use the Pokémon illustrations below to play along.
Come up with clever puns or tongue twisters based on the names of these Pokémon.

↑ **THESE ANSWERS HAVE TO COME FROM YOU!**

Which of these Pokémon is your favorite? Which Pokémon would you like to put together in the same gag? Write and draw your own four-panel gags and share them with others!

Answer for page 137

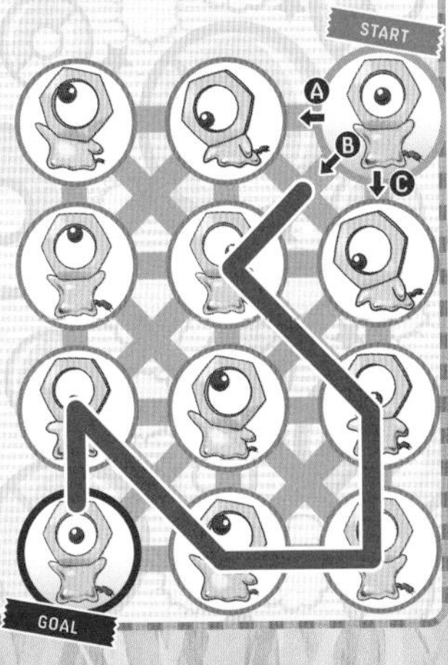
START
A
B
C
GOAL

← **The route that takes you to the goal is route B. A and C lead to dead ends. Pay close attention to the eyes looking in diagonal directions.**

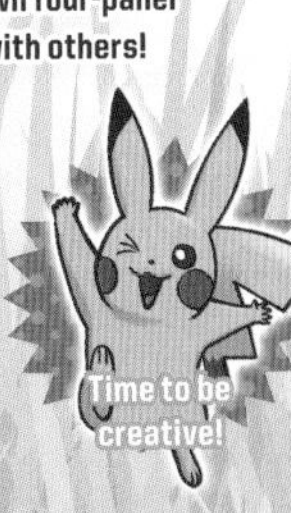
Time to be creative!

Pokémon Index

Use this handy index to find out which gags your favorite Pokémon star in!

Pokémon Pocket Comics: Sun & Moon
VIZ Media Edition

Story & Art by SANTA HARUKAZE (TAK.BR)

©2021 Pokémon.
©1995–2019 Nintendo / Creatures Inc. / GAME FREAK inc.
TM, ®, and character names are trademarks of Nintendo.
POKÉMON LET'S GO! DAJARE CLUB
by Santa HARUKAZE (TAK.BR)
© 2019 SHOGAKUKAN
All rights reserved.
Original Japanese edition published by SHOGAKUKAN.
English translation rights in the United States of America, Canada, the United Kingdom,
Ireland, Australia and New Zealand arranged with SHOGAKUKAN.

Original Japanese Edition
With the Cooperation of/The Pokémon Company, Shogakukan-Shueisha Productions
Editor/Toshiya SUZUKI, Yuta NUKAGA
Designer/Takayuki OSHIDA (Yellow Bag)

English Adaptation/Bryant Turnage, Annette Roman
Translation/Tetsuichiro Miyaki
Touch-up & Lettering/Susan Daigle-Leach
Design/Jimmy Presler
Editor/Annette Roman

Printed in China

Published by VIZ Media, LLC
P.O. Box 77010
San Francisco, CA 94107

10 9 8 7 6 5 4 3 2 1
First printing, December 2021

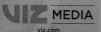

viz.com

PARENTAL ADVISORY
POKÉMON POCKET COMICS:
SUN & MOON is rated A and is
suitable for readers of all ages.